# CONFESSIONS OF THE FUNNY FAT FRIEND

KELSIE HOSS

kh

Copyright © 2022 by Kelsie Hoss

All rights reserved.

No part of this book may be reproduced in any form or by any electronic or mechanical means, including information storage and retrieval systems, without written permission from the author, except for the use of brief quotations in a book review.

This is a work of fiction. Names, characters, businesses, places, events, locales, and incidents are either the products of the author's imagination or used in a fictitious manner. Any resemblance to actual persons, living or dead, or actual events is purely coincidental.

Editing by Tricia Harden of Emerald Eyes Editing.

Cover design by Najla Qamber of Najla Qamber Designs.

Sensitivity Reading by Kelsea Reeves.

Have questions? Email kelsie@kelsiehoss.com.

**Readers can visit kelsiehoss.com/sensitive to learn about potentially triggering content.**

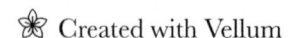

❦ Created with Vellum

*For anyone who's ever felt like the funny fat friend. You deserve to take center stage. <3*

## CONTENTS

A quick note from the author — ix

1. Henrietta — 1
2. Tyler — 12
3. Henrietta — 21
4. Tyler — 29
5. Henrietta — 37
6. Tyler — 48
7. Henrietta — 59
8. Tyler — 68
9. Henrietta — 74
10. Tyler — 79
11. Henrietta — 83
12. Tyler — 91
13. Henrietta — 100
14. Henrietta — 105
15. Tyler — 110
16. Henrietta — 116
17. Henrietta — 124
18. Tyler — 130
19. Henrietta — 136
20. Tyler — 144
21. Henrietta — 156
22. Tyler — 164
23. Henrietta — 170
24. Tyler — 176
25. Henrietta — 184
26. Henrietta — 188
27. Tyler — 193
28. Henrietta — 197

| | |
|---|---|
| 29. Tyler | 201 |
| 30. Henrietta | 207 |
| 31. Tyler | 215 |
| 32. Henrietta | 219 |
| 33. Tyler | 223 |
| 34. Henrietta | 227 |
| 35. Tyler | 230 |
| 36. Henrietta | 233 |
| 37. Tyler | 237 |
| 38. Henrietta | 241 |
| 39. Tyler | 246 |
| 40. Henrietta | 249 |
| 41. Henrietta | 256 |
| 42. Tyler | 261 |
| 43. Henrietta | 266 |
| 44. Henrietta | 269 |
| 45. Tyler | 274 |
| 46. Henrietta | 277 |
| 47. Tyler | 286 |
| 48. Henrietta | 291 |
| 49. Tyler | 296 |
| 50. Henrietta | 304 |
| 51. Tyler | 310 |
| 52. Henrietta | 314 |
| 53. Tyler | 320 |
| 54. Henrietta | 328 |
| 55. Tyler | 334 |
| 56. Henrietta | 339 |
| 57. Tyler | 346 |
| 58. Henrietta | 352 |
| 59. Tyler | 359 |
| 60. Henrietta | 365 |
| 61. Tyler | 369 |
| 62. Henrietta | 373 |
| 63. Tyler | 381 |

| | |
|---|---|
| 64. Henrietta | 383 |
| 65. Henrietta | 391 |
| 66. Henrietta | 395 |
| 67. Tyler | 400 |
| 68. Henrietta | 405 |
| 69. Tyler | 408 |
| 70. Henrietta | 414 |
| 71. Henrietta | 418 |
| 72. Tyler | 422 |
| 73. Henrietta | 426 |
| 74. Henrietta | 431 |
| 75. Gage | 436 |
| 76. Tyler | 442 |
| 77. Henrietta | 449 |
| 78. Tyler | 459 |
| 79. Henrietta | 463 |
| 80. Tyler | 470 |
| 81. Henrietta | 472 |
| 82. Tyler | 475 |
| 83. Henrietta | 480 |
| 84. Tyler | 484 |
| 85. Henrietta | 490 |
| Epilogue | 494 |
| | |
| Bonus Content QR codes | 499 |
| Author's Note | 501 |
| Acknowledgments | 505 |
| Also by Kelsie Hoss | 509 |
| Join the Party | 511 |
| About the Author | 513 |

# A QUICK NOTE FROM THE AUTHOR

*Dear Reader,*

*This book is full of humor, romance, and sexy scenes. Readers 18+ only, please!*

*Love,*
*Kelsie Hoss*

# 1

## HENRIETTA

*Confession: I'm a 28-year-old virgin.*

I WAS BACK IN VESTIDO, bridesmaid dress shopping for my best friend's wedding, and I was starting to see a pattern. A pattern I didn't like.

I met Birdie and Mara two years ago. We'd become fast friends, all single girls in our late twenties, transitioning into our thirties. It helped that we had a mutual love of breakfast food and mojitos.

Then, I witnessed Birdie fall in love with a hot single dad and stood by her side a year later as she got married.

I'd never really been the kind of person to have a lot of girlfriends, always being a loner who was more worried about school and work than fun. It didn't help that my grandma couldn't drive anymore and took up lots of my free time with her appointments and outings.

Or maybe that was just an excuse.

Because after Birdie got married, Mara, a famous romance author and the self-proclaimed eternally single woman, fell in love.

She got engaged.

And now she was six months from getting married.

And me?

You guessed it.

Still. Single.

Still a virgin.

I'd never had a boyfriend in high school, and I'd been too busy working in college to ever make time for a guy. At least that's what I told myself. But the truth was, the guys I met in person just weren't interested in me like that. And online dating at my size? I'd rather help my mom weed her massive garden or... be single for the rest of my life.

Before I knew it, they'd be printing my face on the back of a set of Old Maid cards.

Mara held up a deep-green dress that pinched in around the waist and flowed to the ground. She smiled at the gown, making her brown eyes crinkle at the corners. "What do you think about this one? It would look beautiful on all your body types and skin tones."

Birdie laughed. "I love it. It might actually make me look like I have a waist."

I laughed with her. Even though we'd all been friends

for two and a half years now, I was still getting used to the way she and Mara so easily accepted themselves. I hoped I'd get there someday.

While Birdie was what my gran described as "apple shaped," I was built like a brick shit house. (That's what my grandpa used to call it, before he passed a few years back.) Square and strong enough to throw down on the football field with my brothers and bigger than half the guys I came into contact with.

This dress would look pretty on me, but I wished it had straps to hold up the girls. They did not play well with a lack of support. "Do you think we can get straps added?" I asked.

Mara nodded. "I bet Jonas's tailor could sew some on. She does incredible work." She winked.

I laughed. That boy did fill out a suit better than most. "Then let's get it," I said. It wouldn't really matter which one we got, at the end of the day. I would feel uncomfortable in my body whether I was wearing sweatpants, business casual, or a beautiful dress worth hundreds of dollars.

Mara left, taking the dress to the saleswoman, probably to order enough for all of us bridesmaids. In just a few months, Birdie and I would be standing beside Mara on her big day, along with her future sister-in-law, Tess.

Tess's wedding, just shy of a year ago at Emerson Trails, had been so beautiful that Jonas and Mara had taken the first opening the park had available when she wasn't writing for TV in Atlanta. Bonus that it was during

Birdie's summer break from school, and I had enough PTO saved up to take a few days off for the event.

My phone rang, and I pulled it from my purse seeing my boss's name on the screen. Stepping away from Birdie and Tess, I answered the call. "Hey, Janessa," I said. "How are you doing?"

"Great! I just wanted to let you know that the head contractor's plane just landed, and he'll be at the building in an hour to get his keys."

"I'll be there," I promised. Even though it was a Saturday. Even though I was supposed to be dress shopping. Even though I'd been looking forward to a late afternoon dinner at Waldo's Diner with my friends. I couldn't afford to lose this job.

I put my phone in my purse, and Birdie touched my arm, her wide blue eyes on me. "You have to go to work?"

I pouted. "Yeah, I have to get this contractor some keys. I'm not sure how long it'll take. I might have to miss dinner."

She shook her head, her blond curls bouncing. "We'll wait for you."

"You sure?" I asked, looking to Mara, who was busy chatting with the dress salesperson. Of the three of us, she was easily the most extroverted. "I feel guilty, like I'm already failing my bridesmaid's duties."

"Don't worry about it. She'll understand. And you call us when you get done, okay?"

"You'll fill her in?" I asked.

Birdie smiled. "Of course."

I left Vestido and went to my car in the parking lot. It was cheap and in regular need of repairs, but my dad had taught me enough about cars that I didn't often have to spend money on a mechanic, which helped me tuck away that much more. With my new promotion, I was less than a year away from my savings goal. After that, I had no idea what I would do.

As I drove away from the store, I tried to imagine what life would look like when I finally had the savings I wanted after eight years of scrimping and living with my parents. I'd probably keep my job—I loved managing an apartment building and giving tenants good care and a safe place to live. There were so many shady rental companies out there, and luckily, I didn't work for one of them.

They'd hired me as a move-out cleaner back when I was in community college, getting a business degree. When a manager spot opened, I applied, and they promoted me. Now that the company was developing a completely new apartment building, they'd given me a raise to liaise with the head contractor on the build, and I'd eventually manage the new complex.

It was exciting.

Even if it was a little inconvenient today.

But this would be my first time working with a construction company, my first time having a hand in something from the ground up. I couldn't wait to see how it came to be. (And the extra pay wasn't bad either.)

I reached Blue Bird Apartments and unlocked the main office. The building was fairly old, but I'd spiced up the office and its whitewashed wood paneled walls with lots of plants and some artwork from my mother's studio. She worked at Brentwood University, teaching art classes to college students.

My favorite piece she'd created for me was a colorful chicken in my namesake. *Hen*rietta. It was kind of an inside joke at this point, and my family's entire home was decorated in chicken décor, from our kitschy salt and pepper shakers to the metal napkin holder shaped like a rooster.

At least we'd been able to talk Dad out of putting a weathervane on top of our suburban home.

Since I was already at the office, I worked on printing off some new unit applications, as we had a few coming available soon.

The bell rang over the door, and I stood up to greet the head contractor. Unfortunately, this wasn't him. This guy couldn't have been more than thirty, and he had thick black tattoos swirling down one of his tan arms. Part of me wondered how much his tattoo covered under his tight white T-shirt and jogger sweatpants, but I quickly shut down that thought. He did *not* look like the kind of guy in charge of a multi-million-dollar operation, and I had a diner to get to.

"Sorry," I said. "The office isn't open right now."

"You're here, aren't you?" he replied, the slightest hint of a southern drawl in his voice.

I raised my eyebrows, so not in the mood for sass from a walk-in on a Saturday afternoon.

"Janessa told me to come this way to get my keys?" he said.

My eyes widened. "Janessa?" She was my boss stationed in the corporate office in LA and didn't work with regular tenants... *Shit.* "You're the head contractor?"

"That's me. Tyler Griffen."

"Henrietta Jones. But everyone calls me Hen."

He extended his hand for me to shake.

My cheeks felt hot as I slipped my hand into his. It was large and warm and calloused. So freaking hot. Not to mention his grip was just the right firmness. "Sorry," I said, turning and looking for a key in the lock box as I tried to calm my thoughts. "I thought you were someone else."

When I turned back to him, he had an amused look on his chiseled face. Now that I looked a little closer, I could tell he worked outside. His white skin had a deep tan, like he spent a lot of time in the sun, and his strong jaw had a light cover of stubble. Not to mention, there were flecks of paint on his hands as he reached for the key. Interesting. This head contractor wasn't just a stand-by-and-tell-every-one-what-to-do kind of guy. He must have been highly involved in the work. And that made me even more interested than the tattoos or his defined biceps.

I tilted my gaze down as I realized I was ogling. Clearing my throat, I tucked my relaxed hair behind my ear and said, "Why don't you let me show you around the unit?"

"That would be great," he replied with a crooked smile. "Thanks, Hen."

God, the way my name sounded off his lips. "Is that a Texas accent I hear?" I asked as we pushed out the door and stepped outside.

He chuckled. "It's that obvious? I'm from the Fort Worth area."

"It's subtle," I replied. Cute, I didn't add. "I thought you Texans weren't fans of California."

He laughed. "You can get us to come here from time to time—if the price is right."

I smiled, stopping in front of Unit C. "This is the building you'll be in. There's a laundromat downstairs with a few coin-operated washers and dryers. Your apartment's on the third floor, so we have a bit of a climb. But it is nice and quiet up there, and you have an amazing view of the park from the balcony off your living room."

Usually people weren't so happy about all the stairs, but he rubbed his hands together and said, "Can't wait to see it."

As we hoofed it up the flights, him with ease and me trying not to breathe hard and embarrass myself, I wondered why he was staying here at all. He had to be making hundreds of thousands of dollars a year, and this place definitely wasn't the best he could afford. But I'd already been rude enough for one day, so I didn't pry.

We reached unit 303, and I said, "This is it. Why don't you test the keys?"

He leaned forward, slipping the key into the lock and turning. It opened easily, and he walked in, examining the two-bedroom unit. "It's nice," he said, setting down his duffel bag beside the couch.

He was full of surprises. "I keep trying to talk corporate into replacing the carpets," I admitted, "but they've been freshly cleaned by a great local company. Most units aren't furnished, but they gave me a small budget and I personally picked out some pieces for you so you'll be comfortable while you're here. If you get situated and realize you don't have something you need, give me a call. I'll make sure to get it for you right away."

He turned from his examination of the apartment and laid his eyes on me. They were captivating, a mix of green and gold and brown that I'm sure my mother would have loved to paint. "That's real nice of you, Hen."

God, could he stop saying my name so my heart would slow down?

"Of course," I said, straightening my blouse. I found myself lost without something to do with my hands. "I'll let you get settled in."

I turned to leave his apartment, but he said, "Wait up."

Standing in the hallway, I faced him again. "Did I miss something?"

"Your number," he said with a smooth smile. My heart skipped a beat, and I was about to say something stupid before he added, "In case I need anything?"

"Oh, right." Of course he wanted my number for business, not for any other reason. I reached into my purse hanging from my shoulder. I always kept some business cards with my cell number written on the back, just in case. "This is the office number, but you can use my cell on the back if I'm not in there. My office hours are eight to five, Monday through Friday."

"Great. And we're meeting at the building site Monday at four," he confirmed.

I nodded. "That's Pacific time. In case your phone isn't set to change time zones automatically."

"Good thinking," he said, and damn, why did that compliment have my cheeks all flushed? Good thing my dark skin hid things like that. I could always tell when my white friends were embarrassed just by the color of their cheeks.

"Well, I'll let you get settled in," I said again, turning and walking away.

"See you Monday," he replied.

I walked down the stairs, trying my damnedest not to trip. That was the last thing I needed to do, embarrass myself yet again in front of this person I'd be working so closely with for the next several months. I needed this experience to go off without a hitch. If all went well, Janessa had already hinted I could be traveling around the country, managing new builds for Blue Bird, Inc. *Me*, with my little associate degree that everyone said would never be enough.

I bit my lip, worried if I'd made a good impression. I'd been a little harsh at first. And there was no time like the present to make things better.

On the second landing, I turned myself around and marched back up the stairs, knocking on Tyler Griffen's door.

# 2

## TYLER

I was about to sit down in front of the TV when a knock sounded on my door. After a long flight to yet another place where I knew no one, I'd planned to order takeout, zone out with a show I'd seen a million times before, and fall asleep. But when I opened the door and saw Hen there, my mind went crazy, just like when I'd first seen her moments ago.

She had these sharp eyes that cut straight to the point like she did with her words. Her relaxed, raven toned hair curled past her shoulders and drew my attention down to luscious curves and legs that went on for miles. I knew I couldn't date her—I never dated anyone when I was on location. It would be unprofessional, not to mention futile with me leaving once the project was done—but damn was she something to look at.

"Is there something I forgot?" I asked.

"I was wondering..." She hesitated, chewing on her lip, and I had to force myself to look away from her mouth "Have you eaten yet? I would feel bad leaving you here and not showing you around a little bit. There are a few fast food places nearby, a Chinese place I love down the road, and if you're missing home, I think there's a Texas Roadhouse a few blocks past that."

I let out a laugh. Cute and funny. "Texas Roadhouse has nothing on my dad's grill."

Her laugh was contagious but quiet, like she didn't want to take up too much space. "So, what do you say?"

I wanted to... But I didn't want to give her the wrong impression either. "No better plans on a Saturday afternoon?"

"I was actually on my way to supper with my friends. You can join if you want?"

Relief loosened my shoulders. She wasn't coming on to me—she was helping me feel less lonely. Something I really appreciated, especially in a new town. "If you're sure it's not any trouble..."

"Of course not. It'd be good to get to know each other a bit since we'll be working so closely together." She added, "But it is just a diner. Nothing fancy."

"If it's good enough for you, it's good enough for me," I said, reaching for my duffel bag. "Mind if I change?" She had looked so pretty in her flowy sundress, and I didn't want to look like a schlub in front of her and her friends. Because for some reason... it mattered. She was right. If we'd be working together, it would be good to start things off on the right foot. And if there was one thing I learned from my sister, Liv, it was that if you didn't pass the girlfriend test, you wouldn't be making much progress with the kind of girl that mattered.

"Do you want to ride with me," she asked, "or should I send you the address?"

"A ride would be nice," I said, selfishly wanting more time to talk to her. "I'll be down in a sec."

I couldn't wipe the smile from my face as I threw on the jeans and a fresh shirt. I wanted to get to know her better—for work.

I jogged down the stairs, the memory of her hips as she walked up distracting me. Those hips had looked so fine swaying side to side. I tried to remind myself I shouldn't be thinking of her that way and found her in the parking lot next to the kind of car my mom would call a puddle jumper. She opened her own door and said, "It's unlocked."

I grinned. "You know my dad would have my head for not getting your door."

"Your secret's safe with me, Tex." She shook her head with a small smile and got in, and me? I was grinning like a damn fool. It had been a long time since I'd bantered with a woman I wasn't related to.

When I opened the door and got in, I was immediately surrounded by her perfume. It was like a mix of spring bluebonnets and sugar cookies, and it took all I had not to breathe in deeply.

"The lever's under the seat," she said. "If you want to scoot your chair back."

I'd been so distracted by her fragrance that I hadn't even noticed my knees bumping against the dash.

"Where is it if I don't want to scoot it back?" I teased.

"Ha ha," she said, backing out of the parking spot.

I reached down to the lever, giving myself a little more room. My siblings and I got our height from my dad, who'd hit six-four at fourteen years old. I was six-three, and each of my brothers stood over six feet tall. My sister was taller than most girls at five-nine. I guessed her and Hen at about the same height.

When I chanced a glance around Hen's car, I noticed how nice it looked on the inside. Even though it was an older model, there wasn't a stain or rip in the interior to be seen, nor a crumb in any crevice.

Catching my examination, she said, "I'm saving for a house. A new car's pretty low on the list."

"It's nice," I said, but all I could think was how ridiculous it was that the woman who was "single handedly running this place," according to the Blue Bird corporate office, couldn't afford a newer car along with a decent home of her own. But then again, California real estate was a beast, from what my brother Gage told me. And coming from a billionaire real estate mogul, that was saying something.

She paused at the stop sign before the main road.

"Let me text the girls." She tapped on her phone with its cracked screen for a moment and then set it face up in the console. Interesting. She either wanted me to see a text from some other guy or... she had nothing to hide. As she pulled onto the highway, she said, "It's probably a good thing you came along so we can get to know each other. We'll be spending a lot of time together on this project."

"I'm looking forward to it," I said honestly. "I want to hear about this house you're saving for."

She turned onto the road, quiet for a moment. "I don't need anything fancy..." She took a breath. "But I'm hoping for something big enough that I can stay in for a lot of years to come. Three beds, two baths, a nice backyard but not too big. Of course, it has to have a nice front porch to sit on with my girlfriends. And a garage to hold my tools."

"Tools?"

She nodded. "I'm not the kind to sit by the phone and wait for someone to help."

Damn was that hot. Especially in the way she said it—not bragging, only stating the facts.

"What about you?" she asked. "Do you have a home base, or is it apartments and hotels all the time?"

I shifted, leaning my shoulder against the door so I could face her more. "I have a house back home, but I've had renters in it for the last five years. Don't really have much need for one with all the traveling."

"What's after this?" she asked.

"I've got some ideas."

She raised her eyebrows. "Yeah?"

"I always thought I'd be settled by now, starting a family. It's hard to do when you're moving all the time."

"Hard to do when you're staying in the same place—at least for me."

I was about to ask what she meant, how a catch like her could possibly still be single if a relationship was what she wanted, but instead, she turned into the parking lot of a chrome diner building.

"This is it," she said.

I looked at the sign, taking in the retro design.

**Waldo's Diner.**

For the first time, California reminded me of home.

Back in my hometown of Cottonwood Falls, this was the kind of place where old men would grab morning coffee and sit and talk about cattle prices for hours. I got out of the car, seeing couples and families through the large windows.

She reached for the door, but I stepped ahead and held it for her. At her questioning look, I said, "Making up for last time. A man never lets a lady open the door."

"Who says I'm a lady?" she teased. Her soft, raspy voice made my pulse quicken.

Steeling myself, I said, "No one needed to."

With a small smile, she stepped through the door and into the aisle that went down the diner between the barstools and booths. Even though we'd just come in, a group of women and one older man waved at her from the other end of the diner, smiles on their faces and a few assessing gazes sent my way.

I straightened my shoulders, mentally preparing myself to meet new people. I used to be shy as a kid, and it had taken a lot of practice to get comfortable meeting and working with strangers.

The first woman to slide down the circular booth to make room for us had light skin with dark brown hair and even darker eyes. "Hen, introduce us to your friend." A ring sparkled on her finger as she waved at me.

Hen got into the booth next to her and corrected, "This is my *colleague*, Tyler Griffen."

Ignoring the confounding sting of her correction, I extended my hand to her friend. "Nice to meet you."

She shook it, an impish grin on her face. "I *adore* your accent."

I chuckled. "That obvious?"

She nodded, then gestured at a curvy blonde next to her. "This is our friend Birdie," then she pointed at a thin woman with black hair, olive skin, and a large smile. "My sister-in-law, Tess." I shook their hands.

Then the man at the other end of the booth extended his weathered hand. "I'm Chester. This one's grandpa." He pointed at Birdie.

"Pleasure, sir," I said, shaking his pale weathered hand, spotted with freckles.

He nodded, then grinned at the girls. "Good handshake. I like him."

They laughed, and when all was said and done, I got into the chair next to Henrietta. Everything was going well, until I was enveloped by her scent. Intoxicated was more like it. And damn was it hard to think with her thick thigh brushing up against mine.

Between ordering our food, her friends asked me all the regular questions. Where are you from, how many siblings do you have, what is your job like, and then I got the surprising question from Mara.

"Are you single?" she asked.

Henrietta said, "*Mara*, that's private."

"It's okay," I said, taking a sip from my sweet tea. "Haven't found the one yet. Still looking." I inadvertently glanced toward Hen, who was looking anywhere but at me.

Birdie smiled and said, "You'll find her when you least expect it."

Chester nodded. "And then you'll never be able to let her go."

"Maybe someday," I replied, thinking that was years down the road, when I could afford to stay in Cottonwood Falls and invest in my dream.

Our food came out, and a waitress named Betty set our dishes in front of us, along with all the condiments we could wish for. "I'll refill your drinks," she said. "Let me know if you need anything else."

The service was great, and then when I took a bite of the burger, I knew I'd be frequenting Waldo's Diner while I was in town. "This place is amazing. I mean the service is great, and the food... Tastes like home."

Birdie and Chester smiled at each other, and Chester said, "I'll be sure to tell the owner."

Mara and Tess laughed, and I asked, "What am I missing?"

Henrietta gestured toward Chester. "He's being humble. He owns the place. But it would be our favorite either way."

Chester blushed as much as an old man could and batted his hand at the women. "I'm just good at quality testing the coffee."

"Well, I'm going to get good at testing the burgers," I replied, taking another bite.

Out of the corner of my eye, I saw Mara mouth to Hen, *I like him*.

I focused on my food, desperately hoping this dinner hadn't gone amiss and I hadn't sent Hen the wrong signal. Best not to mix business with pleasure, no matter how beautiful and curvy that pleasure was.

# 3

## HENRIETTA

*Confession: My grandma is just as invested in my happily ever after as I am.*

THE MORE I got to know Tyler throughout dinner, the more I liked him. He had a tight-knit family like mine. The same number of siblings, except he had one sister and two brothers instead of three brothers like me. He was second born, where I was the second youngest. Since his family's farm wasn't big enough to support him once he grew up, he learned a trade and worked his way up in Crenshaw Construction until they trusted him enough to lead major projects around the country.

But he didn't brag. On the contrary, he acted like it was no big deal and asked questions of each of my friends.

In fact, watching the way he blended in intrigued me that much more. He didn't act like a boss—he acted like a friend. And I wondered how that would change on the job.

He walked with Chester to the register, insisting he pay for each of our meals, while the girls and I finished up our drinks.

Mara nudged my side and said, "Hen, you have to get on that!"

My cheeks were just as hot as Tyler's backside. "He's working with my company."

"And?" Birdie demanded. "You're both still answering to your boss, so technically it wouldn't be a huge conflict of interest."

"Maybe a tiny one then?" I deadpanned. Because even though I *maybe* had a crush on Tyler, there was no way a guy like him would ever want a twenty-eight-year-old plus-sized virgin like me. And did I mention I still lived with my parents? Not exactly a great look, especially to a guy like that.

Tess glanced toward him and Chester. "He's a great guy. I mean if I wasn't married with a baby... I'd be getting his number."

Birdie gave her a coy look. "Or building a weak chair for him to sit on."

We all laughed at the joke of how Tess met her husband while she rolled her eyes at us.

Mara shook her head. "I think you need to keep your eyes, and your legs, open."

"Oh hush," I said, swatting her hand. "I'm giving him a ride home. Which is where I *work*. I will see you all Wednesday for breakfast."

They waved goodbye, and I walked toward the register just in time to hear Tyler and Chester talking about the build for the second Blue Bird apartment complex. Chester shook Tyler's hand again and gave me a hug before we left.

Tyler and I walked to my car, and he stopped on his side, looking at me over the roof. "That was great, Hen. Thanks for letting me crash dinner."

I nodded, all my friends' thoughts echoing in my head. "I had fun," I admitted, getting in the car. And my friends were right. He was cute. From the strong edges of his stubbled jaw to the ridge of his nose and the fullness of his lips that revealed a breathtaking smile. And God, the way my name sounded with his accent. If I moved to the South, I'd be in trouble. Pining for men just for the way they spoke.

But Tyler would be my coworker, and I knew better than to chase men who would only break my heart.

I focused on driving, at least until he said, "I feel like I didn't learn much about you at dinner."

"What do you want to know?" I asked cautiously. I had to be careful—revealing too much could be a liability, especially as a woman in the workforce. I'd seen my sister-in-law get shoved out of her job after announcing her pregnancy. Not to mention my younger brother's fiancée constantly got called 'emotional' since her line of work was heavily male populated.

"Did you always want to be in property management?" Tyler asked, drawing me out of my thoughts.

The question seemed innocent enough, minus the way he watched me. It was like he wanted to genuinely hear my answer. And with his eyes on me, it was hard putting two words together. "Not really," I admitted. "I went to college after high school and got my associate degree in business, but I had to work full-time to pay for everything. Once I got a full-time job I liked, it seemed silly to spend all that money to go back."

He nodded. "So you like this line of work?"

"I do," I admitted. When he was quiet, I felt like I had to fill the silence. "Home has always been a special place for me. Somewhere I could go back to after a hard day and always feel safe, loved. Helping other people create that kind of place... it's the dream."

When I glanced his way, there was a small smile on his lips. "I'm excited to build that with you. Especially knowing you'll be the one in charge of the new building."

I couldn't help the grin that spread on my face. Getting this promotion—it was a huge affirmation for me. It meant I'd been right to follow my gut and stop after an associate degree. It meant that my work mattered and was valued by the people I served. And it meant I'd finally be able to reach my savings goal that had always seemed so far away.

Maybe I'd even find someone to share it with.

Someday.

The apartment building came into view, and I parked along the curb closest to his unit. Instead of immediately getting out, he smiled over at me. Not a forced smile, but a real one that took all the air out of the car.

"Thank you for letting me crash your dinner," he said.

I smiled. "Around here, we call it supper."

His laugh was infectious. "Supper," he corrected. "Let's do it again sometime?"

With a silent nod, he opened his car door and got out, then bent down to look at me again. "See you Monday."

I waved, pressing my lips together so I wouldn't squeal. As soon as I got out of the parking lot, I started a group call with Mara and Birdie. But I ended it before I hit send. How juvenile did I look, getting all giddy because a guy I worked with mentioned the potentiality of having supper together again.

I needed to remember who I was—his plus-sized tomboy virgin coworker with less of a chance of hooking up with Tyler Griffen than the Brentwood Badgers had of playing in the finals this year.

With a sigh, I continued toward home.

My family lived on the line between Emerson and Seaton in a smaller ranch-style house with a big backyard. But with so many of us living there, Dad had converted the garage into an extra bedroom, keeping all of our tools in the shop out back.

The light blue house came into view, and I parked under the carport next to Dad's old Buick. That thing had seen more years than I had, but it ran like a dream. No way would he leave it completely exposed to the elements.

When I got out, I noticed a car I didn't recognize along the curb. "Great," I muttered, hoping with all my heart this wasn't another setup. But when I got inside, my fears were confirmed.

A guy around my age, with short coiled hair sat at the table with my mom and grandma while my dad cooked at the stove. He had the distinct look of someone who didn't know exactly how they'd gotten there, but also didn't know how to leave.

At the creak of our front door, all eyes landed on me, and my grandma waved me over. She stood behind her latest attempt at Prince Charming, rubbing his shoulders like a boxer about to go into the ring. "Henrietta, dear, look who I met at the grocery store today! His name is Deshawn, he works at a bank, and he has a *401k*!"

When he waved at me, she pointed at his ringless finger.

Oh dear lord.

Dad gave me a look over Grandma's shoulder that said, *be good*. This wasn't the first time Grandma had brought a respectable stranger over to sweep me off my feet, and it wouldn't be the last. But we all put up with it because she was such a romantic, and well, arguing with her was about as useful as gassing a car in park.

"Hi, Deshawn," I said, hanging my purse up and wishing for the millionth time that I had my own home with my own key and multiple locks. "Which bank?"

"First Bank of Emerson."

"Free cash bags—that's a nice perk," I said. It really did help not to carry around a paper envelope stuffed to the brim with bills.

He nodded, and I took him in. He looked like the kid in school who only showed up so his parents wouldn't pull his keys. With his white sleeves rolled up and half his shirt untucked, he'd clearly been in the mood to relax when Grandma caught him.

She patted his leg. "Tell her about your car. She likes cars."

"My car?" He looked confused. "It's, uh... five years old."

"What kind of engine?" Dad asked.

"Um... gas?"

It took all I had not to snicker at the pained look on Dad's face.

"It's a V4," I said, taking pity on this stranger.

Deshawn gave me an impressed look. "How did you know that?"

"That model brags about good gas mileage. Wouldn't make sense to have any higher." I went to the fridge and got a hard, fruity seltzer, then opened it on Dad's novelty bottle opener before sitting at the table. "That gets, what? Twenty-eight in the city? Thirty-four highway?"

Suddenly Deshawn seemed a lot more interested and a lot less trapped. "Thirty-five..."

Dad and I nodded at each other, and Mom waved her hand, annoyed with us both.

Grandma said, "Enough about cars. Tell me, Deshawn. How many children do you want to have?"

# 4

## TYLER

When my alarm went off Monday morning, I scrubbed my face and got out of bed to hit the apartment gym. I'd checked it out the day before, and it wasn't much. Just a treadmill, an exercise bike, and a rack of dumbbells, but I could make that work. After growing up on a ranch where I had to do chores upon waking, working out seemed the closest thing now. It steadied my nerves and gave me a sense of purpose until it was time to start my workday.

An hour of exercise circuits later, I went back to my place, checking for Hen's car in the parking lot. The instant hit of disappointment I felt at not seeing it there surprised me. Why was I looking forward to seeing her so much?

Blue Bird corporate was meeting Crenshaw Construction leaders at the job site for a groundbreaking ceremony and photo opportunity before the real work began tomorrow.

I showered off the workout and then went to my dresser to retrieve my Crenshaw Construction shirt and a pair of khaki pants. I wouldn't wear this set for an actual day of work, but CC's publicist preferred I wore this outfit for public events.

My phone rang, and I scanned the caller ID. James Crenshaw, my boss and owner of Crenshaw Construction. "Hi, Jim," I said. "Y'all downstairs?"

"Yessir," he replied. "You about ready, or do you need some more beauty work done to that face of yours?"

I snorted. "I'm good, but I could give you a few pointers."

He let out a mix between a grunt and a chuckle. "See you in a few."

I grabbed my wallet from my bedside table and shoved it in my pocket with my phone before jogging downstairs where a black car was waiting. The driver held open the back door for me, which still made me uncomfortable, and I slid in next to Jim. He wore a suit that probably cost more than my first truck, and his salt and pepper hair was combed over to the side.

I shook his extended hand. "Good to see you, sir."

"Same, but I have to say, son, I don't understand your insistence on the cheap accommodations. I pay you enough to stay in a five-star hotel, and you choose a one-bed apartment?"

I followed his eyes, trying to understand why the gray building wasn't good enough. It wasn't the custom-built mansion he and his wife shared back in Dallas, not even close, but the property was well-kept and there were a few modest planter boxes around. "Good enough for a few months," I finally said.

As the driver pulled out of the parking lot, Jim asked, "How are you feeling about the build? Ready to meet the new crew?"

Subcontracting out crews in new locations brought on its own challenges, but I'd discovered a method to make things go more smoothly. "Pizza for lunch and beer after hours always does the trick," I said.

"I've taught you well. Keep it up and you'll be taking over once I retire."

"Retire?" I said.

"When you get to being my age, you think about resting once in a while... And you think about who's going to take over your legacy when you're gone, especially when you don't have any children."

"Jim, I couldn't possibly—"

"Nothing's official. Just the musings of an old man."

I studied him a little closer as he looked out the window. Jim was getting older—well into his sixties with a thinning head of gray hair and plenty of wrinkles and sunspots. I'd only worked closely with him the last four years, but his age was beginning to show. Was he really hinting that I could be the one to take over? I'd thought I'd grown as much as I could in his company, but now? The possibilities were endless.

"It's exciting, isn't it?" Jim said as we pulled up to a vacant lot sporting a giant sign with a mock-up of the building that said FUTURE HOME OF BLUE BIRD LUXURY APARTMENTS.

I nodded in agreement. There was always a buzz that came with groundbreaking. It was full of potential, but if I was being honest, I felt more at home in the day to day of making the project run smoothly than I did in the planning stage or at photo ops.

The driver stopped the car, and while he got Jim's door, I let myself out, taking in the small group of people. A few news vans lined the property, along with sleek cars like the one we'd arrived in. And then there was Henrietta's red car. The sight of it, so different from the rest, brought a smile to my face, and I began scanning the crowd of suits for her.

I spotted her immediately, the sunlight glancing off her dark hair. The blue dress she wore clung to her curves, and I found myself wishing I could be just as close. She was clearly in her element, talking freely with her colleagues, a stunning smile on her face.

Jim put his hand on my shoulder, jerking me away from the thoughts I shouldn't have had. "Ah, there she is.

Let me introduce you to the woman you need to meet." He began walking toward Henrietta, but then stopped short and said, "Tyler, this is Janessa Vogul. She's head of operations of Blue Bird's properties in southern California."

I caught Henrietta looking at me for a moment, but then I heard Janessa say, "Pleased to meet you, Tyler." Her smile fell perfectly in place like she'd practiced it a hundred times before. But the expression didn't meet her green eyes—they were just as calculating, assessing as her smile. I felt like a piece of meat being examined at the butcher shop.

Thanking my lucky stars that Henrietta would be working more closely with me instead of Janessa, I said, "Nice to meet you, Mrs. Vogul."

"Ms.," she corrected with a wink. "And you can call me Janessa."

Jim clapped my shoulder. "Janessa, you'll have to excuse me. I see our publicist. I need a chat with her before we get called for photos."

"That's okay. I'll keep Tyler company," she said.

Jim chuckled, but I wished he would have brought me with him. Instead, Janessa stood just a little too close, like a shark who smelled blood in the water.

"How did we get so lucky to work with you?" she asked, folding her white arms over her chest, like she wanted me to look there.

An uncomfortable chuckle escaped my throat. "I believe Mr. Crenshaw met with the CEO," I said.

She forced a laugh. "I trust you moved in alright. I know it gets lonely, traveling so much for work. I'd love to give you a little company after this. Perhaps get some dinner together? Or a nightcap?"

I raised my eyebrows, shocked at how quickly this woman worked and wishing Jim would come back and save me. I didn't think I could handle dinner, much less an evening with someone who clearly had more than business on her mind. "Ms. Vogul, that's a kind offer, but I'm sorry I have to decline for the sake of professionalism."

She gave me an amused grin. The first expression she made that seemed natural. "Hard to get? I can appreciate that. Let the games begin."

Jim and our publicist, Nancy Finnagan, saved me the challenge of replying. Nancy called out and said, "Can we get the C-suite and property manager in hard hats?"

I hurried away from Janessa, fearing she might be the kind to slap my behind on the way out, and in my hurry, bumped into Henrietta. She swayed in her heels, and I reached to catch her, my hands landing on her curvy hips.

But the feel of her under my palms caught me off guard. She was soft, but solid. And my mind went places it shouldn't have gone in public. "I'm so sorry," I said, quickly righting her and pulling my hands away.

She wouldn't meet my eyes and muttered something about it being okay before grabbing a hat from Nancy.

Great.

Two days in and I'd already made things awkward by practically fondling her on the job site. I'd apologize to her later, maybe with lunch, and hope it would patch things up.

"Over here, Tyler," Nancy said.

I nodded, going to stand beside Jim in the middle of the empty lot. It was mostly mowed weeds and grass underfoot, but soon it would be dirt, a foundation, framing, a building, a home. I couldn't wait to see the transition.

With our hard hats on, Nancy lined us up and began passing out shovels to signify the groundbreaking. Janessa squeezed in next to me, and I had to suppress a cringe. Thank god LA was an hour away, probably more with traffic. Otherwise, I had a feeling she'd be one to make frequent pop-ins.

A professional photographer began snapping photos while the news stations got their shots and filmed B-roll. And then it was time for my least favorite part of any new project—live interviews. I always felt so uncomfortable, preferring hands-on work to talking about work.

But here I was, standing next to a man in a suit with a microphone in his hand. "This is Tim Dugan from Channel Five News, and I'm here with Tyler Griffen, the head contractor on this apartment complex. Tyler, can you tell us a little about the environmental and community outlooks for this project?"

In the background, I heard Henrietta talking with another reporter, and even though I wished I could listen to her, I spoke into the microphone. Time to focus on work.

## 5

## HENRIETTA

*Confession: I hate standing next to skinny girls.*

EVEN WHEN TYLER was out of sight, I could *feel* his presence. He had a way that drew people to him, commanded attention. Including the attention of my boss. She was as high-strung and confident as they came, and my chest ached when I saw her speaking with Tyler. What little chance I may have had with him was long gone. Not that him feeling the girth of my body during his rescue hadn't sealed my hopeless fate.

When we bumped into each other and he'd reached out to catch me, his large hands had landed on my hips, steadying me. His touch had sucked all the air from my lungs, and I'd stared at him, stunned at his strength. But I could see the moment he realized just how big I was. His eyes had clouded over, and he stepped away, immediately apologizing.

I tried to walk away from him as quickly as possible because I just couldn't handle seeing the rejection. But adding insult to injury, we all had to stand in line for photos. Me right next to all of the thin, attractive executives at Blue Bird corporate. All the men were slimmer than me. Even Tyler's aging boss.

And even though they could have been thinking about the weather, I worried they were silently judging me. Most people thought being fat was a moral failing—a lack of willpower against fatty foods. But I'd been fat my whole life, even though half our food came from Mom's massive backyard garden. I was just a big girl. Always had been, always would be.

My friends would kill me if they knew that I was speaking about myself in this way. Mara and Birdie were so much more confident than me, but it was easy for them to be that way. They both had landed men that were obsessed with them. Me on the other hand? My grandma was still trying to set me up at twenty-eight years old, and I'd yet to have a serious adult relationship.

And I knew my grandma's heart was in a good place. She was just trying to get me the same kind of love that she and Grandpa had experienced. But when I walked into the house and she had some guy there, I could see it the instant they laid their eyes on me. What little hope they'd had for a random blind date was quickly replaced with disappointment.

It hurt every time. I tried to keep my mind off of it all as I focused on the television interviews. The corporate publicist gave me talking points, and I'd spent the week memorizing them. But soon, it was time for me to get back to the office.

I didn't bother telling Tyler goodbye before I began walking toward the parking lot with Janessa. She had her hard hat under her arm and a slight grin on her face. "That contractor's something to look at. I'm a little jealous you get to see him every day."

I didn't argue with her because Tyler was handsome in every single way. In fact, I'd never really been that into guys in polo shirts, but the Crenshaw Construction shirt hugged his biceps perfectly, and the collar dipped down to his chest where I could see just the slightest hint of chest hair. For a split second, I wondered what it would be like to feel the crisp curls underneath my fingertips, but I quickly shut down that thought. "He's all yours," I said.

Janessa shook her head. "It's against company policy to have romantic relations with contractors while they're employed by us."

"Oh?" I hadn't even realized that.

She nodded, stopping by her car. "The shareholders wouldn't be happy if they thought we only hired someone because of a romantic relationship. Do you remember Frances?"

"Frannie?" I asked. "I kind of thought we weren't allowed to talk about her anymore." I couldn't remember exactly why she'd been let go from her position managing a complex further south in California, only that it hadn't been on good terms.

Janessa nodded. "She hooked up with a window cleaner, and they had to let her go."

I cringed. How had I been so reckless to think about dating Tyler? I needed this job.

"Her mistake was getting caught," Janessa added with a wink.

I shook my head at her. "It'll be all business around here," I said. "Besides, I don't really foresee him needing a lot from me."

Janessa nodded, opening the door of her car. "Any of the big problems should go up to corporate, but I think you'll be fine with the day to day here."

"See you around," I replied, going to my car. Emotion clogged my throat as I drove back to work. Even though I had been really happy to earn this promotion and a little bit of extra income, I was already wishing this project could be over. Tyler's clear disinterest had only reminded me of my failure in the romance department.

Maybe when I finally had enough money to afford my own place, I would just have a big ol' chicken coop in the backyard and help my nephews and nieces sell eggs. It sounded nice, if not a bit sad. Because if I was being honest, I wanted a man to look at me the adoring way that

Cohen looked at Birdie or the proud way Jonas looked at Mara.

Before Mara fell for Jonas, she used to say, "Some people just don't get happily ever after, at least not in the traditional sense."

And I was starting to think she was right. I was twenty-eight, after all. Shouldn't I have kissed a few frogs by now if I were on the way to a prince?

It was depressing. So I spent the rest of the day at the office trying to avoid those thoughts by doing my normal daily tasks, from offering tours, handling leases, emptying the change in the laundry machines, and so on.

At the end of my shift, I called Tyler while locking up the office. It rang once before I saw his pickup pull into the parking lot. There was a twinge in my chest as I saw him open the heavy black door and step out. Instead of khakis, he was wearing jeans smudged with dirt and a dark blue T-shirt that clung to his muscled chest and arms. With that tattoo peeking out...I almost forgot to hang up the phone.

Not to mention the Griffen Farms hat that was on his head made him look younger, more relaxed. I much preferred this look on him to the khakis and polo from earlier.

"Hey," he said with a smile that outshone the California sun.

I made myself busy tucking my keys in my purse to hide my own smile. "How was the first day on the site?"

"It was great," he said. "We always start off a little

slow to get the guys used to working with a new crew. I always bring in plenty of pizza for a long lunch and have a beer at the end of the day—in the parking lot, of course."

"Clever." If I was being honest, I completely appreciated the taste of a beer at the end of a long day's work. My dad and brothers had made sure of it. "You'd win me over pretty fast with beer and pizza," I admitted.

"Well, I don't have any plans for supper, and I can always go for a second beer," he said.

"Nice use of supper. You're catching on," I teased, but then my mind immediately went to what Janessa had said about dating Tyler being off limits. I needed to be more professional. Not that I had to worry. I remembered the way he looked at me earlier. A romantic relationship was never in a million years going to happen between us. This was work and friendship only.

I was so lost in my thoughts I missed his reply, so I said, "Supper sounds good, but we don't have to do pizza and beer again. If you don't want to."

"Dealer's choice," he replied with a grin. "But I should probably get showered first. Do you want to wait in my apartment?"

"Oh," I said, "no. I can just wait in my car."

He looked around. "It's nearly ninety degrees outside. The air conditioning in my unit is pretty nice. And it doesn't cost you your gas."

At this point, arguing would just make me seem rude, especially since he knew my car AC was on the fritz from the night before. So I followed him up the steps to his apartment. It looked almost the same as it had a couple days ago. But I noticed there were several books and magazines spread out on his coffee table.

"Are you a reader?" I asked, slightly impressed. My mom had to pay my brothers to get their reading done in high school. Literally. Each book report earned them five dollars, and they never made more than twenty in a year.

"From time to time." He gestured at the table. "Feel free to look through them. I don't have anything weird in there."

I laughed. "I hadn't really been worried until you mentioned it, but then again, having brothers should have prepared me for anything."

Chuckling, he said, "There are some things we never grow out of." Tipping his head toward the bathroom, he added, "Should take me about ten, fifteen minutes."

I nodded and sat on the couch I'd picked out myself. It was just as comfortable as I remembered. Add that to a good book and the smell of his cologne that was lingering in the apartment already... Well, it was a great way to pass a quarter of an hour. I reached forward, thumbing through the books and magazines, seeing titles about retirement living bed and breakfasts and interior design. I picked up the first one that caught my eye, *The Homiest Bed and Breakfasts in North America*.

I flipped to the first page and stared in awe at beautiful photography of a bed and breakfast in Montana. It looked like a giant white farmhouse with a chicken coop and a garden with rows of leafy green vegetables out back. With the sun setting over the scene, it looked like heaven on earth.

A block of text flowed beside the picture of the owners. They hadn't been able to have children of their own. So instead, they turned their big home into a bed and breakfast and renovated it over the years to become a great place for guests to stay. They said it was their way of building a family. My heart melted for the ways two people could make a home.

A cute colonial home in Georgia covered the next page. It was magnificent, with giant pillars and vines creeping up the sides of the building. This one had lots of planned activities for the guests, from drives around the Georgia countryside to classes on classic southern cooking. I pictured myself there, running an inn like that, and smiled. It would be idealistic to go along and see their joy at a new experience.

That was one of my favorite parts about working for the apartment company. Getting to see how proud people were of their apartments when they moved in for the first time and knowing I had a part in that... Incredible.

Curious about Tyler's other interests, I set the book down and picked up the one about retirement living. The title, *How Seniors Can Thrive in Community Living*, stared back at me from the cover, alongside a group of women sitting around a table, playing cards.

Why would Tyler have this? His parents couldn't possibly be old enough to need this. But as I opened the book, it opened to a page with a light-yellow sticky note. This section talked about how gardening could be really good for older people. Helping something grow, having regular responsibilities, and enjoying the fruits of their work positively impacted mental health in multiple studies.

My heart ached for the people who didn't have that. I would never let my grandma go to a nursing home, not when she could stay with us. She deserved more than reruns of fifty-year-old TV shows on full volume and six o'clock bedtimes.

The bedroom door opened, and I looked back to see Tyler running a towel through his wet hair. With his arms lifted, his shirt pulled up, showing a sliver of his abs and a trail of hair into his waistband that practically had me salivating.

"That's a good one," he said.

My brain short-circuited. "What?"

He nodded toward my hands. *The book!*

I stood, setting it back on his coffee table. "What got you interested in senior living? Doesn't seem like a normal topic of interest for a construction worker."

There was a laugh in his eyes as he said, "What type of things do you think construction workers are interested in?"

"Oh, I don't know," I teased. "Beer and pizza?"

Laughing, he opened the door for me so we could

leave his apartment. "Can I let you in on a secret?" He seemed to sober at the end, like there wasn't another joke or small talk coming next.

"Sure," I replied, making sure to let him go down the stairs first this time.

He glanced back up at me as he easily took the stairs. "My grandpa moved into senior apartments, and he's having a really hard time with it."

"What do you mean?" I asked.

"Well, you remember me mentioning I grew up outside of Fort Worth?"

"Yeah," I said.

"It's a really small town, and there isn't much for older people there. At a certain age, their homes are too much to take care of, but even assisted living is a little too much. Most people put their relatives in homes in Fort Worth or Dallas and have to drive a long way to see them or they keep them at home with them. But it makes it kind of hard for the family. I know it's been hard on my mom as my grandpa got to that age."

I nodded as we reached the bottom steps and went outside.

"I keep thinking there has to be something to make the assisted living where he is better, so I've been doing some research to pitch to the building's owners."

I couldn't quite find something to say because, honestly, I was breathless. Most men didn't really give two cares about what happened to their grandparents, or their parents for that matter, but here Tyler was reading research books on his time off to make a better home for his grandpa and everyone else. It was incredible.

He held up his keys and said, "Mind if I drive?"

Looking at his pickup compared to my rickety red car, I grinned. "Of course not."

# 6

## TYLER

Henrietta put directions into her phone and told me we were going to an Italian place. It had been a long time since I'd been to a nicer restaurant, usually opting to have food delivered, so I was excited. But to be fair, I was more excited for her company than anything.

Being on the road all the time got lonely. Most of the guys I worked with had families, lives, and not a lot of time to hang out with someone who'd be leaving in a few months. But conversation flowed easily between Hen and me, and I never felt her coming on to me like Janessa had earlier. Even when I went home, it felt like everyone was pressuring me to couple up.

Back in Cottonwood Falls, most people thought marriage and family were the biggest success you could have. So the fact that I was over thirty without so much as a divorce or an illegitimate child under my belt made me the number one bachelor in town, aside from my brothers. The youngest, Rhett, was a perpetual playboy, and my older brother cared more about his Dallas-based business than dating.

And me? I had my job. I could hardly imagine a serious relationship with how much I traveled, and if I was promoted to Jim's position, I'd have more work than free time.

Henrietta pointed at a restaurant with twinkle lights under an awning. "That's it."

I looked at the red sign with swirling white letters spelling La Belle.

Hen said, "Don't ask for pizza or the waiters will laugh at you."

I chuckled. "Thanks for the warning."

We pulled alongside the building, and I gave my keys to the valet driver. As I got out and met her on the sidewalk, she said, "The food really is amazing here. I think you'll like it."

"As long as they serve beer on draft, I'm not too picky," I admitted.

"Not a wine guy?" she asked.

I pulled the hat off as we walked into the building. "I do drink wine from time to time. Just don't tell my dad."

We fell into line behind other parties waiting to talk with the hostess.

"I'm guessing he's a real meat and potatoes kind of

guy?"

"Oh yeah. If the food doesn't come off his grill, it's already at a disadvantage."

"My dad's the same way," she replied. I noticed the way her eyes crinkled around the corners when she talked about her family. "Mom's been trying to sneak spinach into his meals for years."

"Does it work?" I asked.

She laughed. "About as well as an engine without gas."

A server led the group ahead of us toward the dining area, and the hostess gave me a warm smile from behind her podium covered in ivy. "Are you waiting on someone?" she asked.

Confused, I glanced toward Henrietta, confirming she was standing beside me. Her eyes were focused on the floor, so I answered, "It's us two."

The hostess let out a surprised, "Oh," but quickly wiped the look from her face. "Follow me." She reached for a pair of menus and silverware rolled in a black napkin.

When we were alone at the table, I asked Hen, "What was that about?"

She kept her eyes on her menu. "She didn't believe that someone like you would be here with someone like me."

I nearly choked on my spit. "What? That's crazy."

Henrietta gave me a look with a tinge of annoyance.

"Guys like you don't exactly go out with girls like me. Especially not to a fancy place like this."

I studied her for a moment in utter disbelief, wondering what Henrietta had seen. What would make her think that a guy like me wouldn't be interested in her? I knew plenty of guys who liked their girls with curves—myself included.

Any guy, or woman for that matter, should be able to see that Henrietta was a catch. She smelled amazing, had a sexy swell of breasts under her blouse that gave just a peek at her cleavage. And the curve of her hips underneath her pencil skirt was practically kryptonite. Most of all, I liked her smile. It transformed her whole face, lighting it up completely.

"Maybe she smoked some dope before her shift," I said. That was the only explanation.

Henrietta burst out laughing, and the sound was music to my ears. "Dope?" she said with another laugh. "No one calls it that anymore."

"I do." I lifted my menu, glad to see her smile, and said, "What's good here?"

"Everything," she replied honestly. "And be sure to save enough room for the tiramisu after *supper*. It is to die for."

"Good looking out." I flicked my gaze to the drink menu, seeing a decent selection. "Do you want to share a bottle of wine?"

She raised her eyebrows at me. "Wine? What if your dad finds out?"

I shot her a smile. "I usually prefer reds, but we can get whatever you'd like. Perhaps champagne to celebrate our first official day working together?"

She smiled. "I'm fine with either one. I don't really drink much at all unless I'm out at the bar with my friends. One of my friends married the owner so we get free drinks."

"Well, that's the best kind of friend to have," I said.

Henrietta nodded. "That and my dad has a refrigerator full of beer in our garage for after we're finished with projects. But if I had my choice, it would be Cupcake wine."

"Cupcake wine it is," I agreed, just in time for the waiter to come by and get our orders. As he walked away, his notepad full of our choices, I asked, "What kind of projects?"

"Anything, really," she said. "One year we restored an old car. Another year, we built an entire raised garden bed for my mom so she didn't have to stoop so low anymore. And the year after that, we were restoring some of Grandpa's old furniture. You never know what kind of wild-hare idea Dad's going to get. Anything to do with his hands, he'll learn how to do it and be amazing at it."

This woman in front of me was so intriguing. The thought of her restoring a car when I'd only ever seen her in dresses made me want to know even more. "What's been your favorite project?" I asked.

"I think the furniture," she said. "For a while, I would pick up furniture along the road and restore it and then sell it online to make some extra cash. When I was in college it was kind of a nice side hustle."

"You don't do it anymore?" I asked.

She looked thoughtful, like she'd almost forgotten she worked with furniture. "No, I think I just got busy with work and family and let it go. But I should start looking for projects again."

I nodded. "Then what about the garden? What does your mom like to grow?"

"A *lot* of tomatoes." Hen chuckled. "She's always giving away tomato sauce because she says it goes great with just about everything. But my personal favorite is her bed of tulips. She keeps them each year in every color and makes the prettiest little bouquets for our table."

An image of Hen with her nose nestled in tulip petals warmed me in a way I didn't quite understand. And I didn't have time to think about it either, because the server walked up to our table, holding two glasses and a cooler of wine.

We watched as he popped the bottle, and when he poured Hen's glass, she said a sweet, "Thank you."

I thanked him too and took a sip. I stared from the cup to her. "Oh my gosh, this is really good."

Her laugh was contagious. "Why do you sound so surprised?"

"With a name like Cupcake?"

"Fair," she said. Then her mouth dropped, and she slumped low in her chair, lifting a hand to cover the side of her face. "Please don't see me."

"What?" I asked, looking around.

Her eyes darted around, a battle raging internally that I could only see a piece of. Finally, she whispered, "That guy that just walked in. My grandma tried to set me up with him a couple of nights ago."

I did a double take, realizing she'd been talking about the couple who'd just walked inside. The guy was handsome enough, with dark skin and the kind of girl the hostess probably expected me to be with on his arm.

"Did he see me?" Henrietta whispered.

I cringed the moment I saw him noticing. "Yeah."

She sat up, her expression grim. "This is so embarrassing."

I was about to ask for the backstory when the guy walked over with his date and said, "Hey, Henrietta." He glanced at me and said, "Looks like your grandma found someone else to set you up with after all."

God, I already hated this guy. And his date seemed just as stuck up.

Hen opened her mouth, probably to correct him, but I hurried up and said, "Actually, I saw her walking by my work and couldn't let her go without taking her on a date. We've been together about a month now. Although, I don't know how you let a chance with her go." I winked, extending my hand. "Tyler."

"Deshawn." He gripped my hand harder than necessary. No doubt trying to prove dominance. That and the way his eyes were calculating me had the hairs on the back of my neck rising. He was jealous, but only because another guy was interested. It pissed me right off. He had no right to be jealous, especially since he'd turned her down once and then made a joke at her expense. Not to mention he was here with a different girl.

He glanced from Henrietta to me again, completely forgetting about his date. "Your grandma hadn't mentioned anyone else." Then he mumbled, "Not exactly normal conversation in the produce aisle."

Hen smiled at his date, who was growing progressively more stink-eyed. "Sorry, we're being really rude. Deshawn met my grandma at the grocery store the other day. She's getting older, so she forgot I was involved. Hope you two have a good dinner."

Deshawn's date didn't even reply, instead giving Henrietta another annoyed look, and said to Deshawn, "Let's go sit down."

The second they turned around, I could see the air deflate from Henrietta.

Part of me wanted to look away and deny the sadness

in her deep brown eyes. I'd only known her two days, and it fucking sucked seeing this strong, beautiful woman brought down by a man who would hardly give her a second look and a woman who clearly thought appearance was the only thing that mattered.

I gave her a second to gather herself, and then I said, "I hope you don't mind me stepping in."

"Not at all," she deadpanned, taking another drink of her wine.

I waited for more info, then finally I couldn't hold myself back. "So what was this about your grandma and the grocery store?"

She gave me a pained look. "I don't know if your family's this way, but mine is bound and determined to keep me from becoming an old maid. It's not working out."

"Old maid?" I laughed. "You're what? Twenty-six?"

"Twenty-eight," she replied, "but I think they can feel my biological clock ticking. Every time my grandma goes to the grocery store, she comes back with some guy she thinks is going to be my happily ever after."

"Just any stranger?" I asked, thinking my mom could probably take notes from her grandma. She'd been trying to set me up with every single mom who had a child in her fifth-grade classroom.

"Oh no," Hen said, taking another drink. "Grandma gets his credentials first, of course. She only brings home people with a 401k and decent employment of more than two years." She shook her head, an amused look in her eyes.

"What's the rush?" I asked, refilling her glass of wine. I expected that kind of push in small-town Texas but not here, just an hour from LA, where people were getting married and having kids later and later in life.

Our server came back, bringing plates full of buttery, herbaceous food. My mouth watered before I even unrolled my silverware.

As we began eating, Hen said, "My grandma and grandpa had the best marriage ever. They were so close, and I know she just wants me to find something like that. But every time she brings someone by..." She shook her head and continued swirling spaghetti around her fork.

"What?" I asked.

She let out a heavy breath, setting her fork down. "I can see the look in their eyes when they realize who I am." She swallowed hard, looking down at the table again to hide the moisture shining in her eyes.

It took all I had not to get up and walk to Deshawn's table, just across the room, and shake him. What was wrong with these guys that they couldn't see what was right in front of them?

Without thinking, I reached across the table, covered her hand with mine, a strange sense of protection rushing through me. Maybe it was because my sister was full-figured, maybe it was the wine, but I needed her to know she deserved better.

"Do me a favor?" I asked.

She tilted her head in question.

"Don't let those guys make you feel bad about yourself." Her eyes flickered toward our joined hands and then toward me.

She nodded, and it took all I had to pull my hand away.

## 7

## HENRIETTA

*Confession: I'm not used to accepting help.*

THE WALDO'S Diner sign appeared in my windshield, and relief swept through me as I pulled into a spot next to Birdie's car. I needed to talk to my friends, to get their help sorting through the jumbled mess of my thoughts. The run-in with Deshawn the other day and what Tyler had said to me had my mind spinning the rest of the night and into the day. Maybe it was just my lack of any male interaction for the last few years, but I could have sworn I saw something in his eyes...

Shaking off the thought, I turned off my car and walked into the diner. Chester wasn't in yet, but Mara and Birdie both sat at our usual booth. When they saw me, they got up to hug me, and my favorite waitress, Betty, promptly put a mug of coffee in front of me.

"Extra cream, just like you like," she said.

I grinned at her. "That's why you're the best."

She smiled back. "I put a ticket in for the usual. Should be ready to go soon."

"Thanks," I replied.

Mara wasted no time getting to the point. She leaned forward and said, "*Please*, tell us something salacious has happened with the Texan."

My cheeks warmed, but I teased, "Are you looking for more material for your next romance novel?"

She batted her hand. "I'm already fifty percent done with the story. All I need is a good dark moment."

Birdie laughed, "Of course, you have to torture the characters now.

"Right." Mara nodded, taking a sip of her coffee. "They have to suffer a little before their happily ever after. But stop deflecting. He's had to have taken you up to his apartment by now. Right? Maybe flirted a little?"

My mouth fell open. "How did you know that?"

She had a smug grin as she shrugged. "It's a talent. So what did he say?"

I bit my lip, hoping I didn't sound too juvenile. "We went to dinner together last night to celebrate his first day on the job. And he had me wait in his apartment while he showered." At the excited look in Mara's eyes, I added, "*Alone.*"

She pouted, and Birdie said, "You can learn a lot about a guy from his apartment."

"He hasn't been there long enough to have any skeletons in the closet, but he did have an interesting selection of books. He says that he wants to open a senior living apartment in his hometown someday.

Birdie seemed impressed. "That's admirable."

"It is," I agreed, trying to keep the swoon out of my voice.

"Tell us about the dinner," Mara said, a twinkle in her eyes. "Anything happen?"

"Yeah, one of the guys my grandma tried to set me up with walked in with a very hot mean girl on his arm. I'm sure Tyler was wishing that she would have been there with him instead of me."

Mara scrunched up her face. "Why on earth would he want to be with a mean girl when he was sitting across from you?"

I didn't want to say the obvious, so I only said, "The whole encounter was super awkward, and I wish I could have disappeared into the booth."

Birdie asked, "How did Tyler handle it?"

I wrapped my hands around my mug, holding on to it as I searched for the right words. "He rescued me."

With a smile, Mara said, "This is the part I was hoping for."

I shook my head at her. "I think he took pity on me— he pretended to be my boyfriend and made the guy totally jealous in front of his date. He was really sweet about it after too. There was a moment..." I paused, my throat catching with emotion. Tyler had seemed so sincere, and my hopes were getting far too high. But this was the part I needed help sorting through, so I continued.

"He put his hand on mine and looked me in the eyes and said not to let them make me feel any less beautiful than I am. And it seemed like he really meant it."

Both of my friends covered their hearts with their hands and made *aww* sounds like he was some kind of sweet puppy dog.

"He felt sorry for me, right?" I said.

Mara gave me a sad look. "Can I give you some advice?"

Trying to keep from crying, I teased, "I know it's coming anyway, so I don't know why you're asking."

Birdie chuckled as Mara continued. "Let him choose his intentions."

"What do you mean?" I asked.

"You're already assuming you know the 'why' behind what he did, but the truth is, Tyler's the only one who knows."

Her words settled over me for a moment, and I realized she was right. I had already pegged him as just another hot guy who would never be interested in a plus-sized girl like me. What if he had other reasons for doing what he'd done?

Betty saved me from replying by bringing three plates

full of pancakes, eggs, and bacon. The three of us dug into our breakfast, eating our way through the food and moving on to other subjects. Birdie told us about their plans for her stepson, Ollie's, senior year, and Mara shared about the condo she and Jonas were buying in Atlanta for when she had to go there for work.

Catching up with them over comfort food really was a great way to start the morning.

With our food and drinks mostly gone, we all waved goodbye and left the diner. As I got in the car, I realized my mind had settled somewhat. Stewing over the "why" behind Tyler's actions had driven me crazy. Mara's advice gave me permission to simply... enjoy.

I drove toward the job site since I was supposed to check in every day and see if they have all that they needed or if I could get them anything. Janessa had told me that there would be errands to run and communication between Crenshaw and Blue Bird to handle. I was excited to start this new part of my job... when a thump sounded underneath my car and it started pulling to the right.

I groaned as I gently tapped the brakes and pulled onto the shoulder of the highway. That couldn't have been good. Cars rushed by me as I got out and walked around my car, trying to determine what damage there was. And then I found the culprit. I must have hit a rock or something with my tire because it was already completely flat.

I tilted my head back, letting out a frustrated grunt

toward the sky. I didn't have time for this, nor did I have the desire to be late on my very first day checking in on the build site. I was *not* dressed for changing a tire, but I had to get to work at a decent time.

I opened the trunk, trying to ignore the fact that I'd worn my best formfitting green dress and knowing that it would probably be completely ruined by the time I got to the job site. I lifted the storage flap and got out the tire iron, jack, and my spare tire. Thankfully Dad had made me practice changing a tire before I ever got behind the wheel.

I quickly had the lug nuts loosened and the car jacked up. I positioned the tire iron over the lug nuts to take off the punctured tire. Gravel crunched under slowing tire treads on the shoulder, and I looked up to wave them off. I was no damsel in distress.

But the sight of Tyler's pickup and his concerned face through the windshield had me freezing. Now I was really embarrassed. I straightened, wiping gravel off my knees and pulling my dress down.

He hopped out of his truck, his work boots crunching dirt beneath him. My eyes trailed from his boots up his muscular, denim-clad legs, over his green Crenshaw Construction T-shirt, and to the concern in his hazy eyes. "Flat tire?" he asked.

I folded my arms across my chest and nodded. "Bad timing also."

"Can I help you change it? I'd hate to see you ruin that pretty dress."

He thought my dress was pretty? I bit back a smile. "I can handle it. I wouldn't want us both being late to work."

He glanced at his watch. "If we work on it together, I bet we can get there on time."

Everything in me screamed that I needed to be independent. That I didn't want him to see me as any more of a charity case than he probably already did. But then Mara's words came to mind. *Let him choose his intentions.* "If you're sure," I finally said.

His grin was crooked as he stepped closer to me, taking the tire iron. "My dad would whoop me upside the head if I didn't stop to help." He glanced toward all the cars on the road. "I'm surprised someone hasn't already."

"That's not the way out here," I said.

"It should be," he replied simply and quickly spun the tire iron on the nuts. I watched as he easily removed the tire and reached for the donut. I passed it to him, watching his muscles move as he slid it over the bolts.

He tightened the lug nuts in a star pattern, just like my dad taught me. Then he lowered the jack, setting the car firmly on the ground. Tyler knew what he was doing; that much was clear. And if I was being honest, watching his muscles do the job was more than a little attractive.

He finished the bolts, making sure they were secure, and said, "You should be good to go."

"Thanks," I said, taking the jack and the tire iron.

"No problem." He picked up the wounded tire. "Do you want me to take this to get it patched?"

I shook my head. "My brother works at a dealership, and he always gets our tires fixed free."

Tyler nodded, bringing my tire to the back of my car. Once it was in place, he closed the flap over it and shut the trunk. With the job done and us standing on the side of the highway, cars whizzing by, I had no idea what to say. I was used to being alone, used to taking care of myself, but him stopping and helping, inconveniencing himself, I didn't know how to react, how to let him know that it meant the world to me.

So I only said, "Thank you," and moved toward the driver's side of my car. But he reached out, touching my hand to stop me. Just that simple touch sent a jolt of electricity up my arm.

His eyes were warm on mine as he said, "If you ever get in trouble like that again, you can call me."

I was about to tell him I had it handled, but he added, "Can I have your phone?"

"Why?" I asked, completely confused.

"So you can call me next time you're stopped on the side of the road."

My heart quickened. This was a fantasy—someone like Tyler demanding he cared for me. It couldn't be true. But he extended his hand, waiting like there was no world in which he wouldn't get exactly what he wanted.

And maybe it was what I wanted too, so I reached into

my purse, which was still around my shoulders, and handed my phone to him. When he returned it, his name was saved in my contacts with a hammer beside the letters.

Chuckling, I said, "I like the emoji."

He winked. "Just in case there are any other Tylers in your life."

"You're the only one," I said without thinking, and at the dimming in his eyes, I was worried I said too much.

He cleared his throat. "We better go or you'll be late."

A fraction of the light in his eyes returned as he said, almost to himself, "I think I was right on time."

# 8

## TYLER

As I pulled onto the highway, I could not get the image of Henrietta bent in front of her car out of my mind. How the fuck had no one stopped to help her? Where I was from, if you saw a lady on the side of the road, you stopped. You helped. You made sure she didn't get so much as a finger dirty.

But the knees of her dress weren't the only dirty thing around here. I was having less than honorable images of her bent like that in front of me. My mind had me pulling up that dark green dress, seeing the fabric slide over her full thighs.

Someone honked at me, and I realized I'd almost drifted into the next lane. *Fuck*, I needed to focus. My hardening cock was already aching against my jeans, for a colleague I'd barely met. I shifted to give myself some relief and did my best to focus on the road and the job at hand.

We had a lot of work to do to get started pouring the foundation for the project. It would be a lot of moving pieces, and I needed to be at my best. Playing sports in high school had helped me learn how to zone out the crowd and focus on the task in front of me, so that's exactly what I did for the rest of the day. It was harder during lunch when I had less to distract me, and even more difficult on the drive back to the complex.

Was I a creep for hoping to see her car in the parking lot? Or better yet, alongside the road? Probably. If not a creep, then, at the very least, a moron. Nothing could happen between us, I reminded myself for the millionth time that day.

And still, I was more than a little disappointed when I noticed it was already gone. Hopefully she was getting her tire fixed and wouldn't be changing any more tires on the road.

After showering, I got out my tablet and called Mom like I always did on Wednesday nights. When we all lived in Cottonwood Falls, it was our family's tradition to get together Wednesday nights and have supper. Mom always made a delicious meal, and when it was nice outside, Dad grilled the meat to go with it.

On those nights, we'd sit around a table on the cement patio overlooking our family's pasture. I missed that when I was on the road. Especially now, in this apartment with a view of a family playing in the park between buildings. So when Mom's face surrounded by a mop of frizzy blond hair appeared on the screen, it was like a breath of fresh air. A breath of home.

"Hey hon, how you doing?" she asked, setting her phone on the windowsill and washing her hands in the sink.

"Just got settled in here. First couple days have gone well," I answered. "How's everything there?"

She turned the sink off and squinted at the camera, then my view flipped to the window. She showed Dad at the grill, Rhett at the patio table, and my sister, Liv, sitting across from him. My older brother, Gage, was nowhere to be seen. Since his falling out with Dad, he hadn't been around much. But we didn't speak about his absence because it broke Mom's heart.

The camera wobbled as she stepped outside, and I heard her announce, "Tyler's on the phone!"

"Hey, what's that grilling?" I asked.

She turned the camera on the grill, showing blackened steaks and foil packed with what I assumed were peppers and onions fresh from the garden.

"Now you're being mean," I said. I could feel my accent growing heavier the longer I talked to them.

Mom laughed, turning the camera back on her. "You know you can come home any time, right? We miss you like crazy."

"I miss you too," I admitted, that homesick feeling back full force.

She moved again, and I saw her sitting next to Liv. "How's California?" Mom asked. "Are you liking it out there?"

My mind drifted to my new colleague, the one who had occupied far too many of my thoughts as of late.

"That's a smile I see on your face. Did you meet someone?"

I swore my mom could read minds. I didn't want to answer, but my hesitation was all she needed to let out a joyous squeal. "Do you hear that, Liv? Tyler met someone out there!"

My sister waggled her eyebrows at me, and I heard Dad grumble something about California. Rhett added something offensive about bleach-blonde girls in bikinis, and I could hear his protest as my sister slugged him.

I laughed, despite the homesick feeling in my chest. I knew Jim was counting on someone like me to handle the business, but I didn't know how much longer I could stay away from home. Every time I came out on a job like this, I felt like something was missing. But there wasn't anything for me in Cottonwood Falls—not without me coming up with a lot of money. Because I would never ask my older brother for money no matter how much he had to spare or how quickly he'd give it. My pride wouldn't let me do that.

"So when do we get to meet her?" Mom asked.

"I don't date girls when I'm on location," I reminded her, "especially not ones I work with."

"You work with her!" Rhett said in the background. "You dirty dog."

I rolled my eyes. "I do. And even if I didn't, I don't think she's the kind who would move back to Texas with me, and there's no way I'd fit in out here. There was a girl on the side of the road this morning changing her tire, and no one even stopped to offer her help."

"Typical city folk," Dad grunted off-camera. "They're always in a rush. No time to help."

I could feel the rant coming on. Dad loved Cottonwood Falls almost as much as he loved his family, and he never understood why anyone would want to leave town, most of all his oldest two sons. "The job's going well," I said, cutting the rant short. "We got the foundation going today and everything seems to be on track. One of the guys invited me out for a beer Friday night so I think that should be a good time."

"Good deal," Dad said, back to his quiet self.

"How's everything at the school?" I asked Mom. She'd be starting her tenth year of teaching in just a couple weeks. She always said teaching was her second career, since she'd stayed at home until all us kids were in school and then went back to college to get her own degree.

"We got new books for the classroom, so that's good. Although I will miss one student showing me their book that has Tyler Griffen's signature along with a big butt drawn next to it, written in pen no less."

My ears heated at the memory. I'd been such a dumb kid, leaving stupid drawings in all the books. "Maybe I can finally live that down," I said.

She chuckled, and Dad said, "Dinner's ready."

Mom quickly said, "Remember to book your flights for Thanksgiving before prices go up on them."

"Already have one booked," I said. I didn't tell her that Gage had used his extra miles to get it for me.

She smiled. "Good. And hey, maybe buy an extra ticket for that girl."

Mom could dream. Because that's where thoughts like that belonged.

## 9

## HENRIETTA

*Confession: I've gone so long without a relationship that sometimes I have a hard time believing anyone would want to date me.*

WHEN I CAME home from work on Thursday night and saw a different car in the driveway, I steeled myself for another one of Grandma's setups. I ran through the way I knew it would go—he'd see me, look disappointed, suffer through an awkward meal with my family, then he'd go home and I'd never have to see him again. (Hopefully.)

I'd been through it before, and I could do it again. And hey, maybe someday, I'd have a real boyfriend when I ran into one of these setups in the wild.

Just as I'd expected, I walked into the house to find another guy sitting at our kitchen table. Even sitting down,

I could tell he was tall. He had broad shoulders, a solid chest, a short thick beard, and nearly black eyes that unapologetically studied my body. It was different. And to my surprise, it was nice to have someone so clearly appreciate me.

Grandma stood and walked behind him to pat his shoulder. "Henrietta, this is Houston."

He stood and shook my hand. His skin was a little darker than mine, and his hand was so large, it enveloped mine completely, and I was pleased to find out he was a good six inches taller than me. Just as tall as Tyler.

Shaking that last thought, I sat across the table from him. While Dad finished cooking, Mom asked him about his work. He said he supervised workers at a factory that made glass syringes. But as soon as he was done answering, he asked Mom about her garden. Talked to Dad about his work as a journeyman. Had Grandma telling stories about her first car.

He was checking all the boxes—tall, decently handsome, interested enough to ask my family about themselves, and he seemed to be listening to what they had to say. He even complimented my dad on the sautéed squash that we'd been eating from Mom's garden almost every day for the last month and a half.

And when he asked me about work, I told him about my job, steering clear of the hot new contractor who Janessa had forbid me from dating. Ever since he'd rescued me at La Belle, then helped me change my tire the day before, I couldn't stop thinking about him. The way his muscles had worked under his shirt as he made quick work of the job. The way he'd so easily stepped in to help without worrying about how it inconvenienced him. And most of all, the way he put his number in my phone. I pulled it up every few hours the last couple of days, just looking at the numbers, memorizing them, wondering if I would ever get the courage to do something with them.

I was so lost in my thoughts, I almost missed Houston speaking. "Henrietta?"

I looked up from my plate. "Sorry, yes?"

"Would you do me the honor of going on a date with me tomorrow night?"

My grandma was smiling bigger than I'd ever seen, and even my parents seemed pleased, even at how formal the request sounded to my ears. And to be honest, I didn't really have a reason to say no. He seemed decent enough. My grandma liked him. He was single. And, unfortunately, so was I.

So I said, "Okay."

While my mom worked on dishes, Grandma said I should walk Houston to his car. So I did.

The evening sun was hot on us as we walked down the sidewalk. It was a newer Hyundai. Nothing flashy, just... okay.

When we reached his car, he took my hand and said, "I'm glad I got off work early to stop by the pharmacy tonight."

I laughed. "I think my grandma's overjoyed as well. I know they're a lot, so it's okay if you don't want to follow through on the date. I can make up something about you being in an accident or getting transferred from work at the last minute."

His full lips quirked to the side. "Why would you say that? I want to go out with you."

Now it was my turn to be confused. None of the guys Grandma brought home actually wanted to go out with me. "Are you sure?"

He pulled me a little closer. "Your body is bangin', girl. Of course I want to take you out on the town."

Flustered didn't even begin to cover it. No one had ever told me that my body was "bangin'" or even acted like they wanted to show me off. The couple of boyfriends I'd had when I was younger only took me to dark movie theaters or secluded restaurants. It didn't take long to figure out that they were embarrassed to be seen with me.

"If you're sure," I said, smiling slightly.

"I am. I'll pick you up here tomorrow at eight."

That seemed a little late, but I figured he might need to catch up on work since he'd said he left early today. "I can meet you at the restaurant," I offered.

"I like my dates to ride with me."

I shrugged, not mad about saving on gas. "See you tomorrow."

"I'll be here." He kissed my hand, leaving a small wet spot behind.

I waited until he'd driven away to wipe it off.

When I came in the house, everyone stopped what they were doing to congratulate me. Grandma wrapped her arms around me and said, "I am so excited for you! What a charmer!"

Mom nodded. "Can I take you out to buy a new dress?"

Dad said. "Need something good to wear with that car."

I laughed at his last comment. "It wasn't anything special, Dad. I'd be more impressed by a..."

"A what?" Dad asked.

I realized I'd been about to say "a truck." More specifically, a truck like the one Tyler drove. I'd only ridden in it once, but I liked the way it sat high off the ground and I could feel the power of the engine as we drove. But Tyler was off limits, and I had a perfectly decent guy coming to pick me up tomorrow night.

"You know what, Mom? I think I could use a new dress."

# 10

## TYLER

I looked up from the paperwork on my desk to see Henrietta coming into the trailer/office we had set up at every job site.

"Hi there," she said with a smile. She stepped the rest of the way in, handing me a paper to-go cup. "Might not be beer, but coffee's pretty good too."

I smiled, thanking her as I took it. One sip and sugary, creamy liquid filled my mouth. I coughed at the surprising taste. "What is this?"

"A latte," she said, confused. "Do you not like lattes?"

At this moment, I had two choices. Lie and get lattes delivered the rest of the project or tell her the truth. "I'm sorry. I'm more of a black coffee kind of guy. I really appreciate this though. It was awful nice of you to think of me."

She chuckled. "Not that nice, considering I didn't ask your coffee order. I just can't believe it."

"Believe what?"

"That I've met my first person with horrible taste in coffee," she teased.

I let out a surprised laugh. "If you need to fill it with sugar and cream, the coffee must not be very good."

"What kind do you like?" she asked.

I shrugged. "I'm not that picky. Whatever Chester had at the diner was good enough for me."

"Noted," she replied with a smile, then looked down at my desk. "Seems like you're swamped."

"Yeah, it's always heavy at the beginning of a project. Plus, one of the guys tripped yesterday and rolled his ankle. Had him get an X-ray done, so I need to fill out an incident report."

"Was it broken?" Hen asked, genuine concern in her look. "Should I get an ice machine on site for injuries?"

"That's not a bad idea," I said, frustrated I'd never thought of it. We had to use ice from the drink cooler yesterday.

She got out her phone, tapping on the screen. "I'll have one by the end of next week. What else can I help with?"

The way she'd buckled down and gotten to work the last few days was admirable. "It won't set you back at the other apartments?"

She shook her head. "I don't have an appointment for a tour until eleven, so I'm yours until then."

A strange silvery feeling filled my chest at those words, and I found myself searching for a reason to keep her around. I wanted to know her better, understand what this strange draw was all about.

"If you wanted to make copies for me, that would be a huge help," I said, even though I definitely could have made time to do them myself.

"Of course," she replied. "Let me know what needs copied."

I passed her a stack of papers to copy and then sort in the filing cabinets. (James Crenshaw was nothing if not old-fashioned.)

We both got to work, me filling out the lengthy incident report and her moving between the copier and the cabinets. For a while, we worked in tandem—well, she did. I couldn't seem to focus with her delicate, wildflower smell filling the trailer. So I gave up.

"Any plans for the weekend?" I asked, using one of the questions I'd practiced as a kid.

She paused, and I immediately regretted the intrusion.

"Sorry," I said. "It's none of my business." I focused on the report again, forcing myself to read each letter. *Cause of incident.*

"I have a date tonight," she said.

I looked up, finding her standing against the printer

table. She nibbled on the side of her full bottom lip, and my eyes drifted from there to her wide brown eyes.

"Yeah?" My voice sounded rough, even to me.

She nodded. "Another one of my grandma's setups."

That fact made breathing only slightly easier. "Ah."

"Yep. But he seemed nice enough."

Even I knew she deserved more than "nice enough." But if I wasn't willing or able to give it to her, what more was there to say? "I hope you have a good time." Lies. Right through my clenched teeth.

"Thanks," she said. And then the sound of the copier resumed. But it had nothing on the thoughts raging in my head.

## 11

## HENRIETTA

*Confession: I had no idea how I'd react to this kind of guy until I encountered him in real life...*

"YOU LOOK BEAUTIFUL," my mom said when I walked into the living room in my new shimmery green dress. I hadn't been sure about the way it showed off my cleavage and barely skimmed my knees, but Mom and Grandma both assured me I looked beautiful in the store.

Now, with my hair done up and my makeup on, I looked for my dad's approval. His lips stretched to a sweet smile, and he stood, taking me in a hug. "You look beautiful, baby girl. But please," he whispered in my hair, "wear a jacket with that dress."

I let out a laugh as I pulled back. "I'm not so little anymore."

"You'll always be my little girl," he supplied.

A knock sounded on the door, breaking up our moment. Grandma shot me a thumbs-up, and Mom shooed me toward the entrance. With my heart beating quickly, I opened the door to see Houston holding a gaudy bouquet to match the silver shirt he wore with the top showing off ungodly amounts of chest hair.

From behind me, Mom said, "We'll take those flowers and put them in a vase, honey. That was so kind of you, Houston."

I nodded, snapping out of my stupor as Mom reached past me for the flowers.

"Thank you, Houston," I said, his name sounding strange on my lips.

As Houston and I said goodbye, I realized I couldn't wait for the day when I had my own house and wouldn't have the whole family looking over my shoulder and peeking through the curtains at me.

Houston didn't seem to notice as we got to the car. He didn't open the door for me, which I realized I've been coming to expect after only a week with Tyler. And we weren't even dating.

I needed to get a grip. I couldn't date Tyler, and even if I could, he clearly couldn't care less that I was going on a date with someone else. In fact, he'd barely even looked up from his paper long enough to tell me "have fun."

No, I was here with Houston. He'd gone through the trouble of picking me up and bringing me flowers, and I needed to give him a real chance.

I got in, and the car smelled nice. It was clear Houston cared a lot about it by how clean it was. That, at least, was something we had in common.

He took me out to dinner at a steakhouse I hadn't been to before near his work. The food was good, and Houston kept the conversation going, talking about his job, the investment property he owned in eastern California, his family, and basically anything a person could want to know about him. I tried to give him some slack for talking so much because first dates can be awkward. And some people got chatty when they were nervous. But then his foot bumped mine under the table. And when I pulled my foot away, he moved his again so our ankles were touching.

I glanced up at him, wondering if he was having a spasm. Instead, there was a suggestive glint in his eyes.

Houston wasn't nervous at all.

He was playing footsie with me.

And that made me even more nervous. I thought footsie was something that only happened in movies. Yet, here I was, on a first date, with Houston's ankle rubbing against my leg.

Was this supposed to be hot?

Because I didn't feel turned on. In fact, I felt... his ankle on my leg. Just like the way he kissed my hand yesterday, there was no spark. No excitement like there had been when Tyler gripped my hand on the table.

Oh god.

Did I have a complex?

Was I only attracted to unavailable men?

I was mid-spiral when Houston asked, "Do you want to go get a drink? There's a bar I like near here."

And just to prove I wasn't pathetically attracted to a man I could never be romantically involved with, I took him up on the offer.

We drove to a bar nearby, the kind I'd only ever gone to with my brothers to play pool. Smoke made the air hazy, even though indoor smoking had been outlawed ages ago. A few pool tables lined the back area and a small dance floor, and an untouched jukebox that charged $5 per song cast colorful beams over the dimly lit area.

Houston walked up to the bar, and he ordered two rum and Cokes before I had a chance to order my usual mai tai. But I'd drunk Cuba libres before, so it wasn't the end of the world. He started a tab, and the bartender handed him two drinks that were more rum than Coke.

He brought them to a standing tabletop and said, "Let's dance."

I cringed, the drinks sounding good for the first time. "I really have two left feet," I said. The most words I'd said all night, really.

"You just have to follow me." He took my hand, swinging his hips as he pulled me toward the postage-stamp-size dance floor. Then he dragged my hand to his shoulder and made himself far too comfortable, gripping low on my hips.

My stomach churned. Someone braver would grab his hands and pull them back up to where they belonged. But he was bigger than me, stronger, and I didn't want to set him off. That was until he grinded his hips against mine, biting his bottom lip suggestively.

Did he really think I was going to be some cheap date? That he could buy me some flowers and hook up with me in a seedy bar?

I wanted to go home, but I didn't have my car, and the odds of him giving me a ride to anywhere but his bedroom were nonexistent.

"I have to pee," I blurted.

He chuckled low. "Eager for me to join you in the bathroom?"

The greedy way he studied me made me want to puke.

"I'll just be a few minutes," I said and hurried to the bathroom at the back of the bar. I slid the lock shut, and taking a few deep breaths, I had to plug my nose at the stench. It clearly hadn't been cleaned in a long time, and I doubted any amount of cleaner would even touch this smell regardless.

For good measure, I locked myself in a stall in case he decided to follow me, and then I quickly pulled up my messages to text my friends. Hopefully Mara or Birdie could come rescue me, and soon.

**Henrietta:** This date is horrible. He's getting really handsy, and I think he's going to try something. Can you come get me?

I sent a map pin to my location and then held my phone to my chest, praying they would get here soon. I thought about ordering a rideshare, but waiting outside this place at night seemed just as dangerous as spending more time with Houston.

If they didn't text me back in fifteen minutes, I'd suck it up and get an Uber. See what happened when I told him no. It wasn't like he could force me to do anything with all these people around. As strange as it sounded, as long as I was here, I would be okay.

When I walked out of the bathroom, I nearly bumped into Houston, who was standing in the hallway.

"Took you a while in there," he said.

What kind of a comment was that? "Takes girls a little longer," I muttered.

"But not with me." He winked.

When I realized what he was alluding to, I almost excused myself to go throw up. "Can you get me another drink?" I asked instead.

"Sure." He walked toward our table. "But you barely touched this one?"

Desperate to get some time away from him, I tried my hand at seduction, licking the plain rim. "I'm thirsty."

It must have worked, because his jaw went slack for a moment. He cleared his throat. "I'll get that for you."

As soon as his back was turned, I got out my phone. No new text messages.

*Shit.*

I quickly typed in my location for a rideshare, but we were farther away from my house than I thought. It would take at least thirty minutes for a ride to get here. That was too long. I needed to be gone five minutes ago.

I ordered it anyway, hoping I could stall long enough before he suggested we leave together.

He came back with the drink, holding it up. "Why don't you finish these and I'll take you back to my place?"

Shit. Think fast.

"Let's dance," I rushed out. "You—I mean, we were having so much fun doing that." I just had to suffer through, what, five songs? I could do anything for five songs.

"Anything for my sexy girl."

Barf.

He led me to the dance floor, his hands resting even lower on my butt, and began grinding his hips into me. My eyes widened in shock, because I could feel him growing hard.

"Do you feel that, baby?" he said. "You turn me on so much."

My instincts took over, and I shoved him as hard as I could. "Get away from me," I snapped. But he might as well have been a brick wall for all the effect my efforts had.

He chuckled. "Playing hard to get?"

I closed my eyes, wishing I could be anywhere but here when I felt his body pull away from me. I snapped my gaze up, wondering why he would give me space for the first time all night.

And then I saw him. *Tyler.*

He had Houston pushed up against a wall, his hands clenched into Houston's silvery shirt. Even though Houston outweighed Tyler by at least fifty pounds, he cowered away from him.

Tyler jerked his hands and growled, "If you touch her again, you'll die."

Terror was clear in Houston's eyes as he held up his hands and said, "I don't want her anyway."

Tyler shook his head, a vein in his neck throbbing. "Get the hell out of here."

He watched Houston stumble away, out of the bar past everyone who acted like this was just another night.

And then Tyler turned his eyes on me.

# 12

## TYLER

White-hot rage slowly dissipated from my body as I turned to face Henrietta. The sight of that bastard with his hands all over her—I could have fucking killed him. It took all I had to let him leave the bar, sprinting away like the worthless son of a bitch he was.

My hands were still shaking as I approached her, my eyes running up and down her body for any hint of injury. I palmed her shoulders, taking an inventory of her face, her eyes. "Are you okay?" I asked, terrified she'd been hurt in some way before I got here.

She nodded slowly, as if she wasn't quite sure. "How did you know to come?"

Had he drugged her? I searched her eyes, but they seemed clear, as usual. "You texted me."

She shook her head. "I—I meant to text my friends for a ride." She left me, going to her purse at the table and looking through her phone. A stricken look crossed her face. "God, Tyler I'm so sorry. I didn't mean to ruin your evening."

Ruin my evening? She'd been assaulted and she was worried about my Friday night? "Do you remember what I said earlier? If you ever need anything, that means a tire change, a rescue driver, a fucking pack of gum, you call me, okay?"

She nodded slowly again, and then her lips trembled. "I'm just so glad you came," she said, her voice cracking on the last word.

Without thinking, I took her in my arms, holding her as she shook with tears or adrenaline or maybe a mixture of both. I didn't know. I just knew that I wanted to keep her close. Keep her safe. She deserved so much better than this.

When her tears slowed, I asked, "Do you want me to take you home?"

"Not like this," she said, wiping tears from her cheeks. "My mom and grandma were so excited for me to go on this date. And I don't want to disappoint them."

The fact that she was thinking about everyone else at a time like this just showed how selfless she really was. I got pissed all over again at this guy who hadn't seen what he had right in front of him.

"Where do you want to go?" I asked. "I'll take you wherever you want to go."

She pushed her lips thoughtfully to the side. "I have an idea."

I walked her to my truck, keeping my arm around her shoulders to make me feel better about her safety. At least that's what I told myself. Not that it felt good to have her tucked under my arm, her warmth against my side.

I opened the door for her and held her hand as she got inside. Once she was securely in, I grabbed the belt and reached around her to buckle her in.

She started to protest, but I paused. "Let me have this," I breathed. "I need to know you're safe."

She nodded. The belt latched in place, and I let my hands linger for a second. Fuck, seeing her like that, shoving that guy away and the laugh on that sick fuck's face... it had broken something in me.

I pulled my hand away and walked to my side of the truck, my eyes scanning the parking lot for any type of danger. Seeing none, I got in and locked the door.

She looked over at me, a frown pulling at her lips. "You must think I'm pathetic."

"Why would I think that?" I asked, genuinely confused. I thought a lot of things about this girl—more than I should—and none of them included the word pathetic.

"You're always rescuing me."

"What's pathetic is how much I want to," I admitted. Then I cleared my throat. "Where's this place you want to go?"

She tapped an address into my phone. Collie's Bar. It wasn't too far away from the apartments and only about twenty minutes from here. We drove in silence until we reached a building with a glowing green sign with a black and white border collie.

The brightly lit parking lot immediately made me feel less sketchy than that seedy back-alley bar.

I parked and walked to her side, opening the door for her. Although I didn't have my arm around her this time, I walked close to her, determined to help her feel safe.

As we reached the door, she warned, "It's going to be a little loud in here."

I grinned. "How old do you think I am?"

She pretended to think on it. "Fifty?"

I rolled my eyes. "Minus twenty." I pulled the door open for her, and we stepped inside. I gazed around at the big wooden dance floor that had couples swinging about. The bar along the back wall was busy with customers, and barstools lined the dance floor like they were waiting for people to take a break from dancing.

"I'm impressed," she said, tilting her chin up to speak closer to my ear. "Only thirty and in charge of an entire build."

I didn't like to brag, but I gave her what I felt comfortable saying. "I worked hard to get here."

"I believe it," she said.

We reached the bar, and I waited for her order before asking for a beer for myself. I reached into my back pocket to pay for our drinks, but the bartender said, "Henrietta and her friends don't pay here."

The guy turned away to make the drinks, and I gave her a questioning look." Do you have a secret life I don't know about?"

She laughed, the sound music to my ears. "One of my best friend's husbands owns the place." She looked around. "He might be here, actually."

"Oh, nice," I said, glad that I was wearing decent clothes. When I'd gotten Henrietta's text, I hadn't even thought, just got up from my seat in the movie theater and ran.

For some reason, what Hen's friends thought... it mattered to me.

"There he is," she said.

She passed a glass full of beer to me, then held her mai tai and led me down the bar toward silver saloon doors. Standing near the end of the bar was an older guy in a dark green Collie's shirt. He was fit, but his mostly brown hair was sprinkled with some silver streaks, especially around the temples.

He was talking to another employee in a green shirt but paused when he saw us, giving Hen a warm smile and me a calculating look.

Henrietta was definitely well-loved and protected,

when her friends were around.

"Cohen," Henrietta said, "this is my coworker, Tyler. Tyler, this is my best friend's husband and the owner of this bar."

He reached out to shake my hand and gave me an assessing smile. "I'm assuming you're here for a work meeting."

I couldn't help but feel like I was taking my first girlfriend to prom and her dad was telling me to keep my hands to myself. I forced a chuckle and took a deep swig of my beer. I needed to calm all the rage that was still in my body. It was making me jumpy. If I ever came across that guy in a dark alley, I didn't know what I would do.

Henrietta explained, "Blind date gone wrong. Tyler kind of saved the day."

Cohen seemed to loosen up a little at that. "Let's turn your night around."

Hen smiled. "Thanks, Cohen."

He nodded. "How long have you been in town, Tyler?"

"Just a little over a week." I said. "Hen's been a lifesaver, showing me the ropes around the office and helping me get settled in."

"How long are you here for?"

"Nine months," I answered.

"Must suck being on the road all the time," he said. "The guys and I play poker on Thursday nights if you need some people to hang out with."

The thought of a regular poker night made me happier than I wanted to let on. Because guys just didn't do giddy. But I did smile. "That sounds great."

Henrietta offered to send me his number, then she said, "We'll let you get to work, Cohen."

He nodded, and we left him for a two-person table near the dance floor. She slid into her seat and took a deep drink of her mai tai, her eyes tracing the couples dancing.

"Do you dance?" I asked.

She gave me one of her shy grins. "I do the macarena with the best of them."

I couldn't help but laugh.

"What about you?" she asked.

"Two stepping is like a religion in Texas," I said. "Everyone from my hometown knows how to do that and a little swing dancing."

She seemed impressed. "I don't think I've ever been dancing with a guy."

"I'm surprised none of your boyfriends brought you out to dance," I said. I loved taking my girlfriend out on the weekends, when I had one.

Her eyes downturned slightly, and I realized I'd hit a nerve. I just didn't know which one. Had her last boyfriend broken her heart? Or was it about the monster she'd just escaped? I shuddered to think what might have happened if no one had been there to rescue her.

A country song came on before she answered, and I said, "Looks like it's time to learn."

She looked at me in surprise. "Oh, you don't have to do that. I'd hate to crush your toes."

I'd grown up on a farm dealing with thousand-pound animals and this dime piece thought I couldn't handle her size? "Nonsense," I said.

Hesitatingly, she slipped her hand in mine, heat leeching through her skin and slowly up my arm. A thrill went through me at the thought of putting my hands on her hips.

Back in Texas, guys put their arm over their partner's shoulder during a two-step, but I never really liked that. So I settled my hand just where her hip met the curve of her waist and began talking her through the moves. "Slow, slow, quick, quick. Slow, slow, quick, quick."

Despite her talk of two left feet, she was already catching on. "You're doing great," I said honestly.

Still focusing on her feet, as if she could will them into submission, she said, "I just needed someone good to lead."

Good thing she couldn't see my dopey fucking grin.

As she slowly got the hang of the moves, we kept better pace with the song. By the time it ended, she had the most adorable grin on her face. "I think I'm getting it!"

"You're a natural," I replied, loving the way her body felt pressed to mine. Her hand in mine, her flesh under my other hand, moving to the music... it was almost like the song had been made just for us. For this moment.

A new song started, and she smiled up at me. "Thank

you for teaching me, but I think I could use some more practice."

I grinned at her, more than willing to help.

## 13

## HENRIETTA

*Confession: Sometimes, I wanted a hero to rescue me.*

IT WAS NEARLY midnight when Tyler pulled up to my house. The porch light was on, but it looked like the bedroom lights were off. I breathed a sigh of relief. At least there would be no questioning until I had time to work out a story that would satisfy my grandma without breaking her heart.

Blue shadows from the dash danced across the ridges of Tyler's arm as he put the truck in park. When I looked up to his face, his eyes were on me.

He'd caught me staring, but I couldn't bring myself to look away. I could hardly bring myself to breathe.

I swallowed, breaking eye contact. "Thank you for

coming to the rescue," I managed, reaching for my seat belt. "I only wish you wouldn't have to do that so often."

I peeked up to see his response, and he wore a smile on his lips, his eyes taking me in. "What if I said I enjoyed it?"

"Then that would make one of us. I mean, the damsel-in-distress part. I actually had fun tonight at Collie's."

"Actually?" he said, feigning offense.

I playfully narrowed my eyes, unable to hide my smile. "I had fun. And maybe I enjoyed all the jealous looks I was getting too. Everyone wished they would have been on your arm."

He covered his chest with his hand. "Henrietta. Cohen is a married man."

I rolled my eyes, laughing. I adored this playful side of him. Which was dangerous. Adoration was nothing I should be feeling for a coworker. Especially when it could cost me my job. But with Tyler? I couldn't help it. He had this aura of joy around him, and I wanted to bask in the glow.

Which was exactly why I needed to leave, and fast. I reached for the door handle to get out, but he said, "Wait."

I gave him a curious look, and he added, "Let me get that for you."

"That's not necessary. It's not like you were my date." Although Houston certainly wouldn't have opened the door for me.

The quiet before his response unsettled me, but then he said, "I want you to see how you deserve to be treated."

My heart was a puddle on his truck floor.

Without waiting for my response, he opened his door, passing through the headlights to my side. I allowed myself a moment to watch him, the way his arms pulled around his muscles. The strong profile of his face. The contrast of his dark brown hair to his tanned white skin.

But then my door was opening, and he was waiting with one arm up, showing a tattoo on the inside of his bicep. He followed my gaze to the black ink swirling around his muscular arm.

"Is there a story for the tattoo?" I asked, wishing it wasn't midnight. Wishing that he had been the one to ask me on the date. Wishing that the walk to my house was miles instead of minutes.

"A long one," he replied, extending his hand to help me down.

I slipped my hand into his, my heart speeding just as it had when we'd danced before. But now there was no loud music, no other couples to distract me from the heady rush of this man in front of me. Only the pale glow of the streetlights and the soft summer breeze caressing my skin.

He walked beside me to the sidewalk lined with tulips my mom carefully planted from bulbs each year. "Have you ever thought about getting a tattoo?" he asked.

"I've thought about it. There's just never been anything I wanted to look at for the rest of my life."

"So perhaps one on your back?" He winked.

I laughed, gently shoving his arm.

My front porch was approaching way too quickly. We were close enough now to read the embroidery on the porch swing's decorative pillow. *Home Sweet Home*.

Desperate to keep him here a little longer, I asked, "What would a gentleman do on a date now?"

His eyes looked golden in our porch light as he reached for my hands. He held both of them in his, gently pressing my fingertips with his thumbs. "On a proper date, he'd tell you what a great time he had."

The breeze picked up, circling our porch and freeing a strand of hair from behind my ear. He reached up and gently pressed it back.

Between the wind and his touch and the look in his eyes, my breath was gone.

His voice was honey, just as sweet as his words. "This is when a regular guy would lean in and kiss you goodnight."

Involuntarily, I swallowed, flicking my gaze to his lips.

"But you don't want a regular guy," he finished.

"I don't?" I breathed. Because right now, nothing sounded better than a kiss goodnight from Tyler Griffen.

He shook his head, resolute. "You deserve a hero. Someone who would take care of you, even though you're capable of caring for yourself."

My lips parted. Was he saying...

"A hero would lean in, kiss your forehead, and walk

away, because, with a girl like you, he'd know the best is yet to come."

Tyler stepped closer, pressing his lips to my forehead, and with one final sweep of his eyes over me, he turned and walked away.

Shivers prickled down my skin as I turned to the door, fingers shaking on my keys as I pushed them into the deadbolt lock.

Feeling eyes on me, I looked over my shoulder, seeing Tyler smiling at me—*me*—before he opened his pickup door and got inside.

Unsure my heart could take any more, I let myself in and leaned back against the door, smiling wider than I ever had and feeling tears burn my eyes.

Every feeling. Hope. Worry. Longing. Despair. I felt them all as his engine fired up and then faded away.

## 14

# HENRIETTA

*Confession: I want to make my grandma happy. I just don't know if that's possible.*

I TIPTOED TO MY ROOM, where I was in danger of hanging a Tyler Griffen poster on my ceiling like some kind of fifteen-year-old fangirl. This had gone from the worst to the best night of my life, all thanks to him.

Standing in front of my dresser, I pulled out my hoop earrings, hanging them back on my jewelry tree. With them out, I looked in the mirror. My cheeks still felt warm, my hair was slightly askew, and there was a light in my eyes that hadn't been there before.

I wondered what Tyler saw when he looked at me.

The small mole on my cheek? The fullness of my lips? The perfect shape of my waxed eyebrows (the one splurge I regularly allowed myself.) Or did he notice my broad shoulders? My full hips or the extra flesh on my stomach?

The line of questioning was driving me nuts, because I had to know what he had seen that no other guy had noticed.

My door clicked open, and I nearly jumped out of my skin, stumbling backward.

Grandma stepped into my room, wearing her gold and black silk robe, pink silk cap, and a sly grin.

"Grandma!" I hissed at her. "You nearly scared me to death!"

"Seems like the date went well," she said anyway.

I shook my head at her, continuing my routine of unclipping my necklace. The date had been incredible, for reasons she didn't understand.

"Well?" she prompted, leaving room for me to fill in the rest.

I glanced at her. "Aren't you supposed to be in bed?"

"I'm old, not an invalid," she replied, sitting on my bed and crossing her legs. "I had a good feeling about this one."

The hope in her voice nearly undid me. Grandma thought she had done me a favor, but I had to tell her the truth. I hung my necklace on the jewelry tree, then went to sit beside her.

"Grandma, I know you want me to be happy like you and Grandpa, but I have to tell you... I felt really uncomfortable with Houston tonight."

Worry deepened her wrinkles. "What happened? If your father finds out he tried anything..."

"He did," I said. "I actually had to call a friend to rescue me."

Grandma covered her mouth with her weathered hands. "Henrietta, did he—"

"No, no, I'm fine. I just don't think I can do the setups anymore, Grandma."

There was so much sadness and compassion in her eyes as she covered my knee with her hand. "Honey, I never meant to put you in danger. I only mean to help you find someone like my Harold."

"I know you loved Grandpa, but what you two shared, it was magic, Grandma. Maybe..." My throat tightened, and I had to swallow to speak my biggest fear. "Maybe that's just not in the cards for me."

She shook her head, gently running her thumb over my knee. "A partner, a true partner, can change everything. They'll bring out the best in you, force you to acknowledge your weak spots, help you grow faster than you ever could on your own. I'd hate for you to miss out on that because you don't think you deserve it."

My eyes watered again, and I tried to hide the emotion from my eyes.

Grandma didn't miss anything. "You seemed so happy when I came in, and I made things worse. Oh, I feel terrible."

I gripped her hand. "It's not that."

"What is it?" she asked. "Did your friend say something that upset you? You were on the porch for a long time with her..."

"Him," I corrected, and the light of hope in her eyes made me instantly regret it.

"Him?"

"He's a colleague, Grandma. From Texas. Nothing can happen."

"So he's from out of town and has no one to keep him company other than a pretty thing like you?" Her sly smile was back. "He must be lonely then. Invite him over for Kenner's birthday next Saturday.

"I don't think—"

"It's the least we can do to thank him for taking such good care of you," Grandma said. Then she stretched out and yawned. "You know, it is getting late. I think I'll get some shut eye, now that I know you're home safe." She hugged me tight, and I squeezed her back.

"I love you," I said, only the slightest edge of exasperation creeping into my voice.

"I love you too," she replied, giving me an extra tight squeeze before releasing me. "I can't wait to meet..."

"Tyler," I supplied.

"Tyler next Saturday," she finished. "Goodnight, darling."

"Goodnight."

# 15

## TYLER

Growing up on a ranch, I could always count on some hard physical labor to occupy my mind, but now I had to make my own solutions. I worked out the next morning, hoping it would take care of my buzzing thoughts.

But this time, it didn't help like it usually did. No matter how many times I bench-pressed, squatted, or pulled myself up on the bar, I could still see that asshole pressed up against Henrietta. Still feel the soft skin of her forehead underneath my lips.

And most of all, I could feel the pit of guilt growing in my stomach. I shouldn't have taken things as far as I did.

I got on the treadmill and turned it to full speed, sprinting as hard as I could. As if I could forget my own personal rule or the situation we were in. I knew better than to start something I couldn't finish. Yet here I was, ready to break my rule just a couple of weeks into this assignment. I needed a kick in the ass.

I needed to talk to my older brother.

Gage had always been one who knew when to follow the rules and when to break them. He'd pushed my siblings and me to do better and work harder, regardless of who was watching. On top of that, he'd taught us patience—the importance of making the right move at the right time and being certain when we did. It was part of what led to his success in business and made him one of my most trusted advisors.

And even though I didn't want him telling me to back off from Henrietta, I knew I needed him to.

I slowed the treadmill and draped a towel around my sweaty neck. After taking a few deep breaths and drinking a slug of water, I picked up my phone and dialed his number.

After a few rings, he appeared on my screen, dressed in a suit with the blue sky behind him. I'd asked him once why he turned his desk away from the panoramic view he had of downtown Dallas, and he said he wasted too much time looking at the city instead of his work.

"Hold on," he said, not yet looking at the phone.

I continued walking toward my apartment, waiting for him to finish up whatever had his attention.

When I crested the stairs, he said, "Sorry, I'm acquiring a self-storage facility and had to move some things around to make it happen."

"Self-storage?" I asked, my interest piqued. "Is there any money in that?"

"Ridiculous amounts. Everyone's been sleeping on them, including myself."

"Interesting." I pressed my key into the lock and walked into my empty apartment.

"I'm assuming you didn't call me to discuss investment opportunities," he said. "Although, your portfolio is doing well, by the way."

"Of course it is. You're managing it."

"Tyler."

I sat on the couch, still unable to forget the image of Henrietta sitting there, flipping through my books, her eyes lighting with questions, her lips turning into a smile at my answers.

"I'm in deep shit," I said.

A crease formed between his eyebrows. "Do you need money?"

Of course he would jump to the one thing he could solve. "No, I need advice." I propped my phone against a stack of books on the coffee table and leaned my elbows on my knees.

"What's going on?"

I let out a sigh, looking away from my brother. After my dad, he was the person I admired most. "I met a girl."

His lips curled into a smile. "Considering they make up fifty-one percent of the population, it was bound to happen at some point."

I hadn't expected to laugh, but I did. "They're not like this one."

The lift of his eyebrows told me he was listening.

"She's smart and funny, driven, selfless, loves her family and friends, has a smile that makes you forget how to breathe, and her curves..." I closed my eyes. "She's the total package, Gage. But she works for the company we're building for... I can't date her. I *can't*."

When I opened my eyes again, he had a devilish grin on his face, not too dissimilar from when we were kids and he had a prank planned for us.

"What?" I asked.

"You're in deep shit."

"Why do you think I called you!" I half laughed, half cried. I was a drowning man, and damn, if he didn't rescue me soon, I was in danger of sinking.

His background shifted as he stood, pacing his office. "You've never dated women on the job, which I've respected. Makes sense not to rile things up, especially when you're looking for a promotion... Are there any rules against it?"

I shook my head. Waited for him to throw me a raft.

"Honestly, Ty?"

I nodded.

"I don't see the problem."

My jaw clenched. "Don't see the problem? She's from California; I'm from Texas."

"People move all the time."

"Not her. She's saving for her own house."

"And I have so many miles you know you could fly her back and forth every day if you wanted to."

Gritting my teeth, I said, "How's that supposed to work with a family? With children?"

"You're already planning for children with her? How serious is it?"

The tips of my ears got hot, because I was placing a lot of pressure on a woman I hadn't even officially asked on a first date.

Gage asked, "I know you said it's technically allowed, but does Jim have something against it? Or her company? Is it the kind of thing that would be frowned upon?"

"Jim doesn't care as long as I keep things professional. And her boss was practically begging me to take her out, so I doubt there are any rules there."

Gage took a deep breath. "Tyler, I know you're responsible. That's why you went out and made a career for yourself outside the farm. Lord knows Rhett could use some of those brains. But you can't read the future. No one can. Say you go on a couple dates with this girl and it fizzles. That's better than sitting around, beating yourself up over a fictional breakup that may or may not ever happen."

Okay, so maybe he had given me a kick in the pants, but not the kind I had expected. "What if we don't break up?" I asked. "I can't ask her to move to Texas, and I can't move here."

Gage shook his head. "It sounds like you're asking the wrong question."

"What do you mean?" I asked.

He laughed softly, his eyes turning down. "I think the question is, 'How could I miss out on a girl like that?'"

# 16

## HENRIETTA

*Confession: I can't stop thinking about him.*

I STOPPED by Seaton Bakery on my way into work to get donuts and coffee for all the construction workers. Corporate had given me a budget to help manage things like this because they knew happy workers meant a job well done.

Gayle, the owner at the bakery, helped me load up all of the supplies into my trunk. "Are you getting excited for Mara and Jonas's wedding?" she asked.

I nodded. "Knowing them, it's going to be a night to remember. And I hear someone incredible is making the cakes."

She laughed. "We just want to do a good job for them. They're such a sweet couple."

"I'm sure you will," I said. "The cakes at Tess's wedding were fabulous. I had to stop myself from eating everything at the table."

Laughing, she said, "Thanks for saying that." She bumped my elbow. "Who knows? Maybe I'll be making a cake for your wedding soon."

"I love your sense of humor," I teased. "I'm closer to a house full of cats than I am a house full of kids."

"You'd be surprised. Love can always be right around the corner."

Hoping she was right, I replied, "I'll see you at the wedding."

"See you then."

On my drive to the construction site, I may or may not have fantasized about Tyler standing at the end of the aisle, looking incredible in a black and white suit. He was a classic kind of guy—he wouldn't wear any other color. He'd smile at me as I walked down the aisle, wipe a tear away from his face as I got close.

But as I neared the construction zone, I realized I'd just indulged myself in the adult equivalent of writing *Mrs. Tyler Griffen* on my notebook. So I shook all thoughts of marriage and babies from my mind and pulled up next to Tyler's truck.

I couldn't believe how much progress they had already made, taking it all in through the chain-link fence. In a matter of two weeks, they'd begun pouring the foundation. Now, gray cement and a steel frame occupied the space that was dirt and weeds just days ago.

I got out of my car and went to the trunk, grabbing two boxes of donuts. As I walked toward the office trailer, Tyler opened the door and came out. He didn't see me at first, so I had a moment to take him in. The way his tight T-shirt pulled against his biceps. The peek of a tattoo on his arm. The way the morning sun hit his skin, making him look almost golden.

All of it combined was enough to make me drool more than the donuts. But then he saw me, and his smile was even more dazzling.

Catching my breath, I lifted the box of donuts. "I brought breakfast for everyone."

"Well, that was mighty nice of you."

I shook my head. "I don't think I'll ever be used to that Texas accent."

He laughed, taking the box from me. "Here. Let me help you."

I nodded. "I have a few more in the car and some coffee thermoses."

"Great," he said. "I have a folding table in the office. I could set that up in front of the trailer."

"Perfect," I replied. I went to the car and carried back another box. Some of the workers were already beginning to line up around the table, looking at the spread. Seeing them dig in made me feel better—I knew how hard a day of work could be. Sometimes a little thoughtful gesture went a long way.

Tyler came beside me on my way back to the car to get the coffee, and he said, "It may not be pizza and beer, but I think you're winning them over."

I looked over my shoulder to see the guys chatting it up and snacking. "I have my ways," I said.

He replied, "You only needed that smile."

If he wasn't right in front of me, I would have done a happy dance on my two left feet. But since he was, I looked at my trunk to hide just how happy that comment made me. With my facial expression somewhat managed, I handed him a thermos and a stack of Styrofoam cups before grabbing the other thermos for myself.

With everything organized and set up on the table, Tyler poured himself a cup of coffee—black.

"Is there anything you're needing from us this week?" I asked him after a sip of my heavily doctored cup.

"Actually," he said, "if you could bring some paperwork by the city, that would be really helpful."

"No problem," I replied. "I'm really impressed by how much work you guys have done already. I almost can't believe this used to just be an empty field."

He held the Styrofoam rim on his lips as he said, "That's one of my favorite parts of the job."

"What do you mean?" I asked, trying not to be distracted by those lips.

His hazel eyes on me were just as distracting. "In a lot of jobs, you do the work and then you have to do it over and over again. With construction, you can actually see the effects of all the work that we're doing and the lasting results. Fifty years from now, I'll be driving my kids by this building and saying, 'When I was your age, I built this.'"

I pictured Tyler with children, and my mind went haywire. And speaking of children... "So I told my grandma about how you rescued me on Friday. And she wants to thank you personally at my nephew's birthday party on Saturday."

Tyler grinned, his eyes crinkling at the corners. "She does?"

I nodded. "In fact, I'm pretty sure if you don't come, she will call a senior ride and track you down herself."

"Well, I can't disappoint Grandma." He pretended to be at a loss of what to do. Adorable.

I bit my lip, smiling. "I don't think so."

"What time?" he asked.

"It starts at five. Dad will grill hamburgers and hot dogs. We'll put on some TV for the kids and play card games. It'll be fun."

"Sounds like it. Any tips on the gift? How old is he turning?"

"He's four, and you don't need to get a gift," I said. "You've done more than enough."

"There's no way I'm showing up empty-handed." I got the feeling he wasn't going to be talked out of this one, so I said, "Anything Paw Patrol is always a win with Kenner."

"That's a show, right? I don't have any nieces or nephews, so I'm not really up on the kid stuff."

Teasing him, I said, "Are you sure you're not fifty?"

He laughed. "My mom would lose her mind if I reached fifty without a single grandchild for her to spoil rotten."

"I know the feeling."

"The setups?" he asked.

"Yep, not to mention the sad looks at every family get together."

He groaned. "And the wallet photos of every niece/cousin/daughter/cocker spaniel."

I laughed. "Dogs too?"

"Can't have a boatload of kids without a dog," he replied.

"Fair. But I would go with something a little meatier for Texas. Maybe a Saint Bernard?"

"We had one when we were kids. Bernie."

"Cute," I said.

He was about to reply when one of his colleagues called him over.

While he was occupied, I went and refilled my coffee, chatting casually with the construction guys. Most of them didn't give me a second glance, but there was an older guy named Rich who was really kind and got me talking about my work.

I heard Tyler's voice above the chatter as he said, "A few more minutes, guys, then we need to get back to work."

"That's my cue," Rich said.

"Mine too," I replied. "Nice to meet you."

He tipped his ball cap off his head. "You too, Miss Henrietta."

Tyler called me over to the trailer, and I walked into the small space with him. It couldn't have been more than eight by fifteen, but there were a couple of desks and filing cabinets, and even a bathroom in the corner.

Just like the last time we were here together, our aloneness felt so palpable. I could smell his cologne, something earthy and light at the same time. I wanted to reach him to feel his lips on my forehead again. Maybe even on my mouth.

Logically, I knew he was off limits. But that didn't stop my mind and my body and my heart from wanting more with him.

He handed me a couple of manila envelopes and said, "These need to go to the environmental planning office." His fingers brushed mine, leaving a jolt of electricity in their wake.

I quickly took the envelopes and pulled away, not wanting him to see how much of an effect he had on me. In a matter of weeks, he'd consumed my every thought and replaced them with fantasies I shouldn't be having.

"I'll see you tomorrow," he said.

I couldn't wait. And that would be the end of me. I could feel it in my bones.

# 17

## HENRIETTA

*Confession: I still struggle with my self-esteem.*

AFTER WORK, I drove to meet my friends at Vestido for a dress fitting. Mara's wedding was just a couple weeks away, and we needed to make sure that all the alterations had been done correctly.

As I turned into the parking lot, I wished I could ask their advice with Tyler, but this was Mara's time. For the millionth time, I cursed myself for not being more experienced. If I'd dated more, maybe I would know how to make the next move with Tyler. Or maybe I wouldn't be so desperate for love that I was even thinking about jeopardizing my job.

It was a good thing I couldn't ask for advice tonight

while my willpower was nonexistent. I needed to remind myself that I couldn't lose this job. That no man, even one as handsome and sweet as Tyler Griffen, was worth giving up all I'd sacrificed on the way to my goal.

I parked my car and walked to the dress shop, seeing my friends toward the back of the shop. Tess stood on the platform, looking absolutely gorgeous in her dress. I pushed through the door and walked back. "That's amazing on you," I said.

My friends turned to look at me, and Mara got up, giving me a hug. "This is exciting, isn't it? I never thought anything like this would happen for me."

I squeezed her back. "The rest of us did."

She laughed. "Of course you did."

The saleswoman, Venitia, poured me a glass of champagne. I thanked her and took a drink, letting the bubbles warm my mouth and throat on the way down. For the first time today, I felt like I could... breathe.

While the seamstress worked around Tess, I asked Mara, "Getting excited?"

"Honestly?" she said. "I'm looking forward to the honeymoon more than anything. I already feel like Jonas and I are married, with or without the ceremony."

"I could see that." The two of them had been a perfect match from the moment they started their fake relationship—even if neither of them could see it. He kept her feet on the ground, and she kept his feet on the clouds.

Birdie added, "A week in Mexico does sound fabulous."

Mara nodded. "I'm thinking we should all do a girls' trip there next summer, maybe when the show wraps up filming."

I thought through my finances, wondering if I could spare a thousand dollars (or more) to go on a trip. I hadn't been on a vacation in so long, and I needed one, for sure. But I couldn't. My goals were bigger than little frivolities. I had to stay focused.

"Who's up next?" the seamstress, May, asked.

I raised my hand, partially to avoid any more conversations about vacations.

She walked me back to the fitting room and showed me the dress with a little name card on it that said Henrietta. It looked just as beautiful on the hanger as it had the day we picked it out. My problem with clothes was never with the shopping, only with the trying on.

"Let me know if you need any help," May said.

I nodded, steeling myself for any possible outcome. I didn't check the scale anymore, aside from the once a year I went to the doctor—and endured a rant about my BMI that left me crying for days. So there was a decent chance I'd gained or lost since they took my measurements.

I gave myself a mini pep talk and slipped it over my head, surprised at how soft the fabric felt against my skin. Usually when I dressed up, it felt more like being squeezed into a sausage casing, but this gown felt amazing. Even the straps that had been added after the fact looked like they were meant to be part of the dress.

I gaped at myself in the mirror, my eyes watering. I felt beautiful, and it had been so damn long since I'd seen myself that way.

"Henrietta?" May called. "Everything okay?"

"Be out in a sec," I said, trying to hide the emotion in my voice. I pressed the corners of my eyes, stemming the flow of tears, and then I lifted the hem and walked to the podium.

As soon as the girls saw me, they began squealing and clapping. Birdie said, "Oh my gosh, that dress was made for you!"

Tess nodded and bumped Mara's arm. "Aren't bridesmaids dresses supposed to be ugly?"

Smiling, I shook my head, turning and looking at myself in the trifold mirror. Even though I tried to fight it, the tears came anyway. For once in my life, I could see what Tyler saw.

"Oh, Hen," Mara said, coming up and putting her arms around me. "What's going on?"

I shook my head, wiping at my eyes again. "I'm so sorry. This is supposed to be your time."

Birdie said, "She gets a whole wedding for that. Tell us what's going on?"

I bit my lip but finally gave in, telling them about my horrible date and Tyler saving me and the fact that if anything happened between us, I could very well lose my job.

Mara and Birdie exchanged a glance, and Birdie said, "I wouldn't have gotten my happily ever after without breaking a rule."

I shook my head, sitting down on the edge of the podium. "I don't have a thousand students who would be devastated to see me go. They could find someone else in a heartbeat. But it feels silly to even worry about it. I don't know if Tyler feels that way about me or if he was just being nice."

Tess gave me a look like I was being absolutely insane. "Henrietta. He left his plans on a Friday night because you sent him a text message. He threatened to kill a guy, and then kissed you on the forehead saying, and I quote, *'the best is yet to come.'* I don't know what you could possibly be missing here."

"I just—" I swallowed down the lump in my throat, trying to speak. "I never thought something like that could happen to me." I closed my eyes, embarrassed by my low self-esteem. I was almost thirty. Shouldn't I be feeling good about myself by now?

Mara wrote romance novels for curvy women. Birdie was a guidance counselor, helping teens with their self-worth, and Tess was happily married to the love of her life with the most adorable child. And yet here I was, a twenty-eight-year-old virgin, feeling like the kid in gym class who always got picked last.

Mara put her hands on either side of my face and made me look her in the eyes. "Henrietta Jones. You are absolutely beautiful, but you don't have to see that for someone else to realize it."

My eyes watered as I nodded.

Birdie rested her hand on my shoulder. "There are hundreds of jobs out there. There's only one Tyler."

That was a thought that echoed in my mind as I waited for what was to come next.

## 18

## TYLER

I had the Saturday birthday party so firmly planted in my mind that I almost forgot the poker night Henrietta's friend Cohen invited me to. Luckily, he texted me his address about an hour before it was set to start, giving me just enough time to shower off, change, and grab a case of beer from the liquor store on my way over.

I wasn't sure what kind they liked, so I picked a local brew kept in the refrigerated section and hoped for the best.

The directions on my phone led me to a neighborhood with big yards, tall shade trees, and brightly colored houses. The one Cohen had directed me to was a soft yellow, and the yard was decorated with quirky planter pots filled with colorful blooms.

As I got closer, I noticed the garage door pulled up to show a table surrounded by a few guys. They looked my way, and I lifted my hand in a wave before parking along the curb.

I'd had so much practice getting to know new people that it usually didn't faze me anymore. But now? My stomach felt like it used to before an important football game.

And judging by the protective way Cohen had acted at the bar last Friday, this would be an important game. Especially if I followed Gage's advice and gave a relationship with Henrietta a chance.

I took a couple deep breaths as I grabbed the case of beer from the bed of the truck and walked up.

A guy with dark hair, wearing dress clothes with the sleeves rolled up, said, "He brought beer! I like him already."

Cohen lifted an eyebrow and said, "You didn't have to—I have plenty from the bar."

Another guy at the table with gray hair and tanned skin said, "You don't need to buy all the drinks all the time." He stood up and walked toward me, extending his hand. "Name's Steve. I work with Cohen—I'm the bar manager."

"Tyler," I replied, shaking his hand. "I'm working on that new build for Hen's apartments."

"That's what I heard," he said, a slight twinkle in his eyes. "And a little more."

The guy with dark hair took the case from me, setting it in an old refrigerator in the garage.

"Thanks," I said.

He looked over his shoulder. "Nice to meet you, Tyler. I'm Jonas, Mara's fiancé. She said she met you the other day at Waldo's?"

"Yep. Hen was nice enough to let me tag along."

Cohen had a knowing grin on his lips that had me feeling embarrassed. Was I *that* obvious?

"What type of poker do y'all play?" I asked, hoping for a change in subject.

Cohen said, "You'll like it. We play Texas Hold'em."

Laughing, I replied, "Sounds like I'll be right at home."

Jonas pulled out the chair next to him and passed me the deck to cut. I sat down and tapped the top card. He took it back, passing out the cards to each of us. "What part of Texas are you from, Tyler?"

"Cottonwood Falls, a little town outside of Dallas."

Steve said, "Does your family farm?"

I almost laughed, because everyone assumed that I lived on a farm. But I nodded, because I did fit the stereotype, my Griffen Farms hat giving me away. "My family has a beef cattle operation with a small feed yard, and then we grow a few crops to help feed the cattle."

Jonas looked deep in thought. "Does beef come from somewhere other than cattle?"

I laughed for real this time. "No, we say beef cattle, because there can be dairy cows too."

"Makes sense," Steve said. "My grandparents had a farm we went to every summer. It was fun, except the billy goats were assholes."

That made me laugh out loud. "One year my dad got it in his head that goat milk was gonna make us rich. They lasted a year before Mom said it was her or them."

Cohen cracked a smile. "I'm guessing he chose her?"

I nodded. "They've been together thirty-six years. And I don't think she'll ever forgive the goat hoofprints on the top of her car."

Jonas set the deck in the middle of the table and flipped over five cards. "You're first," he said to me.

I looked to my hand... not bad. I swapped a seven for a jack, hoping to make a straight. We went around the table for a while, and I studied each of them, getting a feel for how they played. Cohen was the hardest to read, never giving much away whether he had a good or bad hand.

Steve, on the other hand, kept his good cards close to his chest, removing the smile that was always on his lips otherwise. And Jonas was clearly a terrible liar. His hands twitched when he had good cards, and his jaw tightened with the bad cards.

After a couple hours, Steve and Jonas had dwindling stacks of chips, and between Cohen and me, we knocked them out within a few rounds of each other.

Steve grumbled something about promising his wife he'd get home when he lost, so he said goodbye to all of us before telling me, "You better beat Cohen. He's not used to losing."

Cohen snorted. "Good luck."

It just made me want to win all that much more.

"I'm staying to see this one," Jonas said. "Besides, the girls have taken over my house with wedding craft projects, so I'm in no rush to get home." He shuddered. "So much glitter."

The girls... I'm assuming he meant Henrietta, Birdie, Mara, and Tess. Those four seemed thick as thieves.

But the distraction of Henrietta cost me a couple rounds before I focused back in on the game and won one against Cohen.

"I'll just say it," Cohen said as he shuffled the deck over and over again. "What are your intentions with Henrietta?"

Jonas gave him a look but then watched me for my answer.

"My intentions?" I hedged. Fuck, I was a couple beers in and about to admit that dating her was the worst idea ever—but I still wanted to.

He finished dealing and then flipped the cards over. "You were pretty close on the dance floor."

"She had a bad date, didn't want to go home," I replied, glancing from my cards to Cohen. This hand was good, but was it good enough to win?

Cohen tossed a couple of chips in the pile growing in

the middle of the table. "You're in town on contract, right? Just here for a few months?"

"Nine," I replied, as if it made a difference.

Another round.

"So you're leaving soon," Cohen said.

Jonas's eyes tracked between the two of us.

Instead of answering, I matched his bid and raised it.

Cohen looked from my chips to me. "Henrietta doesn't date. Not seriously, anyway."

"Maybe she hasn't found the right match yet." I traded a card from the pile and replaced one in my hand.

He raised an eyebrow. "And you're saying you could be that match?"

"I'm saying I'm all in," I replied, pushing all my chips to the center of the table.

Cohen studied me before matching my bid with all of his.

When we turned our cards over, I won.

# 19

## HENRIETTA

*Confession: My ovaries have a mind of their own.*

MY STOMACH WAS a ball of nerves Saturday morning. Tyler and I hadn't spoken much outside of work since I dropped off the donuts Monday. But if his forehead kiss the weekend before meant anything, today would be one to remember.

I got up early, taking extra time on my hair and makeup, and then helped my mom peel and boil potatoes for the potato salad. After that, we made deviled eggs, and I ran to the grocery store for chips, soda, disposable plates and silverware, and of course, the cake with the puppy's face printed on top.

As we were putting food into dishes, Grandma sat at

the kitchen island and said, "Is your male friend coming today, Hen?"

All eyes swiveled on me, making me very aware that I hadn't told my parents Tyler was coming over.

Dad's hands stalled over the piping bag he used to fill the deviled eggs. "Male friend?"

Despite the heat in my cheeks, I kept my voice even. "He's a *colleague* who rescued me from that horrible date last Friday. Grandma insisted I invite him."

With a cunning smile, she said, "You know how I love a good Prince Charming, Murph."

Before Dad could reply, the doorbell rang.

"Saved by the bell," I muttered, wiping my hands on a rag to go and answer it.

As soon as I opened the door, my brother Bertrand and his fiancée, Imani, came inside, carrying ridiculous amounts of presents for a birthday Kenner probably wouldn't remember. Mom immediately put Bertrand to work on the potato salad, and I stepped outside to help my other brother Justus, who had just pulled up.

He and Raven had driven a slick red convertible he no doubt borrowed from the car dealership where he worked. Driving new cars, even with the giant stickers on the front, was just a perk of the job.

He popped the trunk and walked to Raven's side of the car. She was eight months pregnant and no doubt needed some help up from her seat. I went to the trunk, grabbing a big wrapped box. "How are you two doing?"

Raven groaned. "If this baby doesn't get here soon, I might lose my mind."

Over the present, I caught sight of her wearing Crocs. "I thought you hated those shoes! You must be hurting bad to have those on."

"You have no idea," she grunted, making her way toward the house with her hands supporting her back.

Justus took the gift from me and followed her to the door. As he passed me, he whispered, "These hormones are killing me, sis."

"Seems like a fair trade—she carries your baby, and you deal with a few mood swings and cravings."

He stuck his tongue out at me, and I patted his back as I walked toward the house, a minivan pulling up.

My oldest brother, Johmarcus, was there with his wife, Laila. They got out of the car, grabbing the kids. She held their nine-month-old, A'yisha, and Kenner bounced up and down with a balloon.

"Look what I got!" Kenner said, waving his arm around to show the string tied around his wrist.

"I love that balloon! And it's red! Your favorite color!"

His smile couldn't have been any bigger as he jumped into my arms for a hug. He wrapped his little arms around my neck, and I squeezed him back, saying, "Happy birthday, four-year-old!"

He let me go before running into the house as Laila futilely asked him to tell me thank you.

"Don't worry about it," I said, reaching for the baby.

That's what we did when they came. I took the kids and gave them a break, and by the way their shoulders instantly relaxed, I knew they needed it. I'd do the same for Justus and Raven when their baby came.

Laila and Johmarcus passed me, going into the house while I slowly trailed after them, holding my niece. A'yisha was only nine months old, but she had the most beautiful dark curls and these big black eyes that constantly sparkled. This had to be my favorite age.

"Hi, baby!" I said to her, smiling wide.

"I usually go by Tyler, but baby will do."

My eyes widened as I looked away from my niece to see the most handsome guy ever walking up the sidewalk. I hadn't heard his truck in all the chaos, but there he was in dark wash jeans, cowboy boots, and a plaid shirt tucked in, showing off his narrow hips and broad shoulders. The bag in his hand with a puppy's face on it and tissue paper sticking out made me swoon that much more.

Damn. I was completely unprepared.

I focused my eyes back on A'yisha and said, "Sweetie, this is Tyler. Tyler, this is my favorite niece, A'yisha."

"Nice to meet you, A'yisha." He reached for her little fingers, and she wrapped her fist around his pointer finger, hanging on. There was the sweetest smile on her lips, showing off her two bottom teeth.

"You are the cutest," he said, his eyes crinkling at the corners.

She babbled back at him, and I swear, my ovaries were

screaming at me, GET A MOVE ON, HENRIETTA! HE WILL NOT LAST LONG! My grandma would probably say the same thing as soon as she met him.

I cleared my throat, hoping for the millionth time he couldn't read my mind, and said, "This is home."

We walked closer to the front door, taking our time. As he took in the simple ranch-style house where I grew up, I wondered what he thought. If it was anything like his home in Texas.

"It's nice," he said. "And tulips." He gestured at the flowers lining the sidewalk. "Your favorite."

My lips turned up. "You remembered that?"

"Of course," he said.

"Henrietta! Who is this?" my grandma asked, her voice as sweet as pie as she watched us from the front door.

A'yisha squealed at the sight of Grandma, and I bounced her on my hip. Grandma was strong, but not that steady. "Grandma, this is Tyler Griffen, my *coworker*."

Tyler extended his hand to her, and she shook it, hearts in her eyes as she sized him up. "We heard all about your heroic rescue last week. I was quite impressed."

Was that a blush on Tyler's cheeks? "I was happy to help."

Her eyes narrowed playfully. "I'm sure you were." Instead of letting go of his hand, she maneuvered him so she could wind her arm through his elbow. "Come now, let's meet the rest of the family."

I nuzzled my nose against A'yisha's ear, making her giggle, and whispered, "When you're my age, I promise I won't make it this difficult."

We followed them inside, and I swear, the entire house went silent at Tyler's entrance. Grandma cleared her throat, as if she didn't already have everyone's attention, and said, "This is Tyler, Henrietta's new male friend."

As if "male friend" wasn't embarrassing enough, my brothers stared him down, three wolves to Tyler's sheep. They didn't know he could bare his fangs when needed. And then there were my sisters-in-law, both pretending they didn't find him attractive. And my mom, all moony eyed, just like her mother.

Dad was the first to speak. "Welcome to our home, Tyler. We're happy to have you."

*Thank you,* I wanted to shout.

And then Kenner yelled, "I'm FOUR!"

It broke the tension just enough to spur some laughter while Grandma marched Tyler around the room, dutifully introducing him to everyone in our family. And since I didn't want to stare in horror, I went to stand by the island with Mom. "How can I help?"

She gave me a knowing smile and leaned against the island. "So this is why you've been so distracted lately?"

"I haven't been distracted."

"Please, I've asked you to take the trash out every day this week and you've forgotten just as many times," she said.

"That was on purpose," I deadpanned.

"And that date you went on last week? I've seen you primp every day for work for longer than you took getting ready for that date."

Okay, so maybe she was right, but, "Was I really that obvious?"

She nodded. "But I can't blame you. He is gorgeous."

Her giggle made me laugh too. "He is. Grandma's going to be real upset when she finds out I'm not allowed to date him."

"What does that mean?"

"My boss, Janessa, said I can't date him, or I could lose my job."

Mom pressed her lips together. "If it doesn't affect your quality of work, what you do in your free time is none of her business. Especially when you don't have anyone in town supervising you."

I was about to argue, but Grandma paraded Tyler our way and said, "Tamica, this is Tyler. Tyler, this is the backbone that holds this family together."

"You can call me Tam," my mother said, smiling as she reached for Tyler's hand. "We're so happy to have you here. Can I get you a lemonade or maybe a beer?"

"A lemonade would be real nice, Tam. Thank you."

"Of course," she said, reaching for the pitcher. I grabbed a red Solo cup for him, feeling Tyler's eyes on me. When I chanced a glance his way, there was a warm look in his eyes and a half smile on his lips.

Warmth flooded my chest as I fluttered my eyelids down and wrote his name on the cup. Giving him a labeled cup felt like giving him a place in our family. And my family was everything to me. No matter how crazy it got when all my brothers were home, no matter how overbearing my grandma's search for my mate could be, I couldn't imagine getting serious with anyone they didn't love.

Dad came out of the garage, carrying a tray of hot dogs and burgers, and said, "Tyler, why don't you come help me with the grill?"

## 20

## TYLER

My stomach was a ball of nerves as Tam loaded my arms with spices and I followed Murphy out to the backyard. Of course, Henrietta's brothers had given me the stare down, just as Cohen and Jonas had, but it was her dad who made me on edge.

He had an easy smile, but eyes that didn't miss anything. Just from our short meeting, I could tell he was the kind of guy who would give you his trust until you broke it, and I wasn't going to give him a reason not to trust me.

As we walked to the grill, I glanced around the yard, seeing garden beds all around the perimeter, filled with lush plants and fruit trees. Catching my gaze, Murphy said, "Will you go grab a few zucchinis from that bed over there? Maybe pull a couple onions. This time of year, it's all we can do to keep up with Tam's green thumb."

"Sure thing," I said, walking to the beds he pointed out. This garden was really something. I was sure if Tam and my mom got together, they'd talk for hours about soil amendments and growing seasons.

"Hose is over there," Murphy said, pointing his tongs to the side yard.

I grabbed the hose and used the spray nozzle, turning it to the center setting to rinse off the plants.

When I returned to the outdoor kitchen area with the produce, Murphy said, "Tam's going to be impressed."

"These are looking really good," I said about the vegetables.

"No, she always says you can tell a lot about a person by the hose setting they use. She'd approve of your choice for cleaning."

I laughed. "She's into garden psychology then."

He cracked a smile of his own. "Something like that."

While he began heating the grill with propane—my dad would approve—he had me chop the vegetables and wrap them in a foil sheet. I was halfway through the first sweet onion when he began talking.

"Henrietta's our only daughter, our baby girl."

I stalled my knife for a little while, then began chopping more slowly. I listened carefully for his words, despite the fact that I could hear my heartbeat pounding in my ears, the sound of child's laughter coming from inside.

"She's got three brothers who would drop anything to be there for her, but she's independent as hell and has a stubborn streak to match. She's fiercely loyal, unendingly kind, and if you take her to a baseball field, she's got a swing that won't quit."

I found a smile on my lips. He was naming a lot of the things I liked about her—except for the baseball swing. I needed to see that for myself one of these days.

Murphy grew quiet, and I found the courage to meet his eyes. When I did, I saw his wrinkles first. The concern for his daughter, but the fierce protection was there in his stare.

"If you hurt my daughter or plan to drop her for another girl the second you go home, I'd appreciate it if you just went back to being coworkers only."

"We are only coworkers," I said.

A humorless smile twitched at the corner of his lips. "Either you're lying to me or yourself. Which one is it?"

My throat felt thick, and I swallowed. "Sir, where I come from, we do things a little differently when we meet a girl, a woman, we really like. I wouldn't dream of getting serious with your daughter unless I first asked your permission. If it's alright with you, I'd like the chance to date your daughter."

Another peal of laughter broke through the silence while I waited for Murphy's answer. He gave me one of those easy smiles again and said, "You have my blessing." I was about to celebrate when he added, "But Hen's opinion is the one that matters."

He turned back to the grill, and I got the distinct feeling our conversation was over. I began salting and peppering the veggies in my foil pouches. Murphy picked up a seasoning container and said, "Son, there is one thing you need to know. When we cook here, we add the flavor." As he added an ungodly amount of spices to the food, the back door swung open.

Kenner sprinted to the trampoline in the corner of the yard, and Hen's two sisters-in-law followed behind. They stood by the trampoline, watching as he tried, and failed, to do a front flip.

"Mind if I cut out?" I asked, nodding toward his grandson. "I think I could give him a few pointers."

He set the foil-wrapped vegetables over the heat. "Not at all, but Kenner's never done well with strangers. Don't let him hurt your feelings."

"I was the same way when I was a kid." I wiped my hands on a dishrag, then walked across the yard. Laila was cheering on her son while Imani checked something on her phone. I asked Laila if she minded me giving Kenner a few pointers.

"That's fine with me," she said, "but Kenner's pretty shy with strang—"

"Cowboys can do flips?" Kenner asked me, coming to the opening in the safety net.

"Only the good ones," I replied with a wink. "I used to

do flips off the horses every summer." Not on purpose, but I'd keep that part to myself.

"Off horses?" he cried, putting both of his hands to his head and falling over.

I chuckled. What a character. "But I started on the trampoline like you."

His eyes went wide. "Prove it."

"Okay, but only because it's your birthday." I kicked off my cowboy boots, set my cowboy hat on the edge of the tramp, and climbed up, hoping I wouldn't embarrass myself too much in front of the adults outside. But then the back door opened again, and I glanced over to see Henrietta walking her grandma out to the table and her brothers close behind with dishes.

Great. Her whole damn family was going to see.

Oblivious to my nerves, Kenner said, "I'll sit off to the side like this. That's what Mama says you have to do when someone else is doing a trick."

"Your mama's right," I said, feeling Henrietta's eyes on me. "So all there is to flipping is tucking your chin and trusting yourself, okay?"

He nodded.

I gave myself a couple warm-up jumps, wishing I wasn't so damn rusty, and then flipped through the air like it was just yesterday that my siblings and I were spending hot summer days with a sprinkler under the trampoline. I landed on my feet, bouncing a couple times, and looked back at Kenner.

"Whoa!" he pealed. "Can you teach me how to do that? My daddy said he's too big to do it."

I laughed, thinking of Johmarcus, who was built like a lineman to my running back. "Well, we all have different talents."

"And flipping is yours?" Kenner said.

Henrietta's voice came. "One of many."

"I have to keep up with my *coworker*," I teased.

Raven called from the folding table, "Keep it up, you two. That's how this happened," she pointed at her belly.

I laughed and got on my knees in front of Kenner. "Can you do a somersault?"

He nodded.

"Show me?" I asked, just like he'd done me.

He bent over and rolled, coming quickly to his feet. I put my hand up for a high five.

"So try jumping before you do that. And put your hands out so they land first."

He gave me a questioning look, but then his little face set with determination, and he jumped a few times before flipping and landing on his hands. Just as he got scared mid-jump, I reached for his legs and flipped him the rest of the way over.

He came back up grinning. "I did it!"

"You did! I barely helped at all!"

"Did you see that?" he asked his mom.

Laila had a proud smile on her face. "You did amazing, honey!"

He turned back to me and said, "I want to try again."

I nodded. "Whenever you're ready."

He did it a few more times with help, and then when he looked up, he grinned. "Everyone's watching me."

I glanced around seeing most of Henrietta's family circled around the trampoline, except for her dad, who was still grilling, and her grandma, who was leaning against a support pole of the pergola.

I focused back on Kenner and said, "You've got this, buddy." I scooted back to give him room, and he balled his little fists at his sides, pursing his lips with determination.

He jumped, swinging his arms to give him extra height, and then used all his force to propel himself forward. He tucked his head, and his hands barely skimmed the trampoline as he flipped over and landed on his bottom.

Everyone cheered as he scrambled up, and then he sprinted into my arms, squeezing me.

"Thank you!" he cried.

I grinned at him. "You did it all on your own, buddy." I climbed off the trampoline and let him bask in all the congratulations and cheering happening around him. But then I felt a hand brush against my arm, and I looked to see Henrietta.

She still had A'yisha on her hip, clearly a natural with the littles in her family.

She smiled up at me, her eyes warm in the summer sun. "That was pretty heroic."

"Nah." I folded my arms over my chest to keep it from puffing up too big. "He was just scared—had to get out of his own way." I thought of me, not asking her out yet. Now that I had her father's permission... there was nothing holding me back. "Actually, speaking of being afraid—"

"Who's ready for lunch?" Tam called. "Gotta eat some good cookin' before we can have cake!"

"CAKE!" Kenner screamed, jumping off the trampoline and running past us.

Henrietta giggled at him, and the sound hit me straight in the chest. I loved her laugh. She nodded toward the table. "Let's grab some food—before Bertrand eats all the deviled eggs."

"Sounds like it'll benefit us and Imani," I said, making her laugh again. "We wouldn't want her to call off the wedding due to excessive flatulence."

"I'll remind her to thank us later." She walked across the grass beside me to the little outdoor kitchen area.

"Why don't you let me hold A'yisha so you can get a plate?" I offered.

She seemed surprised by the gesture. "Are you sure? You are the guest."

"And you're the lady." I extended my hands for her niece.

As she passed the little girl to me, Henrietta said, "If she starts crying, I can trade."

"You think I'm incapable of handling a child?" I

asked, eyebrows raised. I already had her tucked against my side. A'yisha fit easily into my arms, light as a feather and so soft. Instinctually, I put my nose to her crown, smelling her sweet baby smell. None of my siblings had children yet, but my friends who had always welcomed a break.

Hen looked me over for a moment before saying, "I'll be right back."

"How you doing, darling?" I asked A'yisha, smiling big.

She cooed back, and I put my hand up to cover my face. When I moved it away and made a face, she squealed happily. I did it a few more times before Henrietta came back holding two plates.

"I got one for you," she said, holding up a plate packed to the brim with home cooking. I was more excited than I should admit to have food that wasn't cooked in a borrowed kitchen or a restaurant. Plus, it smelled amazing with all those spices.

We sat beside each other at one of the folding tables, and Bertrand and Imani sat with us. Bertrand's plate was half full of deviled eggs, and I nudged Hen's leg under the table. As soon as I nodded toward his plate, she burst out laughing.

"What?" Bertrand asked, his mouth stuffed.

Imani said, "Tyler, will you be around long enough for the wedding?"

Henrietta shook her head. "He's set to go home in May."

"That's a shame," she said. "If you find your way back here in August, we'd love to have you."

I thanked her for the invitation, trying to ignore the reminder about the fleeting nature of my stay here. "How did you two meet?" I asked.

They launched into the story, and I held A'yisha in my lap, wondering if someday, Henrietta and I would be telling the same story with a child of our own.

After dinner, there was cake and candles and singing. And when that was over, Kenner watched TV in the living room while everyone else sat around a long table playing Rummikub, her grandma, Cordelia's, favorite game. Henrietta's family partied like my family did—long and relaxed with plenty of beer and laughter.

I hadn't ever felt so at home on a work trip, but now, with Henrietta by my side, I felt it.

But when Cordelia announced she was tired, that was everyone's sign to go home. Johmarcus picked up a sleeping Kenner, who hung over his shoulder like a sack of potatoes. Laila retrieved A'yisha from the Pack 'n Play, while Bertrand and Justus helped carry out presents. Imani and Raven helped Tam pack up the food and throw out empty beer cans, and then they were gone too. It was clearly a practiced routine.

"Can I walk you to your truck?" Henrietta asked at my side.

I nodded, sad the night had come to an end.

As we walked down the sidewalk, barely lit by a lone streetlight, I said, "You know, I'm the one who's supposed to be walking you to your door."

Johmarcus waved out the window as they drove the van away, and it was quickly followed by the other two vehicles. Hen and I waved back, smiling as we did.

We paused by my pickup, and she looked up at me, moonlight sparkling in her eyes. "Is it bad if I say I wanted a few seconds longer?"

My heart sped at her admission, because I felt the same way. I could have stayed here all night, well into the next morning, and it still wouldn't be long enough. "Henrietta, I have a question to ask you."

Her lips lifted slightly, and I smiled, realizing I was learning all her smiles, all her laughs. This one was shy, patient.

"Will you go on a date with me?" I asked. Never before had I been so nervous to ask, so anxious for the answer... so crushed when her features fell.

There was a war happening on her face, and I didn't know why. Had I read her signals wrong?

"Tyler, I'd love to," she said, "but Janessa said dating contractors is strictly forbidden. I like spending time with you, but... I can't lose my job."

My chest ached as all hope fled my body. With the way Janessa came on to me at the build site, I knew it was a lie, no matter how earnestly Henrietta delivered it. She even seemed genuinely regretful to say no. But I should have known better than to plan an imaginary future with a girl I'd just met. No matter how beautiful and intriguing she was. I'd let myself get invested before I even knew her true feelings.

And arguing the point now would only disrespect her, disrespect her father in saying it was her choice, and her choice alone.

So I dipped my head, attempting to recover, and smiled back at her. "I completely understand. Thank you for inviting me to the party. I'll see you on Monday."

## 21

## HENRIETTA

*Confession: I haven't really been saving for a house...*

THE WALK back to the house was the longest of my life. It took all I had to keep my shoulders square and not show Tyler how much this decision was killing me on the inside. I managed a smile and a wave as his truck drove by, and then I walked inside, expecting to make a quiet escape to my bedroom.

Instead, my mom, dad, and grandma were waiting in the living room. I froze in the doorway, feeling like a goldfish in the bowl. "Why are you all staring at me?"

"Well!" Grandma said. "Did he ask you out?"

My features fell. That's what this was about? "Why would you think he asked me out?"

She glanced at Dad who admitted that Tyler had asked his permission.

I shook my head at the both of them. "I already told you I can't be with him. My job—"

"Your job?" Mom said. "Why are you so devoted to a job when you know you have the skills and experience to do that anywhere else?"

"I just got that promotion, and I'm saving for a house so I can get out of your hair, Mom. I can't be frivolous with my money."

"Stop," Dad said, his tone disappointed. He scrubbed his hand along his chin, not yet meeting me in the eyes. "Henrietta, we need to talk."

My stomach dropped. "What?"

"Sit," he ordered.

Feeling like I was sixteen years old and missing curfew, I crossed from the entryway to the living room, sitting on the chair as the three people I loved and respected most stared at me. And I didn't know how, but I could tell I'd let them down.

Dad said, "Henrietta, I'm no math genius, but your stories aren't adding up. You pay us two hundred a month for utilities, ninety dollars for your car insurance, and your phone is free through our family plan. Your car is paid off, and you fix everything for free at home. You buy all your clothes from the thrift store. Accounting for taxes, gas, and going out with your friends once a week, you have to be putting away, what, two thousand dollars a month? At least fifteen hundred for the last six years since paying down your student loans... Either I'm very confused about the kind of house you're saving for, or you're hiding something."

*Busted.*

"What if I do want a showstopper house?" I asked, lifting my chin.

They all saw right through it.

Mom asked, "Honey, are you in trouble of some sort?"

The worry in her voice almost undid me. I wanted to tell them the truth of why I'd saved so diligently. Why I was determined to put as much away as quickly as possible. But I couldn't without ruining the whole plan.

Grandma said, "Just because Johmarcus got upside-down in a business venture doesn't mean you have to be afraid of money."

"Mom and Dad had to take out another mortgage on the house to help him, Grandma," I said. "If that's not reason enough to be cautious, I don't know what is."

Dad cut his hand through the air. "That was our decision, what your mother and I were willing to do for our child. It was our choice to make, and we made it. That should have nothing to do with your saving habits."

Frowning, Mom said, "Are you waiting to buy a house until you find a boyfriend to move in with? Because times are different now. A real man won't be intimidated by a woman owning her own property and making her own mark in the world."

Seeing my opening, I hung my head. "I am waiting for a man," I admitted, but not in the way they thought I was. I raised my eyes to meet theirs, and my dad shook his head, a heavy expression on his face.

"You just let a good one walk right out that door," he said.

I replied, "I know, but that was my decision to make, and I made it." Then I stood up and walked to my room.

♥·♥·♥·♥

I TRIED to avoid my parents and Grandma for the rest of the weekend, because if they got too close, they'd see that my heart was breaking.

Tyler was the first man in my life who had asked me out, asked my father's permission no less. He'd proven his character when he respected my no without a single argument. He was one in a million, and I was losing him. Had lost him.

I tried to remind myself that I would have lost him when his job was over, but the truth? I'd imagined happily ever after. I'd imagined moving to Texas and celebrating Thanksgiving with his family and Christmas with mine. I'd imagined little children with my skin tone and his hazel eyes pattering through our house.

No amount of logic could take away the ache of that dream gone unrealized.

I kept things strictly business with Tyler at the beginning of the week, hoping he wouldn't see how turning him down had been the hardest thing I'd ever had to do.

But no matter how cheery I tried to be Wednesday morning, my friends knew it instantly.

Birdie took me in, concern in her eyes. "You look... awful. What went wrong?"

Mara nodded. "Did something happen this weekend with Tyler? You haven't replied to any of our messages."

I stared at my coffee and let out a sigh. I couldn't hide this from them just because I was embarrassed. So I told them the story, including my parents' interrogation after I turned Tyler down.

"But I want to know the same thing," Birdie said. "I thought he was the dream guy?"

Mara frowned. "And why is it taking you so long to save for a house? Do you have a gambling problem or something?"

I almost laughed at the absurdity of it. "No, I don't have a gambling problem."

"Then what is it?" Mara asked. "You've been saving as long as I've known you and living with your parents to save costs. Even if you wanted twenty percent down, you'd easily have enough for a smaller house out here." She wasn't judgmental about it. Just confused.

If I told my parents and grandma the real reason I'd been saving, they would talk me out of it, and I didn't want anyone to do that. But my friends could respect my choices. I trusted them. Still, I asked, "If I tell you the truth, can you promise to keep it a secret?"

Birdie and Mara each offered their word.

I took a breath.

I hadn't ever voiced my plan aloud. But I knew I needed to get it off my chest. I needed someone to understand and tell me I wasn't completely insane for letting a guy like Tyler walk away.

"When my grandpa got colon cancer six years ago, it was the worst year of my life. He was diagnosed at stage IV, and he got so horribly sick, he was gasping for air with every breath for months. He deteriorated to skin and bones, but there was so much fluid in his body that his stomach was the size of a beach ball." I choked on my words, on the memory. He'd been such a strong, proud man, but this disease reduced him to nothing.

Birdie reached across the table and held my hand.

"Grandma had to sell her house just to pay for his hospice care. It wiped out all of their savings. The care wasn't great either. The hospice house was so sterile, and turnover was so high you couldn't count on the same workers being there every day. And then the walls were so thin, you could hear all those people suffering around him." My voice cracked, and I hung on to Birdie with all I had. "He kept begging to come home so he could go peacefully in his bed, but Grandma couldn't tell him she'd sold the house. There was nowhere else for him to go. I felt so powerless, watching him suffer and not having the money to do anything about it, especially after all he and Grandma did for me."

My friends waited silently, so I took a deep breath, revealing my biggest secret of all.

"So, I promised myself that I would save all the money I could to keep my grandma from suffering the same fate he did."

Mara covered her mouth, tears in her eyes. "That's why you've been so frugal? Hen, why didn't you tell us?"

I wiped at my own teary eyes. "I got so used to telling the house story around my family, I guess it was easier to keep up the lie."

Birdie squeezed my hand. "That's so selfless of you, Hen, to do that for your grandma. Does she know?"

I shook my head. "If she knew, she'd try to talk me out of it."

"How much do you have saved?" Mara asked.

I bit my lip, knowing the exact number. "Almost a hundred thousand."

Birdie let out a low whistle. "I knew end-of-life care was expensive, but not that expensive..."

"They say to budget for five thousand dollars a month," I said, "and I want to give her two years of really good care in our home, if she ever needs it. I should be able to save the last twenty thousand dollars this year, but by the time I do..."

"It'll be too late for Tyler," Birdie said.

I nodded. "But if I risk my job to be with Tyler and

shit hits the fan, then I have to look for a new job, which could take months. Especially if I want to find one that pays as much as this one."

My friends and I were quiet as the weight of what I admitted hung over us. Because the truth was, some things were more important than following a potential love.

Mara tilted her head, smiling softly. "You know, in business they say short-term loss can lead to long-term gain. It's kind of like with you and Tyler. Even if you're set back a few months, you could gain experience at the very least."

Birdie nodded. "You could find your person, Hen. Tyler could turn out to be nothing—but you'll never know if you don't give him a chance. And if you'd go through all of this for your grandma, don't you think the potential love of your life deserves a date?"

# 22

## TYLER

Gravel crunched under Henrietta's tires as she approached the construction site. I'd love to say it didn't hurt like hell to hear her pulling up, but it did. And maybe I did the immature thing of hiding out in the trailer because I wasn't quite ready to see her yet this morning. She'd been so stoic with me all week, only talking about work and not bantering with me like she usually did. It hurt almost as bad as her rejection.

Rich, an older guy on the construction crew, with white hair and a red face from years of working in the sun, came in and got a couple of folding tables. "Hen brought treats again. I'm really coming to love that girl."

The laugh that passed my lips felt strangled. "She's one of a kind."

He nodded and brought the tables out while I sat

down at my desk, bracing myself to see her. I knew when to accept defeat, and I wanted to respect her answer, but man, it was hard. I was already counting down the days until it was time to go back home so I didn't have to suffer in silence anymore.

The door to the trailer opened again, and this time I heard a different voice. "Hey," Henrietta said gently.

I looked up to see her holding up a giant cinnamon roll on a paper plate and a steaming cup of coffee.

"Want some breakfast?" she asked. "The coffee's black this time."

I couldn't say no to her, not when she was smiling at me like that. "I'd love some."

She passed me the plate, and I was careful not to let my fingers touch hers, not to let the heat transfer from her skin to mine. I'd be a burning man with no way to save myself from the flames.

I set the cinnamon roll on my desk and took a burning sip from the Styrofoam cup. "Is this from Waldo's?"

She nodded. "The girls and I go every Wednesday before work. It's kind of a tradition."

"Nice," I said, wondering why we were making small talk. Why it hurt so fucking much to be in her presence and know I wasn't enough.

"Tyler, there was one thing I wanted to talk to you about..."

My gut dropped. "Yeah? What's up?" This couldn't get any worse than rejection, right? Because I'd made countless moves on her, and now I knew all of them had been unwelcome. I felt like such a creep, reliving the kiss on her forehead, two-stepping at the bar, telling her she was beautiful... A dumb creep at that for misreading all the signs.

"About the question you asked me the other night." She took a breath, her eyes looking everywhere but at me.

"I'm really sorry about that," I began. "I shouldn't have crossed a line, and I promise it won't happen again."

Her eyes snapped to mine. "What if I want it to happen again?"

"What?" I asked, my mind fumbling for a possible explanation.

"I would be honored to go on a date with you, if you're still interested, that is," she said. There was so much vulnerability in her features, and even though I was overjoyed that she'd changed her mind, I had to ask... "What changed?"

She smiled, as if to herself, and said, "Circumstances changed."

That was all I needed—I wasn't about to look a gift horse in the mouth. "Are you free on Friday night?"

She nodded, smiling.

"I'll pick you up from your place at seven?"

"It's a date."

♥·♥·♥·♥

THE NEXT TWO days passed so slowly, I wished I would have asked her out for Wednesday night, but Friday finally, *finally* came. As I got ready to pick her up, I realized just how long it had been since I'd gone on any sort of date at all.

It had to be two years ago... when I realized dating on the job was idiotic.

Not dating Hen felt even crazier, though. Despite how nervous I was.

In fact, I was wearing some of my best clothes, had on new cologne, and I hardly felt prepared to walk out the door. So I stood in my living room, got out my phone, and video called my brother Rhett who had been on so many dates, he had to be an expert by now.

He answered within a few minutes, and I saw his front yard behind him.

"Hey, what's up?" I asked.

"Watering these damn flowers," he said. "Mom planted them last spring, and I know if I let them die, it'd kill 'er." He moved the phone to show the sunflowers in full bloom.

I laughed. "I guess that is one of the benefits of not living back home anymore. No surprised redecorations."

He snorted in agreement. "What's up with you? Job going well?"

"It's fine. Actually, I... uh. I have a date tonight."

"Hot damn," Rhett said, grinning ear to ear. The look

instantly made me regret calling. "It's been what? Two years since Sheridan?"

I lifted my eyes toward the sky, trying to forget my crazy ex-girlfriend. I'd been up-front, telling the girl, Sheridan, that I was only in town for a few months. I'd thought we were just having fun together, but she'd been completely heartbroken and even showed up to my next job site, trying to win me back. Jim had been pissed, calling it a liability. So my no-dating rule commenced.

I cleared my throat. "Two years. Which means I'm rusty as hell. Any tips?"

"On getting laid? I have a few tricks up my sleeve."

"Okay, now I'm really regretting this call."

Rhett laughed. "Girls always loved you. You have that mama's boy charm no one can resist."

I rolled my eyes. "I'm hanging up now."

"Girls like it when they feel like the most interesting thing in the room," he said. "That hot waitress walks by? Don't give her a second glance. Eyes on your date. She says something about her boring job? Ask her questions about it like it's the most intriguing thing you've ever heard. She talks about how her nephew blew his first spit bubble, you're in awe. Got it?"

I nodded, although it seemed easy. Henrietta was like a puzzle, and each new thing I learned about her felt like a piece that would get me closer to the full picture.

"But if you like the girl, which I'm guessing you do because you've never asked me girl advice before..."

I didn't argue.

"You want her falling for the real you and not some lame tip your brother gave you five minutes before the date. Just be yourself, okay? It's enough. I promise it's enough."

I cracked a smile at that. "Thanks, Rhett."

"Any time."

We hung up, and I took a deep breath before leaving the house.

Tonight was going to be big. I could feel it.

## 23

## HENRIETTA

*Confession: No one in my family has any chill when it comes to first dates... especially me.*

BOTH OF MY best friends sat on my bed while I looked at myself in the mirror above my dresser. Birdie had helped with my makeup while Mara picked out my outfit, and even though I was all dressed and ready, I was more nervous than I'd ever been in my life.

I turned toward my friends and said, "Are you sure this is the look?"

We'd gone with an olive-green dress, a denim jacket, white and cheetah print sneakers, and a white headband tied around my hair to match. It was cute, but was it enough for the firework show picking me up tonight?

Mara got up from the bed and put her hands on my shoulder. "Hen, you look amazing, but Tyler already knows what you look like! He already likes you! Remember, this is just for you two to spend more time together and see what happens. No pressure at all."

Birdie nodded from where she sat on the bed. "I totally agree. You two are going to have so much fun tonight. Wherever you go."

I tried to stifle my giddy smile. Tyler was surprising me with the destination of our date, and if I was being honest, I loved surprises. I loved that he was thinking of me enough to plan something he thought I'd love.

I glanced at my watch and saw I only had fifteen minutes until the date. "You guys should probably go so he doesn't find out I needed my besties to help me get ready."

Birdie winked. "Playing it cool, I like it."

I snorted. "Cool is about the furthest thing from how I feel. I need all the help I can get."

Mara hooked her purse around her shoulder. "So not true. Tyler's not going to know what hit him."

I smiled, following them out of my room to the living room. But our quick exit quickly turned into my mom and grandma squealing about my outfit and hair and how excited they were that I was going out with Tyler.

Tears shone in my grandma's eyes, and she put her hand to her mouth. "I remember going on my first date with your grandpa. I wore a dress my mama made for me —little pink and blue flowers on the fabric. He took me to a barn dance out in the country, and we spent the whole night dancing with each other."

Mara asked, "How old were you?"

"Seventeen," Grandma answered, her eyes in her memories. "He borrowed his daddy's car to drive me. We thought we were styling."

The doorbell rang, jerking us out of memory lane. I glanced at my watch and said, "Crap! He's ten minutes early!"

Mom nodded approvingly. "That's the sign of a good man."

"Or an eager one," Mara said with a wink.

I would have laughed if I wasn't so panicked. "He's going to think I'm pathetic if he sees everyone in here! Go hide!"

Grandma raised her eyebrows. "I ain't about to hide behind no couch."

"Please? Just until he gets me to his truck?"

Mom had an amused smile on her lips. "Come on, everyone. We can go out back. I want to show you my verbena."

I waited until they were all safely in the backyard to walk to the front door. I placed my hand on the knob, knowing minutes had already passed since he rang the bell, but I took my time, allowing myself a deep breath.

I'd gotten my associate degree, worked as a professional for eight years... I could do this. I could go on a date with Tyler Griffen.

I opened the door, and the sight of him standing there took my breath away. He held a full bouquet of purple blooms of all kinds, interspersed by greenery and baby's breath. So tasteful and beautiful.

I covered my mouth with my hand, never expecting this. "These are beautiful, Tyler. Are they for me?"

"Unless you know another Henrietta," he said, a teasing smile on his lips.

He held the flowers out for me, and I breathed in the floral scents. Regardless of how things ended, I wanted to remember this moment when I was my grandma's age. I wanted to reminisce on the fact that this handsome man had thought of me, cared for me, in a way that was so unexpected, so wholesome.

"I'll get a vase for these," I said.

Tyler chuckled, pointing toward the back window just in time for me to see Grandma hide again. "Looks like you'll have some help."

My cheeks felt hot as I set the bouquet on the counter. "I'll let them take care of these."

He walked beside me out the door and down the sidewalk, his hand resting gently on my middle back, reminding me he was there but not suggesting any more. I liked it, especially mingled with the smell of his cologne and the fresh sunshine-filled air.

He opened the door for me, helping me in, and then when we were on the road, I asked the question. "Where are we going?"

Glancing my way, he replied, "Not too much longer until you find out."

I watched out the window, practically vibrating with excitement. I was on a date. With Tyler Griffen. The cute contractor with a smile that could replace the sun, muscled arms that would make any woman drool, a laugh that melted my insides, and enough ink to make him interesting without scaring off my parents. How could this be my life?

"What?" he asked, smiling my way.

"Nothing. This just doesn't feel real," I admitted.

And just when I thought the night couldn't get any better, he reached across the center seat, sliding his fingers through mine. "I feel the same way."

I stared at our intertwined fingers, my skin dark against his pale. There were a few freckles on the back of his hand, and a small bit of hair on his fingers. This was a masculine hand, one that spent hours on hard labor. But the tender way he held me... this man was full of so many surprises.

Soon he pulled into the parking lot at the Brentwood Marina, and I said, "The date's *here*?"

"What?" he asked. "You weren't expecting a fine-dining nautical experience?"

I relaxed my brow. "It doesn't seem very Tyler Griffen, farm boy from Texas with the cutest southern twang."

He chuckled, the sound melting me from the inside

out. "It's Tyler Griffen, formerly landlocked redneck who wants to impress the most beautiful girl in California."

My eyelids drifted closed with my smile, and I shook my head. "You are no redneck, you southern charmer."

"On that note, let me keep up my good streak and get your door."

He got out and walked to my side of the truck, and once I was on the pavement, he offered his elbow to me. I looped my hands through, linking my fingers around his solid arm. For a moment, I leaned my temple against his strong shoulder and pretended I was one of those girls who'd been doing this all the time. The kind of girl who had no lack of dates for Friday night and was always treated like a gem. That's how Tyler made me feel, and I was high on the experience. High on him.

He led us to a boat with cursive writing on the front. It said *The Daydreamer*. I smiled at the name. How apt.

A worker dressed in a white suit extended his arm in a welcoming gesture and said, "Welcome aboard."

## 24

## TYLER

As we stepped aboard the yacht I'd reserved for our first date, there was plenty to draw my attention, but all I could focus on was Henrietta. Her eyes were awestruck at the splendor of the boat. And me? Well, I was enamored with her. Seeing everything through her eyes made it feel like the first time.

The maître d', who introduced himself as Jacob, led us to an elaborately decorated table on the deck overlooking the water. Sailboats dotted the horizon, interrupting the space where turquoise water met soft orange sky.

I missed Texas sunsets, all the bright colors meeting waving prairie grass, but this view, reflected in Henrietta's eyes? It had to be my favorite.

"It's beautiful out here," she said as she sat down. "I

don't think I've been on a yacht except for my ten-year reunion."

"They had it on a yacht?" I asked. "My class's reunion was in the school parking lot and involved coolers full of beer."

She nodded with a smile. "Had to make sure we wouldn't escape."

"You'd want to escape? Seems like high school would have been a breeze for you. You're so easy to talk to."

She laughed. "Being just as tall and bigger than most of the guys at my school didn't do me any social favors."

I shook my head, hating to admit it probably would have been the same at my high school. "When you're young and dumb, different things seem important. And then you grow up."

"True," she said, scrunching her nose in the cutest way. "I'm sure you were the star at your school."

I laughed. "In Cottonwood Falls, you go to school with the same kids from the time you're in kindergarten to graduation. They all remembered my awkward younger years."

"We all have awkward younger years," she replied.

"My mom had to drive me to Dallas for therapy because I was so shy, I wouldn't even talk to the teacher."

Now it was her turn to be surprised. "You seem so confident, easygoing."

"Three decades of practice," I replied.

Jacob brought out some wine for us, pouring our glasses full of rosé. They hadn't offered Cupcake on the menu, but I hoped this would be close enough.

She took a cautious sip, her expression thoughtful.

"As good as Cupcake?" I asked.

She hesitated before shaking her head, and I laughed.

"I was worried it would be awkward," she admitted. "Being somewhere so fancy."

"You don't go out much?"

"No, I'm pretty frugal. Pancakes at Waldo's and free drinks at Collie's is about as high-class as I get."

"You'd love Cottonwood Falls," I said. "Everything is like that. If you want fancy, you have to go to the city."

"Do you miss home?" she asked.

I took a drink of my own wine, the bitter liquid sliding down my throat. "I thought I would get used to it, being away, but after four years, I think feeling out of place has just become the norm for me."

"Are you planning on moving back sometime?"

It was too soon to be thinking about how things like this would affect our relationship, but I had to be honest. "If my boss promotes me, I'd be able to move back home and work there full-time. There would be travel for different projects, but I'd have a home base."

Jacob came back with our first course. A salad with a mixture of fruits and vegetables I hadn't encountered. Which left me with a dilemma. I leaned forward and asked Henrietta, "Which fork do I use?"

She giggled, covering her mouth. "I was waiting for you to go first so I would know."

I racked my brain, trying to remember the etiquette lessons I had in sophomore home economics. "I think you go from the outside in."

"Let's do that," she said. We both picked up our outside fork and tasted the salad.

As Hen chewed, her eyes drifted to the water. The sun was sinking quickly. When she looked back at me, she said, "It's funny—you can't wait to get home and I need to leave mine."

I chuckled, wiping at the corners of my mouth with my white napkin. "Your family seems close."

"We are. My brothers come over almost every weekend, and when my grandma can't catch a ride on the senior bus, I take her out. It's nice. But we're *all* ready for me to move out and live my own life. I've been living at home for far too long."

"Have you found a house you like yet?" I asked. The food in my stomach settled heavily. If Hen bought a house here, that would be it. Our fates would be sealed... separately.

"I haven't really looked. I still have quite a ways to go."

"What do you mean?"

She chewed her lip, that same warring expression from the night she turned me down present yet again. "Can I tell you a secret?"

"Of course," I said.

Our main course came out, and as we ate, she launched into this story about saving for her grandma that made me see her in a whole new way.

When I didn't respond right away, she said, "What? You're thinking I'm crazy."

Sure, I already knew she was kind, hardworking. But to know how much she'd sacrificed for her grandma without anyone ever asking... it was amazing. "I'm speechless, Hen," I breathed. "The girls back home—they think of having babies, doing the same thing their parents did before them. What you're doing, what you've done... no one does that. Only you."

She glanced down at her lap like my praise made her uncomfortable.

"You don't like compliments," I observed.

She met my eyes again. "I'm not used to them."

A little rip formed in my chest at the way Henrietta had been made to see the world. "If we make it to another date, I'll give you plenty of practice."

Her laugh tinkled amongst the lap of waves on the boat. "If the food is this good, you know I'm there."

♥·♥·♥·♥

AS WE DROVE BACK to her family's home, her fingers tangled with mine, I couldn't help but think it had been the perfect first date. The food and scenery were good, but getting to know Hen outside of work? Even better. I could talk to her for hours or sit silently beside her for the same amount of time.

I didn't want this date to end. Didn't want to walk her to the end of the sidewalk and say goodnight. But there was something I'd been wondering. And I couldn't stop myself from asking.

I put my truck into park along the curb and turned to her. She looked beautiful with the light from my dash reflecting off her skin, her dark eyes on mine.

"Can I ask you a question?" I asked.

"Another one, you mean?"

I gave her an exasperated shake of my head.

She giggled, nodded, leaning her head back against the headrest.

"When I asked you out... you told me your job had a rule against it. What was really holding you back? I only ask because I wouldn't ever want to do something that made you uncomfortable..."

Two lines formed between her eyebrows. "What do you mean?"

"After the way Janessa came on to me at the build site, there's no way there's a rule against dating contractors."

Her lips parted. "What did Janessa do?"

At the disbelief in her voice, I felt like I should tread carefully. "That first day... she asked me out to dinner and implied we should spend some time together, if you know what I mean."

Henrietta pressed her lips together and shook her

head. "That same day, she told me that I could lose my job if I dated you. I've been fretting over my attraction to you for weeks because of her."

That made so much more sense, the way Hen held me at arm's length. The sincerity when she said no to dating me.

"Why would she do something like that?" Henrietta asked, hurt clear in her voice.

"She saw the way I was looking at you after I told her no." It was the only thing that made sense. "She was threatened by you."

"Threatened by me." Hen snorted. "The girl's a size two, and she felt like she had to threaten my job to keep me away from you."

"You know size isn't the only thing a guy sees," I said.

She raised her eyebrows. "Maybe it's not the only thing *you* specifically see, but that's not my experience with most men."

"What do you mean?"

"Do you know what it feels like to have people make fun of you at the beach for simply existing at your size? Do you know how it feels to walk by magazines and have headlines shouting at you that you need to change? Do you know how it feels to always be the funny fat friend?"

I studied her for a moment, hating anything and everyone that had made her feel like that. "I've never seen you that way."

"How do you see me?" she asked.

I took her in, and only one word came to mind. "Beautiful."

## 25

## HENRIETTA

*Confession: For a woman named Hen, I have a hard time not counting my chickens before they hatch.*

ALL THIS TIME, I'd been so worried about my job, worried about my grandma, worried about my future. When in reality, I'd just been missing out on an incredible guy, all so my boss could call dibs on him, like a child licking a cookie to make it their own. Kenner had more maturity than her, and he was still wearing Pull-Ups to bed.

Tyler was only here for nine months, and I'd missed so much of it just by following the "rules." Well, I was done wasting time, especially when it came to Tyler.

I unbuckled my seat belt and leaned closer.

His eyes flicked from mine to my lips.

A question.

I nodded.

A promise.

My eyelids slid closed, and I felt his lips against mine, felt the slight stubble on his chin as our skin brushed. Electricity, lust, desire, longing, it all swept through me as I got lost in our kiss, tasting the mint on his tongue, feeling his hand grip the base of my neck, holding me in place so he could deepen the kiss.

A small whimper escaped my lips, one I hadn't been expecting or holding in, and that only encouraged him more. Our tongues tangled, removing all the breath from my body as I tried to feel him, taste him, get lost in him.

Tyler was a gentleman, but the way he was holding me, his hand dancing up my hip, barely touching the side of my breast, he was holding himself back. Every part of me wanted to find out what more he could do, discover the ways he wanted to touch me.

I fisted my hand in his shirt over his stomach and kissed him hungrily. I'd made out with guys before, but it had never been like this—so all-consuming, so addicting to where I cared more about his lips on mine than my next breath.

Moisture soaked my panties, and even though I'd never had sex before, my body knew I wanted it. Was ready for it. With him.

He pulled back, his heavy breathing matching my

own. I studied his hooded eyes, feeling all the passion I saw there.

His voice was husky as he said, "I should get you inside."

"What if I don't want to go?" I whispered.

A heated grin hit his lips. "Does this mean I get a second date?"

My smile came all on its own. I nodded. But then my lips turned down.

"What?" he asked.

"It's wedding week."

"And?"

"I'm a bridesmaid. It's a lot of responsibility, and I don't want to drag you along to it if..." I couldn't bring myself to finish the sentence. It was too much too soon.

But Tyler said, "If what?"

"If this wasn't something that's going to last."

His expression grew serious as he took my hand in his. "I can't predict the future, Hen, but until we figure out what this is..." He gestured between us. "I'm in. All in."

I bit my bottom lip, holding back a smile. "In that case, will you be my date to the rehearsal dinner and the wedding?"

He cupped my cheek with his hand and kissed me again, softer this time, only stirring the embers instead of lighting a flame.

A curtain in the front window of my house cracked, letting out enough light for me to know my family was waiting on me. They were just as excited to hear about my date with Tyler as I was to tell them and my friends.

"We're being watched," I whispered.

"Then I should get you to the door like a gentleman instead of doing everything else I'm imagining right now."

A swoop of desire went through my stomach.

This could be it, I realized.

The guy I lost my virginity to.

The guy I loved.

But I couldn't get ahead of myself right now.

Instead, I let him open the door for me. We walked together down the sidewalk, and he kissed me on the cheek at the house, an unspoken promise in the air.

The best was yet to come.

## 26

## HENRIETTA

*Confession: I felt betrayed.*

AS I DROVE to the office Monday morning, I couldn't stop thinking about the bomb Tyler had dropped on me. Had Janessa really lied to me? We'd worked together for eight years, and at this point, I'd considered her a friend. A close colleague at the very least. Would she really have felt threatened enough to lie?

There was really only one way to find out.

When I reached the apartment parking lot, I put my car in park and began searching through my contact list. One of the benefits of never updating your phone? I had every single contact from as far back as I could remember.

Midway through the Fs, I found Frannie's number.

Hoping she hadn't changed it in the last few years, I pressed call.

"Henrietta!" she answered. "Long time no talk."

I could hear her car running in the background. Maybe she was driving to work. "I'm sorry about that," I said. "Have you been doing alright?"

"Great, actually! I ended up marrying that contractor I met on the SoCal build, and we have a kid now. I'm on my way to drop her off at daycare as we speak."

"Congratulations!" I told her. I hadn't been invited to the wedding, but then again, that didn't surprise me. The events of her leaving Blue Bird had been really hush-hush. "I was wondering... whatever happened back then? Do you mind sharing why you left?"

She was quiet for a moment, and I half expected her to tell me to fuck off. I wouldn't blame her one bit. I needed to be a better friend that way. I was about to apologize for interrupting her day when she said, "They didn't tell you?"

"No," I answered. "Well, Janessa said it had something to do with that contractor. What was his name?"

"Jeremy," she answered.

"Right."

"Janessa's full of hot air, but you know that," Frannie said. Her daughter cried, and she shushed her for a moment before saying, "I kept showing up to work late because I was so nauseous in the mornings, so they let me go. If I would have known the reason for my 'stomach bug' was morning sickness, I would have sued them for all they had."

I shook my head, processing it all. "I'm sorry they did that to you. Being pregnant sounds miserable." If I got pregnant, I'd only know the signs because of my sisters-in-law, who way overshared.

"It is, and then you get the best gift ever at the end."

I smiled at the love I heard in her voice. "So it wasn't against the rules for you to date Jeremy?"

"Corporate only cares what you do on company time. They don't give a shit who you're dating off the clock."

"Right." My jaw tensed. So Janessa really had lied to me, just to get Tyler.

"Hey, I'm at the daycare, but if you're ever in Chula Vista, let me know. I'd love to get some drinks with you, catch up sometime."

"I'd love that too," I replied honestly. "I'll talk to you later?"

"Sure thing."

We hung up, and I gripped my phone tightly as I lowered it from my ear. I felt sickened, betrayed. If Janessa had so easily lied to me about Tyler, what else had she lied to me about? I thought back over what I once believed had been a friendly working relationship, rethinking everything.

She'd only been looking out for herself. And maybe it was time I did the same, starting with enjoying this wedding week and spending the weekend with Tyler. I had felt so guilty for submitting my time-off request for Wednesday through Friday since it meant Janessa would have to drive from LA to Emerson.

But now, I didn't feel guilty at all. In fact, the only thing I regretted was having to call and remind her that I'd be off work. I went into the office, putting my sack lunch in the fridge and then checking voicemails.

With my blood at a simmer instead of a boil, I dialed her number on the office phone. It rang a few times before her perky voice came on the line. "Hey, Hen! How's it going this week?"

I stood to pace my office as far as the phone cord would allow. "Construction is still on track. Tyler says we're good on all the permits, and so far, there have been no delays."

"I knew he was amazing," she said, a wistfulness to her voice.

I scowled. "I just wanted to remind you I'll be out Wednesday through Friday. I'm meeting with the maintenance crew tomorrow to make sure they can handle any emergencies that come up, and I'll set up the phone to forward calls to you."

"Have I told you that I love how on top of everything you are? You've always done such a good job for us."

Her words were just another slap to the face. Did she mean any of them? We'd been colleagues for eight years, and suddenly, this office didn't feel like a second home anymore. It felt like a cage. A lie. One I had to stay trapped in to keep my job and save enough for Grandma.

"Thanks," I said, carrying on the act. "I'll call you first thing Monday to touch base on anything I missed."

"Perfect. Have a great day, girlie!"

She hung up, and I sat back down in my chair, defeated.

I really had loved this job, loved this company. I'd put years of my life toward it. Maybe it really was time for a change of scenery.

Since I didn't have any tours scheduled this morning and I didn't have to run rent checks to the bank until this afternoon, I clicked onto the computer and began looking for new jobs. By lunchtime, I had printed off my résumé to go over, along with a few listings I thought would be a good fit for me.

I ate my packed lunch at my desk, crossing out words on my résumé and replacing them with keywords from the job listings like I'd learned to in a professional development class. But I was so busy marking red, the sound of the door opening nearly scared me to death.

I hurriedly swiped my papers aside, setting them beneath a stack of apartment layouts, and smiled up at the intruder.

It was a young guy, barely twenty if I had to guess. "Hey," he said, "I'm here for the tour?"

I nodded, getting back to business. "Come with me."

## 27

## TYLER

The third time in Cohen's garage was far more comfortable than the first time. Especially when Cohen started the conversation by raising his beer to me. "Birdie said you and Hen had a great first date."

Steve crooned happily and Jonas grinned at me, making my ears feel hot.

"How was it?" Steve asked. "Tell me you brought her flowers."

Okay, now my neck and cheeks were red too. "Can't show up to a first date without flowers."

"Sheesh," Jonas said. "You're going to make the rest of us look bad. Better step up my game before Mara calls off the wedding."

"Speaking of the wedding," I said, "Henrietta invited me as her plus one. Are you sure it's okay that I come?"

"Of course. Any friend of Hen's is a friend of ours. And if you keep beating Cohen at Hold'em, you'll be replacing him as best man."

Cohen scowled at him. "Couple weeks of bad luck and all of a sudden I'm getting demoted."

Steve tilted his head back and laughed. "You always were a sore loser."

Cohen good-naturedly brushed off the heckling. "Your deal, Ty."

I smiled slightly at the nickname, beginning to shuffle the deck. The sound mixed with the flutter of cardstock against my fingers was strangely settling. "Any plans for the bachelor party?"

I glanced up in time to see Jonas shrug. "That's more of Mara's thing."

I raised my eyebrows. "A bachelor party?"

"The whole"—he waved his hand through the air—"stripper, drinking, penis-shaped-candy, party thing. We'll be here, having a beer and playing poker if you want to join."

I thanked him for the invitation, and we got back to the game. Drinking, gambling, all the things that would make my late grandma shudder. "Sounds like a good time," I replied, continuing with the game.

When the night was over, with another win for me, Jonas and Steve left, but Cohen held me back.

"What's up?" I asked as the garage door slid shut, blocking us from the outside world.

He scratched the back of his neck. "Well, here's the deal. I don't want to just drink beer and play poker for Jonas's bachelor party, but I have no idea what else to do."

"Steve didn't have any ideas?" I asked.

"We're all pretty laid-back guys. We didn't want strippers or a party bus or anything like that, and going to the bar I own just feels like a cop-out."

I grinned, thinking of the party bus I'd been on for my high school best friend's wedding. There had been more beer than common sense on that thing. "Y'all live minutes away from the ocean. Why not do some deep-sea fishing or a kayak tour or something active like that? Get away from the city and clear your head for a day."

Cohen nodded. "Steve's shit on motorboats—gets seasick—but a kayak could be fine. We can always do beer and poker afterward if Jonas wants... Hell, it's just a couple hours to San Diego..."

I patted his shoulder. "Now you're thinking."

He grinned. "Thanks. I guess I've lived here so long I've forgotten what we have." He opened the side door leading into his kitchen, gesturing for me to follow him.

"Dallas is pretty landlocked, so I'm trying to enjoy the water while I can. We have lakes, but it's not the same." I followed him into a well-lit kitchen area that was far fancier than anything I'd grown up with. They had matching dishes, glass cups, and herbs in kitschy containers.

"Nice place," I said.

He grinned my way. "It's all Birdie."

"How long have y'all been together?" I asked on the way to the front door.

"Almost three years now. One year married. Best years of my life."

The comment made me smile. I hoped to find that someday. Soon.

## 28

## HENRIETTA

*Confession: There are some things even I can't plan for.*

WAKING up Wednesday morning and not having to go to work was a huge relief. I hardly ever took time off, but I had vacation days saved up, and I was excited to spend them with my best friends.

Before meeting Birdie and Mara a few years back, I never really had girlfriends. I was always that girl who hung around my brothers or read books by myself. Then when my brothers started dating, I got girl time with their girlfriends (now wives and soon-to-be wife) when they came over. Now that I had best friends, I wouldn't trade them for anything.

Mara wanted to start wedding week off with a relaxing

day at the beach, so I put on my one-piece, then slipped my cover-up dress over my head, packed a beach bag and left my room to help Grandma with her morning medications.

She wasn't in the living room, reading her Bible like she usually did in the mornings. So I checked the kitchen, thinking maybe she'd gotten her toast, but still came up empty. Worry settled in my gut, making it hard to move. I walked to her bedroom and found her lying on the floor by her closet, her pants half on and her arms covering her face.

"Grandma?" I choked out.

When she moved her hands, I saw the tears on her cheeks.

I hurried to her, kneeling next to her on the floor. "Grandma, are you hurt?"

She slowly nodded. "I fell getting dressed, and my hip... I think it might be broken."

"Why didn't you call for me?"

"I didn't want to bother anyone."

If I wasn't so worried, I would have scolded her. "I'm calling an ambulance," I said, getting my cell from my purse. I tried to keep my voice from shaking as I spoke with the dispatcher and gave them directions to my house.

The person on the phone said not to sit her up until the medics arrived in case there was a spinal injury. And then it was on us to wait.

"Can you help me put a skirt on?" Grandma asked.

I gave her a look. "You trying to get fancy for the EMTs?"

"I can't be seen like this. So... frail." Her voice sounded frail as she said it. Frail, but stubborn. "Please, Hen?"

I couldn't argue with her, so I carefully slid her pants off without moving her legs and then got the most forgiving skirt I could find and carefully shimmied it up her hips. She cringed when I slid it under her backside, but as soon as it was on, she seemed to settle.

"When are they getting here?" she demanded. "Did they send a student driver?"

I let out a relieved laugh as I checked my phone. That was the grandma I knew. "Average response time for our area is seven minutes. It's been five."

As if on time, the front door rang, and I said, "I'm going to let them in, but I'll be with you every step, okay?"

Her eyes watered as she held my hand. "I'm sorry to ruin your day with your friends."

"They're my friends; you're my *family*." I held her weathered hand in mine. "I would do anything for you, Grandma."

She squeezed my hand and then let go so I could answer the door. There were three paramedics in blue uniforms, one carrying a gurney. It all happened in a flash, showing them where she was, following them out the door, and getting into the ambulance with my grandma strapped to a board and her trying not to make a sound with each bump the ambulance hit.

As we drove, I called my mom and dad, telling them we were on the way to the hospital, then I texted Mara to let her know I wasn't coming this morning.

When we reached the hospital, they wheeled Grandma back to imaging and told me which ER room to wait in. I paced the small space, the fluorescent lighting hurting my head just as much as Grandma's helplessness had hurt my heart.

I'd expected, prepared for, Grandma to struggle for a year, maybe two, like Grandpa had, but I hadn't considered a broken bone. If it was bad, she could be in a wheelchair for years. And my parents couldn't help her all day every day to get the things she needed. The thought of my vibrant, spirited, opinionated grandma being relegated to a cold, impersonal nursing home... it made my stomach churn.

I was about to break when the doors pushed open and Grandma was wheeled into the room. They transferred her onto the bed and then helped her get comfortable before saying a doctor would be in to let us know the results of her X-rays, along with her next steps. I just hoped she'd be able to make them at home.

## 29

## TYLER

Since I knew Henrietta wouldn't be by this morning, I ordered coffee and donuts for the guys. She was right—beer and pizza were a great way to make friends, but breakfast was the best way to start the day.

I set up the table myself and then helped the delivery person lay out the food and drink. With it all ready to go, I called the guys over. "Grab some breakfast! We've got a long day of work ahead!"

"You're in a good mood, boss," Rich said, coming up beside me with a donut in hand.

I was beginning to like this guy, even though he still called me boss despite all my protestations. "I *am* in a good mood," I admitted. It's not like I could deny it. I'd worn a smile on my face since my first date with Henrietta, and the thought of going to a wedding with her as her date... It meant we were moving forward. Together.

But then I saw a slick car pull up to the job site. And a heeled leg extend from the cab and settle on the ground.

"Shit," I muttered.

Rich followed my gaze and murmured, "Corporate. Good luck."

It wasn't my kind of corporate. Jimmy was laid back, and anyone else he hired to work with him had the same down-to-earth attitude.

No, this was Janessa, dressed to kill. She had on a sleek black dress that hugged her toned body. Her blond hair was curled, her lips blood red, and her heels the expensive, pointy kind my sister would never wear.

At the sight of me, her lips curled into a deadly, seductive smile, and she crooned, "Tyler Griffen, aren't you a sight for sore eyes?" She was looking at my Crenshaw Construction T-shirt like she wanted to rip it off my body.

I folded my arms over my chest as she neared. "Janessa, we weren't expecting to see you here."

She touched my arm with her hand, decorated with pointy red nails. "Henrietta's out of the office this week, so I wanted to check in. See if there was..." She slowly wet her lips. "Anything you needed?"

I suppressed a shudder. Maybe I would have been into this even a few months ago, but now it made my skin crawl. I wanted to send the clear message that our relationship would remain professional. "We're making great progress here. Pouring the foundation for the second floor this week, and when it cures, we'll be on to the third."

Her eyes traveled over the job site, all my guys back to work with a suit on site. "You have quite the team here, Tyler."

"I do," I agreed. I was happy with everyone and their work. "I think Blue Bird will be pleased with the build when it's all said and done."

"That's why we hired Crenshaw," she said. "James's reputation is stellar. Getting you with the deal was just a perk." She winked.

I studied her for a moment. This was a woman who was used to getting what she wanted, and she had no qualms doing so by any means necessary. That much was apparent from what she'd told Henrietta. I tried not to be annoyed that her lie had nearly cost me an incredible woman.

"Since I'm in town, I was wondering if you might want to get lunch, professionally speaking, and talk over the project?"

I was on a tight rope; I could feel it. If I said no, I'd offend someone very important to Crenshaw Construction. But if I said yes, I'd risk her twisting more words to Henrietta. But at this point, Henrietta had to know I wasn't interested in Janessa, so I nodded and said, "Sure. Where would you like to go?"

She rattled off the name of a restaurant I didn't recognize and said, "I'll be back at noon to pick you up."

I nodded. "See you then."

Giving me a wicked grin, she spun on her heels and turned to walk away. Shaking my head, I walked up to the site where they were starting to pour concrete. This was going to be a long day.

♥・♥・♥・♥

JANESSA WAS BACK at twelve o'clock on the dot, just as she'd promised, and there was nothing I could do to worm my way out of it. So I washed my hands in the on-site bathroom, threw on a polo I kept in the office, and followed her to her car.

It was one of those small, sleek things that made me feel like I was riding in a clown car. I reached for the button and pushed my chair back so my knees wouldn't be knocking the dash as she whipped out of the parking lot.

"How was your morning?" she asked.

"Good, and yours?"

"Learned something new about Henrietta. Turns out she's been fronting rent for people at the beginning of the month."

"She pays their rent?" I asked.

Janessa nodded. "And then they'll pay her on the fifth or sixth when their check comes in."

My eyebrows rose. "For how many people?"

"A couple every month as far as I can tell." She shook

her head as if Hen's generosity was unbelievable. Or stupid. "Her money, though."

"Why not move the rent payment back for those renters if it's the same people every month?" I asked.

"Makes accounting's job harder, and they have enough on their plate as it is," Janessa said, whipping around another corner.

Thankfully, I wasn't driving, because that news about Hen knocked me back. Even though she was saving for her grandma and living frugally herself... she was still helping how she could. The charitable giving part of Gage's business should take notes from her.

"Here we are," Janessa said. She pulled up along a restaurant with big glass windows overlooking a downtown park, then let the valet open her door.

I got out on my side and walked to the restaurant with Janessa at my side. "Are you sure I'm not underdressed for this place?"

She studied me for a moment. "Maybe."

With all that reassurance, I felt like I was a socially awkward child all over again. We walked inside, and I certainly was not dressed fine. I was surprised they didn't kick me back by the dumpster to be rid of me. The hostess stared me down, the server stayed as far away from me as possible, and they sat us at the worst table, way back by the kitchen where basically no one could see us except staff.

Which, unfortunately, gave Janessa an excuse. "I'm

going to sit by you so I can stay out of the way," she said, getting up and moving her chair. Right. By. Mine.

Her perfume, almost clinically strong, wafted over me, and my stomach turned at the scent combined with all the seasonings from the kitchen.

"Tell me, Tyler, how are you liking California?"

My mind immediately went to Henrietta. "It's better than I expected." In every possible way.

"If you think Emerson is great, there's a vineyard farther north I *have* to take you to. They have the most romantic weekend retreats, beautiful rooms overlooking miles of grape vines... It's quite the aphrodisiac."

I tucked the idea away for a weekend with Hen and said, "There are a few vineyards in Texas."

She laughed like that was the funniest thing she'd ever heard.

Thankfully, a waiter came and saved me. I ordered the daily special, and Janessa picked something off the menu, making a million adjustments "to protect my figure," she explained after he left.

My phone began ringing, and I thanked whoever it was on the other end.

Seeing Hen's number, I smiled slightly, then said to Janessa, "Sorry, I have to take this."

## 30

# HENRIETTA

*Confession: I made a mistake.*

TYLER'S VOICE was warm over the receiver. "Am I happy to hear from you."

My lips cracked a smile before quickly falling. I'd hoped calling him would cheer me up, but now it was taking all I had not to cry. I walked farther down the hallway away from the waiting room and stood at a window overlooking the parking garage.

It was full of cars. I wondered how many of those cars belonged to hospital employees. How many belonged to family like me, their world turned upside down.

"Henrietta? I can't hear you."

"I'm here," I said, barely a whisper.

"Are you okay?"

Okay? Not even close. It felt like everything was falling apart. "My grandma fell this morning." I sniffed in a heavy breath, but the hospital smell didn't help anything. "She fractured her hip, Tyler. They moved her to the trauma unit of the hospital."

"Oh no, that's awful," he said. "Did they say what next steps were?"

My voice went on autopilot, relating the same story I had called all my siblings with this morning. Both my parents had been at the hospital almost immediately after we arrived. "Lots of physical therapy. She'll be in a walker once she gets out of here. Mom's already trying to figure out how to get another credit card to have the carpet replaced. I could dip into my savings to replace it, but that would set me back months..."

"I can do that."

I turned away from the window, staring at the white cinder block wall as I attempted to process what he said. Had he really just offered to replace all of our flooring? "Tyler, that's too much."

"It's the least I could do," he said. "I can get supplies cheap, and I've installed hundreds of floors before. Done. What else do you need?"

I racked my mind, wondering what else there was to do. The list had seemed so insurmountable before this call. "We need a rail installed in the bathroom and another rail and a seat in the shower."

"Easy. What else?"

Now hot tears were rolling down my cheeks. A nurse walked by, and I turned toward the window to hide my emotions. I'd felt so alone this morning before everyone arrived, and now I knew I wasn't. "I was supposed to be going away to an overnight spa with Mara tomorrow, but someone needs to take care of Mom's garden."

"I can hoe with the best of them."

The smile in his voice made me laugh for the first time all day. "You're amazing."

"I'm *here*," he said. "Do you want me to come to the hospital?"

The sound of clashing dishes came from the background. "Where are you? It sounds like you're in a kitchen."

"Almost. I'm at lunch with Janessa. She insisted."

My stomach instantly soured. "What is she doing in town so early? I had everything prepped already. Was there an emergency at the apartments?" It would be just my luck.

"I suspect she wanted to make another pass at me without you around. Which, she has, and trust me, it's not working. Although she has been poking around the office."

"Shit," I muttered, then looked down the hallway to make sure no small ears had overheard. I was still alone. I had left my updated résumé and printed off job listings at the office. If Janessa found them, I'd be out a job before I was even close to ready.

"What's wrong?" he asked.

"I need to get back to the office. Can you stall Janessa?"

"Not a problem. I have a feeling she'll be dragging this out as long as possible."

"My hero," I said, a slight smile on my lips.

"Thanks for letting me rescue you for once."

I hung up and hurried back to the room to tell Mom I had an errand to run. Grandma was sleeping, her hands folded peacefully over her chest. Dad had gone to the cafeteria to bring lunch back.

"Hey, you can stop looking at credit cards," I said with a smile.

She looked up from her phone, surprised to see me. "Oh, Hen, what do you mean?"

I told her about Tyler's offer, and his insistence to follow through on it.

Mom put her hands over her heart. "He is one of the good ones."

"I think so," I agreed. "I have to run an errand for work real quick, and then I'll be back for the night. Are you sure it's okay that I go away with the girls tomorrow? I feel bad for leaving her."

Mom glanced at Grandma. "She wants you to go."

"She's not thinking of herself."

A coy smile crossed Mom's lips. "Well now we know where you get it."

Shaking my head, I took the keys from Mom's purse

and left the hospital. It took precious minutes to find her car in the massive parking garage, and my nerves were starting to fray. Tyler had said he would stall, but if Janessa got to those papers before I did...

I didn't want to think about it. I hadn't yet reached my savings goal, and losing this job... I pressed my foot down on the gas and finally, finally reached my office. I parked in front of the main door, one mission on my mind: in and out as quickly as possible.

I fumbled with shaking hands to unlock the door and yanked it open. I quickly crossed the worn blue carpet to the spot behind my desk. Janessa had clearly messed with some papers, but my stack was safely at the bottom of an untouched pile.

Breathing a sigh of relief, I folded the papers in half.

The bell above the door jangled, and I jumped backward, seeing Janessa come inside, followed by Tyler speaking rapidly about a deck that needed structural repair on the opposite side of the complex.

"Henrietta," Janessa said, her eyes narrowing. "What are you doing here? It's your day off!"

"I, uh..." I searched desperately for an excuse and accidently walked into my hanging plant, the pothos leaves tickling my shoulder. Thankful beyond belief, I reached for it, pulling it down. "I just had to bring my plant home! Didn't want it to feel all abandoned and wilt while I was gone." As I had my back to Janessa, I tucked the papers between the two inside pots. Mission complete.

When I looked back at them, Tyler had a small smile for just the two of us. Janessa shook her head, looking around the office. "I have no idea how you keep all these things alive. They'd be dead within a week if I were taking care of them."

"Which is why I wanted to bring it home," I teased. "This one has an attitude."

Tyler laughed. "You and your mom with your plant psychology."

I smiled, but Janessa asked, "You've met Henrietta's mom?"

Shit. Shit. Shit. I had to think fast. But I was coming up blank.

Tyler quickly supplied, "Henrietta's mom brought lunch to the office one day while I came to ask Henrietta a question. I think she loves these plants as much as Hen does."

Janessa eyed us suspiciously. Then she turned to Tyler and said, sickly sweet, "No need to come by the office, Tyler. Henrietta should be coming to you. And if she's unavailable, I'd be happy to make a trip out here."

I closed my eyes, biting back rage. How dare she tell me dating was against the rules when her words were full of innuendo.

"Actually," Tyler said, "I need to get back to the job site. Henrietta, can you give me a ride? I know Janessa is so busy with work. That's one of the things I admire about you, J. So dedicated to your role."

Janessa barely concealed her giddy smile at his compliment and the nickname. "Are you sure? I don't mind taking some extra time. So Hen can have her day off."

"It's on my way," I offered. "No big deal."

Before Janessa could argue, Tyler said, "Thanks, Hen. Janessa, thanks for lunch. Hope you have a great day."

He hurried us out of the office and got into my car so fast, you'd think Janessa was a cheetah on a hunt instead of a thirty-something blonde in middle management.

As soon as we pulled out of the parking lot, he was laughing.

"Your plant needed to come home?" he teased.

I glared at him. "The deck needed looked at?"

He reached across the console and grabbed my hand. "I still feel like I win for getting an extra few minutes with you today."

Butterfly wings tickled my insides.

"How are you?" he asked, bringing me back down to earth.

"I feel guilty," I answered honestly. "On one hand, I'm letting down my grandma by going away with my friends, and on the other hand, I'm missing out on my best friend's wedding week. There's no winning."

"I know I just met your family, but I can tell she won't be alone for even a minute at that hospital."

A smile touched my lips. "You're right."

"So go with your friends and have a good time." He drew my hand to his lips, making it hard to focus on the road. "Although selfishly, I do wish you could stay so I could take you out before the wedding."

My cheeks warmed. "I'd like that too."

He glanced toward the clock. "I do have a few minutes before I have to be back..."

"What did you have in mind?"

# 31

## TYLER

"Pull over up there," I said, gesturing toward a stand of trees I'd noticed before on my drives to work. As far as I could tell, it was an empty lot, and right now, I couldn't stop thinking of kissing Henrietta senseless. Of helping her forget her worries for the day, if only for a few stolen moments.

She swiveled the wheel, following the overgrown trail into a space between tall sycamore trees. With the car parked, I could hear the music more clearly. I reached for the keys and twisted them off. "So we don't start a fire in the grass," I explained.

Her dark eyes were on me as she nodded, her breasts moving up and down with her breath. It was sexy as hell, especially with the lacy dress she had on over a swimsuit.

I trailed my finger from her shoulder to the spot where her suit began to dip into her cleavage. "I like this."

Her voice was quiet as she said, "I meant to wear it to the beach."

"I'd like to see that," I said, coming closer, pressing my lips to hers.

She softened into my kiss, her hands coming to my head and weaving through the short hair above my neck.

Already turned on, I kissed her cheek, tipped her chin back and kissed along her jaw, her neck, the top of her breasts where they began to swell. She kept her hands in my hair, her breath coming in a gasp as I gently bit down.

"Tyler," she breathed.

It was enough to spur me on, to drive me wild. I pulled back on her top, sliding her black suit back until I could see the dark, puckered skin of her areola, the full, hard tip of her nipple. I took it in my mouth, sucking and licking in tandem with my other thumb, swiping over her other nipple.

She let out a moan that made my cock harden. I covered her lips with mine, kissing her deeply, tangling my tongue with hers. I wanted more, these clothes out of the way, her skin against mine.

But I had to back off before I couldn't stop myself. She deserves more than me taking it further in the car. Our first time together was going to be something she'd remember as perfect. "Fuck," I moaned against her lips. I moved her clothes back in place and kissed her gently. "You are irresistible."

"Irresistible?" she asked, a slight smile on her lips.

They were so kissable, I kissed them again. "Irresistible, incredible, the whole damn package," I said. "And this weekend is going to be amazing. For you and your friends. And your grandma should know how much you love her if she doesn't already."

Hen closed her eyes, nodding, and I slipped my fingers through hers.

There was an unspoken understanding in the car. I needed to get back to work, and Hen had things to take care of at home. But the best was yet to come, and damn, was I looking forward to it.

She drove the last couple minutes to the job site, and then when she parked in the small dirt lot, I didn't want to get out.

"Text me if you need anything while you're out of town," I said.

She nodded, biting her lip.

"And call, if you want to talk."

Now she smiled. "Do you like talking on the phone?"

I shrugged, not wanting to give myself away. "When you live on the road so long, you get plenty of practice."

There was awe in her eyes as she looked at me. "I can't believe you're interested in me."

But the words sounded so wrong. I took her face in my hands, not caring if any of the workers saw me. She needed to hear this. "Hen, there are billions of women on the planet, and none of them have ever amazed me the way you continue to do. Please, believe me."

Her eyes softened as she took in the words, and I couldn't stop from kissing her one more time.

"I'll see you at the wedding," I said.

"I'll be the one in the purple dress, walking down the aisle."

"And I'll be the guy sitting there, wondering how in the hell he got lucky enough to be your date."

# 32

## HENRIETTA

*Confession: I'm done keeping secrets from my friends.*

I TOOK a drink from my own bottle of champagne, my toes dangling in the hot tub, a terry cloth robe wrapped around me. Mara, Birdie, and Tess sat with me around the hot tub, in pure heaven as the sun sank down a sky of orange and gold.

A spa day for the bachelorette party had been brilliant. We'd spent the day drinking cucumber water, soaking in mud tubs, getting waxed, having our nails painted and our hair done. Even the bride-to-be seemed relaxed, which was the exact opposite of how my sisters-in-law had been prior to their weddings.

Birdie raised her bottle of champagne toward Mara.

"A toast to your last moments as a single woman. Can you believe you're getting married Saturday? *One* penis for the rest of your life?"

Mara giggled, swinging her feet through the water. "One *amazing* penis. You forgot that word."

Tess covered her ears and started humming, and I giggled so hard my stomach hurt.

Okay, so maybe we were getting a little tipsy.

Birdie laughed. "It must be amazing for you to feel so happy about settling down."

Mara reached out to uncover her sister-in-law's ears and smiled as she rolled the champagne bottle in her hands. "You know, I used to think that settling down was a bad thing, like it was an act of giving up. Settling for less than you wanted. But this feels so much different."

I tilted my head to the side. "What do you mean?"

She set down her half-empty bottle and leaned back on her hands, resting her head on one shoulder. "Settling down is not the same as settling for less. It's resting where you know you belong. Not needing to run and chase and search anymore. It's the best feeling ever."

My heart swelled at the description. I wanted that. I wanted to feel at peace with someone I loved. I wanted to know that my heart was where it belonged. But there was something I still didn't understand. "What about the passion, Mara? You were always about the hot sex and exciting adventures."

"Cover your ears, Tess," she laughed out. Tess

chugged some more champagne instead as Mara said, "The sex is still hot. And let me tell you, there's something to experimenting with someone who makes you feel safe."

Safe? With Tyler, I felt terrified. Terrified of not being enough. Of being disappointing. Exhilarated. Electrified by his touch and the words he spoke about me. and then there was the fear—that all of it was too good to be true. None of that felt safe.

"What is it?" Tess asked, studying me.

I looked up at them, realizing there was one big secret I'd kept from my very best friends. Maybe it was the champagne, or maybe I was tired of the secrets, because I blurted my biggest one: "I'm a virgin."

Champagne flew from Mara's mouth into the hot tub, and if I wasn't so embarrassed, I would have cackled at the stunned expression on her face.

"You're a virgin?" she gasped. "Like you've never done anal before?"

Okay, now my feet and face felt hot. "I haven't passed second base before."

Birdie's jaw dropped. "There's never been anyone? Not even a high school boyfriend or a summer fling?"

I shook my head.

Tess asked, "Are you saving it for marriage?"

The laugh that passed my lips was almost bitter. "No one's ever gotten close enough for that to be an option."

My friends were quiet for the first time that night, and I felt shame washing over me. I was undateable. Unlikable.

Cursed to be the funny fat friend for the rest of my life. And not only that, I'd taken away from Mara's moment, yet again.

Not seeming to mind, Mara asked, "Do you think Tyler could be the one to pop that cherry? Take your v-card. Deflower that perfect little pus—"

"Mara!" I cried, laughing through my horror. Birdie and Tess were laughing too, the sound blending with the hot tub jets. But they quieted, and the question was still there. Could Tyler be the one to take my virginity?

And I nodded, because I had a feeling he could be more than my first time.

He could be the one.

Birdie's eyes widened at a spot behind me, and she muttered, "Finally!"

I twisted to see what she was looking at and saw a guy walking toward the pool area in a suit...with silver buttons on the side of his pants.

## 33

## TYLER

Cohen had booked a kayak tour at La Jolla Beach for Jonas's bachelor party, and I was honored to be included. The fact that the guys treated me like one of the crew meant more than they knew.

There were five of us total, including Jonas's brother-in-law, Derek. I could definitely see myself hanging out with someone like him back home. We rode in Derek's minivan, which Jonas teased him mercilessly for. Apparently, Derek only had one kid, but there were hopes for more on the way soon.

We rolled up to a crowded parking lot near the beach and Cohen led us to a stand farther down the sand. They had racks of long kayaks, paddleboards, and surfboards.

When we reached the place, looking like a bunch of

tourists in our swim trunks and T-shirts, a guy walked out of the shack. "Cohen?"

Cohen lifted his hand.

"Right on, right on," he said. He looked like a complete California surf bro stereotype, from his sun-streaked hair to his tanned skin and shell necklace. "I'm Geoff—with a G—and I'll be leading the tour today. Five singles, right?"

"We're all married, or about to be," Derek said. "Well, except him."

I felt like I was in fifth grade again, the only kid without a little crush to call my own.

Geoff with a G laughed. "I meant single kayaks." He winked at me. "Although, I have a friend I could hook you up with."

"That won't be necessary," I grunted.

"Right on. So pick a yak and let's get on the water."

Steve looked at the kayaks like they were wild animals. "I'm going to need an extra life jacket."

Jonas patted me on the back with an apologetic grin before taking a kayak off the rack. Geoff had us carry them toward the water's edge, and I stood by mine, feeling the rough brush of sand under my feet, the sun on my skin.

I worked so much, I didn't take a lot of time to enjoy or relax. I should change that, I thought. Ask my brothers to go on a trip with me. Maybe they'd agree to Vegas. At least, I knew Rhett would.

Geoff interrupted my thoughts, going through a safety spiel, which Steve listened very intently to, before helping us get our kayaks out on the ocean. We paddled out, following Geoff away from the crowded beach. Steven's knuckles were white on his oar.

The late afternoon sun glanced off the dark blue water, and here, away from the city, there was a sense of peace and quiet I hadn't found since leaving Texas. Between the cool saltwater soaking my skin to the powerful feel of my paddle ripping through the waves, I couldn't help the grin on my face. I felt like a kid riding go-karts for the first time, except this was better because I could have beer after.

Another wave approached, and I paddled to angle my kayak so it wouldn't tip. Geoff pointed out cliffs on our left with million-dollar houses on top. He said the land eroded each year, getting closer and closer to making those houses cave in. The thought that someone could build their home on such shaky foundation baffled me. But then again, a tornado could hit any time in Texas—maybe it was better to know when the end would come so you could be prepared.

Geoff pointed his paddle to a spot north of Cohen's kayak. "Look down there! Three sea lions swimming by."

I paddled forward, careful to give Cohen some space, and spotted three darker spots deep below the water. I wished Henrietta could see this with me.

"We should take the girls next time," I said. "They'd love this."

Cohen splashed me with his paddle.

Wiping saltwater from my face, I said, "What the hell was that for?"

Wearing a grin that looked like one of Rhett's, he said, "You're in trouble! Already thinking of her when you're on a guys' trip?"

Steve grunted from his kayak. "Next thing you know, you'll be looking at dolphin souvenirs for your three-year-old."

Jonas said, "He's speaking from personal experience."

"Obviously," Steve said. "And can I just say, magnet prices are ridiculous these days."

I shook my head at the three. I may have been the only 'single' one here, but I couldn't deny all those thoughts had been on my mind. "Shit, you're right."

Cohen rested his paddle in his lap. "Nothin' wrong with that."

I didn't know if I agreed. Because it meant six months from now, I'd have an impossible choice to make.

At my hesitation, the guide said, "What's with the face? You fall for someone unavailable?"

All the guys looked at me, waiting for my answer. "I fell alright. Now let's find some more of those damn seals."

Geoff said, "Sea lions," and continued on his way.

## 34

## HENRIETTA

*Confession: I'm... beautiful.*

MAGIC WAS in the air as we got ready for Mara's wedding.

The event center at Emerson Trails had separate dressing rooms for the bridal party, and this one had big skylights in the ceiling, bathing us in soft natural light. Mara wore a silk white robe as we had our hair and makeup done, and each of the bridesmaids wore similar robes in black. It was picturesque and beautiful and... inevitable. Like this day was meant to happen exactly this way.

And as I watched Mara get eyeshadow patted on and lipstick painted across her lips, I couldn't help but hope it would be me soon. Me next. Because I was ready for that feeling she described. I wanted to settle. I wanted peace. I wanted my own family for Saturday afternoon barbeques and sports games on the weekends and home-cooked dinners on weeknights. And most of all, I loved the idea of writing my future with a partner at my side. Someone who would lift me up when I was weak and someone I could provide shelter to in any storm.

But today wasn't about me. It was about my best friend. I got her mimosas whenever she ran empty, added polish to a nail that chipped, and when it came time, I'd hold her wedding dress so she could pee. That's what friends did.

The wedding planner, a woman younger than us by a few years, came in and said, "It's time to start getting your dresses on, ladies. Twenty minutes to showtime."

Mara, Tess, Birdie, and I all exchanged glances. Today was the day, and now was the time.

We helped Mara into her dress first, sliding the tulle skirts over her head and shoulders, then flaring them out to the natural-toned wood floor. The hairdresser slipped the veil in her hair, and we stared.

She looked beautiful.

But more than that, she looked *happy*.

With the time left over, we put on our bridesmaid dresses, taking turns zipping up the backs. Birdie handed me my bouquet of white and green flowers and foliage. And I stared at my reflection.

The woman looking at me in the mirror wasn't the funny fat friend.

She was beautiful.

She was happy.

And she smiled. Because now I knew when Tyler looked at me and saw something beautiful, I wouldn't disagree.

## 35

## TYLER

Gravel crunched underfoot as I walked across the parking lot with other guests toward a tall glass building. Past the eaves, I could see acres of rolling grass and trees. The sun shone down from overhead—the perfect day for a wedding.

I'd been to tons of weddings in Texas, and most of them were more casual than this. Everyone around me was dressed in black-tie attire. Back home, most of the grooms wore jeans and boots. Their good jeans, but still. Lots of the ceremonies happened in little churches and the receptions were moved to a shop building that had been cleaned up for the event.

When I walked inside, Derek greeted me, holding his little baby in a light purple dress.

"Got wrangled into being an usher?" I asked.

He grinned. "It's not so bad with my little helper." The baby couldn't have been much older than A'yisha, except his little girl had far less hair.

"She's beautiful," I said honestly.

"I think so too," he said. People were piling up behind me, so he added, "Either side, my man. We're all family today."

I grinned, walking past him. I sat on the edge of a row toward the back so I wouldn't take up the spot of someone more important than me and waited, listened, watched people filter into the seats around me and talk about the bride and groom.

I picked up snippets about the television show Mara was writing for, heard about how Jonas's virtual accounting firm continued to grow. And most of all, I waited to see Henrietta.

And then the music started, cutting all chatter. A man holding a Bible walked to the front, followed by Steve and Cohen. Then Jonas walked up the aisle, an older woman dressed in a purple gown on his arm. He kissed her cheek before leaving her sitting in the front row.

As if my body sensed her, I turned, looking to the aisle. Henrietta approached, moving purposefully in a floor-length dress. Soft fabric swished around her perfect hips with each step, and the bouquet she held at her chest only accentuated her cleavage. But her face stole the show. She had a soft peach blush on her cheeks and her full lips were glossy. And the light in her eyes, in her smile, made her shine.

Our eyes met, and her smile grew, deepened, and for a moment, all the air was gone from the room. All the people had vanished. It was her and me and the sound of the pounding in my chest.

And then she passed me, and the view got even better.

Shit, my girl looked like a million bucks.

My stomach dropped. My girl.

She wasn't my girl. Not officially.

I'd never asked her to be. And I needed to fix that.

Immediately.

## 36

## HENRIETTA

*Confession: I'm not jealous, but I don't mind claiming my territory.*

**THE CEREMONY HAD BEEN ABSOLUTELY** beautiful, but after taking about a million and one pictures with the bridal party, my feet hurt and I had to pee like a racehorse. I made it to the bathroom and took the best restroom break of my life, then checked myself in the mirror. Only a few hairs needed brushed back into place, and I reapplied gloss to my lips, even though doing this in front of other women in the bathroom usually made me nervous.

Two women came in, a little younger than me, and each took a stall.

"Did you see that hottie in the boots?" one said.

I smirked in the mirror. I only knew one guy who'd arrived in cowboy boots.

"Think he's single?"

"Didn't see a ring," the other replied.

I zipped my clutch shut. "He's here with someone," I told them, smiling to myself as they groaned before leaving the restroom.

I planned to walk to the reception area, find Tyler, and ask him to spin me on the dance floor like he had that night he rescued me. Instead, I felt a calloused hand grab my wrist and pull me backward into a dark room.

I was about to scream when another hand covered my mouth. "It's me, Hen."

Tyler's warm voice mixed with his rough grip already had my skin tingling. "What are we doing in here?" I looked around, my eyes adjusting to the dim lighting. "Is this a coat closet?"

"It's a closet no one has entered for the last half hour, and it locks from the inside." His hands skimmed my bare arms, sending goosebumps rising on my skin.

As far as I was concerned, we could stay in here all day. But I wasn't bold enough to say so. Not that forward or sexy. So I swallowed and tried not to let my shallow breathing give me away.

"You were great up there," he said. "I couldn't take my eyes off you."

I grinned, the compliment meaning everything, especially after overhearing those girls. "Thank you."

"But there was one issue," he said, his fingers toying with the thin strap of my dress.

"And what was that?"

He brushed his nose over my neck, making me catch my breath, and said, "I wanted everyone to know you were mine, and we haven't had that talk yet."

"Oh," was all I could manage to say with his lips trailing kisses and nips down my neck.

"Any objections?"

"None." To anything he was doing. "None at all."

His hand tightened around my waist, pulling me closer to him, and I leaned into his kisses, working my fingers through his hair and tugging. He palmed my ass, pressing us together, and—oh my—I felt something hard at his waist. He was turned on by me. *Me.*

Feeling bold, I reached down, rubbing it with my hand, and he moaned in my ear. Heat pooled between my legs, readying me for him.

"Fuck, Hen, if you keep this up, I'll have to take you right here."

I froze, realizing he was ready for that step. And I was too, but I didn't want to lose my virginity in a closet.

Sensing the change, he stepped away from me, his hands completely gone from my body. "I'm sorry. Did I overstep?" he asked.

Guilt immediately racked me. For the secret of my virginity. For the fact that I wanted to keep it a secret. That he thought for one moment I didn't want every single thing he was doing to me and all the ways my body reacted.

"That's not it," I said, stepping closer and placing a kiss on his jaw. On his chin. "What are you doing tonight?"

I already knew the answer.

He smiled underneath my lips. "Any ideas?"

"I'd like to check on your apartment, make sure it's still in good shape—you know, for my job."

"For your job," he repeated, kissing my cheek, nipping the shell of my ear.

I let out a shaky breath. "We should get back…"

And in five minutes, we did.

## 37

## TYLER

Weddings might be my new favorite date with Henrietta. Although she sat at the bridal party's table for the meal, I loved watching her, seeing her smile, meeting her eyes across the room.

And knowing she was officially mine... it made it that much better.

After the meal, Mara and Jonas shared their first dance. They held each other close, Mara gently playing with the hair at the back of his neck as they swayed back and forth. Then the DJ invited other couples to the dance floor.

I crossed the room to Hen. "May I have this dance?"

She smiled up at me. "I'm not sure what my 'male friend' will think."

I laughed, remembering how heady and nervous I'd

felt to be introduced to Hen's entire family as her male friend. But now I wouldn't want to be known as anything else. "I think your male friend will be mighty disappointed if he doesn't get to spin you around the dance floor."

Her chocolate eyes warmed. "I'd love that."

I extended my hand, and she slipped hers in mine. The perfect fit. As we walked away from the table, I spun her twice, and she giggled, her dress flaring around her. On the third spin, she fell into my chest, breathless and smiling.

"I wasn't ready for that," she said with a laugh.

"Well you looked damn good doing it," I said, two-stepping with her. We fell into rhythm together, just like we had that first night I taught her to dance.

She leaned her head close. "Thank you for coming. I know weddings aren't for everyone."

I kissed her crown. "I love being here with you. And you might be surprised—I think weddings are fun."

"Yeah? What do you like about them?"

"Other than the leap of faith it takes to commit in front of everyone you know?"

She chuckled. "Yeah, other than that."

"Hmm." I thought it over for a moment, letting the music wash over us. "I like the cake cutting, and not just because I inherited my grandpa's sweet tooth."

Smiling, she said, "What is it then?"

"You know how they hold the knife together? It's ridiculous and adorable at the same time. And then you get to see their personalities on full display by the way they feed each other."

"What do you think of shoving cake in each other's face?" she asked.

"A waste of perfectly good cake." I winked. "Unless you get to lick it off."

The music slowed, and the DJ came over the speakers. "It's time for our bride and groom to cut the cake."

We walked closer to the table with the cake, getting a better view of Mara and Jonas. The cake was stunning—lots of creamy frosting, decorative frosted flowers, and multiple tiers so everyone would have plenty to eat.

Just like every other wedding, Mara and Jonas approached the cake. A little couple mirroring them stood on the top tier, holding hands. Mara grabbed the topper first and licked the bottom, making me laugh along with everyone else.

"What? I'm not wasting perfectly good frosting," she said.

"Hear, hear," I called, raising my beer. (The open bar was a nice touch.)

Hen giggled. "That's my girl."

Jonas grinned adoringly at Mara, picking up the knife as the photographer's camera sounded with each new picture. She placed her hands atop his, and they cut a chunk from the bottom layer. Jonas put a small piece in her mouth, and she sucked his finger suggestively.

Everyone whooped, cheering and making comments about the honeymoon.

"That sums up their personalities," Hen confirmed with a laugh.

Then Mara held out the cake for Jonas, and after he ate it, he kissed a stray bit of frosting from her lips. I tightened my grip around Hen's waist, and she smiled up at me, that ever-present light in her brown eyes. Feeling like my heart couldn't get any bigger, any fuller, I bent my neck and placed a kiss on her lips.

She smiled up at me, and it was good.

It was so fucking good.

We danced for the rest of the reception, held up sparklers as Jonas and Mara walked away from the venue, and cheered along with everyone else as their car drove toward the airport, cans rattling on the ground behind them.

People around us began dissipating, getting into their cars and lighting the dark parking lot with headlights and taillights.

"Did you drive here?" I asked.

She nodded. "I can follow you to your place?"

I kissed her, hard. "I'll see you soon."

## 38

# HENRIETTA

*Confession: Cleaning supplies turn me on.*

AS I DROVE to Tyler's place, all I could think was... I'm about to lose my virginity. My heart was beating fast and my hands were shaky on the steering wheel, but when I saw him standing against his truck in the parking lot, my worries faded. He'd been the dream guy since I met him—sex wouldn't change that.

I got out of my car, acutely aware of his eyes sizzling over me like no man had ever looked at me before. His gaze wasn't greedy or hungry... It was... appreciative. And oh so sexy.

I noticed something sticking out of the truck bed

behind him, and I nodded toward it. "Bring your work home?"

"Oh this?" He turned toward the boxes as I walked beside him, looking at them.

My eyes instantly watered at the labels.

*Engineered hardwood flooring, oak brown.*

"Tyler, that stuff is so expensive. We have fifteen hundred feet to cover."

He ran his hands over my hair, my shoulders, and hugged me from behind. His breath feathered my hair as he said, "Can you believe me when I tell you it's no big deal?"

I shook my head, the memory of my mom begging with credit card companies fresh on my mind. I turned to face him, linking my hands behind his neck. "It's a huge deal, Tyler. A very, very big deal."

He leaned his head forward, resting his forehead against mine. "Then would you believe me when I told you that you're worth it?"

Butterfly wings tickled my insides, replacing nervous jitters with syrupy sweet emotion. And since there weren't words to show him just how much it meant to me, I tilted my chin up and met his lips with mine. His touch mingled with the breeze against my skin and sent tingles down my spine.

"Come on," he said, his voice a whisper. His lips a smile.

I nodded, biting my bottom lip, and slipped my fingers

through his. Going to his place with him, with our fingers linked, was so different than the first time. I'd been so nervous, insecure, but now he made me feel beautiful, desired, and I was high on the feeling.

He let go of my hand to get his keys and slipped them into the lock before leading me in. His scent hit my nose even stronger, a fresh mix of leather and linen that was just as sexy as the man before me.

"Did you spray your cologne as air freshener?" I asked. "Because I'll gladly buy some off you."

Chuckling, he said, "My sister sells candles, so I bought a few off her. She did a whole scent profile for me and everything."

I closed my eyes, savoring the smell. "She's got some real talent."

"I'll let her know you said so," he replied as he slipped off his suit jacket and went to hang it up in the coat closet. There were three other coats in there—a rain jacket, a Northface outer shell and then a thicker winter coat. Everything he needed and nothing more. I liked that about him too.

I kicked out of my heels, breathing a sigh of relief as my feet flattened on the carpeted floor. "That feels so good."

"I can give you a foot rub," he offered.

"And make me fall in love with you?"

He laughed. "That's the goal."

I shook my head, still smiling, and said, "Can I borrow

a pair of socks? I'd hate for you to be disgusted by my feet."

Acting exasperated, he took my hand and pulled me onto the couch with him. He sat opposite me and took my feet in his lap. I knew I'd hoped for sexy times, but the way this man rubbed my foot... It had to be orgasmic. "That feels so good," I sighed, leaning my head back against the couch cushion.

"You've had a long few days," he said. "With your grandma and the wedding... I bet you're exhausted."

With his words, I felt down to my bones how true that was. "I am. When you're a woman in business, you start to feel like you can't show any emotions, any weakness, or people won't take you seriously. And at home—I know I have it good, being able to live there basically rent free. It feels wrong to complain."

"You have every right to feel however you feel. I love my folks, but I couldn't share a sink with them. My mom's so particular about dishes that she rewashes the plates my dad cleaned after he goes to bed."

"Seriously?" I laughed. "I would just be happy someone's doing the dishes who isn't me."

"You don't like dishes?"

I shook my head. "It's the worst. And knowing all that dirty water is soaking into your skin. Yuck."

"You know they have this fancy contraption called rubber gloves."

"And have my hands soak in their own sweat? No

thank you. And god forbid some of that dirty water gets in there and starts growing something. No, no, no."

He chuckled, reaching for my opposite foot. "As long as you're with me, I'll do the dishes."

I bit my lip. "So. Freaking. Sexy."

Waggling his eyebrows, he said, "You should see me with a toilet brush."

"Talk dirty to me." I winked, resting my head back on the couch.

# 39

## TYLER

Henrietta's eyes slid closed, and her breathing slowly evened out. I smiled, feeling her completely relax in my hands, her legs growing heavy in my lap. I'd wanted to please her tonight, but this, knowing she felt safe enough to let her guard down with me... it was just as good.

I looked at her feet in my hands, soft from the spa day, and her toes were painted with a shiny olive-green paint. For a moment, I sat, watching the rise and fall of her chest, gliding my palm over her shins, just enjoying the peace that came with her presence. Something about having her here made my apartment feel less lonely than it usually did, and I dreaded the moment she'd eventually have to go.

But I didn't want to think of that now. I carefully lifted her legs from my lap and went to my room to get a spare pillow and blanket. When I returned, I gently moved her into a more comfortable position and then covered her with the blanket.

She shifted slightly, nuzzling her head into the pillow, and then settled again. I stood back, folding my arms across my chest. "You're one hell of a woman, Henrietta Jones."

Smiling to myself, I walked back to the bedroom and began taking off the rest of my suit from the wedding. As I slid down my pants, my phone fell out of my side pocket, and I picked it up, seeing a text from the group chat I had going with her brothers.

Johmarcus: I'll be there at seven. See you then.
Justus: Me too. Thanks for this.
Bertrand: I'll be there at half past eight with the lumber delivery.

I texted them back.

Tyler: See y'all soon.

Then I set my phone on the dresser, threw the clothes in the hamper, and walked back to the shower. These apartments weren't fancy, but one thing I could say, the water pressure was top-notch.

I stepped under the heavy stream, letting the pressure wash away all the tension from the day. I'd wanted to take things to the next step with Henrietta, make her scream my name until she clenched around me, but once I saw how tired she was, I couldn't ask that of her.

That memo hadn't reached my dick yet, though. I was so fucking hard for her. I ran my hand down my length, wishing it was her hand instead.

Fuck. I didn't want to masturbate with her in the next room, but this situation wasn't going away any time soon... especially with how good she looked tonight, how fucking sexy she was pressed against the coat closet wall.

I gripped my cock, holding it tight in my hand and closing my eyes. Her breasts would bounce as she worked me faster and harder. Her lips would part, ready for me to enter her mouth so she could taste me on her tongue.

Fuck, she was so hot. And those tits. I'd knead them, slather them with oil and thrust my cock in her cleavage. Harder and faster, her throat humming with pleasure as I tit-fucked her.

Just as I got close to coming, she'd take me in her mouth, hold my thighs with her hands so I had no choice but to nut down her warm throat. And she'd look up at me as she swallowed every. Last. drop.

My cock throbbed one last time before I came all over the shower floor. The next time, it would be with her.

## 40

## HENRIETTA

*Confession: There's not a lot that Grandma's hugs can't fix.*

WHEN I WOKE UP, Tyler's apartment was dark except for a bright slit of light shining through the blackout shades in his living room. And then it hit me: I'd fallen asleep on his couch, in my bridesmaid dress, still a virgin.

I sat up and let out a groan. Gah, I was so pathetic. I couldn't even stay awake to bone my hot boyfriend.

I cringed internally at my use of the word bone. That was such a virgin word to use. Which made sense because… Flower? Still there.

I stood up, wondering where he was and what time it was. A paper crunched between my leg and the coffee table. I picked it up, then went to the shades, drawing them back and squinting at the bright reflection of sun on notebook paper.

*Sorry I had a work thing to get to. The coffee pot is on, and there's a to-go cup you can use. Creamer is in the fridge, and sugar's in the cabinet—help yourself to anything. I had your friend Birdie get an extra outfit for you too, and it's sitting on the counter.*

I glanced toward the counter, seeing a reusable grocery bag there.

*Take a shower, make yourself at home, maybe visit your grandma. I'd love to take you to dinner tonight.*

*- Tyler*

Still stunned at his thoughtfulness, and Birdie's involvement, I went through the tote bag. Everything was there, from toiletries to a fresh pair of *lacy* underwear, a cotton dress, socks, and slip-on sneakers.

I opened up my clutch, which was on the coffee table, and pulled out my phone, seeing a few new texts in the group chat.

**Birdie:** HENRIETTA! PLEASE TELL ME IT HAPPENED LAST NIGHT!
**Mara:** Did you get deflowered?! Details!! (For book purposes of course ;))
**Birdie:** It was so sweet of him to have me get your stuff for you. *swoon*
**Mara:** The suspense is killing me, girl!

I smiled at my friends' messages. They were so excited

for me. I should have opened up sooner about my virginity. But for now, it was still intact.

Henrietta: I fell asleep before we could do anything. So freaking lame.
Mara: Was he bad in bed?
Henrietta: I wouldn't know! He gave me a foot rub and I basically passed out on his couch.

I glanced at my clock, and my jaw dropped open. How had I managed to sleep past eleven o'clock? I must have needed the extra sleep. And I promised myself I'd make the most of my renewed energy tonight.

Birdie: There's still time. You should have seen the way he was looking at you last night. That boy's not going anywhere.

I smiled at the text.

Henrietta: Fingers crossed.
Henrietta: Now get back to your honeymoon, Mara.
Mara: Fine, but text me when it happens. I'll drink a margarita to celebrate. Extra cherry on top. ;)
Henrietta: Gross lol and promise

♥·♥·♥·♥

I WALKED into the hospital carrying three sweet teas. A raspberry flavored one for Mom, peach flavored for Grandma, and blackberry for me. Usually we made flavored teas at home, and we'd sit on the back patio sipping away and chatting about the day.

Today was different.

We weren't at home. We were in the hospital, and I felt the weight of that fact as soon as I got underneath the harsh fluorescent lights. Even though I'd had fun at the wedding, everything was different now, and the future was more uncertain than ever.

When I was younger and had worried thoughts like that, Grandma would say, "Stop with your stinkin' thinkin'." I tried to do that now, taking a deep breath to clear my mind before walking into the room.

Mom smiled at me, taking her tea, and Grandma grinned. "I was just thinking I needed some sweet tea," she said.

I handed her the clear cup with ice crackling against the plastic. "I had them add some extra sugar for you."

"You're bad," she said, giving me an appreciative yet scolding smile.

I took the other open chair by her bed and drank from my straw. Sweet liquid flooded my tongue, making me relax a bit. "How has it been, Gran? I still feel guilty for not being here this weekend."

"Don't be silly," Grandma said. "You can't stop living your life because I'm getting old."

I gave her a look. "Getting?"

She batted her hand at me, and I laughed. "Can't you just let me worry about you?" I asked, exasperated.

"If it involves pittea, then yes," she replied. "Get it? Pitty-tea?"

I rolled my eyes letting out a laugh. "You've done better."

"Well excuse me. My humor lately is almost as bad as the hospital food."

Mom smiled at us, shaking her head. "How was the wedding?"

"Beautiful," I began, telling them all about the event, from the vows they wrote themselves to the best-man speech Cohen gave that had me crying I was laughing so hard. And then, of course, I had to tell them how amazing Tyler had been on the dance floor. "I overheard multiple women saying they hoped he was single when I was in the bathroom."

Mom said, "That's exactly how your dad was. Every girl had their eyes on him, but we've been together thirty-eight years now."

Grandma said, "Well now I do feel old. I remember you bringing Murph home that first time to meet us."

Mom covered her face with her hand not resting on a magazine. "I'd rather forget it."

Grandma cackled and put her hand on my arm. "That boy dressed up, had on suspenders even."

"Suspenders?" I gasped. "I've never seen Dad out of jeans."

Grandma nodded. "Suspenders and these shiny black shoes. Your grandpa gave him one look and shook his head." She lowered her voice. "'Not for my daughter. I need a man who can get some dirt on his hands. I'm not going to be able to run over to fix every leaky faucet and change every tire forever.'"

I dropped my head back and laughed. Of all the stories I'd been told of my parents' youth, I hadn't heard this one.

Mom said, "Murph was absolutely floored. He was stumbling over his words, and Grandpa gave him the side-eye. 'You tongue-tied boy?'"

My stomach shook with laughter. "Poor Dad."

Grandma said, "The next day he drove the car he restored over to the house, wearing his work clothes, and got his second chance at a first impression. Harold loved that boy once he got to know him. You're lucky to have him as your daddy."

After hearing Mara's horror stories and seeing how strained things had been between Birdie and her parents, I knew she was right. "I'm lucky to have all of you as my family." My voice cracked. "I love you."

"Oh, honey," Grandma said. She extended her arms for me, and I stood over her bed, letting her give me one of those hugs that makes everything better even though you're falling apart. As I sat back in my chair, she said,

"We are *so* proud of you, baby girl. And we're happy you've found Tyler. I have a good feeling about that boy."

"Me too," I said.

"In fact," Mom said, looking at her phone.

"What?" I asked.

"Nothing," she said quickly. "I just need you to head by the house in an hour. I want to make some more macramé hangers and all my stuff is there."

I gave her a suspicious look, but she was already flipping back through her magazine, a small smile on her face.

## 41

## HENRIETTA

*Confession: I don't know what I did to deserve this.*

I SENT a text to Tyler before leaving the hospital, letting him know it would be another hour or so before we could meet up for dinner. I needed to get Mom her rope and rings to make those hangers. I should have asked her why Dad or my brothers couldn't do it, since I hadn't seen them at the hospital, but I'd honestly forgotten.

**Tyler: No worries. I can pick you up from the hospital.**

I smiled at my phone before tucking it in my purse and driving to my parents' house. I needed to ask him when we'd be able to get to work on the new flooring. According to Mom, we had a couple weeks, since they wanted Grandma to do physical therapy in the hospital and get stronger before coming home. The fracture was small enough they hoped it would heal naturally, and she could use a walker until she felt more confident. If not, we'd have a whole ramp to install as well, adding the question of someone around to help her

Grandma's life could be a lot longer, and harder, than I had planned for. And that put a knot of worry in my gut. I could be working for another ten years to keep her at home... unless I could find a remote job to stay at home with her?

But that thought was quickly wiped from my mind as I pulled up to the house. All of my brothers' vehicles were there, along with Tyler's pickup, and there was a brand-new ramp leading up to the front door.

Completely speechless, I got out of the car, seeing my brothers and Tyler spilling out the front door onto the porch.

"What do you think?" Dad called, grinning ear to ear.

"You built a ramp!" I barely registered my feet carrying me down the front sidewalk.

Dad clapped Tyler's shoulder. "Wait 'til you see the inside."

Our eyes locked from feet away, and I gave him a disbelieving look. "What's inside?"

Tyler nodded, answering my unspoken question.

It was taken care of. All of it.

I walked up the ramp, and Johmarcus put his arm around my shoulders. "Check this out, sis."

We walked inside, and it was like a new house. The flooring gleamed under the lights, completely beautiful, and all the furniture and trim boards were already back in place. There was even a new recliner in our living room.

"We got a new chair too?" I asked.

Justus said, "Imani's mom had an extra chair with a built-in lift. We thought it might make things easier for Grammy."

I let go of Johmarcus and hugged Justus, his earring scratching my cheek. "Guys, it looks incredible."

Bertrand said, "We did the living room and all the bedrooms."

"How did you work so quickly?"

Tyler grinned and said, "I've asked them if I can hire them for my crew at least ten times. They made the job go so fast."

Dad shook his head and said, "Tyler's being modest. He put this all together, got us here at seven in the morning. Ordered all the materials. This wouldn't have been possible without him."

Feeling my eyes well up, I went and wrapped my arms around Tyler's middle. He held me close while my brothers and dad stayed silent, giving us this moment. I hoped Tyler understood how big of a difference this would make to Grandma coming home and life hopefully getting back to normal. Or at least the newer version of it.

Then it hit me, and all the blood drained from my face. "Does that mean you all went through my room?"

Tyler chuckled, and Dad said, "Don't worry. We hid all your unmentionables."

Unmentionables? Now I was really embarrassed. I let go of Tyler and walked into my room, staring at how all my furniture looked on the new flooring. It was like an entirely different space.

"Well, it does look good," I said.

Tyler huffed, "You sound so surprised."

Laughing, I hit his chest. "It wasn't very clean before I left for the wedding." I frowned. "Speaking of leaving, I was supposed to get Mom stuff to make her macramé plant hangers."

Johmarcus spoke up. "That was just an excuse to get you here. We're all going to the hospital now for a visit. Why don't you stay and enjoy the new floors?"

Dad nodded. "I'm spending the night there with Grandma. No one should be back here tonight. Just eat some vegetables, please. We're up to our ears."

There wasn't any insinuation behind his words, but the meaning was clear. Tyler and I had the house to ourselves for the entire night to do whatever we chose. Trying not to blush, I nodded. "Want me to make you all some supper before you leave?" I didn't want to seem too eager to jump Tyler's sexy bones.

Dad shook his head and clapped his hand on Tyler's

shoulder. "I have to get your mom some food anyway. I'll see you tomorrow, baby girl."

And just like that, they were walking out of the house, getting into their cars, and driving away.

Tyler and I were alone.

## 42

## TYLER

Henrietta faced me, a slight smile on her lips. "I'm sorry," she said, "I still can't believe you did all this."

"I mean, it wasn't just me. Your brothers and dad did most of the work."

She shook her head, stepping closer and taking my face in her hands, kissing me deep. Her kiss drew all the air from the room, made me forget anything else but the two of us.

I wrapped my arms around her waist, deepening our embrace. Yesterday, she'd said this was all too much, but she was wrong. I wished I could show her just how special she was, how any guy worth his salt would have done the same thing I had.

Her hands traveled from my neck, to my chest, and

then down to my belt. My dick twitched in response, already growing hard.

But then my fucking stomach growled.

She giggled as she pulled away, and I tried not to look annoyed at my traitorous stomach. I was already planning my next meal anyway, and it was going to include Henrietta, on her back, screaming my name.

"Let me make you some supper," she said. "I'm kind of hungry anyway."

Well there went my response. If she was hungry, she should eat. "Can I help?" Anything to get my mind off my aching balls.

"You've done more than enough. Sit at the island. I'll get you a beer."

If this girl wasn't perfect already... "That sounds amazing."

She smiled at me before reaching into the fridge and handing me an icy can. "Beer always tastes better after a long day of work."

I nodded. That first-sip feeling always got me. I thumbed the top, and it cracked loudly as it opened. She got herself a beer from the fridge as well and opened it. I held my can out to her, and the aluminum made a soft bumping sound as she tapped her can to mine.

She took a drink and set her beer down on the island before reaching to the vegetable basket. "Do you like bell peppers?"

"Love 'em," I answered.

She grabbed a couple from the basket, along with an onion and garlic clove, then got a cut of meat from the fridge. She cut the meat first, slicing it in methodic motions.

"Do you like cooking?" I asked.

"Love it. I can't wait to have my own kitchen someday. I want a double oven where I can cook loaves of zucchini bread every summer and a big island where everyone can sit when I make Christmas dinner."

I loved the way she talked about her dreams, like they were this fantasyland where anything was possible. I wanted those dreams to come true for her so damn bad. "You like hosting?"

She nodded. "You just got a taste of it at Kenner's birthday party. My family's always coming over and hanging out."

"Same here," I said. "Except there's usually a dumb prank involved. I kind of think that's why I was so awkward. I was used to my close circle of people and new faces made me nervous."

She nodded. "I always felt like I had plenty of friends in my family. It only got lonely at school."

I totally got it. Hen was quiet as she chopped, giving us both time to get lost in our memories.

"You never told me about the bachelorette party," I said.

She grinned. "There was a stripper involved."

I nearly snorted. "A stripper?"

She nodded. "He came in wearing a suit, since Jonas is an accountant." She shuddered slightly. "He did things with a calculator I never would have dreamed of."

I tried to imagine what he must have done and came up blank. But judging by Hen's reaction, that was a mental image to avoid.

"What about the bachelor trip?" she asked. "Mara said you went with them?"

I couldn't believe I'd forgotten to tell her. "We went to La Jolla and did a kayak tour, then one of those bike and beer tours. It was pretty fun. Especially since Steve asked for an extra life jacket in case his first one failed."

Her tinkling laugh mingled with the smell of food in the air. "Sounds like swim lessons are in order."

"If you could get Steve back on the water, that's probably a good idea," I said, watching her liberally season the meat before tossing in the vegetables. While they sizzled in the pan, she got tortillas from the fridge and started some rice in another pot. "Tell me about your mom," she said. "What does she do?"

"She's a teacher, a good one. She won teacher of the year last year."

"That's amazing. I like kids, but I couldn't imagine watching twenty of them all day every day."

"My mom's always been talented that way. She could be in an empty room and still find something fun for everyone to do. And she's one of those people who never makes you feel stupid about having questions. My sister wasn't very good in school, but Mom worked with her every night on her homework because she was too embarrassed to ask for help in class. Helped her self-esteem a lot."

Henrietta tilted her head. "She sounds amazing. My mom's main strategy for homework was to sit us at the kitchen table and stand over us with a wooden spoon." Hen laughed. "Johmarcus especially needed the motivation."

"My brother Rhett was the same way. But Johmarcus seemed to have plenty of motivation today," I said.

"He's grown a lot." She stirred the meat. "Back when he was younger, he was always about to become rich on some scheme. It cost him and my parents a lot."

I nodded. "Some lessons are harder to learn than others."

"True." She turned and retrieved two bowls from the cabinet, then dished them for us. The smell wafting from the dish she passed to me made my mouth water. "This looks delicious, and you made whipping it all together seem so effortless."

She smiled. "You flatter me, Tyler Griffen."

"You make it easy."

# 43

## HENRIETTA

*Confession: I'm terrified of losing my virginity.*

WE'D EATEN OUR FAJITAS. We'd drunk our beer.

I was warm and buzzing with electricity.

And I'd never been more nervous in my life.

I pushed abruptly back from the island and said, "I'm going to use the bathroom."

"Sure, I'll take care of the dishes." He winked.

I shook my head at him because, gah, he wasn't allowed to be sexy *and* kind *and* do the dishes because he knew I hated them.

My breath picked up as I walked to the bathroom and shut myself inside. Was I really going to lose my virginity to Tyler? Tonight? And what would he think when he saw me naked? Would he change his mind? Had he been with big girls like me before? Would he know to expect the stretch marks and dimples and rolls? Or would it all scare him away?

I wished I was more like Mara and Birdie, confident in my size. But even if I didn't have their confidence, I did have them at my fingertips, so I sent them a text.

Henrietta: SOS. I'M ABOUT TO HAVE SEX WITH TYLER AND I'M FREAKING TF OUT!
Mara: What happened? What's wrong?
Birdie: I'm here too. <3
Henrietta: What if he doesn't like my body?
Mara: Henrietta. You're fat. Your clothes don't hide that.

I cringed at her calling me fat. I knew to her it was just a word, a descriptor, but when people had used those three letters to insult you your entire life, it was hard to get used to thinking of the word any other way.

Mara: And being fat isn't a bad thing.
Birdie: Exactly. Cohen loves my curves. Honey, I don't think Tyler would be so into you if he didn't like your size.
Mara: ^^^ I know it sounds cliché, but there's literally more of you for him to love... and play with. ;)

My cheeks were getting hot. Was I really ready for this? What if...

**Henrietta:** What if I'm bad in bed?

**Birdie:** I don't think Tyler will mind practicing with you. ;)

Practice. I could do that.

There wasn't a text from Mara right away, so I locked my phone and set it on the sink. If I stayed in here too long, Tyler would think I was having stomach problems and that would totally kill the mood. And I wasn't about to *almost* have sex for the second time. No, tonight was the night.

I reached into the cabinet and dabbed on some expensive perfume my grandma got me for my birthday a few years back. Then I ran my fingers through my hair, making sure it was perfect. And, of course, I dabbed on just a little bit of lip gloss.

I looked at myself in the mirror and whispered, "You can do this. You have a hot guy who likes you. The whole house is yours for the night. And if it doesn't go well... you can try again. If it doesn't work with Tyler, there will be someone else."

But I already knew that last part was a lie. I may not have known Tyler long, but I knew him well enough to understand that there was no one else like him.

I pushed back from the sink, put my hand on the doorknob, and took a deep breath. Henrietta Jones was not going to be a virgin anymore.

# 44

## HENRIETTA

*Confession: It's time.*

"TYLER?" I called from the bathroom doorway.

"Yeah?"

"Meet me in my room?"

The sink immediately turned off, and I smiled to myself. Maybe that meant he was just as excited as me.

I met him in my bedroom doorway, and we were squeezed into the space, our bodies pressed against each other. He palmed the side of my neck, his hand big enough to cover my jaw too. "Have I told you how beautiful you are?" he breathed, his voice husky.

I looked from his eyes, a dreamy mix of dark green

and brown, to his lips. Full. Pink. And I kissed him. Slow at first, then harder as we walked to my bed.

He lowered me down, straddling me on the bed as he feathered kisses from my lips to my cheek and jaw. His five o'clock shadow scratched against my skin as he worked his way to my neck, my collarbone. And then his hands slid under my dress, his palm running over my thighs, my side, my breasts. His thumb flicked over my nipple, already pebbling in anticipation.

He parted my legs with his and pressed his knee against my center. Moisture pooled between my legs, soaking my lacy underwear as I rode his thigh.

"Tyler," I moaned.

"I know, baby," he breathed, pulling at my dress. He lowered himself until his face hovered over my vagina, and he pulled my underwear aside, rubbing his thumb over my clit. The sensation was so strong, I clenched and moaned.

I'd touched myself before, spent time with toys, but this was already so much better. So much *more*. His thumb kept pressure on my clit as he slid a finger inside me. "You're so wet." His voice was husky before he replaced his thumb with his mouth.

Knowing he was tasting me... savoring me. Fuck, it was hot. My hips bucked, and I moaned, gripping the blanket we lay atop. I might not be good in bed, but Tyler was already surpassing every expectation, meeting every need I didn't know I had.

His tongue worked slow circles around my sensitive

spot as he caressed my insides with his fingertips, hitting all the right places that I hardly knew could feel that way.

And then he hummed against my clit, and I nearly came undone.

"Tyler," I gasped.

He hummed, moving his fingers in and out, sweeping them around.

I tightened around his digits, so close to the edge, until he worked me over the top, and I came undone around his finger, on his mouth. He continued licking it all until the waves slowly faded.

"Tyler," I said again. I was at a loss for words, only able to speak his name. But that was more than enough for him. He got up and took a tissue from my nightstand, wiping his face, and then took off his shirt.

I sat up, still quivering from his touch, and stared at his shirtless body. He was perfect, all hard lines, a dusting of short brown hair, and now I could see all of his tattoos. There was the one on the inside of his bicep and then a pattern that changed from prairie to sun that covered one of his shoulders almost to his neck.

He caught me staring, and I let myself look. He reached for his jeans, undoing the button and slowly lowering the zipper. His cock strained against his black underwear, the tip full, hard under the fabric.

I wanted to feel it, to touch it.

I moved to the edge of the bed, reaching for his underwear, but he caught my hand. When I looked up at him in question, there was a salacious smirk on his lips.

"You, Henrietta Jones, are wearing far too much clothing."

A laugh passed my lips, surprising even me. This, with Tyler, was sexy, hot, incredible, and... fun.

He reached for my hands, pulling me to stand next to him. And then he raised my dress over my head. Blinded by fabric, I could only feel him against me, my stomach brushing against his.

When the dress left my head, I could see him again. He looked in my eyes, his hazel ones so captivating. So open. He was letting me see him, the real him.

And I was letting him see me.

Stretch marks.

Cellulite.

My apron belly and my thighs that rubbed together and my breasts that strained against my size G bra.

It was me.

All of me.

But he didn't look away or step back. Instead, he kissed me. Not like I was something to be devoured or fetishized, but instead, someone to be worshiped. He reached to my shoulder, fingering the white strap of my bra.

"I like this," he said.

I reached behind me, undoing the clasps, freeing my

breasts, and handed it to him. "It's yours." I took a breath. "I'm yours."

He stared at my breasts, then lifted one into his hand, drawing the nipple into his mouth.

I closed my eyes as he sucked. "That feels so good."

He drew his mouth away and said, "I want to make you feel good, baby." He lowered himself, pulling my panties over my thighs, and I kicked them aside as he stood, fully bare to this man I cared so much about.

Who'd given me more than he'd ever know. And I wanted to return the favor.

## 45

## TYLER

Henrietta lowered herself to her knees in front of me. She gave me a coy smile before hooking her hands on the waistband of my underwear and bringing them down, releasing my cock. It was thick and veiny, waiting for her, and when she saw it, she licked her lips.

Fuck, it was hot.

She took it in her hand, giving it a few soft pumps.

"Harder, baby," I said.

She tightened her grip, pumping it for another few seconds before bringing her lips to the tip. Moving her hands to my hips, she slowly took me into her mouth. The soft warmth of her tongue on the underside of my tip, the stretch of her lips around my shaft, was almost too much.

I dropped my head back, moaning. "You know how to make me feel good, baby."

She moaned against my cock, and it took all I had to stay still, not to ram it the rest of the way into her mouth. Instead, I weaved my fingers through the hair at the back of her head, holding it away from her face as she moved over me, sucking and moaning and driving me fucking crazy. And when she looked up at me, like she was checking to see if she was doing a good job...

"Good girl," I encouraged.

She moved faster over my cock, and I could feel my precum sliding into her mouth. I was getting close. Too close. There was no way I was coming on her tongue when I hadn't felt what it was like to be inside her.

I took her hands from my ass and pulled her up, turning her so I could lay her back on the bed. Her tits spread, lulling to the side, so full I couldn't even hold them in one hand. Her stomach flattened into a brown pillow. And don't even get me started on the sexy girth of her thighs. I wanted her on top of me, riding me, pressing me into the bed. But first, I wanted her like this, face to face, with me in control.

Her eyes stayed on me as I lowered myself over her, my cock pressing into her stomach. "You're so fucking sexy, Henrietta," I breathed.

Her lips quirked slightly. She was nervous—I could tell —so I worked my way down, kissing her neck, her collarbone, sucking on one nipple while kneading her other breast, working a hand down to rub her sensitive spot. I was more than fine with taking my time with this beautiful woman despite how hard I was for her. She was worth the wait. And I needed her to *need* me. To beg for me. Because I wouldn't have her any other way.

She ran her hands down my back, digging her nails into my skin, holding on, until she was gasping for air.

"Tyler," she rasped. "I want you closer."

# 46

## HENRIETTA

*Confession: I love Tyler Griffen.*

HE ROLLED a condom over his length and then propped himself up over me. I held on to his shoulders, feeling him press his tip to my entrance. This was it, the moment I would no longer be a virgin. But it was so much more, seeing Tyler's face, inches from mine. Watching him search my eyes as he pressed inside.

I'd heard it could hurt the first time, and I had prepared myself for that. But it was more of a stretching sensation as he sheathed his thick cock inside me. He was slow at first, drawing himself almost all the way out, then pushing all the way in. Pressure built inside me with each thrust.

His lips curled into a sultry smile. "You feel so good, baby."

All the emotions were there, happiness, surprise, delight, and so much more. I hardly had words, so I took his face in my hands, drawing his mouth to mine. He kissed me, hard, as he continued a steady rhythm, in and out. It was all so surreal. My first time. With Tyler Griffen.

I couldn't have asked for anything better. My heart swelled as he continued his pace, filling me in a way I'd never known before. Emotion clogged my throat, and I swallowed, feeling tears sting my eyes.

"I know, baby," he said as tears dripped down my cheeks. He lowered his hips to mine as he ground inside me, then cupped my face with his hand, brushing a tear away from my cheek. His voice was hoarse. "It's never been like this for me before either."

I felt more vulnerable, more seen, than I ever had in my life, with this man holding me. He wasn't shying away from my feelings, from my size, from me. No, he'd embraced me and all that I was.

The swell in my heart grew with the build of my orgasm. "Tyler, I'm coming," I gasped in shock. I never thought I would come with my first time, but the waves were growing. "I'm coming."

"Yes, baby, that's it," he said, pushing harder, faster, until he shuddered over me. Inside me. I whimpered as my orgasm milked his cock, and when we stilled, he lowered himself to lie beside me, his breaths slowing from the gasps he'd taken earlier.

Plastic snapped as he freed himself of the condom. I watched as he tied it in a knot, pulled the plastic to check for holes. Seeing none, he set it in the trashcan by my bed.

I rolled to my side, facing him, as I assessed my body. I felt different, not because I'd had sex, but because I'd been claimed as his. And he'd let himself be mine in the most intimate way. Somewhere in the back of my mind, I wondered if I was bleeding, but I doubted it. My hymen had probably already been broken by a toy or a tampon.

"That was amazing," he said.

I smiled slightly and nodded. "I'm sorry for crying."

He laughed, and I found myself laughing too. "Don't worry about that," he said. "You were so beautiful with your eyes shining."

I covered my heart. "You're perfect. Tell me there's something wrong with you."

"Well, I did have some unwholesome thoughts when you had your mouth on my cock."

I sputtered, laughing. "I mean, that's about the most 'unwholesome' sentence I've heard. What were you thinking?"

He took my hair, twirling it around his finger, then tugging gently. "I thought about taking your head and making you take all of me, as deep as you could, until you gagged on my cock."

Even though I'd already come twice, my vagina clenched. "That sounds sexy."

"Yeah? You're into the dominating type?"

I bit my lip. "I think I am."

"We'll have to try it next time."

My lips lifted with a smile. "There will be a next time?"

"If I have a say in it, there will be a next time, and a next time, and a next time." He nuzzled his chin into my collarbone, tickling me and making me giggle.

I hugged his head to stall him and kissed his crown. "Good. I want that too."

He spread his arms so I could rest on his shoulder, and I curled into the nook, pulling the sheets over my chest. I loved the warmth of his naked body against mine under a cocoon of sheets and blankets. With his arm behind his head, I could see the tattoo on his bicep more clearly. It looked like a windmill, but just the blades... I traced my fingers over the spokes.

He watched my hand, then looked back at the ceiling. "My siblings and I got them together, after Gage's falling-out with my parents."

I watched him, taking in his beautiful eyes. "What was their fight about?"

"Gage wanted to take over the ranch and help Dad grow it so it could be big enough to support our entire family."

"And your dad didn't want that?"

He shook his head. "Dad thought Gage's idea was a pipe dream, something that would drain all our money and break their hearts in the process. And Gage told Dad that he was just scared and using money as an excuse. So, of course, Dad punched back, with his words. Said Gage was greedy and needed to stop talking about land grabbing from other families like us."

My heart already ached for Gage, for the rift all of it must have caused their family.

"Rhett was only twenty, too young to have much of a say, and my sister told Gage to stop arguing. I was already set on getting a job, and nothing I said could convince Dad to change his mind or take it back. So Gage was going to leave, join the military and never come back."

"Wow," I said. "It must have been awful."

"It was. Mostly because it was the beginning of the war in Afghanistan. He would have gotten sent abroad, and so many people were dying. I was selfish—didn't want him to be one of them."

I nodded. "I would have done the same thing if one of my brothers had wanted to enlist."

Tyler took a deep breath. "So I told him to prove Dad wrong. To build a business from nothing and buy a ranch twice the size of Dad's out of sheer spite." He laughed. "Now he's a billionaire with the biggest real estate investment company in Texas."

"Has he bought the ranch?"

Tyler shook his head. "It was never about the ranch. It

was about keeping our family together, rescuing them. And now that the family's all split up, well..."

I trailed the path of his tattoo with my fingertip. "Not really much of a point anymore."

He tapped my nose, making me smile. "But the four of us siblings all got tattoos. My sister's idea. She was only twenty-two, but I think she could sense all of us drifting apart."

"Why windmills though?"

"Because they always move but never leave." He kissed my temple. "You can count on them, day in, day out, to give you water, life. And you can never miss them. Even in a big pasture, it's like a country lighthouse telling you to come back home."

"That's beautiful," I said.

"It is, isn't it?" The slight smile on his lips touched his eyes. "Willa Cather always said anyone could love the ocean or the mountains. It takes a special person to see the beauty in the plains."

"I hope I can see it someday," I said.

"You will," he promised, shifting to get up. "I'm going to use the bathroom. Be right back." He kissed my forehead and got off my bed, walking that beautiful naked body to the door.

As soon as it shut behind him, I rolled and put my face in the pillow, squealing. I'd just had my first time, and it had been *amazing*.

After allowing myself a few moments of celebration, I rearranged myself on the bed, fixing my hair and pulling the sheets and blankets neatly up over my breasts like the women always did in the movies, waiting for him to come back.

As he walked back through the door, I smiled at him, until I noticed the frown on his lips, the crease between his eyebrows. And then I saw my phone in his hands.

"Henrietta, what the hell is this?" He held up my phone, showing a text I couldn't make out. But I could certainly imagine what was on the screen.

"What does it say?" I asked.

He held it up, reading from the screen. "'You should tell him you're a virgin. It will make ravaging you that much more fun for him.'"

I cringed, wishing I could sink below my bed and hide next to the boogeyman. Instead, I lay there, facing Tyler and his critical gaze.

"Is this true?" he asked.

"That you'd have more fun ravaging me? I think you're the only one who can answer that."

His frown only deepened. "Henrietta."

My cheeks warmed, and I felt like a little kid being caught with my hand in the candy jar. But I couldn't lie to him, couldn't keep the secret anymore. "That was my first time."

His jaw went slack, and he scrubbed his hand over his chin as if in disbelief. "There's never been anyone else?

You *are* twenty-eight, aren't you? I didn't accidentally hook up with some teenage intern?"

Now it was my turn to glare at him. "Does this body look like a teenager's?"

A small flame sparked in his eyes, but he quickly put it out, coming to sit next to me and speaking gently. "Why didn't you tell me?"

"I was embarrassed!" I cried. "It's not exactly the best pickup line. 'Hi, my name's Henrietta. I live with my parents, and no one's ever been interested enough to round home base.' You would have run away screaming."

He reached for my hands. "Not true. Especially after I found out how good you could cook."

The joke would have made me laugh if my chest wasn't feeling so tight.

Running his thumbs over the back of my hands, he said, "If I would have known, I would have... I don't know, been more careful with you. Were you crying because you were hurt? Are you bleeding?"

I bit down on my lip, considering my words. "I was crying because I've never felt closer to anyone else than I have to you today. I'm so lucky to know you, Tyler. To be loved by you."

His eyebrows lifted, and I instantly backtracked. "Not saying you're in love with me, but—"

He stopped my words with a kiss, and when he pulled back, he held my face in his hand. "I do love you, Henrietta Jones. I love you."

Tears filled my eyes again for completely different reasons. "I love you too, Tyler."

He kissed me again, and with both of us naked in bed, it quickly became heated. He pulled back, still close enough for me to feel his breath on my cheek. "I'll make sure you never want anyone else."

## 47

## TYLER

We spent all night in bed, drifting between sleep and lustfulness, exploring each other's bodies and making each other feel so damn good. It was heaven, and I knew I'd been a damn fool to think I would ever be okay with goodbye. So when Henrietta was sleeping, around two in the morning, I ordered plane tickets for us to visit home for Thanksgiving, just a couple months away now.

I wanted to convince her that Cottonwood Falls could be home. Show her all the trees that lined the creeks as their leaves changed to orange and gold. Introduce her to my mama and have her drive around to check cattle with my dad. Yell at my brother Rhett for flirting with her and my sister, Olivia, for sharing too many embarrassing secrets. I wanted to show her the high-rise where Gage worked and the incredible view from his office at night.

And most of all, I wanted her to fall in love with Texas like I'd fallen for her, because this feeling I had? Just the *thought* of it ending ripped me to shreds. But I wouldn't focus on that. I'd focus on this beautiful girl and the feeling I had in my chest. Like I had everything I needed right in front of me.

I rolled to my side, taking her in. She slept so peacefully, just like she had on my couch the night before. I loved her awake, but this quiet, serene side of her was beautiful too. If she woke up now, I knew she'd laugh at me for staring, but I enjoyed this immensely. Just as much as I liked lying next to her as I slowly fell asleep.

♥•♥•♥•♥

NORMALLY I'D GO for a run when I woke up, but this was a special morning, and my girl was getting a special breakfast. Even if I had to look through every drawer and cabinet in this kitchen to find what I was looking for.

That yellow box I used to make pancakes at home was nowhere to be found, so I used my phone to look up ingredients for pancakes and got to mixing. I was halfway through the batch when I heard a yawn behind me.

Henrietta was shuffling into the kitchen, her black robe tied at the waist and her gray slippers swishing against the new vinyl floor. With her hair tied in a messy bun atop her head and her eyes half closed, she still looked half asleep.

"Not a morning person?" I asked.

She hmphed. Maybe it was supposed to be a laugh. "Coffee?" she asked.

I nodded toward the pot, still tending to the pancakes. "Did you know your mom keeps coffee in a cookie jar?"

That got her laughing. "It's decorative."

"It's *hidden*," I retorted. "If the can isn't red or blue, I have no idea what to look for."

She stirred in cream and sugar, took a long sip, then said, "All a part of my mom's evil plan to see how we'd handle a relationship decaffeinated."

"Now there's a test," I replied, taking a drink of my own coffee. "But I am a morning person. I like to get my workout in before work, or I'd be too tired afterward."

She shook her head at me. "I knew there had to be something wrong with you."

I tossed my head back and laughed. "You're so grumpy when you first wake up."

Smiling slightly, she said, "Only after I've been kept awake all night."

I winked at her. "I'm more than happy to stay up for those reasons."

"Me too."

I leaned in and kissed her, her tongue tasting like sweet coffee, and then got back to cooking.

She leaned against the counter, watching me. "I was thinking I'd go visit my grandma real quick before work."

I glanced at the clock. It was only six fifteen. "Do you mind if I come along?"

Her smile grew. "I'd love that."

"There's my sunshine," I said. "Just needed some coffee."

She shook her head at me and took another drink. I finished dishing up the pancakes, and we ate in companionable silence before she needed to shower and get dressed. I'd brought a change of clothes to wear, so I put those on, and we made quick work of getting out the door and into my truck.

"It's fun, riding to work together," she said with a smile.

I smirked. "It's fun, knowing I'm your only ride so you'll be forced to stay with me."

She snorted. "As if you'd do that. You're too nice."

"Too nice?" I pretended my chest was hurting. "You wound me."

"It's a compliment. Most guys I know feel like they have to put on this tough guy act, never show an emotion. The way you handle things is... refreshing."

"I'll take that compliment," I said.

She pointed out another turn, and soon we were at the hospital, walking toward her grandma's room. As we approached, I could hear someone talking to her grandma. Hen listened quietly at the door and said, "Sounds like the doctors are here."

She knocked, and the talking paused as we walked into the room. Cordelia lit up at the sight of Henrietta and grinned even bigger when she saw me behind her.

"Hi, you two! Sounds like Tyler was quite the hero yesterday." Cordelia said to the doctor, "He installed vinyl floors and a ramp so I could get around the house easier."

The woman in a white coat smiled at me. "That's great. I was just telling your grandma here that things are on the right track. Inflammation and pain seem to be down, so we'll focus on the steroid regimen and some strenuous physical therapy, since Cordelia says she's up for the challenge."

Hen squeezed her grandma's hand. "Gran's the toughest person I know."

"When will I be able to go home?" Cordelia asked.

The doctor glanced at the chart in her hand. "Other than the hip, you're looking very healthy. Once you're able to make it around this unit with your walker, without anyone assisting, I don't see why we wouldn't release you. I'll recommend outpatient PT three times a week, but there may be an option to have someone see you at home."

Henrietta let out a quiet cry, covering her mouth with her hand. "That's great," Henrietta said. "I'm so happy."

I put my arm around her, holding her close, and she rested her free hand on my chest.

I smiled. "That is great news. But we all knew Cordelia was too stubborn to stick around here long."

Cordelia smirked. "Damn straight."

"Grandma!" Henrietta said at the same time the doctor said, "Right on."

## 48

# HENRIETTA

*Confession: So maybe I'm not as professional as I thought...*

WHEN I GOT BACK to my office, everything felt right. Except for the plant I forgot to bring back with me. The room did feel a little bare without it. And the fact that Janessa had clearly messed with some papers while she was here. It took about an hour to get things back to the way I liked them.

I was glad I remembered those papers when I did. From now on, my searches would be purely digital and on my phone. For the rest of the day, I gave tours, managed the clean out of one apartment and had to serve an eviction notice to someone I'm pretty sure had already abandoned their unit.

But most of all, I looked forward to after work. Tyler and I hadn't made plans specifically, but as he mentioned, he was my ride, in more ways than one. *Wink*.

During the last ten minutes of work, I shut myself in the bathroom and refreshed my makeup, then added a little perfume to my wrists and neck. And when I walked back out, I saw Tyler standing by the door, his hand on the knob.

We both froze, but Tyler's eyes moved first, traveling over my body, something heated in his stare.

Then he slid the lock shut and said, "Close the blinds, and get on your desk."

Goosebumps erupted over my skin.

"Now," he growled.

I fought the giddy smile taking over my face and went to the windows, pulling down each of the cordless blinds. This was something out of a fantasy, and here I was, experiencing it in real life.

A million worries popped up—what if someone came by, or worse, what if Janessa did a surprise drop in? But knowing we could get caught and being too overcome with desire to care made this even hotter.

With the blinds down, I did as he asked, walking around the counter to sit on my desk. His hooded eyes followed my every step. And when I sat on the desk, my skirt riding up, he said, "Good girl."

Did I have a praise kink? Maybe. Because hearing

those words just made me want to do whatever he asked of me that much more.

With a sizzling look in his eyes, he lowered himself to his knees, separating my legs with his shoulders. Just like the night before, he pulled my panties aside and began feasting. The scrape of his five o'clock shadow on my delicate skin was just as sexy as what he was doing with his tongue.

I raked my fingers through his hair as he continued his assault, each second better than the one before.

"Tyler," I moaned as silently as I could, but it was hard to hold back. I gripped the edge of the desk and held on for dear life as he pushed me higher, harder, with just his mouth. And then he added his fingers to the mix, and I came undone, clenching hard and screaming with my mouth closed.

But there wasn't time to recover after my orgasm because he slid me off the desk, roughly turned me and bent me over, and then rammed into me from behind, the pain of his sudden entrance deliciously hot against my sensitive vagina.

He held on to my skirt, using it to pull my hips back to meet his, the slap of his front against my thighs filling the office.

"I love that fucking sound," he growled. "Tell me what you like."

I was nervous to speak out loud, to tell him what I liked when I'd never done that before, but I leaned into the moment, focused on the sensations in my body. How he made me feel. "The slap of your sack against me," I gasped.

"Fuck. And the way your ass jiggles with each thrust? So fucking sexy."

"Mhmm." My moan is almost a whine. All of him felt so good.

He reached up and grabbed my ponytail, yanking my head back. "Tell me more, baby."

The pain was exquisite, only adding to all the other sensations I felt. "I love it when you take control," I said. "When you tell me what to do and make me yours."

"You are mine," he said. "No one else's." He pulled out, turning me around so my ass was pressed against the desk, then hooked his arm under one of my legs. As he came back into me, we were face to face, nose to nose, eye to eye.

"You're mine," he said again.

And that, being claimed by Tyler, was everything.

"I'm yours," I said, my voice shaking with an oncoming orgasm.

"Come with me, baby," he said.

And I had no choice but to listen. My body would obey his every command. I held on to his shoulders as I tightened around him. He shuddered against me, filling me with the warmth of his come.

As we slowed, he kissed me, hard, then smiled against my mouth. "That was sexy as hell."

I never thought those words would ever be used to describe me, or anything I did, but I agreed. "I think my office is better with you in it."

Grinning, he released my leg and helped me stand, straightened my skirt and my blouse and buttoned his pants. Then he brushed back hair that had fallen from my ponytail, tucking it behind my ear. "We'll have to see if that theory holds true everywhere else." He held up his fingers, ticking them off. "My office, my truck, your car, my apartment..."

I couldn't wait to find out.

## 49

## TYLER

If I could only use one word to describe the last month with Henrietta, it would be... *right*.

Spending time with her, getting to know her and exploring how our bodies fit together... I'd never done anything that came so naturally but felt so electrifying at the same time.

We spent almost every day together, and a lot of nights, she stayed over at my place, quickly turning it from a temporary stay to a home. On Wednesday mornings, she had breakfast with the girls, on Thursday nights, I played poker with the guys, and on the weekends, we hung out with her friends or her family. Her family had a *huge* party when Cordelia came home.

But most of all, I couldn't wait for her to meet my family, see my home. Because each day in Emerson felt like a grain of sand falling to the bottom of the hourglass on our relationship, and there was no way I could ever let her go.

I just hoped she'd be okay with spending Thanksgiving in Texas instead of California like she normally did. We were just a couple weeks away, and I needed to ask soon.

Wanting the request to be special—and to stack the odds in my favor—I printed out the tickets and had them wrapped in a beautiful box with a necklace that had a windmill charm hanging at the end of it.

I stashed the items in my office this morning so when she did her afternoon check-in at the build site, I could give them to her and ask her to come along. That would give us two weeks to prepare for the trip. And to meet my family. They could definitely be a lot.

The build was going along smoothly. We'd only had one permitting delay, and that was back on track now, thanks to a guy on my team whose wife worked at city hall. A few papers may or may not have been moved to the top of the review pile.

With the foundation poured, we were working on framing the first level. I liked this part, where it started looking more like an actual building and not like a big mess of concrete, metal, and broken ground.

I checked my watch again and saw it was about time for Henrietta to get here, but when I told the guys I was going back to the office trailer, I found her already standing outside the building, grinning at me. When we got out of earshot of the workers, she said, "You look sexy working like that." She fanned herself. "Should I be worried that I like the sight of you handling wood?"

I snorted. "I like the sight of me handling you better."

She giggled. "I enjoy that also." The fall sun hit her hair, sending rays bouncing off her black waves.

"You look beautiful today," I said, using all my restraint to keep my hands off her. We tried to keep things professional during the workday, but damn was it hard when I knew how hot she could get for me.

"Thank you," she replied.

We stepped inside my office, and she said, "Is there anything I need to bring by city hall?"

"Not today. Our next checkpoint with the inspectors isn't for another few weeks, so things should be light on your end until then."

She pretended to pout. "Does that mean I don't need to come visit you?"

"If your hot ass isn't on the job site every damn day, we're going to have a problem," I growled.

She laughed. "Where's nice guy Tyler?"

"Right here." I pulled her in, kissing her lips. "And I'll stay that way as long as I have my girl at my side."

"Gosh, you're perfect," she replied. And even though I knew I was far from perfect, I liked hearing the word roll off her tongue.

"Hey, there was something I wanted to talk to you about," I said.

Worry instantly formed a crease between her eyebrows.

"It's nothing bad," I reassured her. "Actually, I'm excited about it."

"What is it?" she asked, the crease disappearing.

I walked around my desk and opened the drawer, pulling out the decorative red box.

"What is this?" she asked, taking it gingerly in her hands.

"I've loved spending these last months with you, Hen, and getting to know your family has been incredible. But my family wants me to go home for Thanksgiving, and I can't stand the idea of going without you."

She watched me, a small smile playing on her lips.

"I want you to meet my parents and get annoyed by my siblings and stare at my brother's office and spend a night under the Texas stars with me."

She bit her bottom lip. "Camping? Won't it be cold in November?"

"Makes cuddling that much better."

Her smile grew, and the suspense was killing me.

Not able to take it any longer, I asked, "Will you go?"

She nodded and wrapped her arms around my shoulders. "I'd love to, Tyler!"

I held her close, breathing in her delicate perfume and loving every damn second. Until the door opened. The only time I'd ever jumped apart from a girl faster was when I got caught making out with my girlfriend in high school.

Rich grinned between the two of us, but didn't say anything about what he'd caught us doing. Instead, he said, "We're at the point where starting the next step would keep the guys here for another hour. Do you want to have them keep going or let them out a little early?"

I glanced at my watch, seeing there were about fifteen minutes left in the workday. "You can send them home. I need to show the boss here what we've been up to."

Rich winked. "I'll tell them to get the show on the road." He turned around and left the trailer, and I shared a guilty smile with Henrietta.

"We should be more careful when the guys are on site," I said.

She nodded. "Definitely."

"But in the meantime." I lifted the lid from the box she was holding. "I thought you should have a piece of home to look forward to."

Her eyes softened as she took it in. "Tyler, it's beautiful."

My lips lifted, her reaction to the necklace was like an acceptance of me, my family. "Can I put this on you?"

She nodded, turning and lifting her hair off her neck. I draped the delicate silver chain around her and clasped the back. It fell against her dark skin, and it took all I had not to place a kiss there.

Instead, I let it go and stepped back. As she turned,

she held her hand to the pendant. And when she removed her fingers so I could get a good look, I smiled. "It's beautiful on you."

"Thank you," she said. "Now why don't you show me the site? It's so different every day."

We walked out of the trailer together, saying goodbye to the workers when they passed us toward the small gravel parking lot. As we approached the building, I started pointing out the foundation, how many steel bars had been laid within the concrete to make sure the building would withstand age and weather and even earthquakes.

Then I showed her the steel framing, long beams that would maintain structural integrity, even in hurricane-force winds. She asked really astute questions, and when I was done, she leaned against one of the walls that had been framed in, shielded from the road.

"It's amazing to think people will live here someday. Hundreds maybe."

"Do you think you'll be working here to see it?" I asked. Because I didn't want to ask the real question—will you move to Texas with me? Would you give up everything you have here so we can build a life together there?

"I don't know yet," she answered. "I've applied for a few jobs, but nothing's come back that would match my salary, and I still have eighteen thousand to save."

Not quite the answer I was hoping for, but it was something.

"You know," she said, "it really was sexy, seeing you working earlier." She trailed her fingers up my polo and undid the top button.

My heart was already speeding. "Yeah?"

She nodded, looking up at me before undoing the next button. "I can see your muscles moving under this shirt when you're working. It's hot knowing my man's so strong and capable with his hands."

My dick twitched, already getting hard. Henrietta, here, in her work dress she knew I loved, was a fucking fantasy. But we'd almost been caught in the office just moments before. I needed to make sure everyone had left first.

"Hold on," I whispered to her. Then I stepped away from the small enclosure and looked outside. The job site was like a ghost town. No one was here to see us, and our vehicles were the only ones in the lot.

Excitement ripped through me as I walked back to her. She gave me a questioning look, and I answered by crossing the small space between us and taking her in a kiss.

But instead of letting me continue to kiss her senseless, she dropped to her knees in front of me.

"Hen..." I said.

She only answered by wrapping her mouth around my cock. And I was gone, lost in the feel of her mouth around me, lost in the grip of her hands on my thighs, lost in the sexy suckling sounds she made on my cock and the gagging sound she made when she took me too far in.

And then I was lost in my orgasm, in the heady rush of knowing my cum was spilling down her throat.

She licked her lips and smiled up at me, fire dancing in her eyes. "How was that?"

"Unbefucklinglievable," I said, my voice hoarse.

She laughed. "Good. Now let's go get some supper. Although I am feeling a little full." And then my girl winked.

God, I loved her.

## 50

## HENRIETTA

*Confession: This trip had me more nervous than I'd ever been.*

GRANDMA SAT on her walker by my bed while I packed for my trip to visit Tyler's family. "Are you excited?" she asked.

"Nervous is more like it. I'm going to be meeting his entire family for the first time, and I'm all in my head about it," I replied, taking a dress out of my suitcase for the third time. "I've checked the weather forecast about ten times, and I still can't decide if it'll be warm enough to wear a dress while we're there."

"Then wear pants," Grandma said. "It's not like they're going to see you in slacks and say, 'Nope. Not good enough for our son.'"

I gave her a look. "Is it just me or are you sassier since you got home from the hospital?"

"Why don't you wear some of those leggings with a longer dress shirt? You look so cute in those outfits."

I nodded. She was right. And I was definitely overthinking this. "But what if his family doesn't like big girls?" I asked. "It'll be a long five days if they're disgusted by me."

Grandma said, "You're not asking the right question."

I faced her, waiting for her to explain. She knew it was true—some people thought being overweight was a moral failing. They judged people like me to no end.

She lifted her hands, her elbows resting on the walker, and said, "You need to be asking, 'What if they are warm, kind, loving people? What if I love Texas? What if this brings Tyler and me that much closer together?'" She smiled. "And if you must be negative, you can ask, 'What if I can't stand them?' Because you are incredible, my dear. If they don't like you, there's clearly something wrong with them. Enough with the stinkin' thinkin'."

I set down the shirt I was folding and went to give her a hug. "Thanks, Grandma." But there was still something holding me back… "I feel like I have to address the elephant in the room."

"And what is that?" she asked.

"I'm a Black woman from California, and Tyler's a white man from outside of Dallas, Texas, one of the most conservative places in the country. What if we don't fit in together there? What if the community doesn't welcome me?"

She twisted her lips to the side deepening her wrinkles. "You know the world's changed so much since I was younger. I lived through the Loving case, and some people still think the courts got it wrong…"

My chest got tight in the way it always did thinking about racist people, the bias some people had against me and people like me. Most of the time I tried to ignore it, but now? It was all I could think about.

"You know, it's hard to believe you two have only been together for a few months. It feels like he's been a part of our family from day one." She shrugged. "Seems to me a man like that wouldn't take you anywhere that could cause you harm. And if for some reason, an issue did arise, a man like that would nip it in the bud faster than you could blink."

I nodded, feeling light enough to get back to folding some blouses to put in my suitcase. Tyler would keep me safe, just like he'd protected me that night from Houston. "He's so easy to be around. I wonder if his family is the same way."

"There you go," Grandma said with a wink.

"What are you going to do without me here to boss around?" I asked in a teasing tone, but part of me was worried about her. I wanted her to be safe when I was gone, and I had been filling in the gaps here lately, especially since it was hard to get on the senior ride with her walker. I'd been taking her to appointments and the store when Mom and Dad couldn't.

"It's only a week," Grandma said. "And besides, you know they have special buses for *old, feeble* people like me. I just need to get signed up."

"I didn't call you feeble."

"You didn't deny the old part," she retorted.

"Didn't need to." I winked.

She rolled her eyes.

I scanned my suitcase, deciding I had everything I needed and probably a lot more. "I think that's it."

From the doorway, I heard Tyler's voice say, "Good timing."

He looked so handsome, changed out of his work clothes into a pair of jeans that fit him so well it should be a crime. And with his arm propped up against the doorframe, I could see a sliver of his fit stomach. If he stood like that much longer, I'd need a mop to wipe up all this drool.

Grandma looked between me and him. "I hope you have a great Thanksgiving with your family, Tyler. Although, we call the next one."

I loved the way she assumed we'd be together, because I was hoping the same thing. Even though I had no idea how it would work with him at his next job site, wherever it would be, and me in California. In fact, I tried not to think about it at all.

I'd wanted to move out from my parents' house, but

now that Grandma needed so much extra help... I just didn't know how that would work. Would my family be able to pick up the slack if I moved all the way to Texas? Would I be able to forgive myself if they did?

Tyler said, "Can I carry your bags for you, Hen?"

I nodded, passing him my suitcase and picking up my purse filled to the brim with the essentials.

Grandma extended her arms for another hug, which I gladly took.

"Give my brothers hell for me," I said.

"You know I will," she replied, squeezing me just a little tighter before letting me go.

Mom and Dad said goodbye to us in the living room, wishing us well, and soon we were on the road to Tyler's apartment. It was easier for me to stay with him so we could get up early for our drive to LA.

Instead of eating out, we grabbed some takeout on the way and walked up the steps to his apartment. As soon as we walked through the door, the smell of his leather and linen candles enveloped me, making me smile. "I need to ask your sister to make me some of these candles so I can light them in the office."

"I'm sure she'd love that," Tyler said, squeezing my hand.

He set up dinner at the table, and we ate while he gave me all the details and quirks I might need to know about his family. He said his brother Rhett would flirt with me, his sister would probably want to take me horseback riding (which sounded like a ton of fun), and his brother Gage would probably spend way too much money on whatever we did. But then he said his mom would love me, and I already felt more at ease. He loved his mom more than anyone in the world, and if I passed her test, I had no doubt this relationship would be something that would last.

With dinner done and Tyler doing what was left of his dishes, I excused myself to take a shower. The water pressure here was incredible. I took my time, shaving my legs, brushing out my hair, and then rubbing coconut oil all over my body. I loved using it as a natural moisturizer, and it smelled amazing. Plus, I knew Tyler liked it too.

I walked to his bedroom and reached into his closet for the oversized T-shirts he kept especially for me because he thought they were sexy. I slipped one over my head, no underwear or bra underneath, and walked to the living room.

Where Janessa was edging her way into the apartment.

My mouth fell open, and I quickly turned to leave, but it was too late. We'd been caught.

## 51

## TYLER

I clenched my jaw, mentally cussing Janessa for being so damn pushy. She'd literally invited herself into my apartment to "make sure it was up to par", even though I'd said, multiple times, that I wasn't feeling well.

Of course, now I was caught in the lie, and Henrietta had been caught half naked.

Janessa's eyes widened as she looked between Henrietta and me, processing what she saw, and then her gaze narrowed with recognition. "What do we have here?" she asked.

Henrietta chirped, "I'll be right back." She pulled the hem of her shirt down and hurried to the bedroom, leaving Janessa and me standing alone.

"Well, now I know why you've been turning me down," Janessa said. "Not that I understand the allure."

Protective rage quickly rose in my chest, spewing out my mouth. "Watch it."

She lifted her eyebrows, an amused smile on her lips. "Look at those claws coming out."

My jaw twitched with bitten-back words. If she uttered one more negative comment about my girl, she'd regret it.

But her smile fell back into place, and she said, "Henrietta, how nice to see you in your clothes."

I looked over my shoulder to see Henrietta walking down the hallway toward us. Her hair was still wet, but now she had on a cotton dress and house shoes.

"Janessa, I wasn't expecting to see you here," Hen said, a smile on her face that didn't reach her eyes.

"I could say the same." She stepped farther into the apartment, brushing her fingers along the back of my couch and thumbing away the dust. "I thought we had a talk about dating Tyler being against the rules."

The audacity of this woman, pushing her way into my home and then shaming Henrietta for doing the same thing she had wanted. My voice was tight as I said, "I informed Henrietta of your very direct, and failed, attempts at flirting with me."

Janessa's smile only faltered for a minute. "That was only banter, Tyler."

Henrietta narrowed her gaze. "I called Frannie. She told me the truth—she was fired for coming to work late *because she had morning sickness,* not for hooking up with Jeremy."

"Same difference," Janessa said as if her lies were no big deal.

Henrietta said, "I'm sure the shareholders wouldn't be happy that Blue Bird only hired Crenshaw Construction for your own selfish crush on Tyler."

"That wasn't at all the plan," Janessa sputtered.

Henrietta lifted her chin. "You met with Tyler and his boss prior to hiring. I doubt your denial will prove anything."

Changing tactics, Janessa stepped between Hen and me. "Henrietta, I thought we were friends. Are you really going to let some guy come between us?"

My gut sank, waiting to hear Hen's answer.

"I thought we were friends too," Hen said, a quiver in her voice. "We've worked together for eight years, and you had no problem lying to me because I told you he was cute. That's *not* what friends do. You are no friend of mine."

Any hint of Janessa's fake smile was gone. "Fine. Enjoy each other. Although I have no idea how that's possible."

Henrietta's jaw fell, and I stepped forward, holding my hand on the door so Janessa couldn't open it. She needed to hear this—and Henrietta did too.

"You want to know why I chose Henrietta when you were so clearly interested? I chose her because I could have a conversation with her without feeling like a piece of meat. Henrietta is intelligent and kind and clearly cares about the people who live here and making them feel safe and comfortable. And I don't know if you've seen her curves, but they're sexy as hell. So I will not be having any more negative talk about her from a desperate, jealous woman like you. Especially not in my own damn home."

Janessa grit her teeth before ripping open the door and leaving the apartment. "You'll regret this," she said in the hallway. "I'll make sure of it."

I shut the door in her face.

I turned toward Henrietta, gripping her shoulders in my hands. "Are you okay? I'm so sorry about what she said."

Henrietta lifted her chin and kissed me. "Thank you for standing up for me like that."

"Of course."

"But are you freaking crazy?" she asked, hitting my shoulder. "Janessa is a powerful woman, and she's clearly not above lying. What if she gets the CEO to fire Crenshaw?"

"She can't. We have a contract in place saying we finish the project unless there are legitimate safety or quality concerns. We do everything by the book on site. She's all talk." I wrapped my arms around Henrietta's waist. "Now, can you go put that shirt back on?" I bit the shell of her ear. "I want to see you bent over the couch with nothing underneath."

Her voice was rough as she said, "Whatever you tell me to do, it's done."

## 52

## HENRIETTA

*Confession: I'm still trying to remind myself that I'm not too big for certain things—they are just too small for me.*

MOST OF THE time I could forget my size. But there were certain things that made me hate the way fat people were treated in this world. Clothes shopping was number one—most people relegated you to one tiny corner of the store, and it was even harder when you tried to thrift most of your clothes.

And then there was basically anything that included chairs. Being forced to stand in waiting rooms because you knew you couldn't squeeze your butt between the arms of the chair. Forget amusement parks—the shame of having to exit the ride because you can't fit and then hearing people whisper, or even talk loudly about you as you walk away. It's a form of torture no one deserves.

But then, there's getting on an airplane. Walking down the rows and every person looking away because they don't want you in their row. People skipping by you because they don't want to sit next to you.

This time, though, I had Tyler with me. We'd sit side by side, and he'd already offered to take the middle seat so I could see Texas from the air. I hadn't traveled much, but he said when you flew over the Midwest, you could see little squares of farm ground below. I couldn't wait.

I walked ahead, since he insisted on carrying my bags, and found us a seat a few rows behind the wings. I scooted into the seat and reached for my belt, and then it hit me.

No matter how much I sucked, squeezed, or adjusted myself, my seat belt would not reach all the way around my waist. My eyes stung as I let loose of the clip and looked out the window. I felt Tyler's shoulder brush against me, but I kept my eyes away.

I was so embarrassed. He knew I was a big girl, had seen me naked and told me I was sexy, but this felt way too much like reality compared to the blissful fantasy we'd been living in. This was part of dating a big girl, and I didn't want to find out that he actually couldn't handle it.

He leaned over, resting his chin on my shoulder. "It's kinda nice that the seats are small so we can cuddle the whole way."

"Yeah," I said, but my voice cracked. I really freaking wish it hadn't cracked.

"Hen, are you okay?"

I tried to blink back tears. "I'm fine." Was there a way to fold my belly over the belt so the flight attendant couldn't see if it was buckled?

"Baby, look at me. What's going on?"

I closed my eyes, wishing for a moment that I could be smaller. That this wouldn't be an issue I had to worry about.

"Do you not want to meet my family anymore?" he asked.

The worry in his voice gutted me. And I hated to make him worry when it wasn't his problem; it's mine.

"The belt doesn't fit," I whispered, blinking back hot tears. One slid down my cheek, and I wiped it away.

"Oh, that's no big deal," he said. He turned away from me, and when he spotted a flight attendant walking by, he said, "Excuse me, sir, can I get a belt extender for my girlfriend?"

"Of course," the guy said, like it was no big deal. He handed one to Tyler, and then Tyler passed it to me, and I held the clip in my hand, staring at it.

"Here," he said gently. He took it back and hooked it on his side of me, then he reached across my midsection, finding the other side of my belt. Once it was all clipped into place, he kissed my cheek. "Look, you're all belted in. No need to be embarrassed."

I looked at him, studying his molten hazel eyes and wondering what he saw in me. If he ever wished he was with someone who would... fit better into the way the world expected beautiful people like him to live.

He held my face in his hands and kissed me softly.

And it was better. Already it was better. And he hadn't even said a word. I knew I had to talk to him about something else, to help the worry that hadn't quite left my system since my talk with Grandma.

"Maybe there is something else," I admitted, biting my lip.

"What is it?" he asked.

I ran my hands over my legs, trying to remove the sweat from my palms. "Tyler, I'm Black."

He chuckled slightly. "I know that."

"Does your family know that?"

He seemed confused by my question. "Well, yeah. I sent them a picture pretty soon after I bought plane tickets. My sister thinks you're gorgeous, by the way."

I smiled slightly. "It's just... Texas isn't always well-known for being welcoming to different kinds of people. With you being from a small-town... Not that I'm saying every person who comes from a small town in a red state is racist, but maybe if they don't see a lot of people like me." My eyes were stinging again as I struggled to get out the words, struggled to express my fears. I wiped at my tears. "I don't want to feel out of place when I'm there, and I don't want you to change your mind," I whispered.

Tyler held my face in both of his hands. "I need you to hear this."

I nodded.

"What other people think about you will never change the way I see you, right now. You are perfect, kind, sexy as hell, *and* Black. It's a part of you, just like your family and your heart and that beautiful brain in your head. And *if* we come across anyone who judges you, they have another fucking thing coming. I promise, I won't let anyone tear you down without ripping out their ass hole and pulling it over their head."

I couldn't help but laugh at his violence. Tyler was always a gentleman, but when it came to me, I knew he'd defend me, no matter what it took.

"I'm serious," he said. "But I also want you to know that Cottonwood Falls is different from what you see on the news. The people there look out for each other, no matter if you've been there five days or fifty years. They're going to love you."

"Thank you," I said, my chest finally relaxing. "I needed to hear that."

"Of course. Is there anything else? I want you to be excited, not scared."

"Not at all. It just helps knowing you have my back."

He kissed my forehead. "Of course I do."

I lifted the armrest between us and leaned against his shoulder. "What do you usually do on flights?" I asked, trying to distract myself. "I haven't been on one since I was little."

"I usually just find a movie on the airline's list and watch that." He got out his phone, going to the in-flight Wi-Fi. My eyes widened in horror as he paid the eight dollars for advanced access.

"What are you doing?" I asked. "We can go a few hours without internet."

"But what if you want to watch something they don't have?"

I laughed and shook my head. "We haven't even been through the list yet!"

"Yeah, but what my baby wants, my baby gets. That's worth way more than eight dollars to me."

Tears of a new kind found my eyes. "How did I get so lucky with you?" Because really, I felt like the luckiest girl in the world—he wasn't ashamed of my size, he supported my dreams, and he was even flying me across the country because he wanted me to see his hometown.

He kissed me again, making butterflies dance in my stomach. "I've been asking myself the same question ever since you agreed to that first date." Then he kissed the top of my head. "So, what do you want to watch, baby girl? We have the internet at our fingertips."

## 53

## TYLER

We were midway through our second movie when the pilot said we'd crossed the Texas border. Hen looked away from my phone and leaned close to the window.

"Look at the little squares!"

The joy in her voice made me smile so damn big. I looked over her shoulder, seeing all the farmland below. My chest swelled with pride, knowing that less than two percent of the population was growing food for all of the US and then some. My family was part of that number.

"What are the squares with circles?" Hen asked.

"Those are the ones with center pivots. They're like giant sprinklers that spin around the field."

"Way cool," she said, looking back at me for a moment. "I've seen some farmland in California, but not like this." We watched the landscape go by as it gave way from open space and farmland to the bustling city streets of Dallas.

The pilot announced our descent, and she smiled over at me.

"Will your parents pick us up?" she asked.

I shook my head. "I have a truck in long-term parking. We'll get lunch, and then I'll drive you out to the farm. Everyone's excited to meet you."

Her nervous smile wrenched my heart. But if she knew how much I cared for her, she'd know how little she had to worry. My parents weren't the kind to judge—if we kids were happy, then they were happy. (Even if Rhett had them shaking their heads from time to time.)

We grabbed our suitcases from the baggage claim and then went out to the parking lot. It had been a few months since my truck had been driven, but it was nice and clean and fired right up.

"Why do you keep a truck out here?" Henrietta asked.

"It's just easier not to bother anyone when I come to town. Cottonwood Falls is about two hours from the airport."

"Oh wow," she said. "You really are from the boonies."

"Hey," I laughed.

We joked and talked until we got to the restaurant for lunch, and then we talked some more, and then it was time to take her to the farm. On the drive, I pointed out every special place to me. There was the turnoff that led to a cornfield where I lost my virginity in the back of my truck. (Original, I know.) And then there was the rival school our football team always beat despite having half as many guys on the team. We drove past the movie theater where we took all our dates.

Then I saw something that caught me off guard. A for-sale sign in front of the old schoolhouse. Both of my parents had gone to school in this building, but they built a new school before my siblings and I started. For the last thirty years, the local hardware store had used it for extra storage.

I stopped in front of the building, staring from the sign to the building.

They were selling it.

"What is this?" Hen asked, looking at the brick facade through the window. "Did you go to school here?"

I shook my head. "My parents did... I always thought it was stupid that they filled it with junk instead of using it."

"Using it for what?" Hen asked.

"With all that square footage, it would make a great apartment building. People would go crazy over the historical details inside—if they haven't been completely ruined."

Hen got out her phone, tapping on the screen.

"I know it's not that interesting but—"

She held up her finger, putting her phone to her ear. After a couple seconds, she said, "Hey, we were wondering if we could take a tour of the schoolhouse?... I mean, we're here now.... Great! I'll see you in a few minutes."

I stared at Hen. "What did you do?"

She laughed, pushing her door open. "I wanted to see inside. Why don't we look around until the agent gets here?"

Shaking my head, I followed Hen out of the truck. Life with her was certainly an adventure.

She walked over the unkempt buffalo grass to the big front stoop. "This would be a beautiful common area for an apartment building—you could set up some benches and people could actually get to know their neighbors."

I pictured the peeling paint over the cement done up freshly, maybe even covered with a wooden deck, and rocking chairs lined along the building. Add some hanging plants, and it could be a beautiful place to pass an afternoon with a glass of sweet tea.

She walked to the side of the porch, looking around the back. "The playground is dangerous, but if you took it out, there would be plenty of room for a big community garden and maybe even another sitting area?"

I put my arm around her, loving the way she dreamed. "Imagine it being a senior living building," I said. "Grandpa would love it here, closer to home."

"I love that!" she said, twisting in my arms to give me a kiss.

Tires crunched on gravel, and we looked over to see

Linda Macomb walking our way. I lifted a hand and said, "Hi, Linda."

She peeled off her black sunglasses, revealing light blue eyes. "Tyler Griffen, is that you? I haven't seen you since you were scoring touchdowns!"

I chuckled, turning to Hen. "Linda, this is my girlfriend, Hen."

Hen smiled, shaking Linda's pale hand. "Nice to meet you."

"You too, darling. Let me show you around."

We went into the school, and it was about as rundown as I'd expected. Even though the hardware store had taken out most of their stuff, there was a layer of dirt on the floor an inch thick. All the windows were dirty and cobwebbed. But I'd been right—this place had been built in the early 1900s. So much detail had gone into woodwork back then, before the minimalism trend hit.

As we walked outside, Linda asked, "Thinking of buying it?"

Hen glanced at me, her eyes full of curiosity.

"It's a pipe dream," I said. "I travel too much to ever be able to do it justice."

"That's a shame," Linda said. She reached into her purse and handed me a business card. Her photo on it had to be from ten years ago. "Call me if anything changes."

I assured her I would, and then Hen and I got in the truck. From the schoolhouse, it was a right turn and an easy shot out of town.

"It's so different from Emerson," Hen said, gazing around as we drove down the dirt road that led to Griffen Farms. It was a beautiful fall day, low sixties, and the sun was shining. All the cottonwood trees had brown and yellow leaves, and even the grass was turning from green to yellow. Something about this place just made my heart feel lighter.

"It's home," I said.

"I bet you get so homesick when you're on the road."

I nodded, squeezing her hand. "The air's just different here."

She smiled, then her look changed to surprise. Pointing out the windshield, she asked, "Are those llamas?"

"Alpacas," I said. "When I was about five, the Deans decided alpacas were better than cattle. They've had ostriches, emus, even camels one year. It's always fun to see what they've got going."

Hen giggled. "Who would have thought? Camels in Texas."

"We're full of surprises."

"Any camels on your farm?"

I shook my head. "But Dad did buy a goat one year because he was tired of mowing the lawn."

She laughed. "Don't mention that to my dad. He would actually buy one."

"It's all fun and games until you see goat hoofprints on your car."

"They jump?" she asked, seemingly surprised and amused.

"Oh yeah. And they'll headbutt you if you're not paying attention."

She covered her mouth as she giggled. "I'm imagining a little goat running up on you before school."

"You're not too far off." The metal arch leading to my family's farm appeared on the side of the road, and I pointed it out. "That's us."

I slowed and watched her smile as she read the letters.

*Griffen Farms*

Then she gazed at the white farmhouse farther down the road. "Tyler, it's beautiful! Like something out of a picture book."

I followed her gaze, trying to see it with new eyes. This place had always been home, but it certainly was beautiful. Mom and Dad lived in a two-story white farmhouse with red shutters and a wraparound porch Mom kept decorated with hanging planters full of flowers and spider plants. The grassy yard spilled into a buffalo grass prairie, and just beyond the house, you could spot the red barn and the horse pen.

"It was fun to grow up here," I said. "Like the whole world was my backyard."

She gazed out the window toward the black and red cattle dotting the hillside. One of my favorite views. With the windows down, you could hear the occasional moo.

That, mixed with the breeze rustling the grass, was one of my favorite sounds.

We parked in the gravel drive alongside the house where Rhett and Liv's cars were already parked.

"Do we need to get our bags?" Hen asked.

"I can grab them later." I smiled over at her and said, "I can't wait for you to meet them. They're going to love you."

"As long as you love me," she said.

I gave her a quick kiss to let her know that hadn't changed and got out of the truck to open her door. As we walked to the house, I kept my arm around her shoulders, and she hooked hers around my waist.

I was so proud to bring this woman home. Her wit, her humor, her heart... she was the complete catch.

Before we reached the door, Mom pushed it open and greeted us on the porch. "Honey!"

I let go of Hen to hug my mom, then stepped back, my arm around my mom's shoulders, and said, "This is her."

Mom covered her mouth with her hands. "Henrietta, you're just as beautiful as he said you were." She extended her hand to shake Henrietta's. "My name's Deidre. It's so nice to meet you."

Hen shook my mom's hand. "You can call me Hen."

"Love it," Mom said, holding on to Henrietta's hand. "Come meet the rest of the family."

# 54

## HENRIETTA

*Confession: I love a family man.*

DEIDRE HAD her hand linked with mine as she led me into their home. It was beautiful, with what looked like original hardwood floors, big picture windows with a view of the prairie, and the people inside were just as good-looking.

The one woman in the room close to my age was beautiful with curvy hips and a sweet, heart-shaped face. She had long, brown hair with natural curl, and her eyes were the same shade of green as Tyler's. I liked her instantly.

She said, "I'm Tyler's sister, Olivia, but everyone calls me Liv."

"Nice to meet you," I said, shaking her hand.

A guy who stood a couple inches taller than Tyler's six-foot height stepped forward, laying hazel eyes with thick brown lashes on me. "I'm Rhett, the good-looking one."

Tyler snorted behind me. "More like the cocky one."

"That too," Rhett said, extending his hand. "Pleased to meet you, Hen."

I shook his rough hand and smiled at him. "Same here."

Tyler put his arm back around my waist as the elder Griffen stepped forward. His dad looked so much like him, tall and strong, except he had a brown mustache peppered with gray hairs, and his tanned face was full of wrinkles.

"Jack," he said as he shook my hand. "Glad to have you on the farm."

"It's stunning," I said. "Tyler's told me all about it and how much he loved growing up out here."

Deidre smiled. "He was a good kid when he wasn't hiding in the trees, trying to get out of doing chores."

I laughed, remembering Tyler telling me about that. "There are more places to hide out here than there are in the city."

"One of the many benefits," Tyler said.

Deidre shook her head with a smile. "I thought Tyler, Rhett, and Liv could take you on a tour of the farm while Jack and I get dinner ready. We have some Griffen select steaks we'd love for you to try." She glanced at Tyler. "She does eat meat, right?"

"As if I'd bring home a girl who couldn't house a steak," Tyler said.

Olivia laughed. "He knows better than that."

The banter between them made me smile. I'd only ever seen Tyler around my family or on his own, but seeing him so close with his siblings and parents brought out another side of him that only made me love him even more. I'd always wanted to be with a family man, and Tyler delivered that and so much more.

Deidre asked, "Do you need to get freshened up before you go out?"

Tyler said, "Let me show her the room and bring our bags in."

"Good idea," his mom said.

"I'll get the bags," Rhett offered. "Are they under the shell?"

Tyler nodded and then led me toward the stairs in the corner of the living room. They had a beautiful oak railing, and as we walked up, I imagined all the mornings Tyler had come down these stairs, all the touches that had worn this rail smooth. It was like the house had a history all its own.

"Are we staying in your old room?" I asked as we crested the stairs.

"We are," Tyler said. "I hope my mom hid my 'unmentionables.'"

I elbowed him in the stomach with a laugh. "I'm pretty sure I've seen all of those already."

The wood floors creaked under foot as we walked down the hall. Tyler tapped on one door, opening it to a bathroom that had clearly been remodeled with black and white floor tile and a walk-in shower backed with pretty green tile. "This is the bathroom. You can imagine it was fun to share before school with four kids."

"Just about as fun as ours was to share," I said. I loved that we both had big families, so we understood each other in that way.

He stopped at the bedroom at the end of the hall and pushed the door open. "Home sweet home." I stepped through the doorway, taking it all in, from the full-size bed on a wooden frame to the west-facing windows that gave him a stunning view of the barn and everything that lay beyond it. You could see forever here, and something about that set my heart at peace.

Tearing my gaze away from the view, I saw mostly bare walls. "Where are all the posters of naked ladies?" I teased.

Tyler leaned against his wooden dresser and said, "I told you it's not much."

He must not be a decorator. In fact, I only saw a calendar from nearly ten years ago hanging by his dresser. It was open to a page of a boy standing with a calf on a leash.

"Oh my gosh, is that you?" I walked closer, grinning giddily at the little Tyler. "Oh my gosh, you were so cute!

That plaid shirt was way too big on you, but you rocked those Wranglers!"

"I was fifteen and wore Gage's hand-me-downs half the time," he protested. "But I got on the calendar for winning grand champion with my bucket calf."

"I only understood about half of that," I admitted.

He folded his arms across his muscular chest. "It means I was the best."

"Looking to replace Rhett with the cocky-brother title?" I teased.

"No way," Rhett said, pushing in the door with two rolling suitcases and both of our duffel bags. "Plus, you're losing at the strongest title."

Tyler rolled his eyes. "You're a child."

Rhett stuck out his tongue. "A strong one."

I laughed at the two of them. "Is it always like this?"

"Most of the time," Tyler answered at the same time Rhett said, "When he's home."

While Rhett helped Tyler get our bags unpacked and they teased each other mercilessly, I excused myself to the bathroom. I took my time, looking in the mirror and making sure my hair was okay and none of my makeup had gotten messed up on the plane.

When I came out of the bathroom, I walked down the hall, hearing voices in the bedroom. Rhett said, "Did you see the way Mom looked at her? I think she's already in love."

"It's impossible not to love Hen," Tyler said.

"I get where you're coming from," Rhett replied. "Not in a 'steal yo' girl' way, but a 'man, my brother is lucky way.'"

I smiled at their conversation and made sure the floorboards creaked on my next step.

They went silent, and I reached the doorway. "Ready when you are."

## 55

## TYLER

The second we got outside, Liv ran to the pickup and reached the front door. "I'm driving!"

"Shotgun!" Hen called.

Rhett and I stared at each other, stunned, as our sister and my girlfriend got in the front of the ranch truck.

Liv fired up the truck and craned her head out the open driver's side window. "You snooze, you lose!"

"I feel like I'm five again," I muttered.

Rhett patted my shoulder. "Can't win 'em all."

We walked to the truck, and I got in the seat catty-cornered to Hen, wanting to see all her reactions to the ranch as we drove along. After Rhett climbed in, Liv put the truck in drive and started down the rutted trail toward the barn.

Liv pointed out Hen's window. "This is the barn up

here, and we keep the horses in the pen right next to it, especially this time of year, so we can supplement their feed. That black and white horse is Rhett's. The reddish-brown one is Dad's. And then that darker brown one is kind of like the family horse. Whoever's helping out gets to ride it because it's the oldest and the easiest."

"I call that one," Hen said with a smile.

"We'll take you out on a ride to the creek tomorrow," I said, excited to show her one of my favorite spots.

Liv stopped in front of the gate to the main pasture and said, "Rhett, you grab the gate."

"No way," he said. "Hen's shotgun; she gets it."

"She's our guest," Liv said.

Rhett shrugged, a smirk on his lips. "Rules are rules."

"Come on, Hen," I got out of the truck, and she climbed down too.

"What's this shotgun rule?" she asked, walking to the gate with me.

"When we were younger, we always argued about who got to ride up front, so Dad's rule was whoever sat shotgun had to open the gates. Made it a little less appealing. Especially because some of these are hard to open."

"How do you do it?" she asked, a look of determination on her face.

That's my girl.

I walked up to the barbed-wire fence and pointed at the pole looped through with wire to hold the fence up. "You push your shoulder against that, then move the wire up over the post. After that, you should be able to slip it out and move it to the side. But you're in that dress. I can do it."

"No way will I give Rhett more ammo to tease me with," she said.

I laughed, hands up. "I knew you would fit right in."

She grit her teeth and carefully lifted her arm over the barbed wire, pushing the gate post, and then lifted the wire over the top. "Easy peasy," she said, pulling the gate to the side so Liv could drive the truck through.

"Hen's a baddie!" Liv called on her ride past us.

Hen grinned, and damn, I was grinning too.

We slid back into our seats, and Rhett said, "Hen, if this dumbass doesn't marry you, I will."

He might have been joking, but I punched him in the shoulder just in case. No way was he coming anywhere near my girl.

She tossed her head back and laughed, and with the wind fluttering through her hair, she looked like she'd descended straight from heaven's gates.

Hen held on to the oh-shit handle as we bumped over the pasture, and Liv pointed out everything around us. She told Hen about our neighbors who had been renting their grass to us for the last fifty years so our cattle would have plenty to graze. Then she showed Hen the copse of trees in the corner by the creek that ran in the summer or after heavy rains in other times of year.

As we crested another hill, the feedlot came to view.

"This is where we feed cattle in the winter and after weaning," Liv explained. "Since the grass has been eaten down, it gives us a chance to make sure they're getting good nutrition and are well taken care of."

Hen nodded, taking it all in. "It sounds like a lot of work."

Rhett said, "Twenty-four-seven, three-sixty-five."

Liv nodded. "It's like having three hundred thousand-pound kids."

Laughing, Hen said, "I imagine finding a sitter is difficult."

"We trade off on the weekends," Rhett said. "That way Dad can get a break from time to time."

I tried not to feel guilty for not being around—being a part of this family had always meant helping out—but I reminded myself that it was Dad's choice to keep the ranch small. One call to Gage and he'd have an investor to help expand the operation. They were both just too damn proud.

I must have been deep in my thoughts, because I jerked back when Hen said, "Windmill!"

I looked where she was pointing and saw our windmill in the corner of the far pasture. Its dark iron silhouette stood out against the background of the pasture, its spokes spinning quickly in the breeze.

Liv drove us up to it, parking on the worn-down dirt several feet away from the tank. She stopped the engine and got out. The country played its own kind of music.

The drop of water into the tank. The clod of cows' hooves on the dirt. The rustle of wind against the grass. It was my favorite song.

As we got closer to the cows, they backed away. Hen watched them with wonder. "I don't think I've ever seen a cow this close up."

"That's crazy," Liv said. "They should put them in zoos or something so people can see them."

"Yeah," Hen agreed. "I've only ever seen goats, chickens, and rabbits in a petting zoo. Never a cow."

She looked away from the cows to the tank, tipping her head back to take in the windmill. "How tall is it?"

"About twenty feet," I said.

Hen approached the tank and trailed her fingers through the water.

Liv did the same and said, "In the summers when the creek was dry, we'd come over here to cool off."

Hen laughed. "I bet the cows love Griffen-flavored water."

Rhett nudged my arm, whispering loudly, "Funny too? Get a move on, man."

I shook my head at him. For someone who was so... free with his relationships, he certainly was pressuring me to settle down. But I couldn't blame him. I'd been having the same thoughts myself, in between the fears of what would happen when my time was up in Emerson.

"Come on," Liv said. "We should show her the hay loft."

## 56

## HENRIETTA

*Confession: If I'm being honest, I have no idea how we'll figure this out.*

"NO." I stared at the wooden boards nailed to the wall of the barn, then stared at Tyler. "No way are those holding me up."

While I hesitated, Rhett easily took the ladder up and disappeared through the hole in the ceiling of the dusty barn. It was dim in here, just a few plexiglass windows offering light filled with dust motes. The whole place smelled like dust and composting earth and something else I couldn't quite place.

Liv winked at me. "They're stronger than they look.

See?" She reached for them and started climbing up. The wood bowed a little under her weight, but it held steady.

In my ear, Tyler teased, "I'm here to catch you."

"More like break my fall," I retorted, reaching for a rung at shoulder height. Very aware that a dress was not the best idea for this, I put my foot up on a rung and hoisted myself up, not breathing for fear of falling.

Tyler whistled below me and said, "Beautiful view down here."

I sent him a glare over my shoulder but couldn't help my smile. I faced the ladder again, climbing until I crested the hole in the ceiling. Or floor, depending on your perspective. I kept my eyes forward, seeing tiny cobwebs and even a couple of brown spiders hanging out on the wooden wall. Then when I was high enough, Rhett said, "Here, take my hand."

I let go of my death grip on the wooden rung and squeezed his hand. He easily pulled me closer to him so I fell against his chest. He waggled his eyebrows, and I rolled my eyes at him.

I stepped back, brushing dust off my dress, and looked around in awe just as twinkle lights came on. Liv walked away from the outlet to stand beside me. "What do you think?" she asked.

My eyes were glued to the building. There was a rough wood plank floor, light green and yellow hay bales stacked along the walls, a rope swing in the middle, and even a wooden couch and a refrigerator back against the wall.

"This is like every kid's dream," I said.

Tyler put his arm around me—he must have come up without me even noticing. "We hung out here all the time. Snuck beer out here too when we were teenagers."

"Mom and Dad totally knew," Liv said.

"Don't they always?" I cringed internally, thinking of my first encounter with alcohol when Bertrand bought a bottle of vodka off some guy in the streets of LA. We both drank so much one night when Mom and Dad were out that we puked all over the bathroom. Of course Mom and Dad knew, and our punishment was cleaning vomit hungover. Never would I ever drink that much again.

Tyler said, "I think they were just happy we were getting drunk out here and not going anywhere else and driving afterward."

Rhett tapped his nose. It was fun to see Tyler's gesture on his brother. I wondered what my brothers and I had in common—if Tyler had noticed.

"Check this out," Liv said. She walked to the front wall of the barn, unhooked the latch, and swung the door open. As I approached the opening, I first noticed how high we were—at least ten feet in the air. And then I saw the view. From here, you could see the horses in the grazing pen, cattle on the hillside, and the beautiful farmhouse they grew up in.

"Wow," I breathed. No wonder Tyler loved growing up here. It was incredible, and I couldn't believe I'd gone my whole life up until now without experiencing it.

I looked over at him and laced my fingers through his. He smiled at me, happier than I'd ever seen him. "I'm so glad you came," he said.

"Me too."

Liv glanced at the smart watch on her wrist and said, "We should probably get back and wash up for dinner."

We all made our way to the ladder. Liv went down first, and I gave the loft one last look before following her down to the floor of the barn. While she and Rhett took the truck back to the house, Tyler and I walked the few hundred-yards distance, with our arms around each other.

With the sun sinking down, it was getting cooler, but I felt so warm with the excitement of the day. And as we got closer, I could smell the most heavenly scents coming from the house. "It smells amazing," I said.

"Dad's the best on the grill," Tyler said. "Mom told me they're setting up the heaters outside and we'll eat on the porch."

I smiled. "That sounds so fun. And I love your siblings. Liv is so beautiful and nice, and Rhett, well, he's a handful."

Tyler laughed. "That's one way to put it."

"At least I know he likes me," I teased. Rhett's comments about putting a ring on my finger had been all in good fun. But despite the fact that Tyler and I had been together just a short while, I hoped that's where this was heading. It was like Grandma said with Grandpa—she just knew he was the one.

There was a knowing in my heart that this man beside me was meant to be in my life. Not just for a little while, but forever.

Tyler opened the door to the house for me, and we went upstairs to wash up for supper. Since we were eating outside, I changed into a pair of leggings and a sweater so I'd be nice and warm. When I came out of the bathroom, Tyler was still in his jeans and T-shirt, and damn, did he look good.

"Have I ever mentioned how sexy you are with that tattoo peeking out from under your sleeve?" I asked.

He came to me, putting his arms around my waist. "If tattoos turn you on, I'll get more."

I laughed, running my arm over the swirling pattern. "I like these just fine."

"Come on," he said. "Let's get downstairs."

As we reached the kitchen, I saw Deidre balancing a big dish of mashed potatoes in her arms. Tyler hurried to get the back door for her, and seeing a few dishes still on the island, I grabbed them to walk them outside.

Deidre smiled at me. "You are so sweet, Hen. You didn't have to do that."

"No worries," I said, setting the gravy and corn on the table. "It all looks so good."

Jack lowered a platter full of charred steaks to the table. "Wait until you cut into these. Best steak of your life, I promise."

Tyler chuckled. "One thing I love about my dad is his modesty."

Jack held up his hand, flashing a greasy spatula. "No harm in confidence—where its due." He stared at Rhett as he said that last part.

Rhett said, "I don't know why you're looking at me." And everyone laughed.

"So, Hen, tell us about yourself," Deidre said. "Tyler says you work in property management?"

I nodded. "I've been managing an apartment complex in my hometown for about eight years now. I love it."

"She's being humble." Tyler said, "All the renters there love her, and she won over the guys on my crew faster than I've ever seen."

My cheeks warmed at the compliment. "I think coffee and donuts have more to do with that than anything else."

Deidre smiled between the two of us. "What's the plan when Tyler moves to his next job? Will you do long distance, or—"

Liv gave Diedre a look. "*Mom.*"

She lifted her hands. "Sorry, was that off limits? I was just asking."

Despite the heaters around us, it felt like all the warmth had been sucked out of my bones. The one thing Tyler and I had both been avoiding was staring us in the face. But Tyler squeezed my hand under the table and said, "We'll figure it out. Right, babe?"

I nodded, giving him a grateful smile. "Right."

But for the rest of dinner, there was a sinking feeling in my gut. Some things were easier said than done.

## 57

## TYLER

Hen and I didn't talk much after dinner. Instead, she said she was tired and excused herself up to her room, but she encouraged me to spend time with my family. I stayed up with my siblings for a little while, talking and catching up, but soon I went to join her.

Mom's question had dampened the whole evening, not that I was mad at her. It was a fair question—one I didn't have an answer to. I hoped Hen would be up to talk a little bit, but the bedroom lights were off, and her breathing was slow and steady.

So I slipped out of my clothes, down to my underwear, and slid into bed with her, pressing my front to her back and loving the way her curves felt against me. She was so solid, steady, and I couldn't imagine ever living without her again.

I slept through the night with her at my side and woke with sunlight shining through the sheer curtains. She stirred against me and then rolled over in my arms to face me, her face only inches away.

I dropped a kiss on her nose. "Happy Thanksgiving, beautiful."

She smiled. "Happy Thanksgiving."

"How'd you sleep?"

"Much better after you got in here," she said.

"I hope you didn't mind me staying up."

"Not at all. Family time is important. Especially when you've been away from them for so long." She blinked sleepily and yawned. "Your mom missed you like crazy. I can tell."

I nodded. "What do you want to do today?"

"Eat and watch football? Isn't that what everyone does?"

I chuckled at her response. "We usually do that after chores. I thought we could ride the horses around the pasture this morning. Check in on the cattle that aren't in the feedlot."

Her expression fell. "I know I said I was interested in horseback riding, but isn't there a weight limit? I was too big to go on a trail ride with Kenner last year."

An ache grew in my chest. I hated that she had to worry about these kinds of things. "Our horses are really strong—made for hard work. You'll be fine."

"Are you sure?"

I nodded. "Of course. Plus, I want to see that ass in some jeans." I reached around and grabbed a handful, already turned on.

She shook her head at me. "You're such a horndog."

"Maybe. But I have a gift for you. Go use the bathroom, and I'll leave it for you on the bed."

While she used the bathroom, I set the gift I'd special ordered for her, with some help from her mom, and then got dressed and went downstairs. Mom was in the kitchen, cooking breakfast, coffee gurgling in the pot.

"Morning," I said.

"Morning." She reached for a mug and poured me some coffee. "Still take it black?"

I nodded, reaching for the cup. That first sip tasted amazing. No matter where I went or where I ordered it, coffee never tasted like it did brewed from the well water at home.

"What are your plans for the day?"

"After the game, we're going to the city to see Gage," I said.

A dark look crossed Mom's face. "Can you bring him a loaf of the lemon zucchini bread for me? I have some in the freezer."

"Sure thing." My heart ached for her, caught up in a war between her husband and her son. Mom's rule was always to put her marriage first, but I could tell it was hurting her.

Footfalls sounded on the stairs, and we both looked to

see Hen coming in jeans, a flannel shirt, and her brand-new cowboy boots. I'd gone with square toes and tan coloring with intricate leather work up the wide calves. With her jeans tucked into the boots and her buffalo plaid shirt, she looked absolutely adorable.

I whistled loudly, and Mom clapped her hands together.

"You fit right in on the farm," Mom said.

Hen smiled, doing a spin in her boots. "I can't believe you got these for me, Tyler. How did you know my size?"

"Had a little insider help," I answered with a grin. "Do you like them?"

She nodded, coming to sit beside me. She placed a kiss on my cheek and said, "Thank you so much. That was so thoughtful of you."

"We couldn't have you riding horses in tennis shoes," I said.

Mom offered Hen coffee, and soon we were both done with breakfast and walking to the barn. Liv was already there, riding Fred, the paint horse, around the pen. She trotted easily, perfectly at home in the saddle.

We Griffen kids had to be, growing up with our parents. Dad expected nothing less than our best, and if we ever got thrown off the saddle, we had to get right back on.

When Liv spotted us, she waved and easily slid out of the saddle. As she got closer, Hen said, "You look like a natural up there, Liv! Such a baddie."

"Thanks, girl," Liv said. "We'll have you doing the same in no time."

"I'm willing to try it," Hen said with a hint of doubt in her voice as she nervously rubbed her hands together.

We walked her to the horses lined up in front of the barn and introduced her to Star. She was a pretty chestnut mare, eleven years old with a white blaze running from her nose to her forehead, covered with her shiny mane.

Hen gently patted Star's neck. "That's the smell from the barn. Horses." She breathed in deeply. "I love that smell."

I grinned. Seeing Hen take so easily to my life... it was just that much more proof that we belonged together.

We told Hen about the parts of the saddle, how to use the reins to lead the horse, and then it was time for her to get on. She looked nervous at the size of the horse, so Liv brought out a five-gallon bucket for Hen to stand on to give her some more height.

With the extra lift, we had Hen on Star's back in no time. She gripped tightly to the saddle horn as she slipped the toes of her boots into the stirrups.

I held on to the reins, leading her around the pounded-down dirt of the pen. She rocked atop the horse, slowly getting used to the movements. Liv held up her phone, pointing it at Hen. "Smile big!"

Hen gave her a cheesy grin that made my heart soar.

"How are you feeling about it?" I asked. "Ready to take the reins?"

With a determined look, Hen nodded, and I handed her the leather straps. I went to go stand by Liv, and we both gave her directions from time to time until she was walking in steady circles around the pen.

"Time to speed it up!" Liv challenged. At the nervous look Hen gave her, Liv said, "You're ready, girl! Go for it!"

Hen carefully tapped her heels to Star's sides, and Star walked a little faster.

"Bit harder," Liv called.

With the extra nudge, Star took off at a trot, Hen's legs clinging to the horse's sides.

"I'm doing it!" she cried.

"That's right, baby!" I yelled, pumping my fist in the air. "You're fuckin' doing it!"

## 58

## HENRIETTA

*Confession: I like my men sweet, and their talk dirty.*

MY LEGS FELT like rubber as I stepped on land for the first time. "Okay, now I know why all those cowboys walk funny in the movies."

Liv laughed. "It's a bit awkward at first, but you get used to it with some practice."

Frowning, I said, "No way to practice where I'm from. I don't think I could convince Mom to let a horse have part of her garden."

Smiling, Liv said, "You're welcome back for a practice run any time. I'm sure Ty's already told you about Gage's frequent flyer miles."

"Your whole family is so generous."

Liv smiled. "When you grow up out here, you learn that everyone needs a leg up from time to time, including us."

Tyler was busy unsaddling the horses, but when he was done putting the saddles away and brushing them down, the three of us walked back to the house. Even though the sun was right overhead, the clouds were thick enough to keep the sky a pale gray. The air prickled like there might be rain later.

In a similar way to the ocean, the entire country landscape changed with the weather—it was a sight to behold. The golden grass had a deeper hue, the dirt trails took on a somber feel, and even the wind was subdued.

When we walked inside the house, my senses were completely overwhelmed. Jack was carving the turkey, and Deidre's face was red with heat from baking. Sports commentary played from a radio with an antenna sitting on the buffet table.

"It smells wonderful," I said. "I wish I had enough room in my suitcase to bring this all back with me."

Deidre chuckled, and Jack asked, "How were the horses?"

"Star was a great horse to learn on," I answered. "It was so much fun."

Liv said, "We'll have her running barrels in the rodeo in no time."

I laughed at the thought. "Not a chance."

Deidre said, "Why don't y'all go wash up, and we'll sit down to eat."

We went up the stairs, the insides of my legs already burning. Riding horses was a heck of a workout (and probably the only one I didn't mind). In the bedroom, Tyler sent me a sexy stare.

"Did I mention how hot it was to see you on that horse? I wish I was the one you were riding." He trailed his hands along the waist of my jeans, then linked his fingers through the belt loops, pulling me closer.

A swoop of desire went through my stomach, sending heat between my legs. His mouth was already on my neck, working his way down the slit of my shirt, unbuttoning the top button.

"Tyler," I gasped. "Your family is downstairs."

He ground his hips into me, and I felt his erection, turning me on that much more.

I was beginning to forget the four very specific reasons why I should say no. "What if they hear us?" I breathed, already lifting the hem of his dark gray Henley shirt.

He took his shirt the rest of the way off and spun me, pushing my face into the pillows of his bed. Excitement rippled across my skin as he yanked my jeans down. I loved it when he got rough with me, and mix that with my kink of risking being caught?

There was no turning him down.

I arched my back, wishing he wasn't still out of me. "Hurry," I whispered.

"I'm getting a condom."

"Don't worry about it," I said, my chest tight with the knowledge of what I was saying. What I was offering. "I'm on the pill." But nothing was a hundred percent effective.

He was quiet for a moment. "Are you sure?"

"I am."

Then I heard the teeth of his zipper come apart before he pressed inside me all the way. I bit back a cry from my body adjusting to him, to the delicious pain of his girth, and tried not to moan as he slowly backed out.

He pressed one hand on the back of my head, shoving me deeper into the pillows as he pounded into me again, and my eyes rolled back in pleasure. I could still hear the hum of voices downstairs, oblivious to all the ways Tyler was claiming me above their heads.

He picked up the pace, and when the headboard rattled, he shifted—I assumed to still it with his other hand—and continued his relentless drive into my body.

I reached down, rubbing my sensitive spot as his thrusts continued, and between the force of his hand on me, the pace of his thrusts, and the pressure on my clit, I was close. So fucking close.

"Fuck," Tyler hissed. "I'm coming."

And that was all I needed to push me over the edge. My orgasm racked my body, and I tightened around his cock, raking my hands across the comforter for anything that would keep me from crying out.

As the waves slowed, Tyler bent over me, his torso

pressing into my back, and he whispered in my ear. "My cum's going to be dripping out of you in front of my whole family. Because you're *my* good girl."

My sensitive vagina clenched again around his softening cock. Fuck, he was hot, and he knew exactly what to say to me to drive me wild.

He pulled out of me, handing me a tissue to help me clean up, and then we both got dressed, sending each other heated smiles as we did.

Before we went downstairs, I relieved myself in the bathroom and did the best I could to make sure my hair wasn't wild. There wasn't much I could do about the added brightness in my eyes or extra color in my cheeks.

When I reached the main floor, Tyler was already tucked into the table, an empty seat across from him. I slid into the chair, and he winked at me. Reminding me.

*My cum's dripping out of you in front of my whole family.*

I shuddered, already looking forward to round two.

But I did the best I could to act like I wasn't constantly turned on by their son and brother. Instead, we talked about football, something my brothers had prepared me for with endless hours of conversation.

My phone buzzed in my hip pocket. (Side note: leggings with pockets are the absolute best.) I drew it out below the table and saw my mom was calling me. Probably just to wish me a happy Thanksgiving. I pushed the button to send the call to voicemail.

My phone vibrated again, I assumed with the voicemail notification. But then there was another buzzing. A call from my dad. Were they really that worried about me being away from home?

I pressed the end button again, but then there was a fresh call. From my mom again.

I looked up at Tyler across the table, and he had a worried look on me. "Sorry," I said. "I need to take this."

His family was really sweet about it, and I stepped out on the back porch to answer the call. "Mom, what's going on? Is everything okay?"

Mom's voice shook as she said, "Your grandma fell again. She's back in the hospital, but this time the break was bad. They think they'll need to do a full hip replacement."

My chest froze. I couldn't breathe. Could hardly speak. "A hip replacement? At her age?"

"They think it will help with her pain and maybe her mobility, but the odds of her coming home this time aren't looking great."

I dropped into a chair at the patio table, shivering from the cold, from the news. This couldn't be true. Grandma had been doing great on her walker. "What happened?"

"It was an accident. She tripped over one of Kenner's toys."

Anger made me grit my teeth together. Had no one been paying attention to Grandma? She'd barely gotten out of the hospital, and the second I left, she was back in. I knew what hip surgery meant, especially for someone her age. It meant more health risks, including pneumonia, which could be deadly.

My voice was raw. "I'll find a flight and have Tyler—"

"No, you absolutely will not," Mom said. "You are there with his family, and we have more than enough people here to help if needed. You can come back on Sunday like you had planned."

"Mom, I—"

"Honey, you can't fix this," she said softly.

And that was the thing that broke me the most. My grandma probably wouldn't be coming home. I'd missed her last Thanksgiving.

I glanced through the windows, seeing Tyler laughing with his family. I should have been home, but I wasn't.

I was here.

"Tell Grandma I'll see her as soon as we get back."

"I will, honey," Mom said.

And then she hung up, and I was alone on the porch, filled with worry and fear and something even worse...

Regret.

## 59

## TYLER

"Hey, is Hen okay?" Liv asked.

I turned in my seat to see Hen on the patio, her elbows resting on the table, her head in her hands. My heart dropped to my stomach, and the smile lingering on my lips quickly fell. "Excuse me," I said, pushing back from the table in complete silence and walking to the sliding door that led to the porch. As soon as I got outside, Hen turned to face me, the porch light catching the tears streaking down her cheeks.

I hurried to her, dropping to my knees beside the table. "What's going on? What happened?"

"Grandma—" Her voice broke and she sniffed, looking down at the table at her phone. "Grandma fell again. They think she has to have a hip replacement and she—and she—" Hen began sobbing, and through each cry, she sputtered, "She won't be able to come home."

"Oh my god," I whispered, pulling her into my arms as she continued shaking. I wanted to fix all the pain I could feel rolling off of her. "Hen, I'm so sorry. Do we need to find a way to fly back? I'm sure I could book us something tonight if we need to go."

She shook her head, pulling back to wipe her eyes. "My mom told me I should stay here, that Grandma has plenty of people around, but I feel so guilty. Like I should have been there for her, like I could have prevented it somehow."

"What-if is a dangerous game," I said, accentuating each word so she understood how much I meant what I was saying. "Even if you could have prevented this fall, there's no guaranteeing it wouldn't have happened another time when you were at work or busy with friends. We can only focus on *now*. So tell me, what feels right in this moment? I'll do whatever *you* need. Not what your mom wants you to do."

She bit her lip, her eyes still full of tears. "I don't want to ruin your family's dinner."

"It's just food. It'll keep."

"I don't want to miss out on meeting Gage. I know how much he means to you."

"A million points, remember? He could fly us back tomorrow if we wanted to."

She shook her head at me. "Sitting here and

pretending to be happy when my grandma's lying in a hospital bed feels wrong."

I nodded, already knowing the answer. "Let's go."

We went back inside, and I explained what was going on to my family. Hen apologized a million times, but my mom hugged her and said, "Honey, you don't need to apologize to us. Family is everything."

I could have sworn my dad's eyes misted over when she said that.

Hen hugged my mom back, uttering a quiet, "Thank you."

Liv came upstairs with us, helping pack our bags back up, and then Hen and I were in the truck, rushing to Dallas. After five minutes on a call with Gage, we had seats on the evening's last direct flight to LA.

It was the waiting that was the hardest. Watching Hen lean her head back on the truck seat and close her eyes, picturing god knows what.

I reached across the console to hold her hand, but it felt limp in mine, like she was somewhere else entirely. Selfishly, I ached to be closer to her, to be needed and leaned on, but I was doing the best I could, and that had to be okay.

The three-hour flight to LA was almost as torturous as the hour drive to RWE Memorial Hospital in Emerson. We parked in the parking garage, and I had to lengthen my strides to keep up with Hen's quick pace. We had to go through the emergency entrance since it was nearly midnight, and Hen quickly said to security, "I'm here to see Cordelia Jones."

The guard looked from Hen to me. "Are you family?" he asked.

Hen nodded.

"Trauma unit, room 1431. Follow the red lines."

Trauma. The word sounded harsh on my ears. Cordelia was in a trauma unit from her fall? She was tough, but this... it was a lot.

The side door automatically opened with the sound of metal sliding against metal.

Hen took the visitor sticker from the security guard and said, "Let's go."

I followed her, the halls mostly empty around us save for the sounds of the night shift. But the smell was there—chemical and sweet at the same time. It made my stomach turn. The fluorescent lights were even harsher at night, slightly orange, and eerie against the painted cinderblock walls.

The sound of talking grew louder as we turned the corner and came to the trauma unit's waiting area. Almost all of Hen's family was there. Imani and Raven were there, but I assumed Laila had taken Kenner and A'yisha home for bedtime.

When they saw us, Johmarcus looked up and said, "What are you two doing back here?"

Hen was looking straight at her mom as she choked out, "I'm sorry, Mom. I had to be here."

Tam got up, taking Hen in her arms and patting her back. "I know, baby. I know."

Her dad got up, standing with us, and Hen pulled back from her mom's embrace. "Is there any news?"

Murphy repeated what Hen already knew—that it was a bad break and that there would be an emergency hip replacement the next day. Other than that, it would be a waiting game to see how well she recovered from surgery and which "skilled nursing" facility would take Cordelia.

Hen and I exchanged a look. We both knew that last part wasn't going to be an option.

"I need to see her," Hen said.

Tam replied, "It's just Bertrand in there now. She's allowed two visitors at a time."

I reached for Hen's hand. "Do you want me to come with you and see if he'll trade?"

Hen shook her head, patting my hand with hers. "I'll be okay. You can go home if you want."

My eyebrows drew together. That wasn't even something I'd considered, leaving her when she was going through this. Why would she have thought that's what I would want? "I'll be right out here," I replied.

She nodded and slipped her hand from mine, the absence of her touch making me feel cold all over. Then she left the room and was gone.

I felt a hand on my mid back and looked to see Tam standing next to me. "Don't take it personal, honey. She's always been close with her grandma. I tried to get her to stay there in Texas, but you know how she is."

A faint smile touched my lips. "She loves her family more than anything."

And for a guy who claimed to love her, I was being unforgivably selfish for hoping to take her away.

## 60

## HENRIETTA

*Confession: I can't do this anymore.*

THIS WING of the hospital set me on edge. I could hear moaning down the hall, beeping from various monitors within the rooms. The nurses I walked past didn't say anything, barely met my eyes.

I counted down the numbers until I reached Grandma's room, then slowly pushed the door open. Bertrand sat at the chair next to our sleeping grandma's bed, holding her hand that wasn't hooked up to an IV.

There were two bags there, dripping fluid into her veins. And she looked so frail, her brown skin and silver hair a deep contrast to the stark white blankets and pillow behind her head.

At the sound of my footsteps, Bertrand turned to look at me, surprise clear in his face. "I thought you were in Texas."

"I was," I whispered, folding my arms around my middle to hold myself together. My legs felt weak, seeing Grandma like this again when I thought we were in the clear. It was so much like Grandpa lying in that hospice bed, fighting for each breath.

"Here," Bertrand said, reaching for the wheelchair behind him and wheeling it next to the bed.

I sat in the chair, locking the wheels for stability.

"It was crazy, Hen," he said, his voice low. "All of a sudden we heard this crash and then a scream. I can't get that scream out of my head."

I leaned my head against his shoulder. It must have been awful to witness. "I should have been there to make sure the walkways were clear." Bitterness leached into my voice. We shouldn't have been here on Thanksgiving night.

"It was a freak thing, truly. Kenner was trying to get a toy to come apart, and it slipped from his hands and flung back toward Grandma just as she was getting up to use the bathroom. Johmarcus and Laila feel awful, and Kenner was crying so bad to see his great-grandma hurt."

My anger didn't dissolve at the knowledge that it was a true accident and not just carelessness. It changed. I was mad at myself for not being there to support my family when shit hit the fan. I'd been off galivanting in Texas, riding horses, having sex, being *selfish*. What other moments, tragedies, would I miss if I moved away to be with Tyler?

Bertrand slowly removed his hand from Grandma's. "I'll give you two some time."

"Thank you," I said.

"Of course." He patted my back one more time before leaving the room.

With his footsteps growing quieter, I turned my attention on Grandma. I sat in Bertrand's seat and reached gently for her hand, her palm soft against mine. The skin on the back of her hand looked papery, slightly glossy and cracked with age. When I was little, she'd hold my hand, and I'd press into her fingertips, watching the indentations formed there slowly bounce back in place.

These hands had loved us so well, from cooking treats to serving her husband on his deathbed to holding us when we were down. Grandma had always been there for us. Every football game, every scholar's bowl competition, every graduation and dance recital, she had been there.

And I'd abandoned her.

A tear slipped down my cheek at the pull I felt between my new love and my family who had always been there for me. I'd only known Tyler for months, and I loved him with all my heart. But my family had been there for *life*.

What future could there be with Tyler when he had a job that required such extensive travel? When he wanted to settle in a state over a thousand miles from California? I couldn't ask him to give that up to move here, even if I had a house for us to share. Just like he couldn't ask me the same question.

It was reckless to let my heart become so invested in him when this was the inevitable answer.

So I cried.

I cried for my grandma lying in this hospital bed, her life forever changed.

I cried for my first real love, the man of my dreams.

And I cried for the future we could never have together.

# 61

## TYLER

My phone vibrated in my pocket, waking me up from where I'd slept in a waiting room chair the whole night. All of Hen's brothers had gone home, but her mom and dad were here too, leaning against each other as they slept. My neck protested as I slowly stood, reaching into my pocket to see who was calling.

Jim Crenshaw's name filled the screen, and my eyebrows drew together. He knew I was off work, and we didn't have a meeting scheduled until the following Tuesday. And it was only nine in the morning. I swiped to answer, wondering what he could possibly want.

"Hello?" I asked, my voice rough from a poor night's sleep. Hen hadn't come out all night, and I wanted to know if she was okay.

"You really shit the bed on this one," Jim growled.

My chest instantly tightened. In my ten years of working with him, Jim *never* talked to me like that. "What's going on?"

"Don't play dumb with me, Tyler. I understand needing to get your dick wet, but I never would have thought—"

"Whoa, whoa, whoa," I said, walking away from the waiting room and into the hallway so Hen's parents wouldn't overhear this conversation that had already turned into an explicit yelling match on Jim's end. "Jim, I don't know what you're talking about."

He cleared his throat, and it sounded more like a growl. "I get a call this morning from a suit at Blue Bird, and you know what she tells me? She thinks that you have been acting inappropriately on the job site."

Ice filled my veins. My knees buckled, and I leaned against the cinderblock wall for support.

"But I tell her that's impossible," Jim railed on. "I've been working with Tyler for ten years, and he's the best damn employee I have. So good, in fact, that I'm considering training him up to run the damn company once this project's done. But she demanded a review of the security footage anyway."

I raked my hands through my hair. The fucking cameras. I never thought much about them because we never reviewed footage unless there was vandalism. But Janessa had given him all the cause he needed. *Clients first* was Crenshaw Construction's motto. The first line of our company mission statement. If a client wanted a video review, they got one.

"Imagine my surprise when our security guy sends me a clip of you getting *fucking blown on the job site* BY THE WOMAN WHO'S SUPPOSED TO BE HELPING THE CONSTRUCTION PROCESS RUN SMOOTHLY."

I held the phone away from my ear, easily hearing him shouting even from a distance.

"Now what you do in your free time is your damn business. You can fuck whoever you want. Man. Woman. I don't give a shit. But the second you step on the job site, it's about the project. I can't believe you would jeopardize our reputation like this and risk a *multi-million-dollar project!*"

Fuck, fuck, fuck. "Did they let us go?"

"I saved the deal on one condition. You're off the job, Tyler. You need to pack your shit and go home by Sunday. They're done with you, and so am I."

"Jim, I—" I began, but the call ended.

I stared at the lock screen on my phone, the picture of Henrietta on the horse. I'd had Liv send it to me, and it made me smile so much, I'd put it there. But now I didn't feel like smiling. I felt like an asshole.

I'd never been fired before in my life. Not when I was a teenager baling hay. Not when I was working at a sandwich shop while in carpentry school. And not in the ten years of my professional career. Ten years of hard work, moving around the country, giving all I had to this business.

What was I supposed to do now? Pack up my bags and share Hen's bedroom? Take over a guest bedroom in her family's home while they dealt with the very real changes coming in their beloved grandma's life?

I had savings, but that would get eaten up quickly with rent going the way it was in this town. But I'd do it. I'd spend every last dime and work any grunt job I could find —if Hen would be my last just like I'd been her first. But that was a lot of pressure to put on a new relationship, on someone whose worst fear had just been confirmed.

But I had to ask.

Love isn't convenient. I just hoped she'd think it was worth it.

## 62

## HENRIETTA

*Confession: I wish I could go back to being the funny fat friend.*

I'D BEEN in and out of sleep throughout the night, and when I was awake, I watched the rise and fall of Grandma's chest. The part in her lips as she breathed. The drip of liquid through her IV. All signs of life to be lived.

Grandma blinked her eyes open around nine in the morning. She looked at our linked hands, then at me. Her voice was raspy as she said, "Baby girl, shouldn't you be in Texas?"

Fresh tears slid down my cheeks as I shook my head. "I'm right where I need to be." I opened my mouth to say more, but a nurse walked in saying, "Great, you're awake! I have orders to take you back to pre-op so we can get started on your hip replacement." Another nurse followed behind her, giving me a smile.

Grandma nodded. "Have you reviewed my advanced directives? I have a DNR in place."

"DNR?" I asked.

The nurse answered, "It means do not resuscitate. It's a common request from older patients."

I stared at my grandma, saying these words so casually to a nurse before a major surgery.

"And, yes, we have all of those orders in place," the nurse said. Then she looked at me. "You're free to wait in here or in the waiting area, but it will be several hours before she's back."

I nodded and squeezed Grandma's hand. "We'll be praying for you, Grandma. See you soon."

She patted my hand and nodded to the nurse who began the process of wheeling her away.

Moments after she left, I realized I'd never said I love you.

I fought tears, hoping she'd come back so I could say it out loud.

I sat in her empty room for a moment, looking out the window that only faced a brick building. Part of me wanted to sit here forever, never face the conversation that I knew was coming. I didn't want to have it. Didn't want to face it.

But if Grandma could suffer a broken hip, go under the knife knowing they wouldn't resuscitate her if something happened, I could survive a heartbreak. Especially if it meant Tyler could have the kind of life he wanted without my selfish needs getting in the way.

I stood on shaky legs and left the room, walking down the long hallway to the waiting area. As I walked in, I noticed my parents sipping coffee, eating takeout. Where was Tyler?

My mom said, "Hen! How was she? Did you get to talk to her?"

I nodded, redirecting my attention to my parents. "I can tell she's in pain, but she woke up right before they came to take her for surgery. Did you know she has a DNR?" The betrayal in that statement hit me in the gut. "Why wouldn't she do everything she could to stay with us longer?"

Mom and Dad exchanged looks.

Mom tilted her head. "Watching your grandpa suffer was so painful. She doesn't want that for herself, honey."

Dad nodded. "It's difficult to understand now when you're young and in love and have your whole life ahead of you. But someday, if you're lucky, you will have a new perspective on Grandma's wishes."

It felt like a punch to the gut, that they were all okay with just letting her go. But I didn't want to fight. I didn't know what I could say that wouldn't cause irreparable harm, so I said, "Did Tyler go home?"

Mom shook her head. "He took a call in the hallway."

I left the waiting room, finding Tyler leaning against a

wall. At the sound of opening doors, he glanced over and quickly straightened when he saw it was me.

"Tyler." I allowed myself a selfish moment, falling into his hug as tears fell down my cheeks. Would this really be the last time I felt his arms around me? The last time his lips feathered kisses on my forehead.

"How is she?" he asked, stepping back.

I wrapped my arms around myself, trying to stay strong. "She's going for surgery. And she has a DNR, Tyler."

He didn't seem surprised. "My grandpa has one too."

"Why would she do that?" I asked, hoping he would see my side.

Instead, he replied, "Maybe she misses her husband."

Emotion swelled within me, taking over my every thought. "How could you say that? She's better off dead with her husband than alive with us? No one even knows what happens after you die! What if you're just supporting her to go into oblivion for eternity?"

I stopped, my chest heaving as I waited for his response. The kindness in his green eyes just made me that much angrier.

"It's her decision, Hen."

"It's a bad one," I snapped.

His voice was gentle. "In your opinion."

I glared at him. "What are you doing here anyway? I said you could go home."

A crease formed between his brow, and I hated how

tired he looked with circles under his eyes and scruff on his chin. "I couldn't leave you here, Hen. I wanted to be here for you."

"Why?" I demanded, my voice breaking. "Why are we doing this? Someday, your job is going to be done here, and you'll be on the road again. Were you just expecting me to follow you wherever you go? Give up on being here for my family and my career so I could be some sort of housewife? Why did you do it?" I demanded.

"I couldn't stay away from you," he yelled, his voice tortured. He put his hand on the wall by my shoulder, holding the other against his chest. "I love you, and I don't want this to end. I meant what I said when I told my mom we'd figure it out. I know it's hard to see an answer right now, but if we put our heads together, we can—"

"We can *what?*" I argued, tears streaming down my cheeks. Why was he so fucking perfect and understanding? Why couldn't he be like every other asshole who my grandma tried to set me up with? Why did he make saying goodbye so damn hard?

"We can be together!"

"Until the job is done," I bit back.

He shook his head. "Hen, I got fired this morning."

The words took the air out of my chest. "What?"

"Janessa had them look at security footage of us, and they found some incriminating video. Jim let me go to keep the contract with Blue Bird. I'm supposed to be out of the apartment by Sunday."

My mouth fell open and closed as the words hit my brain, one after another, like hail shattering on a sidewalk. He'd lost his job—and would be moving out of Emerson in two days.

He took my hands in his, my arms feeling wooden as he spoke. "I can get an apartment here, try to find a job. Or I could bring you back to Texas, we could start a life, a family. I know it's soon, but I love you, Hen. I don't want to live without you. I don't want to fuck around with long distance and video calls and seeing each other on the weekends. And I know you have a job here, but Janessa won't stop at me. Not when she has video proof. You could find a job in Cottonwood Falls. Or I could support you. I know the timing isn't great with your grandma being in the hospital, but I know Gage would help us with flights to visit her. You could come visit every weekend if you wanted to. I just want to be with you." His voice cracked at the end because he knew what he was asking. He was asking the impossible.

"We can't live with my parents," I said.

"I'll pull my investments."

"You can't do that," I said.

"Then come with me," he begged, his molten hazel eyes on mine.

"I can't do that," I cried. Our relationship was ending. Right here in the hospital hallways, with families walking by and workers in scrubs acting like my world wasn't falling apart. But it was. Piece by fucking piece. "My grandma could live for years with a broken hip, Tyler. I have savings, but I can't afford to take a gap in employment if I still have a job on Monday. My family's going to need me around to help. My parents still work. My brothers have jobs, families. They can't do it all on their own. They need me."

Tyler's gaze darted over me. "Do they really need you? Or are you looking for a reason to run?"

"You're the dream guy, Tyler, but if you move here, you'll resent me. Maybe not today, maybe not a year from now, but someday you'll look around at your city life and know there's something missing."

His voice was a whisper as he said, "Something will be missing if you're not with me."

My lips quivered. He was taking all the fight left in me. "Tyler, tell me you'd be happy here."

He hesitated. "I'd give it up, for you."

"I can't ask you to do that."

"Then what are you saying?" he asked, his eyes red.

"I'm saying you're a windmill, Tyler, and we both know you don't belong here."

His Adam's apple slid down his throat as he swallowed. "Don't do this, Hen. Please don't do this."

Tears rolled down my cheeks as I shook my head. "We both knew how it was going to end."

"I thought you loved me." His hoarse whisper broke every last unshattered part of me.

"I do," I said. "But it's not enough."

Then I turned and walked back where I belonged, with my family. Tyler was behind me, in my past. And even though I loved him with every broken piece, that's where he needed to stay. After all, if you loved something, you needed to set it free.

## 63

## TYLER

I wasn't waiting around until Sunday. Not when everywhere I looked reminded me of her. Not when all I saw was her face telling me there was no future, nothing I could do to change her mind.

Not when I'd lost everything that mattered to me.

I packed up all my things, shoving them in the suitcases I moved here with, then I texted Gage.

Tyler: Can you get me a flight back to Dallas for tonight?
Gage: For you and Hen?
Tyler: Just me.

There was a pause before he replied.

Gage: Booked.

He sent me a screenshot of the boarding pass, and I locked my phone, holding it tightly in my hand. I was leaving Emerson. Without Henrietta by my side.

## 64

# HENRIETTA

*Confession: I've been preparing for this moment for the last eight years, and I'm still not ready.*

I GAVE my parents an excuse about Tyler needing to change and shower at his apartment, and they let my red eyes and smeared makeup pass without further questioning. It had been a long night for all of us.

While my grandma was in surgery, Birdie called me. I didn't answer. But then she sent me a text.

Birdie: Just checking in to see how it's going with Tyler's family. Are they as sweet as he is?

A small huff of air came out my nose.

**Henrietta:** They were incredible.

His sister was warm and welcoming, Rhett was funny, and even though I didn't get to meet Gage, I knew he'd be just as generous and gracious as Tyler was. And his parents had this quiet agreement about them, like after so many years, they naturally knew how to exist together and keep a home running. I knew they weren't perfect, but Cottonwood Falls could have been named Paradise and it still would have been accurate.

My phone pinged with another notification.

**Birdie:** Were? Did something happen?

I closed my eyes, not wanting to admit what I'd done. Because it was stupid; I already knew it was stupid to let Tyler go. But I had to stand true to the people who had given me everything. If that meant saying goodbye to the love of my life, I'd do it. If it meant working a job under a woman I now knew was truly evil, I'd grit my teeth and make it through.

No matter how much it hurt.

I took a breath and sent Birdie another text.

**Henrietta:** My grandma was admitted to the hospital last night. She's getting hip replacement surgery. And because everything has to go wrong at the same time, Tyler was fired for... indecent activity on the job site. I ruined his job for him and I feel awful, but I couldn't stay with him. He's always said he wants to settle in Texas, and I can't leave my grandma here.

My vision blurred by the end of the message, and I took a shaky breath as I blinked away the ever-present tears. Three bubbles appeared on the screen, and I watched them, waiting for Birdie to tell me how stupid I was, to chase him down and keep him. But then her message came through.

Birdie: I am so sorry, Hen. That's so much to deal with. What hospital are you at? I'll bring you all supper tonight, and I'm sure Mara will help too with anything you need. I love you.

Gratitude poured through me as I typed out my reply.

Henrietta: We're at RWE Memorial.
Henrietta: I love you too.

The door from the trauma unit opened, and a doctor came out in scrubs and a white lab coat. "Are you the family of Cordelia Jones?"

My stomach clenched with nerves as my mom said, "We are."

We circled around him, desperate to hear the news, praying that it was good.

"The surgery went well. With her age, it's hard to tell

how recovery will go, but I'm hoping with good PT she can make a decent recovery and walk again with a walker when needed, but it's more than likely that she'll be in a wheelchair long term, despite our best efforts." He frowned, reaching into his pocket and retrieving several brochures. "Our team is recommending advanced nursing care. These are all state-sponsored facilities that Medicare will cover. Once you decide, they typically have someone on staff who will coordinate discharge from the hospital and get her admitted there."

Mom nodded, taking the brochures. "Thank you, doctor."

I looked up from the brochures and asked, "When can we go see her?"

"I recommend we let her rest for the next few hours as she comes off the anesthesia, but there's no reason you can't go sit with her quietly now until she wakes up."

"Thank you," I said.

He nodded, walking back through the doors. Mom, Dad, and I exchanged a glance.

Mom said, "Why don't you two go sit with her in case she wakes up? I'll call the boys and let them know she's alright."

I took a shaky breath. "I need to talk to you both about something first."

Mom and Dad exchanged a glance, then Mom said, "Here, honey, let's sit down."

I took one of the cramped hospital chairs and looked

across the coffee table at them. "A while back, Dad asked me what I was doing with my money. The truth is, I've been saving for something like this so Grandma wouldn't have to go to a home."

Dad looked dumbfounded while Mom said, "That's really sweet of you, but in-home care is very expensive. Even ten thousand dollars would only get us a couple months of care, three at most."

I nodded. "I've done my research, and I've saved a hundred and eight thousand."

Now Dad's jaw was on the floor. "I knew the numbers weren't adding up, but Hen, this is crazy. You've been living at home all this time so you could save for Grandma?"

I felt embarrassed to admit it, but I nodded. "I know it was hard on you and Mom to help Johmarcus, and we didn't have the money for private care when Grandpa was so sick... I just didn't want to see Grandma's life end like Grandpa's did."

They sat in a stunned silence for a moment, and Mom said, "Honey, you're twenty-eight years old. I'm sure Grandma will understand if you put your life savings toward a home, a family, a wedding."

The realization struck me that two of those things were not in my cards anymore. But I'd decided my course of action at twenty and had been staying the course for eight years. No way would I let my grandma down now, in her moment of need.

"This is what I want to do," I said. "But I'd rather not tell Grandma that I'm the one paying for it. I don't want her to feel guilty or try and talk me out of it. We all know she's so persuasive she'd win."

Dad chuckled, but it was a sad sound. He put his arms around me and held me close. "I love your heart," he said. "Sometimes I wish you would care a little more about yourself. It's good that you have Tyler now. That boy thinks you hung the moon and all the stars."

Mom gave me a small smile. "I noticed he has a picture of you on a horse as his phone wallpaper. It's adorable."

Each word was another twist of the knife in my heart.

About to break down, I said, "I'm going to sit with Grandma."

I walked back to her room, and when I saw her in the bed, her chest rising and falling with the oxygen cannulas in her nose, I covered my mouth to hold back a sob. She'd made it through surgery. I knew this was only the beginning of her recovery, but she'd made it through the first step.

I went and sat by her bed, just thinking. Looking out the window. Wondering what was next for me. Hoping that if I kept my job, Janessa would somehow get fired or leave. And then I felt a hand on my hand.

I looked up, seeing Grandma looking back at me. "Hi, sweetheart," she rasped.

I got up and hugged her gently. "Grandma, I'm so glad you're okay."

"I am," she said tiredly, resting her head back on the pillow.

"Do you need anything?" I asked. "I can ask a nurse to bring more pain meds?"

"I'm a little hungry," she rasped out.

I pressed the call button and asked for some food and a new drink for grandma, and we sat for a couple hours, not talking much as the anesthesia wore off and she became more coherent.

Mom came in and told us she was getting supper and then left. When I glanced back at my grandma, I saw tears streaming down her cheeks.

My heart stalled. "Grandma? Are you hurting? I can ask for more medicine."

"It's not that... It's just, I've enjoyed living with your family more than you'll ever know. The idea of moving to a place I've never been and being away from you all..." She put her fist to her lips, tears sliding down her creviced cheeks.

"Grandma?"

She looked my way.

My voice was shaky as I said, "That's not going to happen. There's a Medicare program that will pay for a home health aide. You can stay with us."

Her lips parted. "You can't be serious."

"I am," I said, crying with her. "You can come home."

Her smile was wide, and she cried happy tears. "Give me a hug, baby girl. That's the best news I've heard all day."

I hugged her tight, hanging on for dear life. "I love you, Grandma."

She smiled at me as I sat back down and said, "Me too. But I want to hear about you. How was your time in Texas?"

"It was amazing," I answered honestly. "If my whole life wasn't here, I'd move there in a second and stare at the prairie all day long."

Grandma laughed. "My little hen wants to live on a farm."

I smiled.

"Maybe you and Tyler will move to Texas together one day," she said, so much hope in her eyes.

I fought back tears and smiled. "Let's just focus on today."

## 65

## HENRIETTA

*Confession: I can do hard things... as long as there's an end in sight.*

IT TOOK all I had to leave the hospital to get ready for work on Monday morning. Partly because I didn't want to leave my grandma's side, but also because I had no idea what would greet me at the office.

Janessa had been on radio silence all weekend. I kept waiting for her to call me, tell me Tyler was fired, that they had hired a new site manager, but... nothing.

So I went home, walked up the ramp Tyler had helped my family install, treaded on the brand-new flooring Tyler had donated, and cried in the shower. He was everywhere. From the renovations on the house to the photobooth strips of pictures I hung up on my mirror. Not to mention the stabbing ache in my heart.

I missed him so much already it was hard to breathe. But I had to be okay with my decision. Okay with the fact that I needed to let him go because I needed to be near my family, and he needed to be near his. He'd offered to move here, but I didn't want him resenting me down the road because he'd given up what I couldn't.

I wore a black dress to work and drove my car down the freeway. When the heat gauge popped up to the danger zone, I got pulled off to the side of the road, waiting for the radiator to cool off so I could add some water. Tyler wasn't there to drive by and save me.

I parked in front of the office, but noticed through the window that there were two people inside... Janessa and a man I didn't recognize. Dread filled my gut. Janessa hardly ever came out here. Especially not this early on a Monday morning. This couldn't be good.

Taking a steady breath to steel myself, I pushed through the door, bells chiming overhead. Janessa turned toward me, an evil smile curling her lips. I'd never really considered her a friend, but we'd worked together for eight years, and I'd never seen this side of her. Just another knife, this one twisting in my back.

"Right on time," Janessa said.

I glanced at the clock on the wall. I was five minutes early. "I wasn't expecting you," I said, still not sure who this guy was. He was muscular, nearly six feet tall, dressed in all black. "Are you the new site manager I'll be working with?" I asked, extending my hand. "I'm Henrietta."

The guy looked at my hand, his brown eyes cold.

I lowered my hand, and Janessa said, "Pierce is a security guard. It's company policy to have two people present during a reprimanding."

"A... reprimanding?" I asked. The word rolled around in my head, still not registering. She wasn't firing me?

Janessa let out a cold chuckle. "Did you really think you could blow the construction manager on site with no repercussions? Corporate was very interested in your unprofessionalism, not to mention your lack of safety gear—and I don't mean condoms. My 'flirtation' with Tyler is *nothing* compared to what you did."

Pierce stood stone-faced, not even flinching at her vulgarity.

"Unfortunately, they said your record has been so good over the last eight years, they didn't want to fire you. Yet. You will be demoted from overseeing the construction process, which also means a cut in your pay. I'll be here every day though to check in on construction—and you."

My mouth opened and closed. I'd been all but ready to get fired and then beg on my knees for my job back. I'd been ready to swallow my pride, show up to work, and do my job, despite the way Janessa had spoken about me in Tyler's apartment, and despite the fact that she clearly had no problem destroying his life out of sheer jealousy. But now I'd have to see her every day? And for how long?

There were a million bitten-back words I wanted to say to her. I wanted to tell her she was lewd, coming on to people who had no desire in her. That she was as fake as vegetable oil butter, treating me kindly until I did something to make her jealous. That she was fatphobic for considering herself the better pick based purely on looks.

But I closed my eyes, thinking of my grandma. How happy she had been when she found out she could come home... I could do this. For her.

## 66

# HENRIETTA

*Confession: I'm afraid I'll forget what it feels like to be loved by him.*

I LIED TO MY FAMILY.

I told them I was spending a couple weeks with Tyler, but the truth was, I was staying with Mara and Jonas. Hiding out in their guest room was more like it. My heart was breaking, and I couldn't hold in my pain all day long, go to work like I hadn't just let go of the best thing that had happened to me, then continue to hold it together once I got home too.

I considered myself lucky to be born into the family I was, but meeting Tyler... it was once in a lifetime. And now that I'd let him go, I couldn't flip the script and beg him back. I'd already broken that trust.

My life fell into a survival pattern.

Sleep in as long as I could.

Go to work.

See Grandma at the hospital.

Go back to Mara's.

Say hello.

Go to sleep.

Mara tried to be there for me, and Birdie even came over to watch movies one night, but I just couldn't. Pretending everything was okay for Grandma took all my energy. I even missed Wednesday morning breakfast because I knew it would be just my friends and me and they'd ask the question: Why? Why did you let him go?

I'd gone over all my reasons in my head, every single day, trying to convince myself I'd done the right thing. If they argued, it would be too easy to do the selfish thing and take him back, ask him to stay somewhere he didn't belong. But I couldn't leave either. Not with my grandma here. Not with my savings goal still unmet.

I planned to spend the entire weekend in bed, save for a couple hospital visits, but Saturday evening, Mara and Birdie both came into my room.

"Get out of bed," Mara said.

I squinted at the bright light. "Thanks for knocking."

"It's my house, and it's for your own good!" she said. Which really made me wish I'd sucked it up and stayed at home.

Birdie sat on my bed. "I know you're sad, honey, but can you let us have a chance at cheering you up?"

I sat up against the pillows, blinking. "I don't want to feel better."

Mara and Birdie exchanged a glance.

Birdie rubbed my shoulder, asking, "What do you mean?"

I took the extra pillow and held it in front of me. "I feel like I deserve to be in pain."

Mara frowned. "That's not true, honey."

"It is!" I cried, frustrated. "You didn't see him as he was walking away, but I did. I ruined everything for him—I cost him his job, pushed him away, because I'm not ready to leave my family, and I'm afraid he'd resent me if he stayed."

Both of my friends wore matching looks of pity. I hated it, mostly because I *was* pitiful. I was a mess.

"And you know the worst part?" I asked them.

They waited for me to continue.

"In a sick way, I want to feel the pain, all of it, because it reminds me of him."

Mara said, "He was your first, Hen. He'll always be on your heart."

"But what if he isn't?" I asked. "What if I'm fifty and I forget what it feels like to be loved by him?"

Birdie pinched her lips together, thinking. "Can you write something? Maybe have a journal you can look back on?"

"Yeah," Mara said. "Or a note on your phone?"

"Not permanent enough," I said.

A small smile grew on Mara's lips. "I have an idea."

We left the house, me still in my sweats, and then she drove up to a strip mall, parking in front of a store with a sign that said TATTOO in bright red letters. There was a sign in the window too. *Walk-ins welcome.*

"A tattoo?" I said.

"You said you wanted something permanent," Mara replied.

Birdie looked over at me in the back seat. "You don't have to do this, Hen."

I shook my head. "I want to."

Without waiting for someone to talk me out of it, I pushed the door open and got out of the car, walking to the tattoo parlor's door. There was a guy in a ball cap at the front counter, scrolling through his phone. At the sound of jingling bells, he looked up, seeming bored.

"Got an appointment?"

I shook my head. "Can I get a tattoo?"

He studied me. "You eighteen?"

"Do I look like I'm eighteen?"

"You drunk?"

"I wish."

He shook his head, reaching under the counter, and then handed me a clipboard. "Fill this out, and then come back to my chair."

Birdie and Mara whispered back and forth as I filled

out the form, and when I was done, I turned to them. Birdie looked concerned, and Mara seemed annoyed.

"Look, I know you're worried about me doing something impulsive," I said, more to Birdie. "But people get tattoos all the time. And if I hate it in a year, I can put a black square over it. Okay?"

"But your job..." Birdie said. "It's already on thin ice."

"They don't care about tattoos," I said.

Birdie pressed her lips together, nodding. "If you're sure this is what you want."

I nodded. Then I followed the guy's directions and sat in his chair.

"Do you know what you want?" he asked.

I nodded, reaching for my phone. I got out a picture and showed it to him.

He studied it for a moment and said, "I can do that."

## 67

## TYLER

I stared at the ceiling of the guest bedroom in Gage's downtown condo, hearing hushed voices in the living room. I closed my eyes, wishing I had it in me to care who his guests were. But I didn't.

I'd lost my job. Lost my apartment. Lost my girl.

My life was looking like a bad country song with no royalty income to go along with it.

And it wasn't about the money—I had savings. I was willing to work hard until I found another good paying job. No, it was the way Hen looked at me and said with all certainty that it was never going to work.

I'd put my whole heart in her despite my fears and doubts. I was willing to work at it and fight until we found something we both liked. And if I was being honest, I would have done whatever it took to have her. Because I was back in Dallas now, and it didn't feel like home anymore. Not without her.

The door to my bedroom opened, and I glared toward the light coming through the door. The first couple days Gage checked in on me, but after that, he let me have my space. I was about to tell him to go away, like a petulant teenager, but then I realized it was more than just him in the doorway.

Rhett was already moving to the big window wall, using a remote to open the blinds. Liv came to me, shaking her head exactly like our mother would. "When is the last time you showered and shaved? Up. Now."

I threw my arm over my eyes to block out the light. "Why's it matter?"

She ripped the blanket and sheets off me—a move my mom used on me in middle school when I was going through puberty and could never get enough sleep.

"I'm not a child," I growled.

"Good, then you can shower yourself," she said.

Knowing Liv would never back down and she could get her other brothers to do whatever she wanted, I got out of bed and stumbled in my boxers to the bathroom. I needed to piss anyway.

Outside of the bathroom door, Gage said, "He's been like this for two weeks. Just leaves the room to get food, and then it's back to lying around. He must sleep fourteen hours a day. At least."

"I can hear you," I yelled, feeling like absolute shit

from all the time spent in bed. But he was right. Sleeping was easier than being awake with the pain of what I lost. At least sleep was black. In my waking hours, all I could see was her face.

Her face.

Telling me it could never work.

Her face.

Pushing me away no matter how much I begged her to let me stay.

Cohen, Jonas, and Steve had texted me, saying they were sorry about the split, telling me to give Hen some time, but I hadn't replied. Hen had spoken. And I'd heard her. The gaping hole in my chest was proof enough of that.

Liv yelled, "I don't hear the shower going!"

I shook my head and got off the pot, flicking the shower handle. Water poured from the rainfall showerhead, and I stepped in. Cold water pricked at my skin, but it quickly warmed. I felt just as tired, just as hollow in the shower as I'd felt outside of it, but now that I was in, I might as well make use of it.

I finished showering and used the disposable razor and travel-size shaving cream to shave my face. When I was done, there was a fresh pair of gray sweats on the bed, which had been completely stripped of sheets, along with new underwear and a white T-shirt.

My siblings weren't going away. Not until we talked.

So I got dressed and walked out of the room into

Gage's open-space living area that had a view of the entire city. The three of them sat at his glass table, looking right at me.

"Join us," Gage said, and Rhett shoved a Styrofoam box and plastic silverware toward the open seat.

"Eat," he ordered.

"You're just as bad as Liv," I muttered, dropping into the seat and opening the box. Inside was some of my favorite food—a pulled pork sandwich and coleslaw. I forced myself to take a bite, but it tasted like mushy cardboard.

They watched me stomach three mouthfuls before Gage said, "Tyler, you can't live like this."

I looked up to him, the hollow ache in my chest bigger than ever. "I don't know how to live without her anymore. It's like the second I met her, she became my air. Every morning, I woke up, waiting for the second I'd see her at work, hear her voice. And now that she's gone, I don't know how to look forward to the next day or how to even have the motivation to get up anymore."

"It's fucking hard," Rhett said, pain ghosting in his eyes. "But you get your ass up and you do it anyway because she's not the only person you love." He tapped at the windmill tattoo on his inner bicep. "We're here too, and it hurts like hell to see our brother like this."

I pushed the box of food away and scored my fingers through my hair. "Shit, guys. I'm sorry."

Liv reached over, putting her hand on my forearm.

"We know you're hurting like hell, but you're not alone. Whatever you need to get back on your feet again, we're here."

I didn't have a plan, not even close. But I would find a way to get up and go. If not for me, if not for Hen, then for them.

## 68

# HENRIETTA

*Confession: I miss him.*

**THEY SAY** time heals all wounds, but it had been two months, and I missed Tyler more than ever before.

Instead of seeing him every day, Janessa made her rounds in the office, watching everything I did and pointing out everything she thought I was doing wrong. It was exhausting. And miserable.

I've never hated my job more or dreaded going to work in the mornings. I hit all my snooze alarms and practically forced myself to roll out of bed each day, praying one of the jobs I applied to would call me back. I only hoped that Tyler had landed on his feet better than I had. I tried to check his social media accounts every so often, but all I'd seen was a picture Liv tagged him in with their other two siblings.

It hurt to see him smiling at the camera, his eyes crinkling in the corners and his perfect teeth on full display. He had his arms easily draped around Liv and Rhett's shoulders, and I would have given anything—almost anything—to trade places with them and feel his arms around me just one more time.

Weekends were easier, though. I could spend the day with my family, which was exactly why I made the choices I did. This weekend, we were sitting around the table, celebrating Bertrand's birthday.

Grandma was in her wheelchair at the table and asked, "Where's Tyler?"

I frowned, aching at the mere sound of his name. I'd been lying to all of them—telling them he was busy with the build or traveling to see his family, but the lies had been harder to keep up with. More painful to tell. "I need to tell you all something."

The table grew quiet.

"Tyler and I... we aren't together anymore. He went back to Texas a couple months ago, and I was just too embarrassed to say anything."

The table burst out into a million questions. Johmarcus wanted to know if he needed to beat him up—typical older brother. Bertrand asked if that meant Tyler wouldn't be coming to the wedding. And Justus wanted to know if he'd left me for another woman, which stung. But nothing hurt more than the disappointed look in Grandma's eyes.

"I thought he was the one," she said.

My lips trembled. "He was." I knew that much for sure.

Everyone was quiet for a moment until Dad graciously changed the subject, saying, "Bertrand, how many spankings is it this year? Twenty-six?"

A look of terror crossed Bertrand's face. "I'm too old for this shit!"

"Language!" Laila hissed.

Dad shook his head. "You're still my child."

Bertrand got up, running from the table, quickly followed by Johmarcus and Justus.

Some things never changed.

## 69

## TYLER

I lay on my childhood bed after a long day of work with a neighbor who needed help building a fence. The labor had been freeing, with hours spent under the warm spring sun, pounding away at the rain-softened earth.

But when the work was done, the pain came back. I always ate dinner at the table with Mom and Dad, not speaking much, and then I went upstairs, took a shower, lay in my bed, and prayed sleep would come quickly.

For the most part, my parents let me be. But tonight, there was a knock on the door.

"About to go to sleep," I called.

"Like hell you are," Rhett said, shoving open the door.

I propped myself on my elbows, staring at him in the dim lighting. "What the hell are you doing here?"

"I'm taking you out."

"On a Wednesday night?"

"Ladies drink free on Wednesday's. Now up."

I shook my head, lying back down. "No way in hell."

"I will drag you out of this house myself, and you know I could do it. So why don't you make this easy on both of us and leave of your own free will." He went to the closet, rifling through the clothes.

"Free will," I muttered. "Doesn't count if you're coerced."

He tossed a pair of jeans and a button-up shirt at me. "Wear this." He walked to the door. "If you're not down in five minutes, I'll come up and get you."

I shook my head. Why were my siblings so damn stubborn?

The door clicked shut, and I let out a groan. I didn't want to go to a fucking bar and have Rhett try to set me up with random women to get my dick wet. I wanted to go to sleep and forget how much it still fucking hurt to know I'd never see Henrietta again.

And I knew it wasn't healthy—you weren't supposed to make someone your whole world, but damn it, she was mine. She was more than that. She was the air that I breathed, the sun on my skin, the ground underneath my feet, and the clouds I loved to get lost in.

If I died still heartbroken, it would be a price I'd pay. Because it was proof that once I had been loved by her. Once I'd been a part of her dreams.

But I could see it in the quiet glances my parents

shared across the table. The way my siblings checked on me throughout the week. I was scaring them. So I quit thinking about myself for a second, got off my ass, and put on the clothes.

Before I knew it, I was riding shotgun in Rhett's truck, praying this night would go quickly.

♥·♥·♥·♥

RHETT PULLED UP TO NOWHERE, the only pool hall in town. It was a big wooden building with a dance floor, rows of pool tables, and enough liquor to drown an army. And since Cottonwood Falls was surrounded by a few other small towns, there was enough business to keep it going. Dad used to say people forgot about liquor when they said death and taxes were the only two certainties in life, and this town proved him right.

And judging by all the trucks in the parking lot, it was just as true on a Wednesday night as it was any other day of the week.

Rhett parked in the lot and rubbed his hands together. "Ready for a little fun?"

I gave him a look. "We both know this is my last idea of fun."

Ignoring me, he got out and started walking toward the building. Heaving a sigh, I followed him into the dusky bar. My first thought was it wasn't as nice as Collie's. My second? That I missed dancing with Henrietta.

"I need a drink," I muttered.

Rhett clapped my shoulder. "On it." We walked to the bar, and he ordered four shots of whiskey. I expected him to take two, but he slid all four to me.

I gave him a look.

"I'm driving," he said.

"And?" I'd done my best to avoid alcohol, because I knew if I started it would be too easy to spiral. Too easy to try and drown out all this pain. But that was all I had left connecting me to her.

"One night," Rhett said.

"Fine, then you take one," I replied.

He picked up a shot glass, easily dropping it back. I stared at the shots on the counter, preparing myself for the buzz of liquor. The dulling of my emotions. And the hangover I knew I'd have the next day.

And then I downed the shots, one after another. I came up coughing, and Rhett patted my shoulder, laughing. "That's how you do it."

I raised my hand and asked for a beer, which the bartender quickly brought. I reached for my card, but Rhett said, "Drinks are on me tonight."

I gave him a look before drowning half of one. The liquid slid down my throat, warming me right along with the whiskey.

"Now," Rhett said. "I see a table right over there."

Nodding, I walked toward the booth on the edge of the dance floor, wishing I wouldn't be able to see the spinning couples so well. I sat down and rolled my cup around in my hands. I was tired, but not physically. Deep in my soul.

"Hey, baby," a woman's voice said, and I looked up to see Rhett extending his hand to a blond-haired, blue-eyed girl, with her shirt low on her chest.

Rhett gave her his signature flirtatious grin. "Look what the cat dragged in."

It took all I had not to roll my eyes.

"Oh hush," she said, sliding in next to him.

Another woman stood by the table, looking a little uncomfortable and far more clothed.

"This is my friend Darletta," the blonde said. She never gave me her name.

Darletta smiled at me. "Is it okay if I sit by you?"

No. "Actually, I need to piss."

I got up, my legs feeling far less solid than earlier, and made my way to the bathroom. But as soon as I got inside and took a good look at myself in the dingy mirror, Rhett joined me.

"What the fuck, Ty?"

I turned to him. "I didn't want a setup, Rhett. I'm not ready to date anyone else."

He swore at the ground, then faced me, putting his hands on my shoulders. "Look, Mom and Dad, hell, all of us, are worried about you. It's been three months, and nothing's any better. Mom's talking about having you go in-patient for a little while."

My eyes widened. "In-patient? Like psychiatric care?"

He nodded. "And honestly, Ty, I'm not so sure I disagree with her."

"I'm not mental, Rhett. I'm fucking heartbroken," I said, my voice rising. A guy walked into the bathroom then, going back to the urinals. I lowered my voice. "You wouldn't understand."

"The fuck I wouldn't. You remember Mags?"

"The girl you dated in high school?" I asked. I barely remembered him taking her to the prom. I was already out of the house at the time.

His jaw clenched as he nodded. "I get it, Ty; I do. But that pain? It can't be all of you. You gotta turn it into a piece." He clenched his chest, right above his heart. "It won't take the hurt away, but if it's all of you, it takes away those parts of your life you do enjoy."

My jaw trembled, and I clenched it, attempting to swallow back the lump in my throat. "What do you want me to do, Rhett? Go fuck Darletta?"

A ghost of his crooked smirk was back. "I don't think it could hurt. But maybe just get used to looking at another person like you're not seconds from falling part."

I glared at him. "I hate you... but thanks."

He nodded, resting his forehead against mine. "You've got this."

# 70

## HENRIETTA

*Confession: I'm twenty-eight years old, and I still need my mom's permission sometimes.*

I HURRIED DOWN THE SIDEWALK, trying not to get completely drenched by this spring rain. I pushed through the door, lowering my denim jacket and sliding it off my arms. But I stopped in the doorway, seeing half a dozen suitcases lined up against the living room wall.

Grandma sat in her wheelchair in the living room, and I was about to ask her what was going on when I heard wheel casters rolling over vinyl. Mom rolled another suitcase into the living room, freezing when she saw me.

"Are you going on vacation?" I asked, my smile fading.

She and Grandma exchanged a look I didn't like at all.

"What's going on here?" I asked.

Mom let out a sigh. "One thing led to another, and the nurse let on that they don't, in fact, take Medicare. Only private payment. Grandma called me and asked for an explanation, and I couldn't lie to her."

Feeling something close to shame, I turned my eyes toward the ground, but Grandma said, "Henrietta, I need you to come here." She patted the couch next to her chair.

Knowing I'd been caught, I went and sat beside her.

She took my hand, holding it in her lap. "Honey, why would you use all your savings on this?"

I met her murky brown eyes, so full of love and affection and... questions. My throat was already tight as I said, "I wasn't able to do anything for Grandpa. But I can do this for you."

"Oh, honey." She met my eyes, then looked over her shoulder at my mom. "The end of your grandpa's life would have been hard no matter where he was. It was better that his last days were spent in a place we didn't have to come home to."

Her words surprised me. "He was so uncomfortable there. He wanted to come home so badly."

She reached up and cupped my face, her wrinkled palm smooth against my skin. "He did go home, honey."

My throat stung, straining against the ball of emotions growing there.

"But wouldn't it have been worth it, to have given him that wish?"

Grandma pressed her lips together thoughtfully. "Generosity is always a virtue, until the cost is your own peace. And don't take that to mean you should never feel discomfort in this life, only that certain sacrifices will haunt you and lead to resentment down the road."

I took in her words, feeling them hard in my heart. "I would never resent you, Grandma."

She shook her head. "Maybe not now. But when you learn you've missed out on the love of your life to stick around here and slave away at a job you clearly don't enjoy anymore?"

My eyes watered at the mention of Tyler. I missed him like I'd miss my right arm. He was a piece of me forever, no matter where we lived.

"It was never going to work between Tyler and me," I reminded both of us. "His family, his home is in Texas. And mine is here, with my family."

Grandma and Mom exchanged another glance, and Mom came to sit by me on the couch.

Mom said, "Hen, you've always been our baby bird, here when we need you, but it's time for you to leave the nest. You are the child, and it is not your job to take care of any of us. It's time you took care of yourself, thought about what *you* want."

I sniffed away liquid and said, "I want Grandma to be happy and know how much we love her. You've always been here for us, Grandma. You deserve the same."

Grandma smiled at me, her eyes watery. "I've lived the

best life, Hen. I met the love of my life, raised a *beautiful* family with him, and gave him my whole heart for fifty-two years. I have children I'm proud of, grandchildren I love to pieces, and great-grandchildren who bring me more joy than I know what to do with. I am happy. And I want you to be happy too."

Mom rubbed my back as I shook with tears. "Tyler made you so happy, honey. I've never seen you so light as you looked with him."

I shook my head. "It's too late with him. He hasn't called me or texted me once since he left."

Grandma laughed. "That boy is head over heels for you. I'd bet he's been moping around just as much as you have."

I laughed through my tears. "I haven't been moping."

"Have too," Mom and Grandma said at the same time.

A car pulled into the driveway, and I looked out the window to see a big white van with *Emerson Senior Living* on the side.

"That's my ride," Grandma said. "Your father is meeting us there to help me move. I want you to stay here and think about yourself for once. But please come visit me before you leave for Texas."

"Leave for Texas?" I asked, just as a knock sounded on the door.

Mom went up to get it as Grandma said, "You need to follow your heart, and I'm pretty sure that's where it is."

# 71

## HENRIETTA

*Confession: I can't believe he remembered.*

I MUST HAVE OPENED my phone a million times to send a text to Tyler. To call him and beg his forgiveness, but I always came up empty.

My family didn't need me. They were setting me free, or rather, shoving me out of the nest, even though the idea terrified me.

I had ninety-eight thousand dollars in a savings account and nowhere to go. I was lost.

After a restless night, I got up to go to work. Not because I needed to, but because I had no idea what else to do. I went to my desk, began drafting the script that was now required of me to write and turn in before every potential tenant toured the building. It was humiliating and tedious, just like Janessa wanted.

Taking a deep breath, I looked out my window, seeing the signs of spring. Buds were blooming on the trees, and the grass had greened up nicely. It was probably time for me to go to the store and see if there were any clearance annuals I could put in the flower box outside my office window that overlooked the small courtyard between apartment buildings.

I studied it, expecting to see plain dirt, but instead...

My mouth fell open, and I pushed up from my desk, running outside. I hurried around the building to the box outside my window. And then I saw them.

*Tulips.*

The flowers had opened into a beautiful shade of pink petals. My eyebrows drew together. How had they gotten there? I knew there was no way the grounds crew had planted them...

But then I remembered a conversation I had with Tyler only days after he moved here. Would he have remembered that? It was the only thing that made sense.

Forgetting my hesitation from the night before, I took a picture of the blooms and sent it to him.

Henrietta: Did you plant these?

I looked at my phone for a moment, wishing he would reply, but the sound of Janessa's voice interrupted me.

"What are you doing out here?" she asked, her pointy heels sinking into the grass as she walked toward me. "Shouldn't you be working? You know, you are on probation. If we see you lazing around, there's a good chance..."

I didn't hear the rest of her words because my phone vibrated. I stared at the screen.

Tyler: I hope they made you smile.

My heart filled, and I covered my mouth, tears stinging my eyes. It wasn't a confession of love, but it was a glimmer of hope. The last shred I had left.

"Henrietta!" Janessa trilled. "Are you really on your phone while I'm trying to talk to you?"

I looked up at her from my phone. "I quit."

"*What?*"

I gripped my phone in one hand, holding it at my side. "You heard me. I quit. I am *done* working under a jealous, controlling, *vile* person." I clenched my jaw in anger. "You had an incredible worker in Tyler. This new guy doesn't care half as much about his crew as Tyler did—that's why turnover has almost *quadrupled* since he left and why production is already a month behind. And now you'll see how much I did for this place." I walked past her, going straight for the office. "Have a nice life."

She followed behind me as I grabbed the few belongings I kept here and threw them into my purse.

"If you walk out that door, there's no coming back," Janessa threatened.

I stood in the doorway, looking at the office. At the kitschy paintings my mom had done for me, at my flourishing hanging plants, and I realized none of it mattered to me. Not if I couldn't spend my time with the people, the person, I truly loved. "The plants need watered twice a week," I said, and then I walked out the door.

## 72

## TYLER

"Something from a job?" Dad asked as we drove down the pasture to build a temporary fence around some corn stalks. We'd move the heifers there once the fence was built to get them some extra nutrition.

I only shook my head. That hollow feeling in my chest was stronger than ever as I realized Henrietta wasn't going to reply. Just like Rhett had said, I moved that pain to a part of me, right at my sternum, but it bloomed now, threatening to take over again. I'd forgotten that I planted those bulbs after our conversation when she told me she liked them.

But the fact that she had texted me after months of silence… I'd been so excited. And now I just wanted to go back to the house and hide all over again.

I'd done well since my talk with Rhett a couple weeks

ago, doing gig work with farmers and ranchers in the area while I decided my next move. I wanted to work in construction again, but a lot of employers thought I wouldn't be a good grunt worker since I'd spent so much time in management. And Jim was a big name in construction around Dallas. The second any employer saw my name on an application for a higher-up position, they called him, and I never heard from them again.

Gage offered me a job on one of his maintenance crews—he wanted to fix everything for me—but my pride turned him down. I'd been the one to mess up my career, and I was the one who needed to put it back together. How? I had no fucking clue.

I felt stuck. Trapped. I wished I would have fought with Hen to stay in Emerson. Rented an apartment and worked whatever job I could get. But it was too late. Months stood between us now. Months and a single text message. And that fact haunted me every single day.

Even home didn't feel like home. It all reminded me of Henrietta, the joy in her eyes as she saw everything for the first time. I knew in my heart she belonged here. That we belonged together.

But I had no doubt she'd find another man there locally. One who wouldn't take her away from the people she loved most. I just hoped he'd love her the way she deserved.

And me? It was looking like our family would have three perpetual bachelors in my brothers and me.

Dad and I spent the day building temporary fence, and after that, I went into Dallas to have dinner with Gage. Even though I was staying in my old room with Mom and Dad, he wanted to meet up once a week for dinner. I think to make sure I was okay. He wouldn't admit it, but I'd scared him.

Hell, I'd scared myself. I was barely climbing out of that hole, hanging on to the edge with my fingertips bleeding in the dirt. But I could see some light. And that hope... it was everything to me.

Gage and I sat in a high-end restaurant and ordered off a menu that didn't even have prices listed.

After the server left, I said, "I need to get a job."

Gage looked at me across the table, annoyance making his lips twitch just like they always did when we were kids.

"What?" I asked.

"You don't want a job. Why the fuck haven't you bought the schoolhouse yet?"

I really fucking regretted telling him about that. He'd called me the night we were at the hospital, and I'd filled him in on our brief trip to Texas. And he'd brought it up every couple of weeks since I moved out of his guest bedroom. Feeling like I was under a magnifying glass, I said, "What did you say about unsecured debt?"

"It's a trap that never pays off. And if you want to argue with me, I'll point you toward the student loan crisis."

"Right. So tell me what lender would want to work

with me when I haven't had a pay stub for months. Hell, half the people I've worked for still owe me."

"You could take a home equity loan—"

"And risk keeping a roof over my renters' heads?" I said. "They have children."

"If you'd just let me—"

I glared at him, cutting him off.

"Fine," he mumbled. "But for the record, you're being fucking stupid. And someone's going to buy that place if you don't get a move on it."

"Noted. But I think you're wrong. It's been for sale for almost six months. I've got time."

He folded his hands on the table. "Number one mistake."

"What do you mean?" I asked.

"You know how I've been able to grow my company so quickly?"

"You're smart," I said easily. "You can always spot a good deal."

"You can be smart as Einstein, but if you don't move, it means nothing. I've grown my business because I don't sit on a good opportunity. When I see something I want, I make it mine."

I looked down at the beer in my cup and took a deep drink. "I think that's enough life advice for one day."

# 73

## HENRIETTA

*Confession: My grandma is my hero.*

I WALKED through the double glass doors Emerson Senior Living. My heart beat quickly, and my stomach turned with fear. Mom had told me move-in went well yesterday, but I wanted to see for myself that it was good enough for my grandma.

The front lobby area was cozy with gilded art, cushy chairs, and plants growing in pots along the wall. As I walked a little farther in, a woman walking by in scrubs greeted me.

"Hi there! Can I help you find something?" she asked.

I picked at my thumbnail as I nodded. "I'm looking for

Cordelia Jones. I can't remember what her room number is."

"She just moved in, right?"

I nodded.

"She's in the room on the right at the end of the hall. Just walk down that way and take the second hallway."

Great. She smiled at me and continued the opposite way. I walked down the tile hallway, breathing in the disinfectant smell. But they also had some type of cinnamon air fresheners going, so it wasn't as harsh as a hospital smell. As I walked farther down the hall, I saw a big room on the left. Half of it was filled with dining tables. A few women sat around a table playing cards.

My eyebrows drew together. "Grandma?" I called. "Is that you?"

Grandma perked her head up, looking over her cards and grinned at me. "Henrietta! What are you doing here?" As I walked toward the ladies, Grandma said, "This is my favorite granddaughter, Henrietta."

The women greeted me, complimenting me profusely and making me feel like a million bucks.

"You're too sweet," I said. "What are you playing?"

Grandma held up the backs of her cards. "Skip-Bo."

"She's a natural," the white-haired lady on her left said.

Batting her hand, Grandma said, "Beginner's luck. But you'll have to excuse me. I need to show my granddaughter around!"

The women waved at her, and Grandma stacked her cards for them, putting them at the bottom of the draw pile. I got behind Grandma's wheelchair, backing her from the table and pulling her away.

"Go this way," she said, pointing toward the rec area. "They have a TV over here, and then there's an instructor that comes in and does aerobics once a day. My physical therapist came in this morning and said I can do all the exercises sitting down until I get stronger."

My throat felt tight, seeing it all. One day here, and Grandma already had friends her age. A place to go work out. A routine.

"Wait until you see the salon," she said with a wink.

"There's more?" I asked.

She directed me down a hall that had a small salon, including chairs where they could get pedicures if they made appointments. Then she showed me the back courtyard with a small community flower garden and a heated pool with sparkling blue water.

"Some people do water therapy," she explained. "I should be able to start that here in a few weeks."

I fought happy tears for her as we walked to her room. It was small inside, but my parents had set her framed photos on the dresser and nightstand, and even hung some on the walls. There was a big window out to the street so she could get sunshine. And she had her own bathroom and mini fridge.

"What do you think?" she asked.

"It's incredible," I said, sitting on the chair across from her. And I meant it. It wasn't perfect, by any means, but so much better than what I had feared. "Grandma, you're so brave."

"What do you mean?"

I looked around her new home. "You're on your own now, in your own place, meeting all new people, even after all the bad things people say about places like this. It's so brave."

She tilted her head, smiling softly. "You'd be surprised how brave you can be for the people you love."

I wished with all my heart I had been braver for Tyler. Brave enough to trust my family to take care of my grandma. Brave enough to let go of my safety net and build a life with the man I loved. Brave enough to ask for what I really wanted and let him give it to me.

Grandma asked, "Did you come all this way over your lunch break just to check on me?"

I bit my lip. "Actually...I quit my job."

Her face lit up with a smile, and she patted her hands happily on her lap. "Baby girl, that's huge! Congratulations!"

"Thank you." I couldn't help the smile I wore. It had felt so freaking good to stick it to Janessa and tell her what I truly thought.

"So when are you going to Texas?"

"How did you know..."

"Lucky guess." She had a sly grin. "So, you are going, right?"

I nodded. "I booked the first flight out of LA tomorrow morning. Mom's dropping me off so my car doesn't break down on the way."

Grandma laughed. "Please tell me you're getting rid of that hunk of junk."

"I'm selling it online. Bertrand told me a regular dealership wouldn't take it," I said with a laugh.

"This is so exciting," she said, her eyes shining.

I nodded. "It's exciting *if* it works out. We haven't even talked for months."

"A few months apart is nothing compared to the lifetime you could have together." She smiled over at a picture of her and Grandpa. "All you have to do is show him that you still care about him. That you're dreaming *with* him now."

I lifted a corner of my mouth. She was so right. It was scary to put myself out there, to go big when he could tell me to go home, but I had to. Because the thought of feeling this ache for him every day for the rest of my life... it was pure misery.

I never should have let him go. I knew that now. It had been a massive mistake, but I couldn't go back in time and fix all my worries, fear, and false sense of responsibility. All I could do now was show him that I'd never make the mistake of losing him again and pray he'd take me back.

## 74

## HENRIETTA

*Confession: I've never been so scared in my life.*

AS I DROVE my brand new (to me) SUV away from the Dallas dealership, my heart was racing. I hoped I wouldn't be driving this car back to California any time soon.

A call came through on Bluetooth, and I tapped the green button on the screen, feeling fancier than I ever felt in my puddle jumper. I answered it, and my dad's voice filled the car.

"Hey, Hen. I just got off the phone with our lender, and they're sending you a pre-qual letter. You're good to put in an offer if that's what you decide to do."

My heart lurched, and I took a few deep breaths to focus on this busy Dallas traffic. Even driving out of town, the roads were packed. I definitely hadn't timed my trip well, leaving the dealership around five.

"Are you sure you're okay with co-signing for me?" I asked.

Dad quickly replied. "Of course we are. I know you'll never need us to help with a payment with how frugal you are."

I laughed. "The vote of confidence is nice."

"Did you splurge on your car?" he asked.

"Yes! We're actually talking on my new-car phone! I went with a Cherokee like Johmarcus suggested. Runs like a dream, and hopefully, I won't be changing tires on the side of the road anymore."

"Good," Dad said. "You deserve to have something nice."

"Thanks, Daddy," I said.

I heard the smile in his voice as he said, "Go get 'em, tiger. Call us after to tell us how it went."

"Pray for good news," I asked.

"We already are."

We hung up, and then I tapped through to call the only romance author I knew. She answered after a few rings, and I said, "Mara, I need some advice."

"Anything. How can I help?"

My cheeks warmed, but I barreled ahead with my embarrassing question. "Well, since you're kind of the expert on grand gestures and couples making up... I wanted some tips on how to do that with Tyler."

Her squeal rang throughout my car. "You're trying to get him back?"

My smile grew. "I'm in Texas right now."

"Oh my *gosh!*" she pealed.

I bit my lip, realizing I should have stopped by to tell my friends goodbye before I dropped everything to start a new life here (hopefully). But thinking of myself was new, and I didn't want to lose my nerve.

"What changed your mind?" she asked.

"He planted tulips in my flower box."

"Is that an innuendo?"

I laughed and filled her in on the whirlwind of the last couple of days.

"Does that mean we won't see you on Wednesday mornings when I'm home?" she asked. She usually videoed in with Birdie and me when she had to be in Georgia to help write for a body positive TV show.

"It means we'll be doing virtual breakfasts, I hope."

"Awesome," she said. "So here's what you do…"

♥⋅♥⋅♥⋅♥

I PULLED up to the old school building on the outskirts of Cottonwood Falls. It was just as impressive as I remembered it. There was traditional brick, big white columns, and big windows wrapped around the building. It would take some work to make my dream come true, but I was ready for work. I was ready to build a life with Tyler from the ground floor.

Soon after I parked, a white pickup pulled in next to me, and through the tinted windows, I recognized Linda from Thanksgiving. She had a new short haircut that accentuated her pointed chin.

I got out of my car to talk to her, giving her a big smile and a wave. "I love that new haircut on you!"

"Henrietta, you are just so sweet," she said. The sad look in her eyes told me otherwise.

A sinking feeling filled my gut. Had word of my breakup with Tyler gotten around town? Was there something, or someone else, I didn't know about?

I shoved aside my fear and said, "Should we go inside and look around? Or can I make the offer now?"

She wrung her thin hands. "I'm so sorry, but the building sold."

Punch to the face. The chest. The gut. "*What?* We talked on the phone this morning. Why didn't you call me?"

"I tried to get ahold of you, but it went straight to voicemail. I left a message."

I must have missed the notification in all the rush of getting off the plane and car shopping. "What happened?"

"We had a cash offer over asking price that the seller couldn't turn down. I'm so sorry. I know you were excited about this."

Despair washed over me. This had been my grand

gesture. My way to show Tyler that I was committed to him, to building a life together regardless of where we were. That I wanted *him* to be my family.

But then I remembered where I came from. My grandma taught me that a stubborn streak can move mountains. My mom taught me anything can grow with a little care. My brothers taught me to go down swinging. And my dad? He taught me how to get my hands dirty and find my own solution instead of sitting around and waiting for a hero.

I was *not* losing this sale.

"Who bought it?" I asked.

She frowned. "I'm really not at liberty to say. You'll be able to search the public records once they're updated."

I reached into my purse, pulling out a hundred-dollar bill.

She eyed it, then me, then took the money. Wordlessly, she tucked the bill in a zipper pocket of her purse, then pulled out a business card.

I held the black cardstock in my hand, desperately reading the information, and my jaw fell to the floor.

**Gage Griffen, CEO**

## 75

## GAGE

My desk phone beeped, and I pressed the button. "Yes, Mia?"

"You have a call from a 'Ms. Jones.' I told her you were busy, but she said it was an urgent family matter."

My shoulders tensed with dread. No matter how hard of a line I'd drawn between my parents and myself, the thought of them passing before we had a chance to make amends... it was a fear that haunted me every damn day.

"Send it through," I said, closing my eyes and hoping like hell it wasn't bad news.

The phone rang, and I gripped the receiver, holding it to my ear. "This is Gage Griffen."

A clear voice came through the phone, strong and in control. "This is Henrietta Jones."

I blinked at the name. "Tyler's Henrietta?"

"I have to know why you bought the schoolhouse. I know for a fact he would never accept a handout from you. Are you trying to take it out from under him?"

I bristled at the harshness in her tone. "I bought it so someone else doesn't do what you're accusing me of. I thought I would hold on to it until he gets his head out of his ass and buys the place himself." In fact, the ink had barely dried on the papers. "How did you find out?"

"I..." She hesitated for the first time since barreling into this call.

"What?" I demanded.

"I'm in Cottonwood Falls. I was going to put in an offer."

"You're *where*?"

"Standing in front of the school right now," she replied.

I reached for the blazer hanging over the back of my chair. "I'll meet you there in an hour and a half."

And then I did something I hadn't done in over a decade—I left the office early for a personal matter.

I rushed past the reception area, and Mia called, "Everything okay?"

The relief I felt throughout my body had me smiling. "More than okay."

I got in the elevator and took it all the way down to the parking garage. My Tesla waited for me in a reserved spot near the door. The car unlocked as I neared, and I got in, tossing my jacket in the passenger seat. The engine quietly revved as I whipped out of the parking garage and onto the road. The sky was already dusky, but I raced through traffic, driving to Cottonwood Falls as quickly as I could. Usually the drive took a good two hours, but I could shave off thirty minutes.

As I flew down the interstate, I dialed Tyler's phone number.

"What's up?" he answered.

"I need you to meet me at the schoolhouse tonight."

"What? Why? I already told you I'm waiting until I find a steady job."

"Indulge me," I said.

I could practically feel him rolling his eyes. "Only if we hit the diner after. I'm fucking starving."

The idea of sitting in the diner where I used to hang out in high school made my skin crawl, but I had a feeling when he found out what was waiting for him, he wouldn't hold me to it.

"Fine," I said. "Be at the school in an hour."

"See you then."

We hung up just as I reached the city limit sign of Cottonwood Falls. Incorporated. Population 8,432.

An unpleasant mixture of anger, guilt, and regret flooded my body at the familiar sights. My life would have been so different if my dad didn't have his head up his ass. I would have been working on the family farm, growing something that had been built over generations.

Instead, I worked in an office, had employees working

for me that I'd never even met before. I hadn't even come into town to buy the damn building, but I needed to see Henrietta for myself. I had to make sure she was honest about her intentions before I did what I wanted to do.

I turned down the streets so familiar they'd been buried into an automatic part of my memory. As I reached the school, I saw a red SUV parked out front, temporary tags on the back. Then my eyes drifted to the front entrance of the school.

A woman with dark skin and ample curves sat on the porch steps, her elbows on her knees and her chin in her hands. An orange security light cast a halo around her, making her black hair appear almost golden. This was Tyler's Henrietta.

Part of me wanted to hate this woman. Wasn't she the one who had broken my brother to the point he wouldn't get out of bed? The one who caused that ever-present glint of pain in his eyes, even months later?

But the way he loved her made me care for her too. I wanted this to work for them—if she was here for good. I couldn't watch my brother go through this again.

Clearing my throat, I turned off the car and got out, walking toward where she sat. With Tyler on the way, we didn't have much time, and I had plenty to say.

She eyed me wearily as I approached. "Are you Gage?"

I nodded.

"You look just like him. But you have your mom's hair color."

"Except mine doesn't come from a box for six ninety-five," I said.

A small smile formed on her lips, but her expression quickly turned serious. "Gage, I want to buy the schoolhouse from you. I have a significant down payment, and even though I don't have a job here yet, my parents co-signed with me on the loan. I'm hoping Tyler will help me turn this into his dream come true.... together."

I studied her, looking for any hint of inauthenticity. In my line of work, most of my decisions were analytical, but there also came a time to trust your gut. And this woman, with her wide brown eyes and lips pulled down with worry? She was the real deal.

"I'm not selling it to you," I said.

Her mouth fell open. "Gage, you have to know how much this would mean to us." Her eyes grew shiny with tears. "Unless he's found someone else." She put her head in her hands. "Oh god, I'm so stupid. I should have called before I—"

I stepped closer, putting my hand on her shoulder. "I'm not selling the schoolhouse to you, because I'm giving it to you."

All her pain was replaced with shock, so easily visible in each of her features. "What?"

"You said you had a down payment. I want you to use that money, and the money Tyler has saved, to build this business. And if Tyler's pride requires him to pay me back, I'll take a cut of the profits over time as an investor. Even if it's annoying."

Now a smile played across her lips. "Gage... that's amazing. Are you sure?"

I chewed the inside of my cheek, not sure how much to give away. "I've never seen my brother happier than when he was with you... or more devastated than when it ended. I'd give everything I have never to see him like that again."

I studied her, waiting to see her response, already knowing I'd be able to read her.

"I may have ended things, but it was the worst mistake I've ever made. If he gives me another chance, I promise you both I'll never waste it."

I saw something in her face, heard it in her words. The truth.

Headlights panned over us, and we looked over to see Tyler's truck pulling up to the school.

## 76

## TYLER

I blinked at the windshield because I couldn't be seeing straight. Gage stood on the front steps of the school with Henrietta.

Seeing her was like a punch to the gut and a drink of fresh water after months in the desert. She was beautiful, even in the dim lighting. The light yellow dress she wore hugged her curves, and her hair fell down her back in soft curls. I wanted to kiss her, I wanted to hold her, I wanted to pool her hair in my hands and breathe in her scent I'd missed so damn much.

But I was hurt too, and that pain kept me sitting in the truck, staring at my brother and the woman I loved.

How long had Gage been talking with her? How long had he known her?

What were they doing here? Together?

Movement made me refocus my gaze, and I saw Gage walking toward me, quickly striding across the distance still in his work clothes. He reached my window and rolled his finger through the air.

My arm felt stiff and heavy as cement as I reached for the button and pushed it down. A fresh blast of cool spring air and Gage's cologne came into the truck.

"What are you doing?" he asked, a slight smile on his face. "Get over there!"

"Gage, I'm gonna need a little more explanation than that. What the hell is going on?"

"I think Henrietta needs to be the one to explain that to you. Call me tomorrow. I'll take you both out to eat somewhere better than the diner."

Despite my protests, he walked to his car and pulled away, leaving just a red Jeep in the lot.

It was just Henrietta and me. She looked at me. I looked at her. She waited on the steps. I waited in the truck. But with my window rolled down, I felt more exposed than I had in the safety of my enclosed truck cab.

She tilted her head, a question in her eyes. *Will you hear me out?*

I had to. Because all the pain this woman had caused me had been from her absence, not her presence. With my body feeling different than my own, I pushed the door open, stepping down and feeling every bit of gravel under my boots.

I kept my eyes on her, silence, pain, distance filling the

space between us, no matter how close I got. I stepped onto the porch with her, enveloped by the harsh glow and buzzing of the safety lights.

"Hi," she whispered.

That little box I'd been keeping my pain in for the last two weeks? It completely shattered with that one word. "Hi," I managed, my voice sounding strangled.

I watched her a second longer, not knowing how to ask the question on the tip of my tongue.

*What are you doing here?*

Instead, I asked something different. "Is that your car?"

She looked around like she'd forgotten completely how she'd arrived. When her gaze landed on the red vehicle, her eyes widened slightly in recognition. "I bought it today," she said. "After I got to Dallas."

"You bought a car?"

A small smile played along her lips. "It turns out my grandma didn't want me to sacrifice the love of my life for her to stay at home."

Those words... they assaulted my heart, pulverizing the already tender muscle. "She didn't?"

Hen shook her head. "My grandma requested to move into a senior living center, and it's great. She already has friends she's beating at cards." Hen smiled softly at the cracked cement beneath us. "And seeing those flowers you planted for me... I realized I wanted to grow something just as beautiful... with you."

It was everything I'd ever wanted her to say, but my life was a mess. And her family was still in California. "Hen, I love you."

She smiled up at me. "You do?"

It took all the strength I had to keep my hands at my sides. I wanted to hold her face and kiss her just to show her how much love I had for her. I only wanted her to be happy with the life she wanted to live. And she'd chosen one without me. "Of course I love you. I love you in a way I've never loved another woman. But you love your family. And even though I miss you like crazy, I can't promise forever to someone who'd put me second. I barely made it through you turning me away the last time. I couldn't make it through another."

"I'm not going anywhere, Tyler," she said stubbornly.

Didn't she get it? We had our window. Our opening where my job wasn't an issue. I'd offered to stay! But my savings were lower now. "I don't have anything for you here!" My voice echoed off the bricks. "I don't have a job. No one in construction will hire me with my reputation, and I don't have the capital for my own business. I'm living with my parents now because I can't kick out my renters. I have nothing, Hen."

She turned toward the school. "What if I do?"

It was like she was speaking in riddles, and the anger and pain in my chest had me letting out a mix between a laugh and a cry. "What do you mean?"

Facing me again, she said, "The reason why my

grandma wouldn't accept my help was because of the life she had with my grandpa. She knew I could have that kind of life... with you."

The buoyancy in my chest was dangerous. The kind that could end a guy if he didn't watch out.

She reached out for my hand, her touch instantly making a lump grow in my throat. "Tyler, I've spent my whole life with my family, being loved and cared for by them. And part of me thought I didn't deserve it, no matter how freely they loved me. I thought I had to earn it, thought I had to protect them because of how they cared for me. But that's not what they wanted for me. And it turns out... that's not what I wanted for myself."

She held her other hand to my cheek, wiping away an errant tear I hadn't realized was there. "Tyler, I want to build a life with you, a family, a home. This building? It's so much more than four walls and a roof. It's a place where we can make our own mark, serve others the way they deserve, and grow our life, *together*."

The dream she was speaking of was everything I'd wanted for us. But I had to tell her the truth. "I can't give that to you, Hen. I don't have a job, no way to get financing for a project this size."

"Now that my grandma's care is covered, I have enough to invest. My whole life savings is ready to create this with you."

I held her face in my hand, tears falling unapologetically down my cheeks. "I can't ask that of you. To give everything you have to me."

Her voice cracked. "Tyler, I already have. My heart? It's yours. My body? My life? Yours. There will never be anyone else like you, no one to replace you, Tyler." She held her hand to her chest. "If I have to renovate this thing by myself until I can prove to you how committed I am, I'll do it."

As she gesticulated, I noticed something on her wrist I hadn't seen before. I took her arm and held it up, giving me a clear view of her skin in the light.

"What are you doing?" she asked.

"Hen, what is this?"

She looked from my eyes to her wrist. South of her thumb, right below the crease, was a windmill. Just like mine.

"When did you get this?" I asked.

She bit her lip, tears filling her eyes. "A week after you left."

My voice was hoarse as I whispered, "Why?"

"Because I knew no matter how much I moved, my heart would always be with you. You're the one, Tyler."

I couldn't hold myself back anymore. I wrapped my arms around her middle and pulled her close to me, kissing her with all I had. Every ache, every tear, every broken dream from the last several months, I poured into our embrace.

"Marry me," I said against her lips.

She looked up at me, her eyes wide. "What?"

"I'm not going another day in this life without you by my side," I said. "Be my wife."

Tears fell down her cheeks as she nodded.

I covered her yes with my kiss, filled with dreams of forever.

## 77

## HENRIETTA

*Confession: I still can't believe I'm getting my happily ever after.*

TYLER WIPED AWAY my tears with his thumbs. "I'm so happy you came here. I never knew how much I was missing in my life before I met you."

I smiled up at him, my lips trembling with emotion. "I knew what was missing. I just didn't know love could be as incredible as it is with you."

He lifted my hand to his lips, kissing my palm, and then he placed his lips over the windmill at my wrist. "Let's get out of here?"

I nodded, despite the worry filling my heart. "Will your family forgive me for the way I hurt you?"

"They love you, Hen. When I first came home, I

stayed with Gage because I knew my parents would tell me to get my ass back to California and win you back."

*What would have happened if he had come back?* I wondered. Would I have accepted him?

No, I decided. I never would have asked him to give up his home for me. Tyler's dreams existed here, and my family would always be there for me. I'd never cared where I was, as long as I was with the people I loved.

"Is it okay for me to stay at your parents' house tonight, on such short notice?" I asked, biting my lip.

"It would be... except I have another idea."

Tyler drove me to one of the three hotels in town, lifting his middle console so I could slide over and sit tucked against his side. After so long apart, we weren't wasting a minute together. He insisted my car would be fine at the schoolhouse overnight, but that was the last thing on my mind.

We walked down the hallway over green and gold carpet to room 106. Tyler held the keycard against the reader, and we stepped into the room. Together. A million missed moments and painful memories filled the space between us.

For a moment, I stood, looking at the bed. He slipped off his cowboy boots, the leather worn with hard work. My own white sneakers were a contrast in almost every way.

That was us. We were different. Him, a tall, strong country boy from Texas. Me, a curvy city girl who'd always been under her family's wing. But together? We created something different entirely. A pair of people who led with love, who served with our whole hearts, and who fumbled through life until we finally got something right. Each other.

"Lie down with me," he asked, lifting the blanket.

I nodded, walking around the other side of the bed to curl in next to his warm body. He was so solid against me, and I slid my hand under his shirt, running it over the ridges of his stomach, the crisp of his chest hair, the slope of his collarbone, the divot at the base of his neck and back down again.

He pressed a kiss to my temple, drawing emotion to my eyes again. It was like my heart had barely scabbed over the last few months apart, and being here with him now pulled me all the way open, leaving me more vulnerable than ever before.

I lifted my face to him, kissing him slowly. Refamiliarizing myself with his taste, the swirl of his tongue against mine, the scratch of his five o'clock shadow over my chin. And then I needed to remember more, to feel more.

I gripped the hem of his shirt, pulling it up, and he helped me, slipping it over his head before moving to my dress, pulling it off. And then we were back together.

Kissing.

Savoring.

*Loving.*

Our middles pressed together, his skin warm against mine. His hands gentle on my hips, my shoulders.

With each second that passed, our kiss intensified, our hands explored. His palm slid against my ass, lifting my thigh so it crossed over his hip, and then there was space for him to gently slide my thong aside, to run his thumb along my slit.

My breath caught as he slipped a finger inside and then lifted it to his lips. He drew his finger in his mouth, closing his eyes. "I missed the way you taste."

Moisture pooled between my legs. "I missed the way you feel," I breathed.

"Not much longer, baby," he breathed, kissing me again, bringing his hand back down and circling his fingers around my clit.

As the sensation grew between my legs, I bucked against his hand. Tears filled my eyes, dripped over my nose and down my cheek as my orgasm built. Tyler was back, he was with me, he loved me.

And then I came into his hand, crying out his name.

With my orgasm still rocking my body, he rolled me to my back and unzipped his pants. Pulled them down just enough to plunge into me.

I stretched around him, my body having tightened up in his absence.

"Baby," he breathed against my lips.

"I love you," I cried, tears flowing freely. "I love you so damn much, Tyler."

"I love you," he said, pumping fast. "I love you."

"I love you."

Our words slowly transformed into breathless pants until his orgasm came and he pumped harder into me, letting go of all he had and filling me completely.

He lay on top of me, letting his orgasm dwindle, then he rolled to the side, opening his arms for me to lie in my nook. I kissed the bulge of his shoulder muscle and then lay in his arms. He wrapped them around me, tracing his fingers gently up and down my side, and one word came to mind.

Home.

This was home.

"I can't believe I get to be your wife," I said, a smile stretching my lips.

"I can't believe you said yes." He froze, then rolled away from me.

His swift distance made my heart stall. "Tyler? Are you alright?" I asked, when really what I needed to know was *are we okay?* Did he realize getting back together with me was a mistake?

There was a deep crease between his eyebrows and his mouth was pinched as he kicked off his jeans the rest of the way and paced the room.

"I fucked up, Hen."

My heart sank, on the precipice of sheer destruction. "What do you mean?"

He shook his head angrily.

"Tyler, you're scaring me."

Almost as if he remembered I was in the room, his expression softened and he came closer to me, kissing my forehead. "You didn't do anything wrong. It was me." And then he was back to pacing. "I asked you to marry me without asking your dad first. How could I have been so stupid?"

All the worry let out of me like a balloon releasing air, and I laughed. "That's what you're worried about?"

A tortured expression pained his face as he looked at me. "That's not how I do things, Hen. I want to do them the right way with you."

I bit my lip, shaking my head. "My dad's happy if I'm happy. And I am, Tyler. So, so happy."

His features lightened a little bit as he knelt by the bed next to me. "I love you. But please don't tell him until I have the chance to ask for his blessing."

I'd do anything for this man, but hiding my excitement from our families? "Okay, but only if you promise to ask him soon."

♥•♥•♥•♥

WOODY'S WAS no Waldo's Diner, but their pancakes were delicious, and they had a table in the back corner perfect for Wednesday morning brunches with my best friends. Only this time, I had news. Big news.

I sat with my pancakes ordered and my coffee

steaming and pressed *call* to be on Birdie's table. Within a few rings, they answered, Birdie and Mara sitting on the same side of the booth with their own pancakes.

Mara jumped right into it. "Tell us how it went!"

I grinned at them, holding up my hand to show them the silver engagement ring on my finger with an oval diamond set in the middle. Classic, modest, beautiful, just like the man who had given it to me.

Their screams came through my phone, making a few of the regulars around me turn their heads.

"You're getting married?!" Birdie cried.

I nodded, smiling so hard my cheeks almost closed my eyes. "He asked me that night I came back. We just got the ring yesterday!"

"That was fast!" Mara said. "The grand gesture must have been really good."

I laughed and filled them in on the confusion of the day, hearing that Tyler's brother had bought the schoolhouse and then talking with Tyler on the porch.

Birdie had her hands laced under her chin, practically swooning. "That is so romantic."

"It's been amazing these last couple days, just catching up on everything we missed."

Mara winked. "And the make-up sex."

My cheeks heated as someone in the booth next to me gave me the side-eye. I scratched my neck nervously, looking down. "That too."

"I'm so happy for you," Mara said.

Birdie nodded but had a frown on her lips. "Does this mean you're there permanently?"

My heart tugged at the question. Birdie had been my first real adult girlfriend. Her moving into the apartments and introducing me to Mara had changed my life in so many ways. Saying goodbye would be too hard. So I'd have to settle on see you soon. "I'll be back," I promised. "Frequently. Apparently, Tyler's brother has a ton of flight miles from his business credit card that he's practically begging everyone to use. And of course I want you all to come and visit us." I told them all about the schoolhouse and our plans for the building.

Birdie said, "I'll take you up on that. Is there even a hotel in that town?"

I laughed. "Two, actually. And a motel."

"Fancy," Birdie said with a laugh.

"Where are you and Tyler staying?" Mara asked. "With his family?"

"For now," I answered. "But we're working to renovate a living space for us at the schoolhouse for us first. We're going to be staying there and managing the property on site so we can give better help to the residents. Tyler thinks he can have it livable in a month, since this is our full-time job now. Bertrand even offered to take a week off work to come help us get settled."

"Your family's all on board?" Birdie asked.

"Oh yeah." I laughed, twirling my engagement ring

around my finger. "They practically shoved me out the door to get him back. They all love him as much as I do."

Mara bumped her shoulder against Birdie's. "We love him too."

Birdie nodded. "If I could have hand-designed a guy for you, even he wouldn't have been half the man that Tyler is."

"He is pretty amazing." I took a sip of my coffee that was already cooling down. "I do have a question though."

"What's up?" Mara asked.

I bit my lip, holding back a smile. "What are you doing a month from now?"

Birdie and Mara exchanged a glance.

"Because I'd love for you to stand by my side when I say 'I do'," I finished.

Another round of squealing had people sending me more looks. In a town this size, I was bound to have a reputation before our wedding announcement hit the local paper.

Birdie said, "That's so soon. Are you worried about planning the wedding?"

"We would have gone to city hall yesterday, but Tyler wants to ask my dad for his blessing before we tie the knot," I admitted. "And Tyler's mom and sister begged for us to have a wedding for our families to get a chance to celebrate and meet each other. So, this was the compromise." My grin spread across my entire face. It was crazy, getting married this soon to the man I lost my virginity to, but on a soul level, it didn't feel crazy at all.

It felt right.

Perfect.

Inevitable.

I just couldn't wait.

## 78

## TYLER

A week after Hen came to Cottonwood Falls, I drove to DFW Airport to pick up Bertrand. The second Hen told him about our project, he said he wanted to come and return the favor for helping his family with their home. Even though I told him he didn't need to, he insisted, and it was probably a good thing he had.

The only problem? I still hadn't called Hen's dad to ask his blessing. I'd already fucked up, and I knew this was a conversation we needed to have in person. But with how hard we'd been working on the schoolhouse, I hadn't had the time to fly to California.

For the last week, Hen and I had worked all day every day to get the top part of the schoolhouse up and running so we'd have our own place to stay, hopefully by our wedding night. But at this rate, we were still a couple weeks behind. And with my chicken-shit behavior, the wedding would have to be pushed back too unless I found a way to talk to her dad.

Except with Bertrand coming, I wasn't sure how much longer we could keep our engagement a secret. What if Bertrand told their parents before I had a chance?

I reached the airport and exited into the cell phone lot to wait until Bertrand texted me that he was ready. My hands were jumpy on the steering wheel with nerves. In an hour, he'd see the ring on his sister's finger. He'd know I'd done things in the wrong order.

**Bertrand: I'm here. Hope you have extra room in your truck. Brought a lot of baggage.**

I laughed at the phone, his text breaking the tension.

**Tyler: You must pack like your sister.**

I put the truck in drive and pulled around the curb, taking deep breaths. Bertrand came into view, standing next to a single duffel bag. Rolling down the window, I said, "What happened to all your bags?"

He nodded his head over his shoulder, and two other Joneses came through the airport doors. My jaw dropped at all of Hen's brothers being in Dallas.

"What the hell?" I laughed out, grinning wide as I got

out of my truck. I hugged Bertrand, Johmarcus, and Justus. And then I saw Murphy walk out the door.

My blood went cold. I had two hours between here and Cottonwood Falls before he saw the ring on his daughter's hand and found out I was a coward.

My knees buckled, and I knelt in front of Murphy. "Can I marry you?"

He stared at me, confusion scrunching up his nose. "You okay, son?"

I shook my head, standing up. "Sorry, I fucked up. Shit. Sorry for cussing. *Shit.*" I was *really* fucking this one up. I ran my hand over my face, trying to give myself an internal pep talk.

"I asked Henrietta to marry me." Shock raised his eyebrows, but I pressed on. "I know I should have asked you first, but I was so excited she wanted me back that my heart spoke before my mind thought. And now that I asked, and she said yes, I can't take it back from her. But I wanted to know if we could have your blessing, despite my lapse in judgment."

Murphy shook his head, grinning. "Her yes was all the blessing you needed." He wrapped his arms around my shoulders. "Welcome to the family."

Hen's brothers joined in the celebration, patting my back and whooping it up. Until a security guard yelled, "HEY! Get a move on."

The guys were still laughing as we piled into the truck and headed toward home.

♥⋅♥⋅♥⋅♥

I PARKED the truck at the schoolhouse in between the plumber's truck and the electrician's van. Gary Johnson, the plumber, had been working around town since I was in diapers, and he'd been thrilled to get his hands on this school to turn it into something of use. He'd been working with us the last week to plumb a new kitchen and bathroom upstairs. When that was all done, he'd plumb bathrooms and kitchenettes in the units downstairs.

Grant Arnold, the electrician, had worked with me on projects in Dallas back when I was starting out on a construction crew. He was cutting us a special price to upgrade the wiring in the entire building. He'd also hang new ceiling fans and decorative lights for each room.

Meanwhile, Hen and I had worked on framing out the bedrooms, hanging up drywall and repairing cracks that had formed in the ceiling over the years. This week, I had hoped Bertrand would help us lay flooring and maybe even install some stock cabinets from the nearest box store, but now that the four of them were here, I couldn't wait to see how much we'd accomplish. I knew firsthand how hard and fast these guys could work.

As we got out of the truck and walked toward the front entrance, excitement rushed through me. Maybe we would get this all done on time for our wedding, which could happen now—with her father's blessing.

Everything was finally falling into place.

# 79

## HENRIETTA

*Confession: I used to think moving meant leaving my home. I couldn't have been more wrong.*

I SCRAPED the drywall knife over a seam, making it disappear in one quick movement. I'd helped Dad with drywall patches around the house, but Tyler had to show me how to hang big sheets of drywall, making walls appear where there had been none. It was heady, seeing something this big come together thanks to the work of my own two hands. I couldn't wait for Bertrand to get here so we could show him all we'd already done.

From downstairs, Tyler called out, "Babe! We're here!"

I grinned, setting down my bucket of joint compound and wiped my hands on my work overalls. I put my hand on the oak stair railing and went down the stairs, excited to wrap my brother in a big hug and show him this life I was building.

But when I got halfway down the stairs and the entrance came into view, I froze. Not only was Bertrand in the entryway, but so were Johmarcus, Justus, and my dad.

My mouth fell open. "What are you doing here?"

Grinning, Dad said, "Came to help you out, but it sounds like we'll be celebrating your engagement too."

I looked from Dad to Tyler, and Tyler nodded.

"Come here, baby girl," Dad said.

I jumped down the rest of the stairs, running to my dad and letting him wrap me in his arms. We rocked back and forth as he spoke into my hair. "I'm so happy for you, honey. He's one of the good ones."

"Thanks, Daddy," I said, stepping back. "I can't wait for you to see it."

He slipped his hand in mine and said, "Show us around."

We walked through the ground floor, which had barely been touched except by Grant to upgrade the wiring. There were six classrooms down here and a massive kitchen. All of it would be converted to six apartments and a common area for mail, laundry, and a small office space.

Then we went upstairs, where there were another six classrooms. Tyler and I had demoed half of them to make room for our future kitchen, living room, and primary bedroom with an en suite bathroom.

We also introduced my brothers and dad to Grant, who was working in the kitchen to wire all the plugs we'd need, and Gary, who was in the bathroom, building plumbing for all the fixtures.

"Holy crap," Johmarcus said as we all stood in the open living area. "You've been busy the last week."

I laughed, looking around at the walls that had been taken down and the walls that were already built up, joint compound drying on the drywall. "It's been a whirlwind. Gary and Grant are helping a bunch, and now that you're here, it'll move so much faster! Thank you for doing this. It means the world." I looked at all the men in my life. It seemed like I'd been crying constantly the last several months between sad and happy tears, but these were happy tears.

I'd been so afraid to move, afraid of losing my family, but seeing them here in my new home, I knew I'd been so wrong to worry. I hadn't lost my family—it had grown. My life was so much better for it.

"Do we need to take you to the hotel to get you settled in?" I asked.

Justus pulled his head back. "Hell no. Girl, you need all the help you can get."

I laughed. "Then let's get to work."

♥·♥·♥·♥

TYLER and I had also made a tearfully happy video call to Grandma and Mom, who celebrated our engagement with us and were already planning what they wanted to wear to our wedding. Mom asked for Deidre's number, and they had quickly started talking by video call, planning the wedding and getting to know each other while Tyler and I worked on the house with my brothers and dad.

In five days, the guys had all the drywall up in the main living areas and had laid hardwood floors with lots of soundproofing so we wouldn't disturb future tenants below. Now Dad and I were on the way to the nearest box store to pick up my cabinet order. The kitchen was going to be kitschy and cute with light blue cabinets, vinyl countertops with a Calcutta marble pattern, and a big island in the middle with room for family, just like the kitchen at home in California.

Tyler's parents had loaned us a horse trailer to carry all the cabinets from the store, and I had to smile at the way my life had changed. At least Dad had rented a trailer way back when I was a teenager to teach me how to pull one; otherwise I'd be completely lost.

He sat in the passenger seat of Tyler's truck, music playing softly through the speakers as the sun shined down on us.

"The skies seem bigger in Texas," he said, gazing out at the landscape blurring past, blue skies before us, dotted with puffy white clouds.

"Haven't you heard? Everything's bigger here," I teased.

He chuckled. "You seem happy here. Like you were always meant to be here."

I felt that way, but it made me happy that my dad noticed, that he didn't hold it against me that I'd decided to move here. "It felt like home the moment I arrived." I'd already met so many people. Apparently, in a small town, any major project called for random visits just to see what was going on.

I'd met the hairdresser, two bank tellers, some teachers, and a handful of other townspeople. They all welcomed me warmly and were so happy to hear that Tyler was back for good. Not to mention Liv had already invited me to go out with her and her friends. My community here was growing so quickly. But most of all, I had Tyler by my side.

We reached the store, and I pulled up along the big garage doors for pickup. An employee came out and took my order number and ID and said he'd be back to load them up in just a little bit.

I smiled and nodded, then sat back to wait with my dad. When I glanced at him, he had a thoughtful expression on his face.

"What are you thinking about?" I asked.

"I'm realizing this might be one of our last chances to talk before you get married next month."

My heart wobbled at the truth. I was getting married in May and then Bertrand would be married in August, just a couple months from now. All of us kids were grown, out of the nest, even if it was later than most. "It'll be just you and Mom in the house."

He nodded. "It just hit me that there's so much that I haven't told you about marriage, about life."

I reached across the middle console, covering his hand with mine. "I'm only a phone call away, Dad. You can call and tell me any time."

He glanced my way with a somber smile. "But there are some things I want to tell you *before* you get married."

"Sure," I said. "I think I need all the advice I can get."

His chuckle rumbled in his chest, and then he sobered. "Mom and I always saved our big arguments for after you kids were asleep, but I don't want you to think we never had any fights."

"You were never that coy," I replied. "Mom would always burn your toast the day after."

He laughed. "A small price to pay for some of the dumb stuff I've done. But you know, I'm thankful for those arguments. Everyone thinks that getting married is supposed to be a happily ever after where you feel only love and never pain, but it's not."

My eyebrows drew together. My parents were some of the happiest, most in love people I knew. "What do you mean?"

"Do you remember when Justus tore his ACL playing football? After the surgery, the doctor told him that his left leg would be stronger than his right, even though that was the one that had been injured. Because the strength, the healing, comes in the repair."

I nodded, understanding what he meant.

"When you and Tyler have arguments, because you will, don't look at it like a break from the ideal life you want to live. Look at it as a chance to make things stronger than they were before."

"Of course," I managed.

"And forget about all that nonsense everyone wants to sell you about marriage being fifty-fifty. People get so caught up in making things equal that they forget marriage isn't just a contract on a piece of paper. It's a commitment to serve each other in sickness and in health. Richer and poorer. There will be times Tyler's too sick to do the dishes." Dad winked. "That means you'll have an opportunity to serve him by finishing them up. There will be times when you've had a hard day with the kids, if you decide to have children, and he'll be there to pick up the slack, even if the bedtime routine is usually your task. Don't get caught up in keeping score, because in a marriage, you're both on the same team."

"Oh, Dad…"

He smiled, reaching across the cab to bump my chin with his thumb. "He's lucky to have you, Hen. Don't you ever forget that."

"I promise, I won't."

## 80

## TYLER

A bachelor party hardly seemed necessary when I'd been ready to marry Hen a month and a half ago, but here I was, riding around a lazy river outside of Waco with my brothers and Cohen, Jonas, and Steve.

This place was really cool, actually. Some couple had bought property and dug out a massive lazy river and a pond with slides that launched you ten feet in the air before plunging you in the murky water. You could bring your own floats and coolers of beer, and it kind of felt like a high school party with legal alcohol.

After smacking my face and ass in the pond a few times, I decided I much preferred the lazy river where we could float on inner tubes and drink beer at the same time.

Gage said, "Is this your first day off since Hen came back?"

I took a drink, thinking it over. "Actually, yeah..."

"Dang," Steve said. "Tell your boss to give you a day off more often!"

I laughed. Henrietta and I weren't the boss of each other. We were a team, equal partners, just like it was always meant to be. "It's hard work; don't get me wrong, but it doesn't feel like work when I'm with her."

Rhett splashed me with water. "Whipped!"

Cohen and Jonas laughed, and Steve said, "There are advantages to being whipped."

Rhett just shook his head, drinking his beer. "I'll take my wet and wild weekends, thank you very much."

Gage rolled his eyes at our brother, then changed the subject. "I have the sign scheduled for delivery, by the way."

"Perfect," I said.

Cohen asked, "Does she have any idea that you're doing this?"

"Not a clue," I replied with a smile.

Jonas lifted his own beer toward me. "Hats off to you, man. We knew you were a good guy, but this seals the deal."

My chest swelled with pride. Almost a year ago, I'd met these guys and wanted to impress them, wanted to show them that I was worthy of Hen. Earning their approval, along with their friendship, meant the world to me. Because in one day, I'd be giving Hen my last name and every last breath I had as her husband.

## 81

## HENRIETTA

*Confession: Maybe I'm a glutton for pain.*

"WHERE ARE YOU TAKING ME?" I demanded of my two best friends. They had me blindfolded in the back seat of my car. I'd agreed to a surprise, but that was before I'd been back here for thirty minutes.

Birdie laughed. "We're almost there."

I shook my head. "If you guys brought me to some weird strip club that's open in the middle of the day…" We had all agreed to bypass the stripper since Liv and all three of my sisters-in-law were coming over later for a grown-up slumber party, but Mara was kind of a wild card. Especially since they asked me to go on a pre-bachelorette-party party with them.

"We're here," Mara squealed.

I reached up and pulled off my blindfold. "No fucking way."

Birdie and Mara were both giggling, but my mouth was open. "What are we doing at a tattoo parlor?"

"Well, you made the last one seem so fun that we thought it was time for a repeat."

"I cried like a baby the whole time," I deadpanned. It turned out I was *highly* averse to pain.

Birdie smiled. "You're not the one getting the tattoo today."

I looked around, wondering who else was here. "Is Tyler getting another tattoo?"

"Nope," Mara said. "Jonas texted me a few minutes ago and said they're all in Waco."

That still didn't answer my question. I gave them both a confused look. "Who is it then?"

With a nervous shrug of her shoulders, Birdie said, "It's us."

"Both of you?" I asked. "I know Mara has ink, but I thought you didn't like tattoos!"

"It's not that I don't like them," Birdie said. "It's just that I've never known what to get before."

"What are you getting?" I asked.

Mara grinned, holding up her phone. On the screen was a cute line drawing of a chicken.

My mouth fell open in a surprised smile. "You're

joking, right? This is a prank and we're all going to get margaritas?"

Birdie laughed. "I'll say yes to a margarita after this if it's half as bad as you made it look." She grabbed her purse, reaching for the door handle. "Come on. We have an appointment."

The three of us walked into the tattoo parlor. It was a bit nicer than the one I'd been to for my windmill tattoo, but the tattoo artist up front seemed just as disinterested. I wondered if that was a thing they were taught or if I was just two for two.

The guy with sleeves covering his arms led us back to a chair, and one at a time, my friends got tiny little hens on their ankles. When they were done, the black ink permanently on their skin, I said, "Wait."

Birdie chuckled. "It's a little late for that."

I looked at the tattoo artist—his name was Gabe. "Can you give me one too?"

He shrugged. "Sure. My next appointment flaked."

I grinned. "Great."

Mara took my arm. "Are you sure?"

"I can handle a little pain," I replied with a smile. "And besides, I want to remember my best friends forever."

## 82

## TYLER

"Not like that," Liv said, gesturing her arms at us as we set up white folding chairs behind the house for the wedding. "It has to be a semicircle so everyone can see you two."

Rhett grumbled, but the rest of us adjusted the chairs for the third time until it fit Liv's expectations. With the chairs in place, Liv, Mom, and Tam flitted around the chairs, adding small bundles of flowers to the ones on the aisles.

We'd all decided to go with a wildflower theme, and with all the blooms thriving in Texas, we had plenty to choose from. It was already looking incredible. Dad had paid for a tent rental so there'd be some shade, and then he'd put up twinkle lights around the tables for the reception area.

In true Texas fashion, we had a hog roasted for barbecue, and some of the ladies from town volunteered to bring sides as a gift. There would be plenty of beer and soda covered in ice, resting in tin tanks.

But I didn't give a shit about any of that as long as Hen was happy when we left for our honeymoon in Cancun tomorrow. According to Mara, it was *the* place to go.

With the chairs set up, Liv had us roll out a burlap aisle and stake it to the ground so it wouldn't blow away if the wind picked up. But she had nothing to worry about. It was a perfect July day with crystalline blue skies and the sun gently setting. It was like the whole world knew this moment was always meant to be.

I kept moving chairs, but I didn't get as much yelling from Liv. "Pretty quiet over there," I said, looking up. Then I realized why everyone had stopped talking. Gage stood at the back of the house. Mom was frozen with flowers in her hand, staring at him. Liv and I looked between the two, waiting to see what would happen. And Tam? She looked like a woman slowly backing away from a rattlesnake.

Gage cleared his throat and said, "How can I help?"

Mom let out a strangled cry and walked inside.

All of Gage's features pinched as he watched our mom rush into the house. "I should..." His sentence trailed off.

"I'll handle it," I said.

He and Liv nodded, and I put a hand on Tam's shoulder just to let her know everything was okay before following our mom inside. I followed the sound of her quiet crying to hers and dad's bedroom on the main floor off the living room.

She sat on her bed, one leg bent on the mattress and the other dangling over the edge. Her curly hair fell in her face, and she had her hand pressed to her mouth, trying—and failing—to quiet herself.

She looked up at me for a moment, then back at the bed, her shoulders shaking.

I took a breath and sat beside her, rubbing a hand on her back. This was the woman who'd lain next to me after every bad dream, made sure I always had a hot meal at night, who pretended she didn't see me cry the day I moved into an apartment away from home.

She was the strongest person I knew, and I hated seeing her like this. "Mom..."

Her eyes were red as she looked at me. "I'm sorry."

I shook my head, rubbing her shoulder. "Don't be sorry."

"It's just... I... his hairline changed."

"Don't tell him that," I teased.

She laughed despite herself, but then her expression fell again. "How many years is it going to be before we make amends? Will I be old and gray before I get to have my boy over for dinner again?"

"You'll never be gray," I told her, brushing back a curl. "There's hair dye for that."

She gave me a look.

"Maybe today will be a chance for him and Dad both to get some perspective. But no one ever said you had to join in on their fight."

She reached to the nightstand for a tissue and blew her nose. With it clear, she said, "I know I'm supposed to be giving you advice today, but I don't think you're the one who needs it."

I chuckled. "I've messed up plenty of times."

"You have, because that's what people do, but it's more than that."

"What do you mean?" I asked.

"You remember when you were younger and you had such a hard time meeting people?"

I nodded.

"One day in therapy, I don't know if you remember this, but you said something I've thought about for years. You said, 'It's not that I'm afraid to meet people. It's that I don't know if I have enough room.'"

I smiled slightly, the memory fuzzy.

"You were so worried that if you met too many people you wouldn't be able to give them all of yourself. You wanted to remember their names, their favorite colors, have enough time to play with them all on the playground... It made you so anxious that you choked up every time you met someone new. And then it happened at school and kids picked on you for being shy, and it all snowballed from there."

Her fingers toyed with the tissue, rolling it in a ball. "I

always knew you'd make the best partner to someone, because anything you do, you give all of yourself."

My eyes felt hot with tears. I felt seen in a way I rarely did. "That's exactly what I want to give to Hen."

She reached up, hugging me close. "I love you and your big heart, Tyler Jay."

"I love you too."

## 83

## HENRIETTA

*Confession: Everyone talks about cold feet on their wedding day, but mine were toasty warm.*

I STOOD in the hotel conference room where we were all getting ready and looked at myself in the mirror.

I was a *bride*.

The wedding dress I'd bought in Dallas with my mom, grandma, and best friends just a couple days ago couldn't have been more perfect. Everyone had told me it was crazy to wait until the last minute and buy a dress off the rack, but if I was being honest, I didn't care what I wore as long as Tyler was standing at the end of the aisle, ready to say *I do*. Our marriage and the people celebrating Tyler and me were so much more important than having the "perfect" dress.

But despite the last-minute trip, we'd found *the* dress. It had been tucked at the very back of a sale rack as if someone had stowed it away there for me. It was a pure white, floor-length gown with off-the-shoulder straps and lacy fabric that nipped in at my waist and flowed out, giving the illusion of an hourglass figure I'd never had before.

Underneath the dress, I wore the boots Tyler had given me. The intricate leather design matched the dress perfectly, and I couldn't pass up the chance to wear a gift from my husband-to-be.

Grandma appeared in the mirror, pushing her wheelchair behind me. "You are a beautiful bride," she said.

"Thanks, Grandma." I turned to smile at her and noticed something in her hands. A velvet blue box. "What is that?"

Her weathered hands rested atop it, her gold wedding band still shining on her left hand. I came from a long line of happy, meaningful, fruitful marriages, and I couldn't wait to carry on the tradition.

"You know the saying," she said. "Something old, something new, something borrowed, something blue?"

I nodded. I hadn't thought about it much in the rush of the last couple months. Just having my friends and family here and knowing I'd be married to the man of my dreams had been more than enough for me.

But she pulled the box open, showing a beautiful hair comb made of what I guessed was sterling silver. Several blue jewels rested in its ornate design. "My grandma gave this to me on my wedding day, and I want to pass it on to you. So it won't be borrowed, but it is old and blue."

I covered my heart with my hands. "Grandma... it's so precious. Are you sure you don't want to keep it?"

Her lips trembled as she shook her head and said, "May I?"

"Of course," I breathed. I knelt next to her, resting my hand on the arm of her chair. Her fingers were featherlight as she pressed the clip at the back of my hair, above the intricate bun Liv had done for me.

"Perfect," she said, removing her hands.

I hugged her tight, then turned to look in the mirror. My mouth fell open as I saw myself, really saw myself. I may not have been small in any way. I may not have the perfect smile or a high-level corporate job.

But I looked every bit worthy of the woman to be Tyler's wife. And I was so glad he agreed.

The door to the conference room opened, and Mara, Birdie, and Liv came back in from taking bridesmaids photos. Mom followed them in with the photographer we hired. She posed me in front of the window and snapped photos of me with my wildflower bouquet picked directly from the pasture behind the Griffens' family home.

When the photographer lowered her camera, Mom smiled at me, tears in her eyes. "It's time."

I'd never been more ready for anything in my life.

## 84

## TYLER

Mom stood in the doorway of my childhood bedroom. "It's time."

All of the groomsmen had changed up here, then gone outside to help with last minute details or directing guests to the best places to park and sit. It was just me up here now, and I still couldn't get this handmade boutonniere Liv made to rest straight on my lapel.

"Let me," Mom said, replacing my hands with hers and easily maneuvering the pin into place. "There you go."

I gave her a grateful smile. "Thanks."

She put her arm around me, looking in the mirror above my dresser. "You look very handsome. I'm glad you decided to go with suits."

"I think Hen's family would have been horrified if I

walked down the aisle in jeans." I chuckled. But the truth was, I wanted to look my best for her. When she saw me today, I wanted her to see a man who loved her, who cared for her, and who would always put his best foot forward.

Mom looped her arm through mine. "Let's get down there."

We walked together down the stairs, and my brothers waited for us in the living room. I could already hear the guitar playing outside. My best friend from high school had a way with the guitar, and it sounded beautiful even from in here.

I walked Mom down the burlap aisle to her chair, giving her a kiss on the cheek as she sat next to Dad. I stood at the front of the aisle next to the pastor. Matthew Cole had gone to school with me, and now he preached at the cowboy church outside of Fort Worth.

I looked over the guests in folding chairs. There were about fifty people, half friends, half family, all here to witness me tie my life to Hen's forevermore.

And then the music on the guitar changed.

Laila nudged Kenner out the door, and he sprinted down the aisle to me, the ring pillow waving in one hand. A gasp went throughout the crowd, and then a chuckle when he reached me.

"Hey, buddy," I said to my nephew-to-be.

"I can run really fast in these shoes. Did you see?"

I chuckled. "Yeah. I saw. Are the rings still there?" I

really hoped they'd tied them good, because I didn't want to be searching for gold bands in the grass.

Seeming to remember his job, Kenner held the pillow up to his face. "Yep." He handed the pillow to me, and I double-checked, just in case.

Still there.

"Great job, Kenner. Mission accomplished." I stuck my fist out for him, and he tapped his little knuckles to mine, blowing it up afterward. As he sprinted back to his mom, the guests chuckled too.

Mara and Rhett walked out of the house next, her hand on his arm. The deep blue dress flowed around her as she stepped down the aisle holding a small bouquet of wildflowers. Birdie and Gage stepped out after, both smiling as they followed along.

And then everyone stood. The back door to the house opened, and my heart stopped.

Henrietta walked outside, her arm looped around her dad's. There might have been music playing still, but I couldn't hear it.

The woman I loved, the woman of my dreams, was walking toward me. Her long white dress fit her perfectly, and were those...? I grinned, seeing the toes of her boots peeking under her dress. But it was her smile that captivated me.

Her beautiful brown eyes were shining in the Texas sun, and her smile was even brighter. This woman was mine. And this day?

It was ours.

I barely dragged my eyes off of her long enough to hear her dad say, "Take care of her, son."

"I will," I promised.

He put her hand in mine, and I held her other hand too, running my thumbs over the back of her hands.

"Hi," I whispered.

"Hi," she said with a smile.

My throat felt tight, and I couldn't get any words out as the pastor started talking about weddings, about love and matrimony and the holy bond that tied us together.

We exchanged rings.

Henrietta repeated her vows, each promise a balm to my heart.

And then Matthew said, "The groom wishes to say something before he speaks his vows."

Henrietta whispered, "Tyler, I thought we weren't writing our own vows."

"This is something extra," I replied before taking the microphone from Matthew. I reached into my jacket pocket and held up the piece of paper I'd been staring at ever since she said yes. But instead of looking at her, I faced our guests. I faced her family.

"The second I met Henrietta, I knew there was something different about her. Something special. And that knowing kept me chasing after her, made me want to learn everything about her. The time we spent together, the more I could see her heart for you all, the people she loves most. I knew anything between us would require a sacrifice. I could give up on my dreams of settling here to be with her. Or she would have to move away from the people she loves so much to be with me." My throat got tight, guilt eating at me even though I knew we'd both made the right choice. Even though our location could change, our love for each other, and our families, would not.

"I think you know what decision we made together. And even though this union is between myself and my beautiful bride..." I smiled at Henrietta, and her smile in return settled me again. "I'd be remiss to think it didn't involve all of you too. I've seen the way Henrietta loves you, and through her eyes, I've come to love you just as much. I want to promise you that even though Hen is becoming my wife, she'll always be your friend, your sister, your daughter and granddaughter too. I promise to always make time for your bond and value it just as much as she does. I am so grateful to be joining your family today, just as Hen is joining mine."

I saw tears streaming down her mom and grandma's cheeks. Even her brothers' and dad's eyes were red. As I turned back to Hen, I noticed tracks of moisture streaking from her eyes.

I passed the microphone back to Matthew and reached up with my thumbs, wiping her tears away. She held my wrists, whispering, "I love you."

My jaw trembled as I rested my forehead against hers. "I meant every word."

"I know," she replied.

Matthew continued the ceremony, and I put all my heart into the vows as I promised my life to the woman across from me.

And when he said, "I now pronounce you man and wife. You may kiss the bride," I wrapped my arms around my wife and made our first kiss as a married couple one we'd remember for the rest of our lives.

## 85

## HENRIETTA

*Confession: I may always be a funny fat friend... but I'm also so much more.*

SPARKLERS LIT our path as Tyler and I left the reception to his truck that Liv had decorated. Flowers lined the truck bed, and the back window said JUST MARRIED surrounded by hearts.

He opened the door for me and helped me in, making sure my dress was fully inside before closing the door. When he got in, he leaned across the middle seat and gave me a kiss before pulling away.

I watched out the window, seeing the twinkle lights fade away. Tyler turned right out of their drive, and my eyebrows drew together. "Weren't we supposed to go that way to get to Dallas?" We had a one-night stay before our flight tomorrow at a place Tyler described as a "ritzy mix of character and culture."

A smile danced along his lips, illuminated by the green dash lights. "We have a stop to make first."

My eyebrows drew together. "Did you forget something at the school?"

"Something like that," he replied, turning down another dirt road.

I shook my head at him, smiling. "Married for four hours, and you're already keeping me on my toes."

He squeezed my hand, lifting my knuckles to his lips. "I hope you're ready, because I plan to do that every day for the rest of my life."

"Of course, Mr. Griffen," I said, loving the way *our* name sounded on my tongue. "But is it okay if I change there? I'd rather not waltz into a fancy hotel still in my wedding dress."

"You can get naked any time you want," he said, his voice husky with desire. The wedding night was something we'd both been fantasizing about for the last month and a half.

I bit my lip. "Keep looking at me like that, and we won't make it to the hotel."

His eyes were hot on mine for a moment before he looked back to the road. We pulled into town and took the familiar city streets to the schoolhouse. We still hadn't decided on a name for it. I thought it should be something like Cottonwood Estates, but he'd wanted to make it more personal to us.

Luckily, we had a few months left of construction to get the units completed, and that was plenty of time to decide.

He parked in front of the schoolhouse, and I got out, going to the tailgate to get my bags from the truck bed.

"Are you insane, woman?" Tyler chastised, coming beside me. "Let me get your suitcase. You go inside."

Shaking my head at him, I lifted the hem of my skirt and walked toward the school until my eyes caught something different.

Underneath the new antique security light, there was a sign.

*The Hen House*

I stared at the letters, my jaw slack, until Tyler came to stand beside me, wrapping his arm around my shoulders.

"What is this?" I asked.

"It's our home," he replied. "What do you think of the name?"

I looked from him to the sign and back again. "You want to name it after me?"

He palmed my cheek, cradling my face in his hand. "*You* are what makes this place a home. You did it at Blue Bird, and I have no doubt you'll do the same here. You're done fading into the background, baby. It's time to have you front and center, right where you belong."

Tears came to my eyes for the millionth time that day. All my life, I'd thought I was destined to be the funny fat friend. Always taking a back seat to other people and their needs, their stories. But this man, my husband, had shown me, every single day, that I could be so much more.

I kissed his lips, rejoicing in my role, not as the funny fat friend, but as his wife, as the main character of my own happily ever after.

# EPILOGUE
## HENRIETTA

*Confession: I love the life we're building together.*

### Christmas

TYLER and I walked up the sidewalk to my parents' house, wheeling a suitcase packed to the *brim* with presents for my family.

Instead of knocking, I opened the door and walked inside. Even if I lived in Texas now, this place would always be home, and my parents made sure I knew their door would always be open.

"UNCLE TYLER!" Kenner yelled, running to Tyler

and wrapping his arms around his legs. A'yisha toddled behind him, saying, "Unca Tya."

I shook my head, scooping her up and saying, "What am I? Chopped liver?" I tickled her sides and she giggled, making me grin.

Our other greetings may not have been as enthusiastic as Kenner's, but they were filled with love all the same. My parents hugged me tight, Raven's pregnant belly pressed into me as she gave me a side hug, and I kissed my new nephew, Tevon, on the forehead. "You are just precious," I said, setting A'yisha down and taking the five-month-old in my arms. A'yisha toddled away, going to play with Kenner.

The party continued, as if we hadn't missed a beat in our relationships, with eggnog being passed around, cartoons playing on TV for the kids, and a competitive card game going on at the table. Grandma was winning.

"Dang, Cordelia," Tyler said. "Those ladies at the home must be whipping you into shape."

Grandma kept her poker face as she reached for another card from the stack. "It's the other way around. Someone needs to keep them on their toes."

"Speaking of keeping people on their toes," I said…

Everyone turned to me, and I grinned. I'd been bursting to tell everyone the news since we walked in, and I couldn't wait any longer.

"I'm getting another grandbaby?" Mom cried.

I laughed, shaking my head. "Not yet." I exchanged a grin with Tyler, who'd been very eager to practice the act, even if we planned to enjoy marriage just the two of us for a little while.

"What's going on then?" Johmarcus asked.

I grinned, saying, "We're opening up other locations of The Hen House!"

"What!" Bertrand said. "That's awesome!"

I nodded excitedly. We'd opened our location just a few months ago, but the concept of boutique senior living in a small town had taken off with the media. Turned out people loved the idea of having a homey, comfortable place for their parents and grandparents to live where they could have their privacy and enjoy activities like gardening while still having a nurse check in on them from time to time.

"We caught the eye of an investor," Tyler said. "They cut us a deal to find and restore five older buildings across Texas, and if this goes well, they want to partner with us to make it a nationwide franchise."

My family cheered for us, and Dad got up from the table to walk around and hug us both. "I'm proud of you two."

"Me too," I admitted. After stopping college with an associate degree and working the same job for so long, I thought just being a property manager was my future. But Tyler had shown me there could be more to life. Especially with my best friend, my partner, my husband, my *home* at my side.

♥⋅♥⋅♥⋅♥

WANT to see where Henrietta and Tyler are three years down the road? Get their free bonus scene today!

Everyone thought Gage Griffen would be the eternal bachelor, but he'll find his happily ever after in **Hello Billionaire**! Grab your copy now!

Get the free bonus story today!

Start reading Hello Billionaire today!

## AUTHOR'S NOTE

Being the funny fat friend is *hard*.

I remember boys befriending me. I thought they might like me... until then asking for one of my classmate's numbers.

I remember going out to bars with my college friends and watching all of them get asked to dance while I stood on the sidelines, holding purses and drinks like a dutiful friend.

It hurt, every time. It made me look at myself and then look at them and ask... Why are they so much better than me?

I used to wish that once, just once, a guy would approach me first, because he was interested in *me*.

I got lucky, as I started dating my now husband in my senior year of high school. I wasn't single for long. But I imagine, if I had been single until twenty-eight, being the funny fat friend would have been even more difficult. Add in online dating, with the instant rejection of swiping at a picture, and you have a recipe for low confidence.

When you're the friend that is always overlooked, you start wondering things about yourself, and then you start assuming things about other people.

He wasn't interested in me because of my size.

He's only paying attention to me to get to my friend.

He wants to take me out because he has a fat fetish.

A guy like that would never be seen with a girl like me.

These thoughts are there to protect you, to make sense of rejection and loneliness. But soon the voice in your head isn't so nice. And when a guy like Tyler shows you genuine interest, it can feel suspicious.

That's why I love what Mara said to Henrietta.

*Let him choose his intentions.*

When you place the responsibility for someone else's feelings or perspectives on your shoulders, you lose every single time. Just because you have grown up in a society conditioned to scorn fat people and view them as less than, just because you've navigated life in a bigger body and struggle to love yourself, doesn't mean you're not worthy of love.

You deserve love and affection at any size, even if you're having a hard time loving yourself.

Self-love isn't a lightning moment where all of a

sudden it all comes together and years of self-deprecation are undone.

Instead, it's a puzzle. You put little pieces together, one at a time, until you realize you were building a picture of yourself. Even when there are holes, pieces missing, you can start to see yourself for who you are. Who you could be.

For Henrietta, there were lots of little pieces that came together. She had friends with great advice. A love interest who told her how beautiful she was. A family to support her. A beautiful moment at a friend's wedding in her bridesmaid dress. And finally, the freedom to be herself, without the expectations she'd picked up along the way.

And I'm here to tell you, it's okay if you only have a few pieces of the puzzle. It's okay if you look at a photo of yourself and have a negative reaction or opt for sleeves on a summer day. It's normal not to have it all together.

But I also want you to look for those little pieces that will show you more of your true, beautiful, worthy self.

Because you deserve to see the full puzzle, no matter how long it takes.

## ACKNOWLEDGMENTS

Oh my goodness! This last part of the book is always so fun, and I'm going to savor a few minutes thanking all these wonderful people who helped bring the book to you!

As always, I want to thank you for reading this story. The reason I write is to make readers like you feel beautiful, exactly as you are. I hope you felt the love in every page.

My family is my biggest supporter and biggest motivator. Although my boys would rather I write more children's books about poop and farts, they make me feel like a rock star when they brag about their mom being an author. My husband and I are likely qualified for a circus act at this point with all the juggling we do. I'm so glad he believes in me and my business, even when I have doubts. My siblings have always encouraged me and helped spread the word about my books. I love them for believing in me and my work.

The group members in the Kelsie Stelting: Readers Club who read my YA books and then encouraged me to write curvy adult stories... thank you! I was so terrified of writing spice, but I've found so much fun and freedom in these last three stories. You've changed the trajectory of my career, challenged me, and encouraged me to be an even better writer. Thank you times a million.

I'm dedicated to writing a cast of diverse characters that reflects the real world, and as a white woman, I couldn't do that without tons of help. Thank you to my sensitivity readers, Kelsea Reeves and Angela Leafi, for helping me get Hen and her family right. You make the world of fiction better with your voices.

My writer friend, and soon to be partner in crime, Sally Henson, has encouraged me to write adult books and throw myself into these stories. I love how she pushes me as a person, a mom, and a writer. Love you Sal Gal.

Two other writer friends have chatted consistently with me about promoting my books and spreading the curvy girl love to the world! Anne-Marie Meyer and Judy Corry, thanks for being a sounding board and source of encouragement!

My editor, Tricia Harden, has seen me from sweet country YA romance to spicy and tender adult books, and I have loved having her walk beside me every step of the way! She is the best cheerleader, friend, and mentor with the biggest heart and most wonderful soul. Thank you for being you.

The cover on this book came to life thanks to Najla Qamber and her team. I love how responsive, understanding, and creative she is. She's so dedicated to helping my vision become a reality, and I absolutely adore her for that! Thank you much!

Maddie Zahm, although I don't know you, I loved listening to your song. It was an inspiration to see you help curvy girls feel seen and heard with your words.

To all the lovely ladies in Hoss's Hussies, I adore you. Thanks for making such a fun space for adult women to hang out and lift each other up. You help me see the good in people and are the kind of friends I love to write about.

## ALSO BY KELSIE HOSS

**The Confessions Series**

Confessions of a High School Guidance Counselor

Confessions of a Smutty Romance Author

Confessions of the Funny Fat Friend

**The Hello Series**

Hello Billionaire

## JOIN THE PARTY

Want to talk about Confessions of Being a High School Guidance Counselor? Join Hoss's Hussies today!

Join here: https://www.facebook.com/groups/hossshussies

# ABOUT THE AUTHOR

Kelsie Hoss writes sexy romantic comedies with plus size leads. Her favorite dessert is ice cream, her favorite food is chocolate chip pancakes, and… now she's hungry.

You can find her enjoying one of the aforementioned treats, soaking up some sunshine like an emotional house plant, or loving on her three sweet boys.

Her alter ego, Kelsie Stelting, writes sweet, body positive romance for young adults. You can learn more (and even grab some special merch) at kelsiehoss.com.

facebook.com/authorkelsiehoss
instagram.com/kelsiehoss

Printed in Great Britain
by Amazon